THE PARTY WORKER

Omar Shahid Hamid has been a police officer in Pakistan for sixteen years and is a senior member of the Karachi Police's Counter Terrorism Department. In 2011, following an attack on his offices by the Pakistani Taliban, he took a five-year sabbatical to write books and worked as a political risk consultant. He has been widely quoted and regularly featured in a number of publications including *The New York Times*, *USA Today*, *The Wall Street Journal*, *The Times*, *Le Monde*, *Reuters*, CNN and BBC. His first novel, *The Prisoner* (2013), was longlisted for the DSC Prize for South Asian Literature 2015 and is now being adapted for a feature film. His second novel is *The Spinner's Tale* (2015). In 2016, Omar returned to active duty as a Counter Terrorism Officer.

D1155774

Also by Omar Shahid Hamid

The Prisoner

The Spinner's Tale

THE PARTY WORKER

OMAR SHAHID HAMID

PAN

First published 2017 by Pan
an imprint of Pan Macmillan India
a division of Macmillan Publishers India Private Limited
Pan Macmillan India, 707, Kailash Building
26, K. G. Marg, New Delhi – 110 001
www.panmacmillan.co.in

Pan Macmillan, 20 New Wharf Road, London N1 9RR
Basingstoke and Oxford
Associated companies throughout the world
www.panmacmillan.com

ISBN 978-93-82616-96-2

Typeset by Manmohan Kumar
Printed and bound in India by
Replika Press Pvt. Ltd.

For my son and co-writer Suleyman, who will always
be the best story of my life

PROLOGUE

NEW YORK CITY

Watch the ball. Watch the ball on to the bat.

He sees the sunlight glint off the metal surface of the baseball bat as the boy swings it in desperation and, not having heeded his silent admonition, fails to connect with the ball altogether. Asad Haider holds his head and sighs as the dejected Little Leaguer walks back to the dugout. And then he smiles at himself, wondering why it should matter to him whether the boy connected with the bat or not. It's not his boy, nor is it his game. He has never played baseball, only cricket. But there is something about games involving bats and balls that never fails to draw him in. Even at a time like this, as he stands in Central Park waiting for the most important meeting of his life.

In fact, that isn't true. The most important meeting of Asad Haider's life occurred yesterday, when he betrayed the man and the Party that have been his life for the past twenty-eight years. This meeting is simply a follow-up, the claiming of an insurance policy to ensure that he stays alive after his great betrayal. The emotion of yesterday has passed, and Asad Haider doesn't ponder over what has happened. The only thing that is important now is to keep his guard up and be prepared for whatever comes next.

He discards the half-eaten hotdog and walks away from the playing fields in Central Park, towards the 79th Street exit on the Upper West Side. He is a tall man, and he retains the taut, muscular body of his youth, making him look younger than his forty-five years, despite his shock of salt-and-pepper hair. His most striking feature are his eyes, grey-green, almost reptilian, as they dart around scanning the hundreds of New Yorkers who have rushed to the Park today to enjoy the first real hint of spring after a bitter, cold winter.

Even on a day and in a place like this, surrounded by casual revellers celebrating the sunlight by shedding their clothes and inhibitions, Asad Haider stands out, his body a coiled spring, ready to react instantly to any kind of situation.

He pauses at the Park entrance and looks across Central Park West to his destination, the Museum of Natural History. He waits a full five minutes, taking everything in. Then he spots his contact – a slightly overweight Pakistani man wearing a battered old New York Jets jacket – get out of a taxi and walk up the steps of the museum. The man seems a bit puzzled by the location, but that is a deliberate move on Asad's part. He has spent enough time as the Party's chief hitman to not leave anything to chance. He wants a meeting in a place that is guaranteed to be unfrequented not just by members of the Party, but by Pakistanis living in New York in general. Yes, absolutely no better place than a museum. Asad approaches him from behind and taps him gently on the shoulder. The man, surprised and extremely nervous, turns around sharply, bringing him almost face to face with Asad.

'Javed Gringo sent you?'

Despite the sunlight, it's still a cold day, but Asad can see beads of sweat trickle down the man's forehead. 'Yes. Who are you? I mean, are you Asad Haider? How did you know how to spot me?'

Asad frowns slightly. Gringo certainly hasn't sent the brightest operative. The questions are unnecessary and the man should already have the answers. 'Your jacket. Gringo said you would be wearing a New York Jets jacket.'

'Oh yes. Of course, of course. But you are Asad Haider, right?'

It's at this point that Asad Haider starts to suspect something is not quite right. He doesn't answer the question but looks around to see if he can spot anything unusual. But the rest of the world seems impervious to their meeting. He looks back at the man, and notices that his hand is shaking. Asad slowly starts backing away from him.

'Wait, where are you going? Wait, I've got something for you here, from Javed Gringo. It's in my pocket, just wait a second.' Asad turns his back and increases his pace as the man puts his hand inside his jacket, pulls out a pistol and starts firing, his hand still violently unsteady.

Asad has almost broken into a run by the time he hears the first shot. For a brief instant, he thinks he might just be able to outrun the bullets. But then something hits him with the force of a freight train, and he goes down hard.

*

Watch the ball.
'We have a forty-five-year-old male, South Asian origin, multiple gunshot wounds in the chest and lungs. Heartbeat's there, but very faint.'

Watch the ball on to the bat.
'Do you see any retina reaction? Mr Hay-dar, can you hear me? Don't try to speak, just nod once if you can.'

Nod. Once. You can hear her.
'We're going to lift you and turn you round, to see if the bullet has exited. You may feel some momentary discomfort.'

No discomfort. Pain. And not momentary either.

'Okay, wheel him into the OR stat. Mr Hay-dar, we're taking you in to operate on you. You have a bullet lodged in your lungs. But it's going to be fine. I'm just going to insert this IV into your arm and you'll feel better after that.'

The white light is blinding. Blinding like the sun on that cloudless day in Karachi. Drenching you in sweat. Blinding you. Forget that, just watch the ball. Dark and red and hurtling towards you. And then the ball becomes larger, and darker, and redder, until it blots out everything else.

*

WEILL CORNELL MEDICAL CENTER, MANHATTAN.

'How long has he been up? Why didn't you call us right away, Nurse?'

'Detective Russo, he regained consciousness two hours ago but his vital signs are low. He can barely nod his head, leave alone talk. I'm afraid you'll have to wait.'

'Ah, Nurse Ratchet, you're killin' me. Do you realize that it's been forty-eight hours since a major homicide incident, a sixty-five-year-old woman is dead, three other people are injured and I haven't even got a basic statement from the sole survivor and eyewitness? Come on! You gotta give me something.'

'I'm sorry, Detective. Dr Bose has strictly said that the patient is not yet stable enough to meet police officers. He'll be back on rounds in thirty minutes. You're going to have to wait.'

'Can you at least tell me the nature of his injuries?' Anthony Russo rubs his forehead with his chubby fingers. The nurse looks positively Amazonian, towering over his short and portly frame.

'One bullet lodged in his left lung. It was taken out when he was operated on, but his lung collapsed and he still can't breathe without a ventilator. The second bullet grazed the left side of his skull, but no permanent damage. And the third bullet went through his right wrist, shattering the bone.'

'That's a total of nine shots fired, if you count the three that hit passers-by, the one that killed the old lady, a stray that lodged in a tree and a live round that was found near the body. It must have jammed and dropped out.' Russo's partner, Carlos Cardenas is a tall man in peak physical condition, an eleven-year veteran of the NYPD and a recent recipient of the coveted gold shield. His well-defined muscles strain against his grey suit. Ten years younger than Russo, his jet-black hair makes a striking contrast to his olive skin. Despite having moved to the United States twenty years ago, his accent is more Puerto Rico than New York.

'What do we have on the other victims?'

'Kirsten Parker, twenty-eight, female Caucasian, a graduate student at Columbia, bullet lodged in her left buttock as she was trying to run away. Murtala Touray, thirty-six, Nigerian immigrant, he has a hot dog stand just outside the museum, bullet shattered his ankle. And Whitney Tesfay, twenty-one, who was in the museum with her family, received a superficial wound on her arm caused by a ricochet. They were all discharged from here on the same day. The dead woman is Nathalie Wlodachek, sixty-five, a professor of Jewish Studies at NYU, got hit straight in the head by a stray. Eyewitnesses say a South Asian or Hispanic man met our friend on the museum steps and the guy pulled a weapon on him. The bullets are from a 9mm pistol, make as yet undetermined. The gunman opened fire indiscriminately, killing Mrs Wlodachek and injuring the other three, and he also shot the victim at close range.'

'Jewish studies, huh? Jeez, that's all we need. On top of everyone crapping themselves about a shooting at the Natural

History Museum, fucking Fox News has set up camp on Central Park West, calling this a race crime. Where's this guy from?'

'I think he's from Pakistan. The other nurse just handed me this box of his personal effects.'

'You think this is a jihadist lone wolf type of thing?'

'I don't know. Our friend seems to have been the target. Let's find out what this guy's all about.'

Carlos Cardenas places the box on the counter of the nurses' station. Although the patient's clothes have been cut up in the ER, the rest of his effects are neatly placed in ziplock bags in the box.

'Okay, let's see what we've got.' Anthony Russo has always enjoyed this part of the job. Trying to put the pieces together without knowing what the final picture looks like. 'One pair of jeans, one white cotton dress shirt, or what's left of them. Label on the shirt says Rizavi Tailors, Karachi. Wasn't he wearing a jacket, or did the paramedics have to cut through that as well?'

'No, here it is, black leather jacket, looks expensive, the paramedics didn't cut it, but it did soak up a lot of blood.'

'It's going to be a pain in the ass getting that stain out at the drycleaners.' Russo chuckles at his own joke but draws no response from his partner.

'Okay, so these were the items inside the jacket. A Pakistani passport in the name of Asad Haider. Date of birth, 12 August 1970. He's got a ten-year valid US visa, issued from the US Consulate in Karachi last month.'

'Where else has this guy travelled in the past three years?'

'He's got stamps for Dubai, Iran, Iraq. Iraq? This guy has been to some shady places. Al Qaeda, you think?' Cardenas hands over the dog-eared green book to Russo.

'If it was Iraq alone, then maybe. But Iran and Iraq together are a Shia combo. Must have gone for pilgrimage. Besides, if it had been, we would have had the Feds and the spooks shitting all over us from day one. And we haven't heard a peep from them.'

'Hey, you know your Islamic radicals, Tony.'

'That's what three years in the counterterrorism intelligence unit will get you, kid. This is interesting. There seems to be some kind of sharpened stud in one of the pockets. Looks like one of those studs that you get on old-fashioned knuckledusters. Remember those? We used to get a lot of punks wearing those in the early 1980s when I was a rookie.'

'Tony, back then I was in high school in Puerto Rico, man.'

'Stop reminding me of how old I've gotten. What else have we got?'

'This looks like a ring, with a large semi-precious gemstone embedded in it. Some kind of Arabic inscriptions on the ring. The stone itself is chipped and looks in bad shape.'

'I've got his wallet here. Brown leather, Montblanc. Classy. Contents include $500 in crisp new $50 bills, subway Metrocard, and a black-and-white picture of an old woman dressed in South Asian clothes. A mini booklet of what seem to be Quranic or religious inscriptions in Arabic. Another piece of paper that seems to be torn off from a poster, I would guess it's some kind of political leaflet or flier. Again a lot of printed words in Arabic or Urdu, written under a picture of an orange-and-black flag. It must be some kind of party flag or something.'

'Wait, there's something else in the inner pocket of the jacket. It's a laminated photo ID. Seems old. The plastic edges are frayed. This guy was good-looking in his day. Under the picture, it says Asad Haider, Party worker, United Progressive Front. Party card no. 005. You've seen the crime scene, Tony. What does this all look like to you?'

'Looks like a hit, Charlie. And it seems our friend in the ICU was the target. So until we speak to him, we can't draw any conclusions about anything. Nurse, when can we speak to the doctor?'

'Dr Bose has just started his rounds. I'll bring him to you.'

Dr Bose enters through the ward's swing doors like a big shot movie director walking onto his set. He is a dark-skinned South Asian man in surgical greens with a slightly receding hairline and extremely hairy knuckles. He rubs sanitizer on his hands before offering Detective Russo a firm handshake.

'I'm Dr Bose, deputy chief of Trauma Medicine here. The nurse tells me you wanted an update on the gunshot victim in ICU.'

'Yes sir, Doctor. It's been forty-eight hours since a major shooting incident in the city, right on the steps of the Natural History Museum, and we believe your patient is the key witness. In fact, we believe that he was the probable target of the assassin. When can we speak to him?'

'Look, he is stable now. We've just moved him from the ICU into a semi-private room. Luckily, none of the injuries were critical. He is conscious, but extremely weak from loss of blood. Plus, he still can't breathe independently. The ventilator is supporting him till his lung fully reflates. And even if he could talk to you, there would be a lot of disorientation and some degree of short-term memory loss because of the head injury. I understand your desire to solve this case, but you can take a look for yourself, the patient is in no condition to deal with an interrogation.'

He can see the three men through his half-open eyes. He wishes he weren't so tired so he could understand better what they are talking about. There is the dark-skinned doctor in his surgical fatigues. He remembers him from the operating theatre. Probably an Indian. The two other men, who, by their bearing, seem to be police officers. Cops are the same all over the world, you can spot them a mile away. They all walk the same way, that self-important strut that presumes that people should move out of their way because nobody's business is as important as theirs. It's like a police strobe light for pedestrians. It reminds him of how much he hates cops.

The throbbing in his head returns and he shuts his eyes tight to keep out the pain. The men are still talking, standing by the nurses' station in the corner of the ward. One of the cops, the stockier one, is holding a shiny object in his hands. It takes him a moment to understand what it is. The knuckleduster stud. He shuts his eyes again and lets his mind drift back. To Nishtar Park. Twenty-eight years ago.

*

Watch the ball.
Carefully, straight from the bowler's hand. The pitch is a minefield, a crumbling concrete strip with cracks right across the surface, and bits of rubble dislodging every time the ball pitches on it. And the bowler is a magician, a practitioner of the dark art of leg spin. He makes the ball dance like a cobra, darting this way and that, spitting venomously at the batsmen. He's already gotten five of them with googlies and leg breaks and sliders.

Don't think about that. Don't think about anything else. Stay in the moment. Watch the ball, watch it right on to your bat. Make room, and cut it delicately. The bat is a scalpel, not a cleaver. There, see it running down to third man. You can hear the non-striker shouting at you to run, so you respond, but your eyes remain on the ball, admiring your artistry. The fielder races along the boundary, but you know your own skill, you know he will never reach the ball.

It is a hot April day in Karachi. He can still feel the heat searing him two decades later in the New York hospital. The humidity is so extreme, it takes on a life of its own. At noon, you think it is not possible for it to get any hotter, until two hours later, you find that it is. You take off your batting glove with its torn webbing and rub it in the gravel beside the concrete pitch, just so the dirt can absorb some moisture so the bat won't slip in your hands. The cheap wristbands you bought last month are already soaked through with sweat, so you wipe the rivulets off your brow with the one remaining dry corner of your shirt.

The batsman at the other end, your captain, says something to you but it doesn't register. It doesn't matter, it can only be some inane observation. The bowler returns to the top of his mark, licking his fingers and massaging the red ball. Here he comes again. Watch the ball. It's tossed up. Move forward, bring the bat in a full arc and connect. There, it is now a red dot hurtling through the sky, over the bowler's head, out of the ground for a six. The perfect shot. Suddenly, the heat doesn't matter. Your captain's prattling doesn't matter. The bowler's prior performance doesn't matter. Your name is Asad Haider, you are nineteen years old and you are the best batsman in the world. That is all that matters.

'That Asad Haider is the best batsman in Nishtar Park.'

'Arre choro yaar. That boy can only play on these dead pitches. Besides, he's a bloody charsi. Always high as a kite. No proper coaching either. He wouldn't survive five minutes on a real turf wicket.'

'Still, I've never seen anyone with such a natural eye. And just look at the grace in his shots. And the pitch isn't easy. The old concrete slab is falling apart. It's not easy to maintain your technique on that surface.'

'Arre, who ever heard of a six-foot-four-inch opening batsman. All the great batsmen were short men. Gavaskar, Bradman, Miandad. That's what makes them compact players. This boy should have been a fast bowler with his height. But saala lazy hai. He doesn't want to work hard. Just wants to bat and smoke charas.'

A third voice pipes up. 'He's nothing more than a khatmal goonda. Goes around the area with his little band of khatmals, shutting down shops and threatening the traders every time the Fiqah-e-Jaaferia decide to call a bandh.'

'Saale badmaash khatmal thugs. Such are the times we live in, that every time something happens to one of them anywhere in the city, these pups who've barely started shaving start bossing around respectable people. At least, we didn't have this kind of thing when Bhutto was still alive.'

'Bhutto was a Shia too. He didn't do anything to restrain them.'

'Yes, but all this started when Zia put his hand on the mullahs. Then this lot started acting up.'

'It was the bloody revolution in Iran. That's when things started going bad. Besides, these fellows have the biggest mullah. That fellow Khomeini.'

'Don't you dare blaspheme against the Imam! We will tolerate a lot of your rubbish but we will not accept any insult against the Imam. And you better be careful. Half of us living around Nishtar Park are Shia.'

Aleem Siddiqui walks into the small makeshift pavilion that has been set up under a bright red shamiana at the very moment that the cricketing debate turns into a sectarian confrontation. His trademark polyester shirt is plastered to his back and two huge sweat stains expand like ink blots under his armpits. It is not just the heat that makes Aleem sweat. It is fear as well.

Getting between the two offensive debaters, he ensures that neither will be able to deck the other. 'Excuse me, sirji, I am very sorry but can someone please point me to where Asad Haider is? Has he left the ground already?'

The intervention defuses the tension. The Khomeini hater and his friends drift away, while the Shia whose sensibilities were offended points Aleem to the far corner of the shamiana, which the teams have converted into a temporary dressing room, by scattering various pieces of kit. Sitting just outside the open flap of the tent, with his back to everyone else, is a broad-shouldered young man. His muscular forearms strain against the delicate cotton material of his white cricket shirt. His hair is cut severely short and a carefully maintained stubble growth covers his dark face. His eyes are bloodshot, giving him a dangerous aura. The unmistakable whiff of cannabis emanates from the cigarette that hangs from the corner of his mouth.

'Asad mian, adab arz hai. Thank God I found you, I have been looking for you frantically for the past couple of hours.'

'Arre, Aleem bhai, you should be careful about who you're looking for. Didn't you just hear, I'm a dangerous khatmal thug.'

'Actually, Asad mian, that's exactly the kind of person I need at this moment.'

The sarcastic smile on Asad's face disappears and he views Aleem Khan with renewed interest. 'Why, Aleem bhai, what's wrong?'

'My friend Mohammed Ali is in trouble. The mullahs at the university want to beat him up.'

'Who is this fellow? Has he come for one of our nets in the past?' Aleem is four years older than Asad but despite that, they do cricket nets together every Tuesday at the university's practice ground.

'No, no. He doesn't play cricket. Mohammed Ali, Mohammed Ali Pichkari is his full name. He's an MComm student at the university and my best friend. But he is very politically active, and the Jamiat's unit on campus is incensed that he is going to give a speech criticizing them. So they've threatened to kill him if he shows his face on campus today.'

'So tell him not to go for classes today.'

'Asad, Mohammed Ali is a man of his word. If he has promised people that he will speak on campus today, then he will speak on campus today, and if the intent of his speech was to criticize the mullah parties, then that is exactly what he will do, to hell with the consequences. He doesn't care about their threats.'

'Sounds like an impressive fellow. So what do you want me to do about it? You know I only come and practise with you guys to tune my batting. I'm not enrolled at the university.'

'I need your help to protect him on campus. Look, the others from our little group have no experience of this sort of thing. They are all intellectuals who can quote Karl Marx verbatim, but they don't know how to be tough. When they heard of the Jamiat's threats, they all ran away. You know student politics. You've been with the ISO. You have a reputation for these things. If you come with me to stand by Mohammed Ali, then the Jamiatwallahs will think twice before doing anything, because they will assume that we are backed by the Shia student groups.'

'This is your same friend whom everyone calls the Don, right? But, Aleem bhai, why should I do this for someone I don't even know?'

'Look Asad, you know me and trust me, right?'

'Sure.'

'Then believe me when I tell you that Mohammed Ali is a special man. He is worth taking a stand for. He has the courage to say the things that have to be said. Trust me on this.'

Asad Haider looks at Aleem and holds his gaze, astonished by the sincerity and passion in his eyes. He takes one final drag of the charas-filled cigarette and throws it away. From his cricket kit bag he takes out a pair of black leather knuckledusters, the metallic studs shining in the sunlight.

'You have your bike, right? You can drop me home afterwards.'

1

THE ASSASSIN

The 20th Precinct's station house is, unusually for Manhattan, located in a quiet residential area, on West 84th Street on the Upper West Side. Walking down the leafy street, it sneaks up on you amidst the town houses, tucked away behind an Eastern Orthodox Church. There are no squad cars parked outside, or any other sign of hustle-bustle. In his twenty-five-year career, Tony Russo has never experienced such serenity outside a police station.

The 20th is an unusual precinct in many regards. Although its jurisdiction covers many New York landmarks like the Lincoln Center, the Museum of Natural History and of course, Central Park, it is considered a 'soft' posting, especially for detectives. While there are plenty of law and order duties, serious crime is negligible in the area. The brass and the pencil pushers at One Police Plaza treat the 20th as half training centre, and half pre-retirement home for washed-up old-timers who've spent too many years in the war zones of the city.

Anthony Russo supposes that he must fit in the latter category. He certainly isn't a newbie. Washed up isn't how he would necessarily describe himself, but he can understand if that's the conclusion an outsider would draw. He doesn't have a lot of things going for him. He's overweight, short and not particularly good-looking. His suit looks like it was stolen from a homeless person. One of his precinct captains once famously described him as looking like he put his clothes in a washing machine, while he was still wearing them. His tie, which wasn't fashionable even when he bought it in 1988, has mustard and mayonnaise stains all over it. His personal life is equally chaotic with the debris of two divorces and numerous failed relationships, all sacrificed for the job.

But Anthony Russo doesn't mind what people say about him. He wears the scars of a thousand public and private battles with honour. Besides, he made those sacrifices willingly because he loves his job. He knows he will never change, the job will always be his first love because he is so damn good at what he does. For one thing is certain. Anthony Russo, whatever he may look like and whatever people say about him behind his back, is one of the best investigative minds on the force.

He loves the thrill of the hunt. Chasing down leads, putting together clues. To him, criminal investigation is an art form and he is its leading artist. That's why he does the job. He isn't driven by some inner desire to do good. Not like those college kids who rushed to fill the application forms a month after 9/11, because they wanted to 'do something that mattered'. He sees them around station houses, these 9/11 babies, having been on the job now for eleven or twelve years. They all wear smart suits, speak three languages and go to the gym five days a week, all the while harbouring dreams of being 'talent spotted' by the FBI or the CIA. A bit like his partner.

That really isn't fair to Charlie, thinks Russo as he parks his car and enters the precinct building. Carlos Cardenas may be many things, but an idealist he isn't. His is the classic immigrant's story. Eldest son in a Puerto Rican family that moved to New York twenty years ago. Parents ran a bodega in Spanish Harlem, saving every penny to ensure their eldest boy went to college. When the money ran out after three years at City College, Charlie joined the force, and went to night school to finish college after donning a uniform. Like most immigrants, Charlie has a burning desire to improve himself. That's what had made him one of the youngest detectives in the force.

Cardenas is already in the office as Russo walks in, even though Russo has come in an hour early to catch up on the case. 'Jeez, Charlie, don't you ever go home?'

Charlie Cardenas grins sheepishly. He looks sort of like a younger version of Jimmy Smits, if Jimmy had curly hair and wore glasses. 'Sorry, Tony. Just trying to catch up on this case. I came in a couple hours ago.'

'Isn't Juanita getting pissed at you?'

'What am I gonna do, man. It's work. I wanted to get some background on this group, this United Front Party, and it's a lot easier to get things done when it's nice and quiet, before the hordes come in.'

'So, what did you find?'

'There's a lot of material on these guys, Tony. I'm surprised you didn't hear of them in your stint in the CTU. They have an extremely informative website. They claim to be the biggest political party in Karachi. The Party leader is a guy called the Don, who has been based out of Brooklyn for the past ten–fifteen years. They currently form the government in Sindh province.'

'Wait a minute. If they're in power, why is their leader based out of Brooklyn?'

'Apparently, this guy moved here years ago, when the Party was in opposition, on the grounds that the Party was being victimized politically. He never moved back when they came to power. The Party's website claims that since the Don has taken such an uncompromising stand against Islamic radicals in Pakistan, there is a constant threat to his life. You sure you never heard of these guys?'

'Usually the guys we heard about in CT were the ones who wanted to blow up shit, not the guys who opposed them, Charlie. They really call their leader the Don?'

'Yeah, that's what they call him. Real name's Mohammed Ali. The Party's official website has a whole section on the reason behind using the word Don. Most of it is kind of self-contradictory. They spend three paragraphs insisting that it has no criminal connotations, and how it reflects the respect that the Party has for its leader. And then they got a testimonial from somebody who says it's actually not 'Don' but 'Dawn', as the leader represents the dawn of a new era. Sounds a little kitsch, but I'll give them one thing, these guys are very wired. I did a quick search of the websites for other Pakistani political parties and no one else comes close to the level of organization of these guys. They have constant tweets coming in from Party leaders, right down to ground-level information like which roads have traffic congestion in Karachi at any given time. And their ministers are filing good governance reports. Basically these guys are on overdrive on the PR side.'

'So what you're telling me is that this Don guy is basically like the Pakistani Bloomberg? The mayor of Karachi?'

'More Michael Corleone than Michael Bloomberg. Our friend was also running armed gangs and ordering hits on his political opponents and on cops, in addition to his mayoral duties.'

'What do you mean?'

'Well, while the United Front is a legitimate political party, it's pretty evident that they seem to have been involved in a lot of bad shit. They've been accused of running a militant wing that was involved in the killings of hundreds of their political opponents, as well as government officials and cops over the past twenty years.'

'Cops?'

'Yeah, the cop-killing tag is a major one. Anti-Party blogs claim that the Party's militants have systematically targeted and murdered police officers that were involved in operations against the Party. According to one blog, the number of killed cops is close to 450.'

'Jesus Christ! What about this guy in the hospital? Anything about him?'

'It seems that this guy was the head of the Party's militant wing. According to these reports, he's wanted by the Karachi police in hundreds of cases.'

'What kind of cases?'

'Rioting. Arson. Burning cars. Assault. Murder of political opponents. Murder of police officers, allegedly. Never been arrested though. But, apparently he's a legend in the Party. Supposedly a real nasty piece of work.'

'When did he arrive here?'

'According to the stamp in his passport, just two days before the shooting.'

'So obviously, this is somehow connected to his activities with the Party. No one else would have a motive to shoot him in broad daylight in the middle of Central Park. What's the Party's set-up here?'

'Their website details all of their North American operations as well. They got branch offices in San Francisco, Houston, Boston, Atlanta and Chicago. But their international headquarters is right here in Coney Island Avenue. Apparently, the Don is supposed to be a local big shot. There are some articles that refer to him as the unofficial "Mayor of Little Pakistan". Runs the party single-handedly from here.'

'I still don't get it. Why the fuck does he live here, if he's such a powerful man in Pakistan?'

'Not sure.'

'Okay. Well, let's pay Mr Mayor a visit. See if he can enlighten us about what the fuck went on over here.'

The journey to Brooklyn takes the better part of an hour in morning traffic. The reason for the locality's nickname of 'Little Pakistan' is evident from the minute the detectives' unmarked Ford Crown Victoria turns onto Coney Island Avenue. Stores selling South Asian groceries are interspersed with dozens of naan–kebab joints and shops displaying colourful sweetmeats in their windows. The Party headquarters itself is an unimposing three-storey building flanked by that most unlikely culinary fusion combination, an Afghan–Chinese restaurant on one side, and the morbidly convenient Geo Funeral Home and Grocery store on the other. There are no Party flags or buntings, or even a sign that would identify the building as the headquarters of the largest political party in a city of twenty million inhabitants.

Russo and Cardenas park in front of the building and walk in through the glass doors to a small reception area. The inside of the building can only be described as 1970s' kitsch, a throwback to old-style US government offices. The only thing missing to complete the look would be a photo of Jimmy Carter on the wall, thinks Russo.

Although a check of building records has confirmed that the United Front Party owns the entire block, the only thing that denotes the Party's presence is a small framed picture of the Don placed on the side of the reception desk. Cardenas recognizes him from the dozens of pictures he has scrolled through on the Party's website, but unlike those pictures, which usually depict the Don giving a fiery speech at some rally or the other, wearing dark glasses and kurta-pyjama, this photo is a remarkably sedate one. The same man is dressed in a sober dark suit and red tie, and the sunglasses are replaced with a pair of trendy spectacles, the very image of middle-class respectability.

The receptionist is a balding middle-aged Pakistani man wearing a faded pink Polo shirt, eating biryani from a plastic container. He speaks with an exaggerated American accent that seems to be put on to hide his otherwise poor English. 'Yes, what can I do for you?'

'I'm Detective Russo, and this is Detective Cardenas. We wanted to have a word with Mr Mohammed Ali Pichkari regarding a murder that we're looking into. I'm told his offices are here?'

The receptionist is visibly unnerved at the sight of their badges. 'Wh-what kind of murder? What does this have to do with the Do – I mean with Mr Pichkari?'

'A Jewish lady was killed and four other persons injured in a shootout in Central Park three days ago. You must have heard of it, it's all over the news. According to eyewitness accounts, one of the injured persons, Asad Haider, seems to have been the intended target. We understand that Mr Haider was a member of the United Front Party. We wanted to ask Mr Pichkari some questions related to that.'

Russo can see sweat pouring down from the pink-shirted man's bald pate. His hand trembles as he picks up a phone, dials a number and starts speaking to whoever is on the other end in a very harassed tone. Russo and Cardenas do not understand what he says because he speaks in Urdu, but it is obvious that their presence has spooked him. Half a minute later, four Caucasian men in dark suits, wearing identical sunglasses, walk out of the lift. All four are bulky, buffed individuals, looking like bouncers at an upscale club. They position themselves in front of the reception desk, and the lead heavy holds up his hand inches away from Anthony Russo's face and speaks in a heavy Eastern European accent. 'This private property and ve private security. Pleez leef the premises immediately.'

'Hey Sunshine, this is police business so stay out of it and get your hand out of my face.' Russo flashes his badge again, but the heavies don't budge.

'I repeat, this private property, please leef or ve vill escort you out.' The bouncer's hand touches Russo's chest and he flashes the weapon under his coat with the other. Russo shoves him back violently, twisting the man's arm and slamming his head on the edge of the reception desk, while drawing his sidearm at the same time. The other three instinctively reach for the holsters under their jackets, but, realizing midway that the men in front of them are police officers, hesitate. Cardenas beats them to the draw by pulling out both badge and gun.

'Okay, place your hands in the air, now! This is NYPD official business and you are obstructing it by attempting to assault a police officer, so back the fuck down!' Cardenas's authoritative voice seems to have an impact on the heavies, who stare at each other, not knowing what to do. Their leader meanwhile, is whimpering, having dropped to the floor after being assaulted by Russo.

'Okay boys, you just entered a world of hurt. Assaulting an officer, obstruction, carrying a concealed weapon. You're already looking at ten–twenty years each. Have a think about that as you listen to my partner's instructions and lay down your weapons, place your hands on your head and move towards the back wall. Now. That means you too, Mr Receptionist. And I want to know exactly who you just called.'

There is a look of terror on the receptionist's face, but just as he shuffles from behind the reception desk towards the wall, the front door slams open and a silver-haired woman in an exquisitely tailored Chanel suit and Hermes scarf walks in followed by two other equally well-dressed men.

'I'm sorry, Detective, I'm going to have to ask you to let these men go. My name is Kira Daniel, senior partner at Daniel Simms Gold. These men behind me are my associates. I'm the attorney for Mr Mohammed Ali Pichkari and for the United Front Party and I'm here to inform you that these men have legitimate permits to carry firearms in the city of New York. They are private detectives hired for the personal protection of Mr Pichkari and of these premises.'

'Yeah, too bad they don't have a permit to pull out their weapons on police officers. We're taking them in, you can follow us to the precinct if you like. Charlie, call in a paddy wagon and some uniforms to get these guys moving.'

'I'm sorry, Detective … Russo, is it? My client has been under considerable personal threat from his various political opponents in Pakistan. There have been several assassination attempts on his life in the past. All of this information was recorded in his asylum application, as well with the NYPD and a local judge. These men are all ex-military professionals, trained to respond to unusual events. Under the circumstances, their reaction to you showing up was a perfectly legitimate one. If you wish to arrest them, you need to get a warrant. Now, what business do you have with my client?'

'Your client is a material witness in a homicide investigation, so I suggest you call him up and get him down here now. Otherwise, I'm going to start digging around your friends over here, to see how long a rap sheet each of them has. Private detectives, my ass. I don't know any branch of the military that these guys come from. I'm guessing these guys are mafia heavies from Little Odessa.'

'Detective, these men may not be US military, but they are ex-military. Russian ex-military. And you have no probable cause, nor any evidence, to allege any underworld connections for these men. This is their private investigator's licence.

Furthermore, my associate, who's just walked in, has brought a restraining order from a judge. My client is not obligated to speak to you about any issue unless you have a valid warrant. Now we can do this the easy way, or the hard way. The easy way is that you gentlemen walk out of here and pursue any potential inquiries by contacting my office. If you do not vacate these premises in the next five minutes, I'm going to file a personal complaint against both of you with the commissioner's office. And trust me, if I do that, you can be sure to face a disciplinary proceeding. The choice is yours, but I suggest you walk away from this one.'

Russo can see the normally effusive Cardenas fuming as he stares down the super lawyer. Russo is pissed too, but he hides it better. Slowly, he holsters his weapon and gently puts his hand on Cardenas's shoulder. 'Come on, Charlie, we're gonna go and talk to the judge about this one. Don't worry, Counsellor, we'll be back, and then you can file whatever goddamn complaint you like with the commissioner's office.'

Russo gets behind the wheel of the car and pulls away from the building. He pulls into a side street a couple of blocks away, where he is sure that the car cannot be spotted from the building. They watch the Russian heavies deploy themselves at the entrance of the building, giving menacing looks to anyone who crosses the street in front of them. A group of South Asian men pour out of the building, systematically spread out in two-man teams and begin scouring the nearby shops and alleys.

'What are they doing, Tony? And where did that posse of Pakistanis come from?'

'They're looking to check if we came with backup, and if we left anybody behind. Very slick. Too slick for some normal goddamn political organization. I'll tell you one thing now, Charlie, and I'll bet my next pay cheque on it. However this case pans out, we'll find that our friend Mr Don has something to do with it. Come on, let's go and talk to a judge.'

*

It is a bright day outside. The sunlight streams through his hospital room window as the tall nurse, the one called Ratchet, stands over him with a guilty expression on her face, holding his iPhone in her hand.

'Mr Haider, I'm very sorry. When you were brought in, your phone fell off the gurney as we were wheeling you in. One of the custodial staff picked it up, but didn't report it immediately. We wouldn't have found out, but the individual in question had a … change of heart … when he read the text messages. We haven't informed the police, we figured you would do that when you're well enough to meet the detectives. I, uh, I'm sorry on behalf of the hospital. Not just for the phone, for everything. If you wish to call the police and press charges against any member of the hospital staff, you are, of course, within your rights to do so.'

He has been conserving his strength, not revealing the extent of his recovery, but he still feels extremely weak and is barely able to talk. He tries to focus on what the nurse is saying, but instinctively, without fully understanding, shakes his head when she mentions the police. But what text message is she talking about? He doesn't remember any incriminating messages on his phone. Years of murdering people at the behest of the Party have taught him never to keep a record of such activities. When it was necessary to communicate on such matters, he and his hit teams would do so in code. If he wanted to order a hit, he would tell them to go and meet the person. So what could it be that so shocked a janitor to prompt him to return a stolen phone? And what did the nurse mean by saying she was sorry for everything? What has happened?

And then the realization hits him. Nani Amma. Mumtaz. Her husband. And her six-year-old daughter. The Don's anger at him had to find a target. Of course, he knew that his life would be under threat, but he should have realized that the Don would never settle for him alone. Wasn't that the principle he himself had set down, when he established the death squads? Never kill just your opponent, but eviscerate him. Strike as widely as possible against his family and friends to ensure that no one raises their head. That's how you spread fear in a city of twenty million. It's funny that you never think you will become a victim of your own terror one day.

He was so proud of his 'system'. He used to argue with Javed that the CIA and Mossad could learn a thing or two from them. Javed Gringo was his protégé, his masterpiece, the perfect killing machine, the younger brother he always wanted. And now Gringo is also the murderer of his family. Just for a moment, Asad Haider wonders how he did it. How he could kill an eighty-five-year-old woman who had fed him with her own hands? Did he even think about that when he pulled the trigger? And Mumtaz? The girl he had delivered countless bouquets of flowers and boxes of chocolates to on Asad's behalf, when it was too dangerous for Asad to be seen in public. Was that the excuse Gringo used to get into her house? Could Gringo have been so heartless? But there is no doubt that it would have been him. The Don would not have trusted anyone else with such a sensitive task. And the text message on the phone, sent by the ward boss of Soldier Bazaar, confirms it.

He clicks on a picture of Mumtaz stored in his phone. It was taken a couple of years ago, when they took a holiday together in Phuket. He would ask her what she told her husband when they went on these trips together. Her reply was that as a travel agent, trips to conferences in exotic locations were a part of her job, and her simple husband never suspected.

In the picture, she has a playful expression, her body wrapped in a blue sarong she would never dream of wearing in Karachi. Dusky skin, pouting, thick lips and the full figure of a middle-aged woman who has borne a child. No one would call her beautiful in a classical way. The picture reveals her as she was. An average-looking, middle-aged woman, who did not have the money to spend on tummy tucks and botox injections to eliminate her physical flaws, like so many of the wives of Party leaders. But to Asad Haider, she was the most beautiful woman in the world, the only one he had had eyes for for twenty years.

He closes his eyes and feels a constriction in his chest. Breathing becomes more difficult. He is dimly aware of monitors beeping alarmingly and nurses rushing into his room, shoving needles in his veins. He doesn't care any more. He wants to die. Maybe they can finally be together in the afterlife. After all the things that kept them apart in this world, that's the least they deserve. But then, if there is a thing as karma in this world or any other, that's the last thing that'll happen. Not after all the lives he has destroyed.

And now he is reaping the whirlwind of what he himself sowed. His family murdered in cold blood by men trained by his own hand. If he were a religious man, he would think that this was God's intended punishment for him. He shuts his eyes and hot tears flow down his cheeks. But the faces he sees flashing in front of him are not of his loved ones. They are of his victims. Asad Haider has a photographic memory, which is what made him so good at what he does. But it also means that he remembers the face of every single one of the sixty-four people he has murdered.

His friend Aleem used to say that every favour the Party doled out would fetch them ten votes. Not only would the beneficiary

vote for the Party, but he would also get his immediate friends
and family to vote for them. But the formula works the other
way round too. For every person Asad Haider has killed in the
past twenty-eight years, he has destroyed ten other lives and
created ten more people who hate him.

Aleem. It comes back to him. The cause of his misfortune.
The man Asad refused to kill, the first time he had refused an
order from the Don in twenty-eight years. Why did he refuse?
What was so different about Aleem? It wasn't as if Aleem
was a saint. Asad should know, he has killed plenty of saints.
Besides, Aleem had his vices. The mistress in Bahadurabad, the
under-invoiced tax returns that officials turned a blind eye to,
the admittedly modest business favours gained through Party
ministers. But at the heart of it, Aleem was a good man, and his
friend. So when the Don accused Aleem of colluding with the
Agencies, Asad could not bring himself to believe that.

Or perhaps it was the fact that Aleem had foretold his own
death. A week before flying to New York, Asad had met him
in Dubai. Since Asad's exile it was Aleem who would check
up on his family in Karachi, and look in on him whenever he
was in Dubai on a business trip. Asad loved these visits. Aleem,
through his witty stories, titbits of gossip and vivid descriptions
of how the city was changing, allowed him to smell the shit in
the gutters of Karachi. But his last visit, just a couple of weeks
ago, had been different. Aleem had been withdrawn, almost as
if reconciled to his fate. Asad had put it down to illness. Aleem
had suffered a couple of heart attacks, the reason why he had
stepped back from Party affairs some years ago. But it was when
he told him of his impending visit to the Don, an event of
some excitement since Asad hadn't physically met the big man
in years, that Aleem had finally opened up.

'He is going to order you to kill me.'

'Are you delusional? You're losing your mental faculties, Aleem. You need to get tested for dementia or something.'

'No, I am serious. That's why he has called you in person.'

It had been Aleem's absolute solemnity while saying this that had shaken Asad.

'Okay, let's say I play along with your silliness for a minute. Why would the Don want you dead?'

'Things have changed a lot, Asad. You sometimes don't get the entire picture because you are here in Dubai. Plus, of course, you were always the one whose devotion to the Don was blind. That is why he craves you. None of us could match that. But the Don, my best friend, is a different man in New York. He sees conspiracies being hatched against him at every corner. It doesn't help that the only person with access to him is Raja. He poisons Mohammed Ali's mind. He believes I am a threat to him because the Agencies might use me to replace him.'

'That's crazy, Aleem. You haven't been involved in Party affairs for years. You don't represent any kind of threat. And even if Raja has made up some bullshit story, the Don could always fly you to New York and clarify things with you in person. He would hardly tell me to kill you. We are all closer than family. That's not what we do with our own.'

'Isn't it? Are you sure we don't do that to our own, Asad?' Aleem had stared at him pointedly. Asad had been forced to turn his gaze away, and neither man said anything more about it.

'You mark my words, Asad. He will order you to kill me. My only request to you is that you ensure that the Don's anger towards me does not extend to my children. They have never been a part of this thing of ours. Let them live their lives as normally as possible after my death.'

'Aleem, believe me, the Don would never order it, and I would never do it.'

'If you refuse him, someone else will do it. And that will also be the end of you, because he would never forgive your refusal. Personally, I would much prefer to be killed by a friend like you, rather than one of the Party's random thugs. But whatever happens, please try and save my family.'

*

When he awakens again, it is dark outside. There is still a dull pain in his chest, but looking at the IV tubes running out from his forearm, he knows he is not dead. His mouth is very dry and he wishes he could have a drink. A real drink. Whisky would be great right now, a peg of Jack Daniels on the rocks. He is an exception in being a bourbon drinker, a taste acquired in his years of exile in Dubai, during the first operation against the Party. Most Karachiites don't understand why anyone would drink anything other than Johnny Walker Black Label. Asad has often wondered if the fixation with Black Label is driven by the laws of demand or supply. Is it because that's all that bootleggers can readily get hold of, or because its constant presence has been driven by a conscious need for upwardly mobile social climbers to acquire the taste for it as another trapping of success, a marker that they have finally 'arrived' in the city?

There were so many of those in the Party. Men and women who when they first arrived at Party headquarters wouldn't have known the difference between Black Label and sewage water, but now act as if they had spent all their lives in Scottish distilleries. How easily people change their tastes as they acquire wealth and power. And how much wealth and power has the Party given to a select few.

His survival instincts finally start kicking in. Asad Haider has always understood his own body very well, a by-product of a lifetime of being a sportsman and a bodybuilder in his youth.

He realizes that he has lost an enormous amount of blood and it will take time to recover his full faculties, if a full recovery is even possible. But he also knows that, somehow, he has to stay alert. The Don must know by now that he has survived. He wonders if the Party has sent someone to check up on him, or to finish the job.

He moves his arms and legs, exercising them, ensuring that they are still in working order. His biggest problem is that he is still breathing through the oxygen tent. He isn't sure why, but he does remember overhearing the Indian doctor say it was something to do with his lungs. He tries to calculate how much of an impediment it would be if there was permanent damage to the lungs. Could he still run out from here, if the Party sends another assassin after him? Probably not.

After all that has happened in the past few hours, a part of him wants to just lie down and accept what comes his way. But the other part, the survivor, will not accept this. After almost three decades of being a predator, Asad Haider does not know how to play the role of the victim. He is not going to be like the scores of people who accept their fate at the hands of this Party. The Don took away everything good in his life, so he will take away the thing that is most precious to the Don. His power. He knows that he is perhaps the one man in the world who can actually follow through on this.

Asad Haider draws a long breath and decides to call the nurse. As he tries to raise his head, he spots the visiting card on the edge of the table. It has the logo of the NYPD. Probably left by one of the cops. And that gives him an idea. He will force himself to make a full recovery. And then he will destroy the Don.

2

THE OLD MAN

'He survived. Saala, nine shots and he still survived.'

The old man's hands shake as he puts the telephone receiver back on its cradle. It's an ancient rotary dial phone. Like everything else in the house, from the Bombay Blackwood chairs to the vintage Victrola gramophone, it is an antique. A relic from a bygone age, much like the owner of the house itself. Byram Dinshaw is eighty years old, and has lived in the house on the corner of Katrak Parsi Colony in Soldier Bazaar all his life. In fact, there has been a Dinshaw living on this property now for almost a hundred years.

The young woman sitting across the table from him in his office-cum-study seems intrigued, but not overly concerned by his reaction. She continues to ferociously chew her gum, much to Byram's irritation.

'Who survived, Uncle?' She makes a small pink bubble with the gum, and then pops it quickly.

'Eh, can you bloody well stop doing that? You're not a bloody goat. I never allowed my son to chew gum when he was your age.'

'Sorry, Uncle.' Unperturbed, the girl takes the gum from her mouth, wraps it in tissue paper and looks around expectantly for a place to dispose it of. As she gets up to throw it in the dustbin near the door, Byram gets a chance to appraise her again. She is an extremely attractive girl, with silky black shoulder-length hair, an oval face and lips that seem to be locked in a perpetual pout. She is fashionably dressed in a tight-fitting sleeveless shalwar kameez that shows off her slim figure. Not quite size zero, but not far from it. A bit too thin for his liking, thinks Byram, but then this is what girls look like these days. And she is *so* young. Byram estimates that she couldn't be a day over twenty-two or twenty-three.

'Asad Haider survived.' Byram cannot hide the disappointment in his voice.

'Who's Asad Haider?'

'Are you joking? What the hell are you doing here if you don't know who Asad Haider is?'

'Is he with the Party?'

Byram's face looks like it is going to explode. Somehow, he manages to restrain himself. 'No, he is not with the Party. He *is* the bloody Party.'

The girl ignores Byram's apoplexy and shrugs. 'I've never heard of him. And I know the names of most of the Party's ward bosses in Gulshan and Jauhar. So he can't be that important, right?'

'Eh chokri, what's your name again?'

'Sadia. Sadia Ali.'

'Asad Haider could order the killing of all the bhenchod ward bosses in Gulshan and Jauhar with the snap of his fingers, Miss Sadia bloody Ali. They all bloody well report to him. He is their mai baap.'

Sadia remains unconvinced. 'But, Uncle, if he is such a big shot, he should be the chief minister, or at least a minister. His name has never even come on the news.'

'The channel owners would never let his name come on the news. They're not stupid, they don't want to end up in a body bag. And as for the CM, he is nothing in front of Asad Haider. Any chutiya can be the chief minister. Any one of the Party's sixty-seven MPs in the assembly can become chief minister tomorrow, if the Don puts his hand on them. Today it is Colombowala, tomorrow it will be some other Johnny. But not everybody can do what Asad Haider can. He runs the militant wing of the Party.'

'Oh, okay.' Sadia Ali nods her head slowly, absorbing this new piece of information in a very deliberate manner. To Byram, though, this only seems to make her look even more stupid.

'So, Uncle, where does this Asad Haider live? Some bungalow in Defence?'

Byram slaps his forehead in frustration. 'No, he lives in Dubai. He's lived there for years, because it's too dangerous for him to live in Karachi. How the hell do you not know this basic information? What world are you living in, that you think you can join our organization without having a basic knowledge of these facts?'

'Sorry, Uncle, don't get upset. Just asking a question, how should I know who this Asad Haider guy is? And if he's so powerful in the Party, as you say, then why does he have to stay away from the city? I mean the Party runs the city, so what's the danger for him?'

'The Party may be the most powerful force in the city, but it doesn't control everything. There are so many who have been wronged by Asad Haider, who would try and kill him at the first opportunity. Jihadis, Lyari gangsters, the people whose families he destroyed. And don't forget, the Agencies would also love to nail him.'

Byram shuffles as quickly as he can and steps out of his office into the veranda of the house. The house has a majestic old-world feel to it, but it is also evident that its glory days lie in the distant past. Empty cardboard boxes, piles of sawdust and mountains of packaging material are strewn all over, giving the place the look of a godown. As he steps into the light, he covers his eyes from the harsh midday sun. He curses under his breath when he notices that the gardener hasn't cut the grass in the lawn. Good help is impossible to find. Not like the old days. The lawn was his wife's pride and joy. She would tend to it herself every day, growing jasmine, marigolds and roses. Every day they would take evening tea together in the garden. Byram would return from the bakery laden with fresh zeera biscuits, steaming chicken patties or plain cake slices oozing with rich butter. He can still smell the jasmine in the early evening time. Freny loved her flowers. Since her death, he has tried to keep the lawn neat, but gardening was never his thing. Besides, it makes him miss her too much.

The rest of the house is also in a similar condition – kept in a state of minimum maintenance, but the personal flourish is gone. One could say that it doesn't have a woman's touch any more. The Gizri stone on the outer walls looks weatherbeaten and the floral patterns on the cement tiles on the floor are faded. As he climbs up the wooden staircase, Byram notices a thin film of dust on banisters that haven't been polished in years. Freny would never have allowed that. The servants got hell if she saw one speck of dust in the house, and all the wooden fixtures got a coat of polish at least once a year. He has learned to live a far more minimalist lifestyle. He only gets the sweeper to clean the outside of the house once a week, and he has stopped bothering altogether about the polishing. He doesn't see the point of it any more.

Sadia follows him up the stairs, looking at the framed pictures that adorn the walls. There is a black-and-white photograph of Byram and his wife on their wedding day, the woman fair

with plump cheeks almost as pale as her wedding gown. Byram
looks dashing in a tuxedo with a full head of hair and a cigarette
hanging from the corner of his mouth. There is another picture
of the couple with a young boy.

'Wow, Uncle, nice picture. You look handsome. When was
it taken? And where's Auntie? And your son? What does he do?'

'Eh chokri, mind your own business.' Byram turns and gives
her a hard stare that literally stops her in her tracks.

The upstairs section looks a little more homely. It is cleaner,
with dozens more photographs on the walls and on tables. There
is even a vase with fresh flowers in the hallway.

Sadia finds the photographs fascinating. They tell a tale of
an older, gentler Karachi, a city that no longer exists, except in
the minds of the remaining few who lived through it. There
is Byram getting off a tram near the Port Trust building. The
road behind him is spotlessly clean, in contrast to its present-day
state with piles of plastic bags and paper polluting it. And as for
the tram, Sadia doesn't remember a tram ever having operated
in her twenty-three years of living in the city. Another picture
shows the family at a picnic near a lake, with Byram holding a
small boy on the hood of his 1970 Mazda. There is another one
of Byram in a tuxedo with his wife, helping another couple cut
a three-tiered cake in a hotel ballroom. Everyone in the picture
is immaculately dressed, the men in suits or tuxedos, their hair
shiny with Brylcreem, the women in dresses or glamorous saris.

Charmed by the pictures, Sadia decides to make another
attempt to break the ice. 'Uncle, where is this lake? What a
lovely scene. I would love to go there.'

He looks at her for a long minute and does not answer.
Finally, he turns his back and walks into one of the rooms. The
room is spartan, with a thin mattress on a narrow bed, a side
table next to the bed and a single chair. The largest piece of
furniture in the room is a five-foot-tall file cabinet. 'It's Lake

Haleji,' Byram finally answers as he takes a bunch of keys from his pocket and starts to unlock the cabinet drawers.

'Oh, it's so beautiful. Hard to believe na, that there is such an amazing spot so close to Karachi. These days, we just never get out of the city. And I didn't even know that there used to be a tram service in Karachi. When was that picture taken, Uncle?'

'1966. And yes, there used to be a first-class public transport system in this city, until the bloody maulvis and Partywallahs fucked things up.' Byram withdraws several files from the cabinet and dumps them on the bed. 'Here, this is the file. You need to summarize the contents and put them on the, what do you call it, the Internet ...' As he is leafing through the file in his hand, a white-uniformed nurse enters the room and silently beckons him outside. Byram takes care to cover the files on the bed with a sheet to ensure that the nurse can't glance at the subject headings. 'Don't touch anything,' he says to Sadia, then walks out, leaving her in the room alone.

Sadia sits down on the cane chair and places her feet on the bed, picking up the file closest to her toes. It is titled THE PARTY – EARLY YEARS. 1982–87. It has several photographs and press clippings attached to it. The photos show the same group of people, five men and a woman, at different events. Standing at rallies addressing students, donating blood in a volunteer medical camp, sitting cross-legged listening to a naat khwani. She thinks she recognizes one of the men. Despite his camp hairstyle and ridiculously flared trousers, the Don's steely-eyed expression is unmistakably the same as in the thousands of posters of him that are plastered all over the city.

'Eh chokri! What did I tell you! I told you not to touch anything. And get your feet off my bed.'

'Arre, Uncle, is this really the Don? He looks so young. And who are the others? They all look so young and vibrant.'

'Young and vibrant, my foot. Each one of those bastards has rivers of blood on their hands. Even the chokri, Zaibunissa. Bloody bitch.'

'But who are they?'

'Arre, are you pretending to be thick, or are you actually like this? You say you are dedicated to destroying the United Front, but you don't recognize the founding members of that same party?'

'I recognize the Don, I mean, he's pretty hard to miss. He's just gotten fatter since then. But I don't know any of the others.'

'Look here, this one, in the tight pyjama and kurta, that's Imam. He was a left-wing student leader, a real firebrand. His father was a famous poet. He met the Don in university and became the Party's second in command. He was an organizational genius and the brains behind the Party's early electoral successes. His stature in the Party was second only to the Don's. That's why the big man had him killed in 1994. This one, wearing the suit and tie, is Aleem. He's a businessman, one of the Party's earliest and biggest financial backers. But he also went into the background after Imam's murder. That one, with the Charlie Chaplin moustache, is Guddu. No one knows what happened to him.'

'And the girl? Zaibunissa?'

'She was the Party's women's wing organizer. Very vocal, very charismatic. But then she sort of retired from politics. Now she is the wife of the chief minister.'

'But Uncle, I've seen the CM's wife on TV. She's always wearing a dupatta on her head, very pious-looking, always organizing Quran khatams and dars at the Chief Minister House. She doesn't look anything like this jeans-wearing girl from the photo.'

'Siasat. Politics changes everybody. She made a political choice. Or maybe she got scared when she saw what happened to all the other founder members of the Party, so she made the smart choice.'

'Wow. And the Don himself? What's his real story?'

'You mean apart from the saala airbrushed version that the Party keeps presenting? In the several biographies and dozen-odd documentaries that they have commissioned about his life? Which they paid for from various government department budgets? That's all bloody lies. The Party's ability to create bullshit about itself never ceases to amaze me.'

Sadia picks up another photo from the same folder. It shows the young Don, giving a fiery speech, his arms gesticulating wildly and his face contorted with effort. Next to him stands another man, taller than the Don, with an athletic build. He stands with his muscular arms folded in front of his chest, and has such a ferocious expression that it makes Sadia shudder to just look at the photograph.

'Uncle, who's this? He looks scary.'

'That's Asad Haider, our target. He is a Shia chokra. He's from around this area only. Used to do odd jobs for one of the Shia student groups, till he became the Don's bodyguard in university. And then, when the Party was formed, he created the militant wing. Nearly every person that the Party's ward bosses have killed, the order came from him. And he's the bastard who survived an assassination attempt today. He is the reason you are here today. Here, this is his file, with details of all his illegal activities. You need to start leaking these details anonymously on the Internet.'

Sadia is silent and stares down at the picture again. 'Did he really give the final order for every killing?'

'Yes, you stupid girl, why do you make me repeat myself? And what is it to you if he gave every order, or if he just gave 90 per cent of the orders? Get on with your work.'

Tears start streaming down Sadia's cheeks. 'Because I want to know if he was the one who gave the order to kill my brother.'

The girl's reaction takes Byram by surprise, but he is unmoved by it. He has seen too many people shed tears because of the Party. 'Who the hell was your brother?'

'Inspector Dilawar Ali.'

Even Byram remembers that name. 'The police officer who conducted all those raids against the Korangi ward. He gave evidence in court, despite threats from the Party, didn't he? And then he was suspended. Damn, I can't remember what that famous case was.'

The tears are now flowing uncontrollably, leaving a snaking trail through Sadia's layer of foundation, like a dry river bed cutting through a mountain range. 'The Bilqees Mai case.'

'Yes, Bilqees Mai. The old woman whose two young sons were shot dead in front of her eyes by the ward boss because they had dared to put up posters critical of the Don and the Party in Korangi Dhai Number. And then she went to the police station to lodge an FIR against the ward boss for her sons' murder, despite the fact that she was threatened and beaten up by the ward boys. But the local thana wouldn't register the case until Inspector Dilawar Ali took over.'

'The old SHO was afraid that the Party would have him removed, or that the local ward boss would kill him if he registered the case. Then, Bhaiya took charge. He not only registered the case, he arrested the ward boss and ensured that he was convicted. We started receiving threats at home. People calling up in the middle of the night, telling my mother and me to call off my brother, otherwise we would be raped in the street. I told Bhaiya, but he always said nothing would happen to him or us, because he was fighting for a just cause, and God helped those who fought for just causes. Four times they tried to kill him in Korangi, but every time he survived without a scratch, and instead killed several of their people. But then the government changed again and he was suspended. For three years, he sat at home because the Party could not countenance having one of their opponents get a posting. Half the time he didn't even receive his salary. He was miserable, but he said he would never go and beg their ministers for a favour, even though a couple of them had been in college with him.'

'So what happened?'

'One day, Bhaiya received an order, to go and take charge of Clifton police station. We couldn't understand it, because he had not done any sifarish, nor had he received any advance intimation of this order. He assumed that maybe the Party had decided to call a general amnesty for police officers who had worked against them. Perhaps their stance had softened somehow because recently we had read that Akbar Khan, who had been SHO in Orangi when Bhaiya was in Korangi, had also been reinstated.'

'The next day, Bhaiya put on his uniform again. He used to look so smart in his uniform, not like the other police officers, who look fat and ungainly. He took great pride in his appearance. He got into his car and drove to the end of our street ...' – it takes great effort for Sadia to continue telling the story through her sobbing – '... and that's where they got him. They were waiting for him. There were about fifty of them, all armed with Kalashnikovs. They didn't want to leave any chance of his surviving. They fired 400 rounds into his car.'

Finally overcome, Sadia weeps bitterly. Byram stands in front of her, uncomfortable, not knowing what to do next. The only thing that occurs to him is to ask an irrelevant question. 'If they were going to kill him, why did they get him posted as SHO of Clifton?'

'I don't know. Different people said different things. Somebody told us that the Party got Bhaiya posted because the Korangi ward boss had said he wanted to kill him in his uniform. Another one of Bhaiya's colleagues said it was because they wanted to reinforce the point to the police, that they would never forget or forgive those that had stood against them, and that it was done this way to show that a policeman's uniform wasn't a shield against the Party. Uncle, do you think the order to kill my brother was given by Asad Haider?'

The question is an earnest one, and Byram remains silent, not knowing how to answer it. Should he tell her that the order to kill her brother almost certainly would have come from Asad Haider? That a simple ward boss, of Korangi or anywhere, would not be able to pull the strings to arrange a fifty-man hit squad? Nor would the ward boss have been able to arrange Inspector Dilawar's posting to Clifton. These are things that only Asad Haider could have got done, in the blink of an eye. So the correct answer to her question would be, yes, you silly girl, of course that bastard Asad Haider ordered the killing of your brother and you are bloody silly to think it could have been anybody else. But he cannot bring himself to say this. It's not just a matter of propriety. Byram has always been a blunt man. But a lifetime of pursuing the Party has also made him a careful man. He does not want to reveal everything to this girl whom he has met for the first time today, who claims to want to join the Others, but hasn't a clue about the way the Party works. So he just shrugs his shoulders non-committally.

'Is that the reason why you joined the Others? Revenge for your brother?'

'Yes. I hate them for killing Bhaiya. But why do you work against them?'

Again, Byram pauses. He has been expecting, and trying to avoid, this question for some time. And not just with Sadia. He doesn't like exposing his feelings and motives to anyone in the world. When he was a young man, he never let his father know about the plans he had to expand the family's little bakery business into a catering industry, until he finally got control of the business. He never let his mother know how madly he fell in love with Freny the first time he met her. She was the only one with whom he has ever shared his hopes and dreams. He has always been a patient man, waiting for events to unfold in his favour.

But some things become unavoidable, and he supposes he must give the girl standing in front of him, still crying, some answer. Wordlessly he shuffles out of the room, beckoning her to follow him with a tilt of his head. Two doors down from his, a larger door opens into a bigger room. Inside, the stout nurse who had called him earlier sits in a corner reading *Khawateen Digest*. In the middle of the room is a large, adjustable hospital bed. A bank of monitors and several IV hangers have been placed next to the bed. And in it lies a man. It is difficult to determine his age, but the pallor of his skin, the bruised patches where IVs have been connected and disconnected repeatedly, and the atrophying of the leg and arm muscles seem to indicate that this man has been in this condition for some time. The man breathes through an oxygen mask, and though his eyes are open, he does not seem to detect their entry. He lies there, lifeless, staring at the ceiling, listening to the pumping sound of a dialysis machine and the beeping of the monitors.

Byram finally turns to Sadia and speaks. 'Because of him. Because of my son.'

3

THE JOURNALIST

Call me Ismail. Ismail Naich. I read that in a book once. Not the Naich part, obviously, but the first sentence. They say that a book must have a catchy opening line. This line was from a book I picked up in Urdu Bazaar a few years ago. I think it was called *Moby Dick*, and it was about fishing or something. Why would I be reading something like that? True, it's not the sort of thing I would read under normal circumstances, but at the time I was preparing for a job interview with an American TV channel. Even though the job itself had no English requirement – they were setting up an office in Karachi and wanted a local crime reporter – I thought I would impress them with my knowledge. So for a brief period, I had started reading English novels. I remembered the opening sentence because the character had the same name as me. I never got the job with the American channel, but I thought at the time that if I ever wrote anything greater than a crime bulletin, I would try working that line in.

I am a journalist by profession. Chief crime reporter for the *Daily Ahsaas*. If you haven't heard of the paper, I wouldn't be surprised. It's an Urdu language tabloid, what we call an 'eveninger' in Karachi. It targets the growing middle class of this city, feeding them a diet of stories about government corruption, police encounters and steamy accounts of liaisons between various actors and actresses. How successful it is as a newspaper is a matter of some dispute. We claim to have a circulation of one million, but judging from the bundles of copies that are returned to our offices every day for pulping, I doubt whether so many people actually read us. The primary aim of the paper is to act as a vehicle to push forward the interests of our owner, Mr Liaqat Khujli, of Khujli Builders fame. Being a builder in this city is no easy job. The profit margins are good, admittedly, but there are so many other problems. Political parties demanding bhatta, building control officials asking for bribes, gangsters threatening to kidnap you for ransom, and if nothing else, these bloody civil society NGOs start petitioning the courts if even one brick from one of your buildings falls out. So, as you can imagine, a builder like Mr Liaqat Khujli, who has taken a few shortcuts in life, needs all the help he can get. Thus, he decided to establish a newspaper. A free press can be a very useful weapon. Every time anyone wants to look into your affairs, you smear them with a strategically placed corruption story, or an editorial about the fascistic tendencies of certain NGOs. It's like having yellow journalism on demand. Also, with a newspaper, political parties court you. You can always trade favours for endorsements or support.

So what was a respectable journalist like me doing working at the *Daily Ahsaas*? Well, first of all, I'm not particularly respectable. Never have been. Like most Karachiites, I'm not originally from Karachi. I'm from Hyderabad, and I got into journalism not out of some altruistic desire to discover the truth, but rather because other options had dried up. I like to think that I was always a people person in school and college, which meant that I always preferred hanging out with friends to studying. That meant I would never have the grades to be a doctor or an engineer, or to even sit for the civil service exams. My father tried to use sifarish to get me appointed as an assistant sub-inspector in the excise department, because the minister was from our village. But even that fell through because someone else paid the minister a bribe for the same job, and cold hard cash always works better than old village ties.

So I went to Jamshoro University and studied journalism because there was no other choice. Being a small landowner, my father always understood the need for connections with government officials. After all, small landowners are totally dependent on these things. Thus, he figured that if I couldn't be in the government, it was good to be in a profession that had daily interactions with government officials. So that was my main motivation to be a journalist. To make contacts that would be helpful for my father and elder brother.

I started my career at a small paper in Hyderabad, which would make the *Daily Ahsaas* look like a paragon of journalistic ethics. Being a journalist for a small tabloid is a bit like being a hunter. You are expected to feed yourself, as your salary will never be enough to live on. Thus, to augment one's income, you go out and find a shikar, a target that is ripe for extortion or blackmail. A respectable, pious businessman who has kept a woman in the red light district for years, and is scared that the exposure will ruin his standing in decent society, is a perfect target. A police station in charge who has been ripping off his superiors by giving them a smaller share of the beat, and is now petrified of them finding out, is another good example. In short, I trade in rumours. Most of them cannot be substantiated, but that doesn't matter. In this business, if enough people read about it, the rumour takes on a life of its own. And the people I target are more worried about their izzat than the truth.

My career in journalism coincided with the big media boom in Pakistan. The only problem was that this boom totally passed me by. Despite the presence of dozens of new news channels, in every language and dialect, none of them wanted to hire me. That's the thing about practising my type of shikari journalism. Once you get labelled as a journalist who accepts lifafas of cash, serious media groups don't want you. So you end up doing more and more of the same thing to make ends meet. I didn't mind, after thirteen years on the bottom rungs of my profession I had come to terms with staying in my present station in life, as long as the lifafas kept coming, but recently the lifafas had also started drying up.

It was this desperation to find fresh shikar that took me to Rafiq Rangoonwala's door. Rafiq seth was one of the big wholesalers of medicines in Botal Galli, the medicine seller's market near Kharadar. These medicine wholesalers are real big fish, though you wouldn't think it if you looked at them. Sitting in dirty crowded shops, conducting business on grubby slips of paper, dressed in crumpled shalwar kameez, you could never imagine that each one of these bastards is worth millions of dollars. Yes, that's right, dollars, not rupees. They are all khepias, smugglers running vitamins and Viagra into countries like Myanmar and Indonesia for huge profits. Hence Rafiq seth's name, Rangoonwala. As a young man, he had made a name for himself doing runs to Myanmar in the years when the country was closed to the world. No matter what their political ideology may be, the elites in any country will still want their dicks to get hard and their hearts to run well.

Rafiq seth made a lot of money and finally settled down as one of the major players in Botal Galli. General secretary of the Medical Wholesalers Association, with five children, two wives, a palatial home in Defence and important contacts in the underworld. What everyone did not know about Rafiq

seth was that he was one of Baba Dacait's biggest supporters.
He had a special deal with the gangster, whereby in return for
a reduced extortion rate and a promise not to kidnap members
of the Medical Wholesalers Association, Rafiq seth promised
Baba support from the association. This was important for Baba
because what I had uncovered in the course of my inquiries,
and what no one else yet knew, was that Baba was preparing
the ground to enter politics. Why he would want to do that was
beyond my understanding. He already enjoyed all the power,
without having to put up with any of the bullshit of politics.
Nonetheless, he wanted to throw his hat in the ring, and Rafiq
seth was apparently helping to prepare the ground for him.

Who is Baba Dacait? If you don't know that then you must
have been living on the moon for the past five years. Or in
France. Baba Dacait is Karachi's biggest gangster, the king of
Lyari. Everyone knows his name, but very few people have
actually seen Baba. Since he was a wanted criminal, it wasn't
exactly easy to arrange interviews with him. He had become
the biggest thorn in the United Front's side in the past five years,
because he had challenged the hegemony of the Don in this city.

Which was exactly why his plans for entering politics were
so bumbard. The Party would go absolutely crazy, and would
never forgive anybody who aided Baba in this endeavour. And
this is exactly why I believed that my knowledge of all this was
my lottery ticket. While Rafiq seth supported Baba, he also
couldn't afford to alienate the Party, which was in government
after all. This is why he would want evidence of his involvement
with Baba to be kept under wraps, and would, I thought, pay
me handsomely to do just that.

I got to Botal Galli that day, mentally having already
put down a deposit on a new flat in Bahria Town, the new
development that everyone was trying to get into. Upon
introducing myself as a journalist, I was immediately taken to the

back of the shop, past rows of medical supplies lining the walls, to a small cubicle that served as Rafiq seth's office. The man himself sat there behind a small desk, piled with slips of paper, and eyed me suspiciously. He was a huge man, at least six feet tall and 300 pounds heavy, and his ability to fit into that small cubicle office was in defiance of all the rules of physics. Rafiq seth was bald, with small, beady bloodshot eyes, and he wore a wrinkled safari suit that struggled to restrain his girth. The only acknowledgement of modernity in the office was a brand new iPhone that lay on the table next to an old Nokia 3210.

Rafiq seth wasn't a talkative sort, and he continued to stare at me silently while the office boy poured hot steaming tea into a chipped cup and set it in front of me. Finally, after several moments of silence, I decided to lighten the mood.

'Rafiq seth, kem cho?' I knew he was a Memon from Gujarat, so I used the only Gujarati phrase I knew. 'How is business these days?'

He grunted and placed his hand on his chest and then pointed upward, signalling, I presumed, that all was well with God's grace.

'Mashallah, mashallah, I have heard you are doing very well this year. But Rafiq seth, what are you doing in this old office? A man of your influence should be in a modern office block with glass windows or something. You are a big man, Rafiq seth, there is no harm in showing that. And what are you doing with this old Nokia set? This is not up to your standards, you should donate such things to poor people like myself.'

I had thought flattery would soften him up, but his face remained as inscrutable as ever.

'I'm a small man, this place is fine for me. It keeps me close to the work here in Botal Galli, and I am much more accessible to the other members of the association. You know Karachi, bhaijan, show a little flash and you get on someone's list for kidnapping or extortion. I have been mugged thrice on the

Mauripur road, that's why I keep the old Nokia, to give away in case I am held up again. But what can I do for you, Ismail bhai? What does a reporter from such a big newspaper want from a nobody like me?'

'Rafiq seth, I am doing a story on reports that some of your association members adulterate the medicines that they sell. It will be a pretty embarrassing story for the association, so I wanted to give you the chance to comment before it came out. I personally didn't want to do this story because I have great respect for your reputation, but my editor is a real kameena. But maybe I can get him to hold off on it. He, and I, would be greatly relieved if we knew that you had paid your zakat.'

'Ismail bhai, I think someone is wanting to trick your paper. Alhamdulillah, none of our members have ever indulged in adulterating any of the drugs they sell. And tell your editor not to worry, I pay my zakat every year. Full amount, no cheating. But I am sorry that you had to take so much trouble to come out here, chasing a false story. If you like, I can give you one or two hundred rupees for your taxi fare.'

'Okay. What about yourself? You're very close to Baba Dacait, aren't you? I've heard you go and meet him in Afshani Galli every week, where even the police don't go. It's interesting that all the other market associations in the area are always complaining to the government about Baba's extortion threats. But your association never complains. Some people say it's because you have a setting with Baba. If all of this were to come out in an article, I am sure that members of the United Front would read it with great interest. Maybe you should dig a little deeper in your pocket, because I don't think I'll be able to stop anything with just taxi fare.'

For the first time, a thin smile stretched across the fat bastard's face. I knew I had him. The Party would never forgive him for becoming so close to Baba Dacait.

'Ismail bhai, how much zakat would you like me to pay?'

'Rafiq seth, this is going to be an ongoing issue, because I will have to ensure that no other reporter gets hold of the same information that I have managed to get. It will probably be best to set up a monthly payment. Let's say, two lakhs?'

'Ismail bhai, this is too much. Give some discount. How about 50,000?'

'Rafiq seth, I won't be able to manage things in 50,000. Make it at least one lakh.'

'Okay, give me a couple of minutes, let me see what I can do. Please sit and have another cup of tea. Can I get you a hot kachori or samosa? They have very nice ones in this area.'

I gladly agreed to another cup of tea and a kachori. After all, this was time for celebration. I had never before secured such a large, regular payment in any of my scams before. So I sat back in my chair, dipping the kachori in my tea, and took the Bahria Town brochure out of my pocket. I always wanted to live in a housing complex that had a swimming pool. Not that I knew how to swim, but it looks so nice in the background.

Rafiq seth was gone a while, at least twenty minutes, but when he got back he was accompanied by two dark sheedis, wearing T-shirts and carrying pistols. This time, the fat bastard had a wide smile that showed all his thirty-two misshapen teeth.

'Ismail bhai, sorry but I considered your offer and have decided to reject it. You do what you have to do, but before you go, you should know that these men are Baba's men. He is quite interested in your attempts to blackmail me, and him. Bhenchod, did you think I was born yesterday that any chutiya can walk in off the street and hustle me?'

I like to think of myself as someone who has seen the dark underbelly of this city, but it is one thing seeing and hearing about such incidents, and something totally different when you find yourself in one. The urge to piss in my pants was a strong

one as the sheedis dragged me out of the office and blindfolded
me with a strip of cloth. I was thrown into the back seat of a
vehicle, with one of the men sitting half on top of me, poking
me with a pistol. The ride was an extremely bumpy one, and
with every bump I prayed that the gun would not accidentally
misfire into my stomach. I assumed that we were going to Lyari.

Finally, after about twenty minutes in which every inch of
my body was jolted and bruised, we came to a halt. I was pulled
out of the car and led into a house. I was shaking with fear. I
wasn't even sure if these were actually Baba Dacait's men or if
that bastard Rafiq had sold me to some kidnapper. Every story
I had ever heard about Baba's exploits filled my brain. Hadn't he
cut off the tongue of one of his lieutenants when he suspected
him of becoming a police informer? And then shot him ninety-
nine times? What about the kidnapee who had tried to escape
and been mailed back to his family, limb by limb? No one could
ever confirm whether these stories were real or folk tales, but
they were all I could think of during that drive.

Suddenly, the cloth was taken off my eyes. In front of me was
a man sitting on a comfortable sofa. He was short, very short,
like a jockey, and he looked like a sheedi, with his curly hair
and dark skin. His most striking feature were his eyes, bloodshot
and bulging, with a stare that seemed to sear into your soul. He
wore a dirty T-shirt and shalwar, and was smoking a long thin
cigarette – nothing about his appearance would make anyone
believe that this was the notorious gangster Baba Dacait. For
all I knew, he could have been the tea boy at the dhaba across
the street from my flat. But then he spoke, and in an instant,
it became clear why this man was one of the most feared men
in the city.

'Do you know who I am?' The voice was raspy but deliberate
and menacing, making the respondent fear that the wrong
answer could cost him his life.

'Ye-yes sir. You are Baba Dacait, right?'

'And who are you?'

'I'm nobody, sir. I'm just a small-time reporter with a wife and three children.'

'Then what makes you think you can try and blackmail me?'

'Sir, I would never dream of blackmailing you. I made a mistake, I was desperate for money, so I went and concocted this story in front of Rafiq seth. Please forgive me.'

In this time, the guards standing next to me, whom I had barely noticed, searched my pockets and handed over the contents to Baba. In truth, there was hardly anything there, just a tattered old wallet with a few hundred rupees and a stack of business cards that I had collected over the years. The men had gone through everything, and one of the guards pointed out one of the cards to Baba and whispered in his ear. Baba's face stiffened, and then a sort of curiosity came over him. From what I dared to try and see, the card in Baba's hand was the one from the American channel I had interviewed with. I had kept the card of the manager I had met, because I thought at some point I would be able to show off my contacts with an American channel to somebody. I had never imagined that this would happen in the circumstances I was now in.

'This channel is an international channel, yes? An American channel? How do you have their card?'

'Sir, I interviewed there for a job, earlier this year.'

'But you still have contacts there?'

'Yes.' I should probably have told him the truth. After all, I had no idea what Baba's views were on American TV channels. He could have been a raving anti-American mullah, but something about his tone, and the look in his eye, told me that this could be my way out of this situation, if only I kept my wits about me.

'How good are your contacts?'

'Sir, what do you need? I am sure I can assist you in any way possible.'

'I want to give an interview.'

'Sir, if you don't mind, can I ask you a couple of questions?' The risk I had taken seemed to have been rewarded. A tilt of Baba's head sent his men scurrying to get me a chair, which I was then shoved down into. Baba never took his eyes off me, but a second tilt signalled that I should continue speaking.

'Why do you wish to give an interview? I have heard that you are interested in entering politics. Is that the reason? If that's the case, I can help you. I have been a journalist for a long time and I understand the media. And if you want to master politics, you need to master the media.'

I could see that my response had aroused Baba's interest. Suddenly, a cup of tea was placed in front of me, a clear sign that I had gone from kidnapee to honoured guest.

'Go on.'

'Sir, the Don and the Party will always try to distort what you say. They are very powerful, they have large segments of the press in their pocket, either through money or intimidation, and more than that, they are experts at media manipulation. Just look at what they have done with you. They have been successful in painting you as a criminal. Why should you be regarded as a criminal and the Don regarded as a politician, when he is as much of a criminal?' I realized my mistake immediately. 'I mean, not to say *you* are a criminal, sir, but I mean in terms of public perception. This is why you need to do more than just an interview. I mean, an interview is a start, but you need to launch a media campaign, that will show you as a protector of your community, while showing the Party as the terrorists and criminals.'

'What will I have to do to start this media campaign?'

'Sir, start with your interview. But make sure you get a journalist who is sympathetic to you, not someone who will leave from here and twist your words. But if you really want to get into politics, what you have to do, is write an autobiography.'

'Auto-what?'

'Autobiography. A book about your life. All great politicians write one. It will give you a chance to tell the world about your life, your experiences and your philosophy. Tell people how you came to your current position in life. You can achieve a lot more in a book format than in a short interview.'

Baba gave me a stare that turned my blood to ice. 'Do you think I am a chutiya? You want me to admit to all of my crimes, so that the police can use this as evidence against me? So that the Party can have more propaganda about me? Rangoonwala was right, you must be a Party spy.'

'No sir! No sir! I have no affiliation with the Party. I hate them. They take bhatta from our building every month. I hate giving it to them but I do not have the strength to fight them. Please sir, let me explain my point to you. Writing about your life, about your struggle, humanizes you. The police can't do anything against you, even if you reveal some parts of your life in a book. The police are not bothered about evidence. They follow power. If they see you as a political force, then it doesn't matter how much head money they put on you. You will become untouchable. All the great politicians have written books, in which they talked about their crimes. Sardar Clinton admitted to having fucked that fat girl. Mandela was convicted as a terrorist, before he became the President of South Afreeka. Today's criminal becomes tomorrow's leader, if you play your cards right.'

'Who is Mandela?'

'He is a fellow who freed the black South Afreekans. He spent thirty years in prison, and then was elected President. Sir, you can be the Pakistani Mandela, a man who fought for his people, who endured all sorts of hardships and false accusations, but did not falter in his mission.'

Finally, I could see the bulb go on in Baba's head. He had fathomed the possibilities of my proposal. Even though his facial expression hadn't changed, I knew from his eyes that I had him. Now was the time to move in for the kill.

'Who will write my auto-graphy?'

'Auto-bio-graphy. Well, sir, you don't have to worry on that account. I will.'

4

ANTHONY

Simon Sole looks exactly like the name sounds. Short, sharp and well put together. He looks like a man who likes simplicity and order. His clothes are all in primary colours, a grey suit, white shirt and blue tie. The well-tailored suit jacket does little to hide the bulging muscles underneath.

That's what gives him away, thinks Anthony Russo. The body is a little too well maintained to be the product of a casual gym rat. These biceps were forged in the crucible of war. An attempt has been made to grow the hair long, but somehow Russo can detect that it's a scalp used to a military cut.

The final giveaway as to the identity of the visitor is the fat class ring that he wears. Again, nothing unusual in this, after all, many Ivy Leaguers wear their class rings, but Russo has already spotted the insignia and motto of the United States Air Force Academy. Yup, Simon Sole smells like CIA all the way.

Of course, he doesn't admit to that when he shows up at the precinct the morning after their visit to Little Pakistan. 'Detective Russo and Detective Cardenas?' He pronounces Cardenas with an accent, like someone who has spent time in

Central America. 'Simon Sole, I'm with the State Department. I heard you guys had a bit of a run-in with Mr Pichkari yesterday.'

'We never got to him, we only got as far as the front door, before they sic'd a $400 an hour lawyer on us. But what does this have to do with State?'

'Ah well, as I'm sure you would have found out, Mohammed Ali Pichkari is a high-profile asylum seeker from Pakistan. He has been in the United States for some years now, but he continues to head one of the main political parties in the city of Karachi. As you can imagine, due to our interests in the region over the past few years, the State Department maintains a liaison with these kinds of individuals. Say, if you guys have a couple of minutes to spare, let me buy you a cup of coffee.'

They go to the old-fashioned diner on Columbus Avenue, the one that's patronized by all the cops in the precinct. At ten in the morning, it's empty. A delivery truck is parked out front, despite the fact that deliveries aren't allowed at this time. Such are the perks of being the precinct's watering hole.

'So, what's good here?'

'The coffee's decent. Try the meat loaf, if you're feeling adventurous. Charlie and I don't usually eat here. He's a healthy boy, nothing but green salads and fruit for him, and me, I like ethnic food so I go to the Lebanese place round the corner. So tell me, Mr Sole, what kind of black ops does the Don run for you guys?'

Simon Sole smiles a disarming smile, taking time to sip his coffee before answering. 'We're not in that business, Detective Russo. We just occasionally consult with him and members of his party on regional issues. His party, the United Progressive Front, was the first major political party in Pakistan to condemn 9/11. Since then, they have remained an integral part of a coalition of liberal, moderate groups that promote a stronger alliance with the US. They talk our language, that's why we dance with them. There's no cloak-and-dagger stuff involved.'

'And you're the guy who liaises with him? Did he tell you about yesterday? Did they have some kind of problem with NYPD officers coming to ask them a few questions? What is this guy hiding, if he hires an expensive lawyer and asks the US government to go bat for him?'

'Detective Cardenas, I think there's been a sort of cultural misunderstanding. Yes, Mr Pichkari's people did get in touch with us after your visit yesterday, but their intention isn't to intimidate you in any way. These guys have been on the run for years. They're a part of the government now in Pakistan, but for long periods they were being persecuted by the military, intelligence agencies, and rival political parties. Most of them have been in and out of jail like it was a revolving door. So you can imagine that their response to two police officers showing up at their doorstep would be panic. Where these guys come from, when cops show up at your door, they're not there to ask you questions, they're there to take you away.'

He takes another long sip from his mug. 'Look, the truth is, they've received threats from their rivals in the past. The fact that the guy who got shot was one of their ex-members has made even more paranoid. Mr Pichkari had incidentally called in his attorney for a consultation on whether or not he should ask for police protection. And then you guys showed up. Scared the shit outta them. Hell, they called us up, asking if the US government had turned against them. They thought we sent you guys there to rough them up.'

'A bit convenient, don't you think, that they had their attorney all ready with restraining orders? Almost like they were expecting somebody to show up asking questions. What have they got to hide, Mr Sole?'

'Detective Cardenas, this is exactly the kind of thing that they were worried would happen. People drawing the wrong conclusions from their actions, especially law enforcement. The

Party keeps a fleet of lawyers on retainer because they have such complex legal problems. Asylum applications for their activists, tax relief for their charities, and yes, expert criminal lawyers in case the Party becomes a target for their opponents. Hell, if I had the number of enemies that Mr Pichkari has, I'd do the same thing.'

'Mr Sole, do you think I'm stupid? Your friends aren't as innocent as you make them out. All you need is a Google-search to figure that out. They've got plenty of blood on their hands.'

'Detective Cardenas, you ought to know better than anybody else that political parties in places like Pakistan are accused of all sorts of crimes, but the reality is a lot greyer than anything you'll come across on the Internet. I mean, isn't it the same with political groups in your native ...'

'Bushwick? Is that what you were going to say? I certainly hope so, because that's the only place I'm a native of, Mr Sole, and the only parties we have there are Republicans and Democrats. You probably have me confused with some other Spic. We all fucking look the same, don't we?'

Anthony Russo observes the exchange between his partner and Sole without interrupting. A lesser man, a less professional man, would have reacted to Charlie Cardenas's insinuation. The only visible sign that it even registers on Simon Sole is a slight reddening of his ears. This one is a very cool customer, thinks Russo. 'Tell me something, Simon. You mentioned that Mr Haider is an ex-member of the Party. According to our information, he's still in the Party.'

'He was formally dismissed last month, though he had been suspended a year ago. It seems Mr Haider was involved in activities that did not fit in with the Party's image. But because he had been a comrade from the early days of the Party, Mr Pichkari and the disciplinary committee kept delaying their decision.'

'So they admit that our friend in the ICU is a close associate of Mr Pichkari, aka the Don?'

'Of course. That's why they're so worried. They believe that anyone who would want to kill this Haider fellow is likely to be gunning for the Don. Their theory is that Mr Haider was probably approached by one of their political rivals, who wanted to try and use him against the Don. But Haider probably refused, hence the attempt on his life.'

'If that's their theory, then why don't they come down to the precinct to tell it to us? The fact of the matter is that I have one dead and four injured in a shooting in the middle of Central Park. I have half of this town's media breathing down my neck, the mayor and the commissioner want this thing solved yesterday, and your friends are running dangerously close to obstruction of justice by not cooperating with an NYPD investigation. I bet you I can get a warrant today and go back to Coney Island Avenue and crawl over *your* Don's ass with a microscope, and no fuckin' Park Avenue lawyer in a Chanel suit will be able to do squat about it. Not when I bring the Channel 5 news truck with me. So you go tell your buddies that the ball is in their court.'

'Well, this is exactly why I'm here. Of course, they want to cooperate in every way. But they're nervous about coming to a police station. It doesn't play well for them back home. But I'd be happy to arrange a neutral venue, perhaps a hotel or some other discreet location.'

'No go. You tell Mr Don or whatever the fuck he calls himself that if he doesn't want a couple of squad cars going down to his offices again, he needs to come see us in the precinct.'

Simon Sole purses his lips, silently seething at Anthony Russo's stubbornness. 'I don't know if the D … I mean, if Mr Pichkari can talk to you guys himself. I hear he hasn't been too well and doesn't meet too many people these days. But they can definitely send a team to talk to you, brief you about all the internal stuff that Haider was involved in and why he was thrown out, those sorts of things.'

'Yeah, sorry, but I'm going to have to see Mr Pichkari personally.' Russo folds his hands across his chest with a finality that indicates the meeting has come to an end.

Sole flashes a brilliant smile and gets up to leave. 'Well, I'll see what I can do, guys.'

'Thanks. We'll see you around.' Russo's eyes follow Simon Sole as he exits the diner and gets into an unmarked black SUV that magically appears from nowhere and drives off.

'What do you think, Tony? Who does our friend really work for?'

'Well, let's put it this way, Charlie, I'll bet you every dime in my pocket that the State Department's never heard of Simon Sole. He's a spook. And I'll also bet you that ain't even his real name. These fucking spooks can't even come up with a believable cover name. I mean, who the fuck would believe a name like Simon Sole?'

'Great. So now all we have to figure out is why the CIA are interested in our case.'

*

Simon Sole gets back to them the next day, only this time he comes from higher up the chain of command. The precinct captain, Brian Ash, receives a call from the first deputy commissioner, informing him that a meeting has been arranged with Pichkari for the following day, but with the proviso that Sole will remain present throughout.

The day is unseasonably warm for March. By prior arrangement, Sole meets Cardenas and Russo at the station house. He gets into their car, and speaks through a lapel radio, instructing his black SUV to drive through Brooklyn.

'I guess lapel radios come in quite handy at the State Department, don't they? For all that diplomacy.' Russo cannot resist having a dig at Sole's flimsy cover. But Sole doesn't answer, preferring to sit in the back of the unmarked vehicle.

'Thanks for agreeing to this, Detectives.'

'How did you get your buddy to speak to us?'

'We just calmed him down, and explained that the best course of action was to cooperate with the NYPD. They wouldn't dream of impeding a police investigation.'

Cardenas turns onto FDR Drive and the conversation dies down till they cross over into Brooklyn. As they turn onto Coney Island Avenue, Sole tells them to follow his SUV, which drives right past the Party's headquarters.

'We're not going to the Party offices?'

'No, Detective Russo. I thought it would make more sense for us to meet Pichkari at one of his apartments close by. The Party owns several condos in the Brighton Beach area, and they keep moving Mr Pichkari around. Their security procedures are quite elaborate.'

'They really believe that someone will try to kill him in New York?'

'Oh yeah. The Party is obsessed with his safety. They believe that the forces allied against them in Pakistan are extremely powerful. And after this incident, I don't disagree with them. They're very suspicious of newcomers in the local Pakistani community. That's why Pichkari lives in Little Odessa, surrounded by Ukrainians and Russians. You've seen his security people. Also Russian. The Party doesn't trust Paks.'

Oceanview Avenue is in the heart of Brooklyn's Russian neighbourhood. A South Asian entering here would stick out like a sore thumb. The black SUV pulls up in front of one of the newer condo buildings on the street. They are greeted by a dark-skinned man in a safari suit, and another well-dressed Caucasian man who is unmistakably a lawyer. They seem nervous, but are relieved to see Sole jump out of the back seat of the police car.

'Detectives Russo and Cardenas, let me introduce Mr Raja and Mr Lowenstein. Mr Raja is the Don's political secretary. Sorry, I keep slipping, I mean Mr Pichkari's secretary, and I believe you already met Mr Lowenstein on your last visit. He was one of the attorneys who accompanied Ms Daniel.'

Raja is a thin, wiry man, whose hands look skeletal. He wears wire rim glasses and keeps his hair long, combing it in a weave to cover a bald spot. In the stiff wind, strands of his hair fly about, giving him the look of someone who has just been on an electric chair.

They are led into what looks like a newly developed condo complex, one of a number that are supposedly changing the face of Brooklyn. Russo spots one of the Eastern European bodyguards from their visit to the Party offices, standing around in the lobby. Another rides the elevator down and escorts all of them to the penthouse.

'Simon, we just want to clarify a few things before the officers meet Mr Pichkari. He usually doesn't meet anyone at such short notice. He has a fixed routine, and gets very agitated at any changes to that. He is also on high doses of medication for stress and various other ailments. So please try and refrain from intensive or intrusive questions, as this can be emotionally traumatic for my client.' It is the lawyer who breaks the nervous silence in the lift.

'Do you want us to keep our hands visible at all times, and refrain from making sudden movements as well?'

Cardenas chuckles at Russo's response, the lawyer stiffens visibly, Sole remains impassive as ever, but the other man, Raja, looking more nervous than ever, totally misses the sarcasm.

'Yes, yes, the Don is a patient. He has depression caused by the death of his comrade Asad Haider.'

'He's not dead. Yet. But someone certainly tried their best to ensure that he wouldn't survive.' Cardenas's tone and stare stun Raja into silence.

'Yes, yes, of course. Sorry, my mistake. Actually, some of our other Party workers were also killed in Karachi, so I got confused. But still, the fact that one of his closest colleagues was shot in this manner, here in New York, has deeply shocked the Don.'

'The other issue, Detective Russo, is that, as you can imagine, due to his very public profile in Pakistan, my client is constantly in the spotlight. Everything he says or does is placed under a microscope. Several times in the past, innocuous statements made by him have been misconstrued in Pakistan, and resultantly, he has been slandered and painted in a negative light by the media and his political rivals. Therefore, he is extremely paranoid about being misquoted. We would appreciate a commitment from you that any statements made by my client in this interview will be confidential and not leaked to the press in Pakistan.'

'I'm sorry, Counsellor, this is an interview that pertains to a murder investigation. I can't promise you anything.'

'Well, then I'm afraid I can't let this interview go forward.'

'Well, you can do that, Counsellor, and Detective Cardenas and I will happily turn around and go back to the precinct. But then we'll go to a judge and get a warrant, and we'll do it very publicly, and so the next time we come around, there'll be about a dozen TV trucks parked outside, so your whole point of keeping this under wraps will be wasted. I'm under no obligation to give you a commitment on anything beforehand. You're just gonna have to trust me.'

Before the lawyer can splutter a response, Simon Sole interjects. 'I think that's fine, Counsellor. After all, the detectives have no reason or inclination to talk to the Pakistani press anyway. They're just trying to do their job.'

The lawyer gives Sole a nervous glance, but gives in. 'I suppose it's okay if you think so.'

'I think it'll be fine, Counsellor.'

The elevator deposits them to the building's penthouse. The floor-to-ceiling glass windows would afford a panoramic view of Brooklyn, but they are covered with dusty tarp shades that look as if they haven't been drawn up in years. The entire apartment, which had been originally designed to enhance light and brightness, has been converted into a darkroom. Even this early in the day, the entrance hallway is lit with dim tube lights. The Russian bodyguard takes them through the cavernous apartment to the door of the master bedroom. He leaves them at the entrance and steps in to announce them. A second later, they are ushered into a massive room. The first thing that hits them is the smell. Dank, musty, like dried sweat, cum and dust mixed together. Russo cannot imagine how someone can live in this room. All natural light has been blocked out by heavy curtains that cover the huge bay windows on one side of the room. Another wall is adorned with eight large flat-screen TVs, their cables spewing out from behind them onto the floor. All the monitors are tuned in to various Pakistani news channels. On the wall opposite the TV screens is mounted a picture of the Don that covers virtually the entire wall. Having gone through hundreds of similar pictures during his research, the image is a familiar one for Cardenas, but its sheer size is intimidating. The dark Ray-Bans covering the eyes, the Stalin-style crew cut, flecked with strands of grey hair, and the moustache whose bristles look razor sharp at that size, betray more than a hint of menace.

The only furniture in the room is a gigantic bed. Two ashtrays propped on the bed overflow with ash and cigarette butts, dribbling their contents onto the sheets that look as if they haven't been washed since they were bought. And in the middle of the bed, propped up by half a dozen pillows, sits a man whom Cardenas struggles to recognize as the same person in the giant poster, or the dozens of other Party photographs he has seen.

Mohammed Ali Pichkari, aka the Don, seems a lot shorter in real life. And portlier too. The body, normally dressed in perfectly cut suits, is revealed in all its folds of fat that cascade onto a protruding potbelly. The famed crew cut is gone, replaced by a mop of dishevelled hair that struggles to hide a thinning and receding hairline. The eyes, without the Raybans to cover them, are bloodshot with dark circles under them that spread to sallow cheeks. His hands shake slightly as he attempts to take a drag from a lit cigarette, causing the ash to fall on his filthy tobacco-stained fingers. In fact, the Don's overall appearance is that of a sick man, an image that is given further credence by the presence of a very pretty nurse who reveals an ample bosom through her tight, one-size-too-small uniform, while leaning over to take his blood pressure.

Raja, the secretary, whispers something to him in Urdu which causes him to look at Cardenas and Russo with some degree of trepidation. But it is Sole who makes the introductions once again.

'Mr Pichkari, good to see you once again. I am sorry you aren't feeling well. Let me introduce you to these two gentlemen. They are Detectives Cardenas and Russo of the New York Police Department. They're the ones investigating the incident at the Natural History Museum, in which your colleague Asad Haider was injured. They wanted to ask you some questions about him. But perhaps we can get Mr Raja to get us some chairs so we can all be a little more comfortable.'

The Don nods slowly as if absorbing all the details of Sole's statement. After an abnormally long pause, in which he stares at the two detectives, he finally says 'yes', although it is unclear whether the affirmative answer is his acknowledgement of the information provided by Sole, or simply permission for Raja to get chairs. Either way, Raja and the Russian bodyguard disappear and reappear with four chairs. Without taking his eyes off Russo and Cardenas, he extends his hand, gesturing for everybody to sit. Russo notices that while the four Americans take their seats, there is no attempt made by Raja to get a fifth chair for himself. Instead, he positions himself behind the Don's bed, while the bodyguard escorts the pretty nurse out. She flashes the Don a brilliant, Pepsodent smile, revealing a set of perfect teeth.

For the first time, there is a glimmer of warmth on the Don's face, as he returns the smile and fixes his eyes on the pretty nurse's ass as she walks out of the door, oblivious to the four men now seated beside his bed. Another elongated pause, as he continues to stare at the door for a full thirty seconds after her departure. Then suddenly, with a feral swiftness, his eyes bulging from their sockets, he turns to Cardenas and speaks in a voice that is barely above a whisper.

'Is he really alive?'

'Yes, Mr Pichkari, if you're referring to Asad Haider, he is. He received three bullets in his body but nothing vital was hit. The doctors believe he will make a full recovery shortly.'

Again, a vacant look as if his brain is processing the information. 'Thank God. Can I see him?'

'I'm afraid not right now, sir. He's in a critical condition and we still believe that there is a threat to his life, so he's being guarded in isolation. Can you tell us a little more about your relationship with him?'

The Don raises his right arm slowly and stares at it. 'My right hand,' he whispers.

'Excuse me, sir?'

'He was like my right hand.'

Russo stares at Cardenas quizzically. 'But Mr Pichkari, we were told that he'd been thrown out of the Party.'

'Everyone makes mistakes.' The Don looks down at his feet, but makes no further attempt to expand upon his answer.

'What do you mean by that? Who made a mistake? Do you mean it was a mistake to eject him from the Party or that he made mistakes?'

No answer, as the Don keeps staring at his toes. Finally Raja, who has been standing unobtrusively behind the bed, pipes up.

'Asad Haider is one of the Don's oldest companions, from his student days. He was virtually a founder member of the Party. He was expelled from the Party recently. The decision was taken by the politburo almost a year ago, but the Don was personally very distressed and did not want Asad to be expelled, so he kept requesting the politburo to delay its decision and give Asad Haider a second chance. But in our Party, even the Don can only request the politburo, he cannot dictate to it. So they announced their final verdict a month ago.'

'Why was he expelled?'

'How is this relevant to your investigation?'

'Excuse me, Counsellor, but what is or is not relevant to my investigation is up to me.'

Raja remains silent, looking at the Don, seeking guidance on whether to continue or not. The Don finally glances back at him, shrugs his shoulders and then breaks the silence himself.

'Corruption. The curse of the Third World. No matter what we do, the temptation is always too great. Within the United Front, I have always tried to enforce a kind of ruthless accountability. I have always told all my Party members that we cannot ever afford to be seen to do what everyone else does. All these other parties with industrialists and landlords. We are a party of the working class that has always fought for the rights of those who cannot buy their justice. That's why we could never afford any blemishes on our reputation. But I am just one man. I cannot ensure that every single Party member of mine is doodh se dhula hua. Washed with pure milk. You understand what I am saying?'

Cardenas and Russo both nod dubiously.

'And I am also a mortal. A man with weaknesses. My biggest weakness is my love for my old comrades. I know. Raja scolds me about it all the time, but what can I do. It's my personality. If it's there, it's there.'

Russo looks at Raja and thinks it inconceivable that he could ever look the Don in the eye, much less scold him.

'We had heard the first complaints about Asad years ago. The problem was he always loved the finer things in life. Try as I might, I could never make him a malang like myself. I ignored it for a long time, as initially the amounts were not too significant, and in those years we had to face the brunt of a government-sponsored genocide against us. Asad was often holding up the Party on his own. I told myself, a man has to eat from somewhere. It is often better to look the other way. But then, the genocide ended, we became part of the government, and the amounts kept getting bigger. To the point where Tariq, our Party's chief minister, came to me and said Asad's corruption was hindering his efforts at good governance. And not just financial corruption. Moral too. Here, in New York, I received calls from irate husbands and fathers, saying he had romanced their wives and daughters, had his fun with them, and then discarded them with no regard for their izzat. This may not be so important here, but in our culture, this is a very big thing. And some quarters were even casting aspersions that I had some personal motive in protecting Asad. No one has ever made such an allegation against me. My first reaction was anger, but at heart I am a simple middle-class man, who is constantly scared of having any mud thrown upon his personal reputation. The politburo decided, I did not interfere. I only asked them to delay the decision to expel him, as I hoped Asad would perhaps repent, turn over a new leaf. Until finally, last month, Raja and the other politburo members came to me and said that I was subverting their democratic right by clinging to this fantasy of Asad. Well, I am a democrat, I always have been, so I told them to do what they wished.'

'Was Mr Haider given any opportunity to refute the allegations that were made against him? What proof did you have of his misdeeds?'

'Proof? What more proof can you have than when an eighteen-year-old girl flies all the way from Karachi to New York with her family, and sits in the very chair you are sitting in, in this very room, and says Asad Haider promised to marry her, promised to make her rich beyond her dreams, only so that she would agree to enjoy carnal relations with him. And then he abandons her, in a pregnant state! Eighteen years old, with her life in front of her. Abortion may be an easy solution for you here, but in our country, oof tobah, it is against Islam. Oh, the shame of the poor girl!'

The Don swoons dramatically, raising his fist to his head and closing his eyes, reliving the girl's torment.

'It's the same with the money. We have a very finely tuned system of checks and balances in the party. We had documentary proof of Asad's corruption, we had statements from the people he took money from, we have everything. Raja will tell you, he keeps all the records. But you ask, why did we not confront him with the evidence? It was not because we thought it was flimsy. This too can be blamed on my soft-heartedness. I did not want to put Asad on trial. I did not want his family's name to be smeared in this scandal. I have too much respect for his grandmother, who was one of my earliest supporters. Also, Asad was a hero to an entire generation of Party workers. They would all be shattered to find that their idol had broken almost every tenet of the Party oath. I thought it would be better for all concerned if we just simply expelled Asad, instead of hanging him publicly.'

'Did he come to see you after he arrived in New York?'

'Yes, yes, he did come. He came two days before this shooting incident.'

'What did he say to you?'

'He was angry. I explained to him the reasons, but still he was angry. The Party was his life. He sacrificed everything for it. He was angry at me personally. He forced me to return to him the aqeeq that his grandmother had given to me the first time I went to their house. It broke my heart because I have worn that amulet for all these years. I cried. Then he cried. And then he walked out. He left us and immediately the dark forces arrayed against us targeted him. I should never have allowed him to walk out of this room. I should have kept him with me, here in this very apartment. I would have fed him with my own hands, I could have reformed him. Oh Raja! Why didn't you stop me!'

The Don starts to sob gently. Cardenas looks at Russo, unsure of how to proceed, but Russo is unflustered and continues to probe.

'Mr Pichkari, who do you think would have a motive to try and kill Mr Haider?'

Immediately, the Don's tears dry up and a thoughtful expression comes over his face.

'My enemies are innumerable. Anyone who has ever stood in the way of progress in Pakistan is my enemy.'

'But why do you think *your* enemies would want to kill Asad Haider?'

'Isn't it obvious? Because to my enemies, there was no difference between him and me. They wanted to get to me through him.'

'But he no longer had that relationship with you, as you yourself have stated. He had been expelled from the Party, right?'

'Yes, but the world didn't know that. We had kept it very quiet. No official announcement had been made by the Party.'

'Could you expand upon who these enemies could be?'

'Where should I begin? The government in Pakistan, the deep state, the secret intelligence agencies, the Taliban, the gangsters of Lyari, all are my enemies, all have sworn to destroy me.'

'But excuse me, sir, aren't you a part of the government? Isn't your party the ruling party in Sindh province?'

'Yes, but there are other parties. The federal government, some of our coalition partners. They believe that it would improve their bargaining position if I were somehow weakened. And the intelligence agencies in Pakistan are under nobody's control. I am not under their thumb, so they would dearly like to teach me a lesson.'

'And the Taliban as well you said?'

'Yes. The United Front is the most liberal and progressive political party in Pakistan. We represent the aspirations of the proletariat. And we have always been secular. That has been our inviolable creed. I was the first leader to dare to speak out against the religious parties. I was still in university then, and Asad was the one who ensured that nothing happened to me while I gave my speeches. Ask Mr Sole, when 9/11 happened, what did I do? When no one else in Pakistan was willing to speak out against these jihadis, I spoke up. I supported America's actions against the Al Qaeda without reservation. That is why I am number one on the Pakistani Taliban's hit list. They would go to any lengths to assassinate me.'

'Sir, don't you think it's frankly a little far-fetched that the Taliban would send someone all the way to New York to assassinate you or any of your colleagues?'

'If nineteen Arab men can smash airplanes into the World Trade Center, then why is this so unbelievable? These religious fundamentalists will go to any lengths to eliminate anyone who stands in their way. And what better symbolism than to murder one of my closest friends, here in America, to send me a message that even in New York I am not safe.'

By now the Don has worked himself up into a rhetorical frenzy, thrashing his arms about, his pitch rising and falling like that of a skilled political orator. Simon Sole looks on impassively, but Raja has an increasingly worried expression on his face, as if he is worried about what will come out of the Don's mouth next. He rushes out to get a glass of water and shoves it into the Don's hands.

'Don, please relax. The nurse said your blood pressure was high.' Unheeding, the Don grabs the glass, gulping down the water almost violently, with no concern as it spills out of the sides of his mouth onto his shirt and on the bed.

'Detectives, I think it may be time to wrap this session up. I am aware that the Don was very busy today but still carved out some time to talk to you guys. He has also, as you can see, not been well, and I'm sure talking about this unfortunate incident wouldn't have been good for him. Besides, it seems to me as if you've covered most of your points. I am sure that if you do have anything else, we can always arrange another meeting.'

It is the first time that Sole has spoken, but his intervention is decisive. He gets up from his chair and the Don immediately calms down and becomes silent. Cardenas is about to object but Russo gives him a look to stop him, and turns to Sole and shrugs.

'Fair enough. Yeah, I think we have sufficient material for now. Thanks for your time, Mr Pichkari.'

'Detective, I would like to know if Asad is being taken care of.' The Don's voice has returned to its low pitch.

'He's in one of the best hospitals in the world, Mr Pichkari. The doctors say he'll be fine.'

'I would like to pay for his treatment. Would you inform the hospital, please? Raja will take care of the details. It's the least I can do for one of my oldest friends.'

Raja stays in the flat while the rest of them take the elevator down.

'I hope that went some distance in assuring you that Mr Pichkari has nothing to hide. He's just in a very difficult situation,' said Sole.

Russo waits till the elevator reaches the ground floor and the lawyer says his goodbyes and walks away. Once on the street, he pulls out a half-smoked cigar from his jacket pocket and lights it. 'My apologies. I'm old-fashioned, I still like a nice stogie. Tell me something, Simon. You really believe his paranoia about the Taliban trying to get to him here?'

'He's not wrong, you know. We monitor a lot of this stuff, and it's amazing how many of these sorts of plots come within an ace of succeeding. And it would be a huge PR victory for them if they managed to get him or one of his close associates here in New York. Now I'm not saying that's necessarily the case here, but it's worth looking into.'

'Okay, Simon, straight up, since you know Pakistani politics so well. Who do you think did it? Who could order a hit in New York?'

'You putting me on the stand, Detective?' Simon Sole grins widely. 'If you ask me, and this is completely off the record, I think the most likely suspect would be the Pakistani intelligence services. They tolerate Pichkari, but they don't like him. As he said, he's too independent a politician for them. And they don't like the fact that he cooperates with us, without going through them. They would have reckoned that killing Haider would scare the shit out of the Don and make him come to them. So they've certainly got motive. Plus, they really hate Haider. I think it goes back a few years, when they allege that he kidnapped and killed some army officer. They never forgave him for that. When the criminal cases against all the other Party leaders were withdrawn, Haider's cases weren't. He had to live in Dubai because the Party thought the Agencies would either lock him up or bump him off in Karachi. So if I were you, I'd start my investigation by looking at them.'

5

ISMAIL

'Who was the first person you ever killed?'

My question caught Baba off guard. It was two days after our first meeting. I had rushed back to my editor, and made all the arrangements. He couldn't believe that I had landed the scoop of the year. Baba Dacait never gave interviews. Most people in the city had never even seen him, because TV teams were too scared to venture into Lyari, and Baba had never been keen to invite them in. But, this would all change. I finally had my foot in the door of the big time, and although I still wasn't sure exactly how to use it to my advantage, I knew that I wasn't going to let go of my opportunity.

Thus, having got a guarantee from my editor that he would run Baba's interview on the front page with a banner headline, I had sat down to work out what I would ask him. I did know that I didn't want to use up all the good material just for the interview in the newspaper. The real nugget was a book. I had never written one, but I knew that was the thing that would make us huge. I wasn't even interested in Pakistani publishers. I had my eye on the international market. All I needed to do was learn how to write in English. But that was just a technicality that I could figure out later.

I had arranged a time and a place to get picked up with Jameel Jheenga, Baba's second in command. I wanted to be discreet, I certainly didn't want the police to get word that I was meeting with Baba Dacait. But Jheenga didn't seem too concerned. As he said on the phone when I mentioned my apprehensions, 'Even if they did want to get to Baba through you, they would still have to come in to Lyari to arrest him. And for that they need to grow balls.'

There was logic in Jheenga's words. Still, to be on the safe side, I did tell one police officer about my meeting. I'd known the head of Special Branch long before he became a big afsar, when he was wallowing in a third-class side posting for years, complaining that no one ever gave him a plum assignment. When I first met him, he was Superintendent of Police of the Railways, trying, and failing, to catch ticket dodgers on the Khyber Mail. No other journalist would give him a lift because he had no career prospects. But because I was just starting out as a reporter, I used to visit his office on the assumption that a professionally dead contact in the police was still better than absolutely no contact at all. Subsequently, Ahad sahib's kismet had finally awakened and he became head of Special Branch. Because I had stuck with him in the bad days, and even kept in touch when he was posted to Gilgit, he had regard for me. He would occasionally call me to his office, and give me a small stipend for information. At times, when he wanted to put something out in the media, he would pass it on to me, to either publish under my name or pass it on to a slightly more reputable reporter.

I told him about Baba because I thought I might get some indication from him about how I could benefit from this entire situation. Ahad sahib called me to his house, in the police officers' flats in Bath Island. He heard my entire story without interrupting, and when I had finished, he encouraged me to meet Baba and establish a relationship with him. If Ahad sahib thought that, then the risk was worth taking.

So, on the appointed day, I showed up in front of the Kutyana Memon Hospital, on the edge of Lyari. I was picked up by Baba's boys in a black Toyota Corolla with tinted windows. Their treatment of me was more deferential this time round. I wasn't obliged to put a bag over my head, and one of them even tried to make small talk with me.

I was not too familiar with Lyari, now I at least had a general idea of where we were going. We passed through Khadda Market, honking our way through a road jammed with hawkers who barely left room for a car to pass, lining their rehris on the footpaths and on the road itself, selling stolen mobile phones and fake replicas of Barcelona and Arsenal football shirts. Right past the front gate of Baghdadi police station, where the sentries did not blink an eyelid at a car with four armed men, their weapons clearly on display. Then onto Cheel Chowk, where the renowned Superintendent Akbar Khan had his final, famous shootout with Baba's men. And finally into the narrow lanes of Kalakot, the heart of Baloch Lyari.

The road widened as we approached Gabol Park, the legendary home of generations of Baloch footballers. Even at this time, just after noon on a sweltering April day in Karachi's heat and humidity, I could see a group of footballers practising their ball control, with what seemed to be a curiously misshapen ball. Baba sat on one of the concrete steps watching this group, occasionally shouting out a word of advice or encouragement to them. He wasn't alone. Armed men surrounded the place, their M-4s and AK-47s at the ready, wearing wraparound shades in the same style as the American soldiers in Afghanistan and Iraq. Baba was a careful man. He had even posted men on the surrounding rooftops as lookouts. One of his bodyguards stood behind him with an umbrella, while an attendant had laid out a small table with bottles of mineral water and soft drink cans next to him. Baba beckoned me to sit, and without exchanging any pleasantries told me to start.

Which is when I popped the question about his first murder that brought the interview to a spluttering halt. Baba stared at me with his cold eyes, and I was sure at that moment that he was seriously considering whether or not to kill me.

'What do you think you are doing?'

'Sir, please, I told you when we last met, I know what I am doing. If you want to challenge the Don, if you want to make a new image for yourself in this city, and make people think that you are a community leader rather than a gangster, you cannot hide your past. Admit to the things you have done. The point we are trying to make with this article is that you are a real man who knows the real problems that everyday people face. You are not like these drawing-room leaders who sit in Defence and Clifton, or in Islamabad, in their safe high-walled houses, with their armies of servants and lackeys, sipping imported sharab and pretending they know what life is like in this city. Nor are you like the Don, who may have come from these streets, but has lived so long in New York that he doesn't remember the smell of a ganda nala. Only you can make a connection between these two worlds, because you came from the streets and your power makes the Defence–Cliftonwallahs fear you.'

Baba scratched his curly stubble that, with his complexion, made him look like a West Indian cricketer. I could feel heavy beads of sweat on my forehead and a growing wet patch under my armpits.

'My mother.'

'Sorry, sir?'

'My mother was the first person I ever killed.'

An overwhelming feeling of relief swept over me as it dawned on me that he wasn't going to kill me, making me momentarily ignore the significance of what he had said.

'Okay. Why don't we talk a little about your childhood, so the readers can better understand what you went through while growing up?'

'Childhood. Heh.' At this Baba turned to one of his men, who handed him a bhara hua cigarette. He took a long puff and exhaled, the pungent sweet smell of opium floating across the football field. And then he smiled.

'My father was Badal Boxer. He was the most feared badmaash in Lyari thirty years ago. He had been a boxer in his youth, and a good one. That's where the fear came from. People say he used to hit so hard that you never fully recovered from a fight with him. By the time I was born, he had a monopoly on selling charas in Lyari. I was a mistake, the child of his old age. My mother was a local prostitute and my father's fourth wife. But he never brought us into the family home, thinking perhaps that it wouldn't be appropriate for an ex-prostitute to sleep under his roof.'

'So you grew up as the prince of Lyari, son of the famous Badal Boxer.'

'No. I never benefited from my father. He died when I was six or seven. His empire crumbled because he had never bothered to organize it in his life. His other sons, from his earlier wives, fought among themselves. Rivals encroached upon their territory. My father was a fool to trust his idiot sons. That is why I will never pass on my empire to my children. Whoever wants all of this will have to prove he can sustain it.'

'But what happened to you and your mother?'

'We got nothing. My mother returned to her profession and I started selling drugs. I have been in this dhanda since I was in short pants. I worked my way up from nothing. After my father's death, we moved into a small quarter in Afshani Galli, near here. Today, I own that whole street.'

'Mashallah, sir. These are exactly the kinds of details that people like to read about. A real success story, working your way up on the strength of your own abilities. This is great stuff. But why did you kill your mother?'

'Because she was a whore. She did not respect the fact that she was the widow of Badal Boxer. She went back to her whoring ways, throwing away her dignity and mine.'

'I … I still don't understand, sir.'

'When I started selling drugs, I used to sell very small amounts, just a few dozen pooris and packets a day, mostly to locals in Lyari. Some years after my father's death, I was negotiating for a larger deal, one that would line me up with buyers from outside Lyari. But I didn't have the quantities that the buyers wanted. So I had to go and ask my idiot half-brothers for the charas, on credit. When I went to them, they mocked me for dreaming big dreams that were beyond my station in life. After all, who was I to think that I could do such deals. When I said I was a son of Badal, they laughed and said no, I was the son of a whore, who even now was fucking someone in my house. They said I was beghairat, and they would never deal with someone who had no honour. I went home and found they were right. My mother did have a customer in there at that moment. She used to schedule her punters for the mornings, when I was out in the streets. So I took a knife from the kitchen and killed them both, the whore and her punter.'

'How old were you?'

'I was thirteen. I remember because the judge cited my age as the reason for sending me to the bachcha jail instead of the big jail. I spent five years inside, but after that, nobody ever called me beghairat again.'

'So what did you do when you got out?'

'I made good connections inside, so when I got out I had big deals lined up to distribute charas throughout the city.'

'Where did you get the drugs from? Did your stepbrothers give them to you?'

'No, this time I didn't ask anyone. I just took what I wanted and killed anyone who got in my way.'

'What happened to the other sons of Badal?'

'By the time I got out, most of them were dead, or had taken whatever little money was left and moved out of Lyari. There was only one left in the business. Khalid Black Label.'

'Why did they call him that?'

'Because you never saw him without a bottle of Black Label in his hands. He was a drunk, trying to cling on to the crumbs of Badal's empire. I had Jheenga kill him. His daughter cleans the toilets in my house today.'

'So you got your revenge.'

'Yes, but he taught me a very important lesson, one that is at the heart of everything I do today. Maintaining your honour is the most important thing in life.'

'This is good, this is very good. Makes you look like a man of principles. But tell me about your personal life, sir. What do you like to do in your spare time? Do you watch TV, play any sports? Are you a boxer like your father? I see from your exhortations to the players on the field that you are very knowledgeable about football.'

'I love football. I remember, one year, when I was a boy, the World Cup was on. I would sell drugs all day long, and in the evenings I would see the matches on the TV at the chaiwallah hotel downstairs from our quarter. There was a player, Maradona, he played for that country, Argenta, Argenti, something like that. But he was a genius. They won the World Cup that year.'

'Argentina. Yes sir, Maradona was a class player. But you never got the opportunity to play yourself?'

'No, I was too busy selling drugs and killing people. But now I try and promote the game in the local community. I paid for the renovation of this park, I pay for the kits of all the boys who practise here. Getting involved in football is good, it keeps the kids away from drugs.'

'That's very admirable of you, sir. But can I ask you a question, if you don't mind? Your business is drugs and guns. In your youth, you sold drugs in the streets. But now, you want the children of Lyari to stay away from these things? Wouldn't that be bad for your business?'

'I sell drugs, but I don't sell them to children. Not any more. That's my dhanda, and I will continue to do my business. But I have pushed it out of Lyari. To the richer areas of the city. I don't want the locals to be corrupted by these things. Lyari will never get out of its present state if our own youth keep getting addicted to drugs. I have it myself, but I am an adult. I smoke teriak, I don't drink people's blood, like this bastard Don and all the other politicians.'

'So would you say you are a man with a social conscience? You want to be a sort of … a sort of social worker, helping the people of Lyari with their problems.'

Baba thought about that one for a second, and then smiled. 'Social worker. Yes, I like that. I am a social worker.'

I was writing all of this down as fast as I could in my notebook. As I scribbled, one of Baba's henchmen came to him with a newspaper, and pointed to the headline in an animated fashion. I could see from Baba's puzzled expression that he couldn't read, and I understood just enough Balochi to figure out that the man was trying to explain the headline to Baba. Suddenly, he turned to me and thrust the paper in my lap, causing me to drop my notes to the ground.

'You are a journalist. What does this say?'

I scanned the headline. It was a super banner, a headline that took up nearly half the front page. The paper was one of the city's largest selling Urdu dailies, much bigger than the *Daily Ahsaas*.

'Sir, it says that the Don has blamed you for the death of one of his oldest friends, who was killed in his home a few days back.'

'Tell me his exact words.'

'Uh, it's not very complimentary.'

'The exact words. Now.'

'Okay. "The Don, in a statement released from New York, said that he held the gangster-terrorist Baba Dacait responsible for the brutal killing of his friend and old party stalwart Aleem Siddiqui and his family, who were all murdered in their home. He claims that Baba had sent a death squad to kill Aleem because he was an easy target, since he had retired from active politics sometime ago, and he held no official government post. The Don has warned the government that the police's inability to capture Baba Dacait has encouraged the Lyari gangsters to expand their operations to other parts of the city, and he has given an ultimatum demanding Baba's arrest."'

Baba didn't say anything, but there was something terrible in his eyes. He got up from his chair and, assuming the interview was over, I got up with him. But he urged me to sit down again.

'I have something to attend to. Stay here.'

Wordlessly, I sat down again and opened one of the soft drink cans. My throat was parched and I continued to sweat profusely in the afternoon heat. I put the cold can to my forehead for some temporary relief. Most of Baba's entourage had walked off with him, leaving me to be chaperoned by a single guard, whose front tooth was missing. He wasn't really paying attention to me, preferring to fiddle with his Kalashnikov. Not having anything better to do, I decided to make small talk.

'Is that a good gun?'

He seemed surprised to have me address him. 'Why, you want one?'

'No, I'm just curious. You see so many of them in the city, I just wondered if it was actually a good weapon.'

'It's the best. You can drop it in a pool of mud for a week, take it out, and it still works beautifully. Much better than these chutiya American rifles.'

Not being an expert on the subject, I merely nodded. In the distance, the footballers continued to practise, regardless of the heat. I could tell they were good, but hindered by a less-than-perfect ball.

'Arre bhai, Baba spends all this money on getting these boys kits and renovating the ground, why can't somebody fill some air in the ball? It's so misshapen, it's spoiling the passing rhythm of the players.'

My toothless friend smiled at me. 'That's not a ball.'

I tried to focus on the ball to see what he was talking about. Then it finally dawned on me. It wasn't a ball they were playing with. It was a human head.

The long sip of Coke that I had just taken came rushing back out of my stomach. I doubled over, gagging on my own vomit. My friend laughed heartily, more than a little amused at my reaction. He shouted out some comment that made the footballers pause and laugh as well.

'Who is it?'

'One of three madarchod Party wardias who we caught last night trying to sneak into Lyari. This one had a lot of attitude, said he was the ward boss of Paposh, and said that if we didn't let them go immediately, the entire Party would be swarming all over Lyari. So Jheenga decided to shut him up by taking his head off.'

Just as I got back on my feet, another one of Baba's henchmen came running across the field. I was being summoned by Baba.

After my experience, I was happy to get away from the field. Trying my best not to look at the footballers, I walked with the guard towards some buildings nearby. The buildings were old storage godowns from the time when most of the goods that came into the port next door were stored in Lyari for convenience. There was a hustle and bustle on the road, people going about their business, not really bothered by the sight of several heavily armed men congregating outside the godown. It was all perfectly normal for them.

It's only when I entered that the smell hit me and made me thankful that I had already emptied the contents of my stomach. The smell of singed flesh. I'll never forget it, or the scene that lay before me. Two men were hanging from hooks in the ceiling, a pool of blood and bits of bone and gristle collecting under them. Their legs seemed limp and were at odd angles, almost detached from their bodies. Kneeling in the pool was Jheenga, an electric drill soaked in blood in his hand, his chubby face looking absurd with safety goggles on it. Above him stood Baba.

'Is the bastard still alive?'

Jheenga shook his head. 'No, Baba. He lost too much blood from the drilling. I think we must have punctured an artery or something. He bled right out.'

'I told you to keep these madarchods alive. I wanted them to remember what happened with them.'

'Sorry, my first time using an electric drill. I didn't realize it would cut through the bone so easily. Mistake ho gaya. I'm a fisherman after all, not an electrician. If you want, we can hit their Ranchore Lines ward office and kidnap a couple of new ones.'

Baba ignored the question and turned to me. 'I want you to see all of this and document it. That bastard sitting in New York blames me for things I never did. He says I killed his friend. I don't even know who that madarchod was. I am not ashamed of what I have done, but I am nobody's fool. I am not part of some scheme that the Don has to take advantage of his friend's death politically.'

'But sir, if you haven't done it, then why kill these ward boys? They are minor Party functionaries.'

'Because I want to show the Don that when I actually want to kill somebody, this is how I do it. I don't hide behind anything. Jheenga, throw the bodies out in Lyari Nadi. But leave a note on them, warning the Don not to think of entering Lyari again. Everyone else in this city may be scared of his Party, I'm not. He can go fuck himself.'

6

BYRAM

'Saala bhenchod, it's a fucking pain to get into your office. The bloody buggers ask for my ID card on every floor.'

The office of the head of Special Branch is on the sixth floor of the Police Head Office. It is the only office on that floor, isolated from the comings and goings of the rest of the building. The silence here is in complete contrast to the hustle and bustle of the floors below, but this is supposed to be by design. Special Branch is the provincial government's premier intelligence agency, and also its oldest one, dating back to the British Raj. It is not meant to be a department where people come to air public grievances, so every Tanveer, Daud, or Haroon does not get to the sixth floor. In fact, you only come here if you are summoned.

The current incumbent, Abdul Ahad Mallick, has been in this post for some years, and as is his wont, he often meets with people from all walks of life in this office. The very rich, the very poor, the pious and the scandalous. Anyone who can provide interesting titbits of information about the ebbs and flows of the city. So the appearance of a foul-mouthed old Parsi

does not surprise anyone. Besides, the staff knows Bhenchod
Chacha. He has been coming here for years.

The office is simple with standard issue furniture and standard
issue décor, not as ostentatious as the offices of the inspector
general and the Karachi police chief on the floors below.
There are no laminated floors or wood-panelled walls, nothing
to denote that the occupant of this office is the third seniormost police officer in the province, and its chief spy. The only
item in the room that hints at the work done here is a massive
and highly detailed map of the city, with Karachi's 100 police
stations all marked with pins, and different shadings indicating
areas controlled by different political groups. The map covers
an entire wall of the office, and half of it is covered with a tarp,
to hide it from prying eyes.

'Come, have some tea. Why didn't you take the lift?' Abdul
Ahad Mallick offers Byram a chair and places a cup of tea in
front of him. He is a short, squat man with keen, intelligent
eyes that hide behind a pair of gold-rimmed spectacles. Despite
his careful combing and healthy application of Brylcreem, his
hair's natural curliness cannot be totally hidden. As Special
Branch isn't supposed to be a uniformed assignment, he wears
a smart suit, but with an ugly bright pink tie. It makes Byram
think that policewallahs must lose all sense of civilian dressing
since they wear uniforms all the time. Or maybe they're just
collectively stupid.

'Arre saala, the bloody lift man keeps telling everyone that
they can't get on as it's an officers-only lift. Bhenchod, you police
buggers get so much budget and eat double that in corruption,
hasn't it occurred to anyone to get a few extra lifts installed in
this head office?' Byram's hand shakes as he lifts the teacup.
His heartbeat is up from having climbed all six flights of stairs, but
he is glad to note that he isn't wheezing and out of breath. A
testament to his daily two-kilometre walk in Nishtar Park.

Mallick smiles indulgently. He has known Byram for years and is well used to his profanities. 'We have had to increase security after the recent suicide attacks on senior police officers. These bloody jihadis can hit us anywhere.'

'Saala chutiyas. I've never understood how one can be willing to give one's life up over religion. Over any cause for that matter.'

'You're willing to give your life up for a cause. You risk your life every day working with us. You and all the others. All of you are driven by your hatred of the Party. It's the same with the jihadis. Speaking of which, how is the girl? I want you to train her well. I think she will be an invaluable asset.'

'Saala, what rubbish have you sent me? Who are these new kids? They were in diapers when we started working against the Party. Some of them are in diapers even now. They have no sense, no samaj, of this work. I don't trust any of them. And especially this chokri. Bhenchod she didn't even know who Asad Haider was! You know the Party is trying to infiltrate all sorts of people to find out who opposes them. That bloody bugger in New York is shitting himself with fear, so he's pushing them harder. We can't afford to take any risks. I don't trust her.'

'I don't trust anyone. Ever. Not even you, Byram. But she's all right. She went through the vetting process. Besides, she's a victim of the Party, like everyone else. Her brother was a police officer, an inspector who had been active in the operation against the Party. They killed him last year. She told you the story, didn't she?'

'Yes, she did. That doesn't mean anything. How many police officers has the Party killed, and how many of their families stood up for revenge? Zero. Because after losing one relative, these families don't want to receive another bori at their houses. So how come this slip of a girl decides to do this? How do you know she hasn't been planted here by the Party?'

'Byram, I've checked her background myself. I knew her brother. He served with me when I joined for my first posting here as an Assistant Superintendent. He was a good man, and a fine police officer. He kept in touch with me, even when I was posted out of the province. He was a good brother, very fond of her. Wanted her to study and be financially independent. That's why he made her study IT, so that she could have an opportunity to go abroad. He had also told her that if anything ever happened to him, she should come to me. She got in touch with me about two minutes after the last bullet was fired into her brother's body. I have been guiding her ever since. The Party hasn't gotten a chance to get close. They were extremely gratified that the family didn't make a big issue of it in the media, and they think I was the one who kept the case out of the news. I've got it all under control. So what are you really worried about?' Mallick takes a plain Marie biscuit from a plate and bites into it.

'I'm *really* worried about ending up in a gunnysack, like that brother of hers.'

'You haven't ended up in one so far, and you've been doing this for years. That's why you are so good at it, and that's why I need you to train people like her. We need her. She knows how to exploit the new social media business. This Facebook, Twitter, all these sorts of things. Anything we want to put out about the Party, any kind of propaganda, she can do with the click of a mouse. Relax, Byram. Besides, I've got your back.'

Byram snorts contemptuously, spilling some tea onto his shirt. 'And who will back you? What is your status in the power structure? Who listens to you? Saala, try and impress someone else with this sixth-floor bullshit. You've been dumped in this sideline post for the past six years. How come nobody proposes your name for IG or Karachi police chief? Even your juniors have gotten to those posts, but you remain stuck here. That bhenchod CM of yours, Colombowala, doesn't even call you for the daily briefings any more. How many people realize that you were also a founding member of the Party? In fact, you joined before the bloody CM and the entire fucking cabinet. The great Guddu Bihari, right hand of the Don in his university days. Why do you go to such lengths to hide that fact now? Ashamed that people will ask why you've not been able to use your connections? Ashamed of a wasted career?'

Not many men can surprise the head of Special Branch. But Byram does. Guddu's eyes widen perceptibly, and it takes him half a minute to respond. 'How do you know about that? Very few people outside the Party politburo know about my past association.'

'Arre charya, first you try and lick my ass by telling me how good I am at what I do, and then you are surprised at how I know such things? I've lived in this city for seventy fucking years, and I've been studying the Party for the last twenty-five. My bloody pubic hair has gone white doing this kind of work. You don't think I would have researched the origins of each and every member of the Party? The Party may want to cover these things up, you definitely want to cover these things up, but I know, chutiya, I know. So now, why don't you be honest with me and tell me what the issue is with you and the Party.'

Satisfied at having achieved total surprise, Byram takes a long gulp from his teacup and sets it down on the table, staring at Guddu, challenging him to respond. Guddu takes a packet of More cigarettes from his side drawer, and lights one of the long, brown cigarillos. He takes a couple of puffs, filling the air with a menthol smell as he contemplates Byram.

'Arre saala, this brand is for ladies. If you keep smoking it, you'll go impotent.'

The comment forces Guddu to laugh. 'It's an old wives' tale. I have three children already. Besides, since you have pointed out that I am already professionally impotent, physical impotence will not make much of a difference.'

'So, what happened?'

Guddu takes several long puffs of the cigarette before answering. 'Nobody has called me Guddu in a long time. The Don came up with that. He used to make fun of my being a Bihari all the time. Not in a bad way, just to tease. To be honest, in those days there were many people on campus who were far more cruel in their comments about Biharis. We were always looked down upon as crude, uncouth refugees from East Pakistan, not cultured like the UP-wallahs, not rich like the Memons or Gujaratis. We were a bit of a historical embarrassment, a reminder of the nightmare of 1971. The Don was never cruel about it though, unlike Imam. Imam was a regular little shit. He belittled me in order to hide his own Rampuri origins. His father had educated himself and become a man of letters, but before that, they had been village butchers for five generations. But to hear Imam talk, you'd have thought the sun shone out of his asshole. But the Don was different. He is a Marwari, so he didn't have the same hang-ups as Imam. We would never have gotten together if it hadn't been for him. We were all drawn to him, like moths to a flame. Imam, the intellectual; Aleem, the only son of an overly busy father, constantly seeking attention; Zaibunissa, the firebrand feminist, who had the misfortune of coming of age in Zia's Pakistan, when she really belonged to the sixties. And me, politically ambivalent, but looking for a cause to support, less out of ideology and more for the sense of comradeship.'

'What about Asad Haider? He was also there in the beginning, right?'

'That's another myth that the Don propagated when he wished to rewrite history in his own image. When Asad became his favourite son, when he became the embodiment of the loyal Party worker, it was important to convey that he had been a true believer right from the start. So everyone's roles had to be adjusted. My part was, of course, cut out from the script, and Imam's was downgraded, although it could never be fully eliminated. Aleem had to acquiesce to his father's demands to drop out of politics and take over the family business. And Zaib chose domesticity. Or rather, the Don chose it for her, getting her out of the way by marrying her off to Colombowala, to become the dutiful housewife to the man who is today our chief minister. But we were the originals.'

'Why did he cut you out? He didn't trust you?'

'Oh, he trusted me for a long time. In the beginning. I was the one who arranged his first meeting with the Khakis. It happened a couple of years after we left university. I had sat for the civil service exams and joined the police. But the others had to face the brunt of the backlash from the Jamiat's student activists, who were incensed at the Don's success in creating a grassroots liberal political organization. Their thugs chased us off the campuses. We were almost wiped out. Asad had created the structure of the wards, and wherever the Jamiatwallahs found a ward member on any college campus, they would put them in hospital. It was the early years of Zia's martial law and the religious parties, as you know, were his creatures, so the police supported them completely. Every time they beat one of our boys up, the police would register a case against the United Front. And the maulvis made sure that Asad's and the Don's names were mentioned in each criminal case, whether they had been physically present or not, just to keep them on the run from the law. When I returned from my training and took charge in my first posting as ASP Sardar, the Don and Asad were in hiding and already had twenty–thirty cases registered against them. The Jamiatwallahs knew that neither of them had the money to post bail. And even though the evidence was negligible in almost all the cases, arrest would mean that those two would spend years in jail.

'The Corps headquarters used to be in my area, and I was friendly with some of the Corps commander's staff officers. It was the last days of martial law, so it paid to be on their good side. One of them, Brigadier Fazli his name was, knew about my history with the Party, and approached me to bring the Don in to meet with him. He said he wanted to talk about the Party's political future. The maulvis were getting too big for their boots and the faujis wanted to cut them down to size, using us. Their offer predictably divided opinion amongst us. Imam wanted to have nothing to do with the military. Asad thought it could be a trap. And Aleem believed, not incorrectly, that it was either very good news or very bad news when the military started paying attention to you in this country. I thought the Party was out of options and so we really had no choice but to heed the summons. Imam and Asad thought I was advocating for the meeting out of some scheme for personal advancement, but the Don agreed with me. As a strategist, he knew he had to play this hand.'

Guddu taps out a long strand of ash from the cigarette and takes another puff, evidently enjoying the recollection. 'Back in those days, before we had these bloody suicide bombers, you could simply drive up to the front gate of the Corps headquarters. There was no barbed wire, or snipers or tank traps. They used to have just a couple of sentries on duty. And I was virtually a daily visitor there, so they all knew me, but that day, right up to the point where we walked into Brigadier Fazli's office, I was full of trepidation that they would grab me along with the Don and throw me in a cell somewhere. After all, it was a martial law government. What difference would the disappearance of one ASP make?

'The brigadier's office was huge, built to intimidate and overwhelm all visitors. At the furthest end of the room sat the brigadier, wearing an immaculate uniform. The orderly guided us to these two chairs across the table, which were positioned in such a way that the brigadier would always appear to tower over his visitors. Everything in that office was done to convey a message. After having made us wait in the outer office for almost an hour, the brigadier didn't address us immediately. Instead, we kept sitting for a full ten minutes, in complete silence, before he looked up from the files on his desk. But when he spoke, he was very direct. He laid out the hopelessness of the Party's position. I remember thinking, if things were so bad, why was he bothering with us? But the Don read his game immediately. And with equal bluntness, without wasting a moment, he responded by asking the brigadier what the military wanted us to do, and what we would get in return. I still remember, the brigadier smiled proudly, as a teacher would at a student who has proved himself to be particularly bright, and then he said, "You will get the keys to this city." And that was the moment that the Party's rise actually began.'

'Saala, so the Don accepted the deal without even blinking?'

'He accepted the deal without even pausing for breath. Up till that point, I had still, somewhat naively, believed in the Party's rhetoric. That we stood against military dictatorship, against a feudal political system. But the Don's performance that day rid me of these childish notions. The only thing he has ever believed in is power.'

'So that's why he sidelined you. Because he had been naked in front of you.'

'That wasn't the only reason. Initially, I handled all government contacts in the early days. After the meeting with Brigadier Fazli, things happened quickly. All of a sudden, our penniless Party was awash with wealthy donors wanting to back us. In this city, everyone keeps an eye out for which way the wind is blowing. And after that meeting, the wind started blowing undeniably towards us. That's when our current CM got involved. What is the term they use in the financial markets? Early-bird investor? That's what he was. Subsequently, he has reaped the profits.

'The Don insisted that we had to have a massive public event, as a sort of coming-out party, something that would make everyone sit up and take notice of the Party. So he planned the legendary first jalsa, at Nishtar Park. Because of my Party background, the government made me in charge of the security arrangements and all liaison with the district administration. Do you remember the jalsa? We took the city by storm. I have never been as proud of anything in my life as I am of that day.'

'Yes, I remember. There was a buzz around the entire city a week before the event. Everybody wanted to know who this young chokra was, who called himself the Don, and had the balls to take on the maulvis. My wife insisted that we had to go and see for ourselves. Nishtar Park is just two streets away from my house, but that day the entire area was so clogged with people and Party supporters that it took us over an hour to get to the park.'

'You mean, *you* attended the jalsa? I would never have guessed that you were ever a Party supporter.'

Now it is Byram's turn to smile. 'Arre saala, at that time, after ten years of bhenchod martial law, it was a breath of fresh air. It was freedom from having a government-approved version of life shoved down our throats. Relief from that bastard Zia and his lies. It was a festival, a mela. It had been oppressively hot the whole morning, but just before the jalsa began, it started to pour. I remember thinking at that moment that God favoured this fellow. If the heat had continued, the crowd wouldn't have stayed. When the rain came, it became a massive outdoor party, with music and dancing. My wife and I were drenched, but we danced like we hadn't in years.' Byram starts absently humming an old tune. 'You know that song they came up with, the one that was copied from some pop album …

Dil dil United Front, Dil dil United Front,
Aisi tanzeem, aur rahnuma,
Phir kabhi, mile ga naa
Dil dil United Front

(Heart, Heart United Front,
Such a Party, and such a leader
Will not be found again.)'

Byram's recitation is impressively melodious. 'Saala, brilliant idea. Who came up with it?'

'Aleem. He paid some wedding singers to convert the pop version into the Party version. He wanted to plug into the new youth culture to give the Party a hip image. A young leadership for a new generation in contrast to the religious parties, with their legions of ancient white-bearded leaders. It was us showing the world that you didn't need to be old to lead. After all, the Don wasn't even thirty at the time.'

'My wife made me buy the cassette the next day. She would insist on listening to it every night, for the next three months.'

'Yes, that night was a success beyond our wildest dreams. We were immediately flooded with membership requests and donations. Rich, poor … people sent whatever they could. So many women sent us their gold bangles, we had to actually assign Zaibunissa to find a jeweller who would buy them off us in bulk. Asad bought guns to arm the wards, so no one would dare to rough them up again. And Imam organized a brilliant election campaign, reaching out to first-time voters, getting the wards to organize neighbourhood committees, youth committees, elders' committees, a committee for any and every segment of society. It seemed as if the whole city was behind us in that first municipal election. But most importantly, the military kept its end of the bargain and remained benevolent. The religious parties formed an alliance against us to try and stop our momentum, and still most of their candidates lost their election deposits.'

'Yes, saala, that was the only election you fellows didn't rig.'

'In truth, we became victims of our own success. Since that first result was so overwhelming, the Don decreed that we couldn't ever afford to get a result that was less than that first one. But after that first election, we thought we were going to change the world. When it became clear that the city's mayorship would be ours, the Khakis encouraged the chief minister to call the Don to the CM House to talk about an alliance. But the Don wanted to do everything *ulta*. Instead of putting up an experienced politician for mayor, he selected a twenty-seven-year-old engineering student. He even refused to go to meet the CM at the CM House. He insisted that the CM should come to *his* house, in Lines Area, to pay homage to our electoral success. He sent me to inform the CM of his demand. Me, a lowly assistant superintendent of police, going to the CM and telling him my friend refused to meet him unless he came to a hovel in Jut Lines! Can you imagine? In his wildest dreams, the CM would never have imagined going to Jut Lines. But he did it, because as a politician he understood the need to salute the rising sun. He and many other politicians were to make that journey in the years ahead. But on that first visit, we were so disorganized that no one had accounted for the fact that the CM's huge Mercedes couldn't come into the narrow alley that led to the Don's house. The car had to stay on the main road, with the CM awkwardly waiting inside, while Aleem and I begged the Don to at least come till the main road to receive the chief minister.'

'Saala bhenchod, when you were doing all this running around for him, then why did he sideline you?'

'Because for the Don, loyalty means complete subjugation. It means never dissenting, never protesting, never even asking for personal favours unless he offers them of his own volition.'

Byram nods in understanding. 'Ah, now I see. So what did you ask for that he was unwilling to give?'

Guddu smiles at the memory. 'You will be shocked when I tell you. It was over a girl.'

'A girl? You asked him for a girl?'

'You make it sound so sordid, Byram. It wasn't like that. There was a girl I liked in university. Her name was Afshan. Afshan Illahbadi. She was a poetess. She liked me as well, but it never went anywhere beyond holding hands and having a few cups of coffee in the university canteen, furtively glancing around to see if there were any maulvis watching us. Then I left to go to the Police Academy. In my absence, the girl fell under the Don's spell. She was bewitched by his oratory. So much so that she even gave him her favours in bed, a courtesy that, I must say, was never extended to me. The Don toyed with her for a bit, but quickly lost interest and moved on to other prey. Afshan took it badly. She became depressed, dropped out, started· writing sonnets about her love for him. That's the condition I found her in when I returned from the academy. I was still interested in her, so I professed my love for her and coaxed her back to her normal state. I wanted to marry her. It seemed like the perfect time. We had just won the municipal election and I was going to be promoted and made one of the five district SPs in Karachi. With our government installed in the city, it made sense for me to have control over a chunk of the city's police force. I made the mistake of asking the Don for his blessing. I knew he didn't have any interest in Afshan any more, but still, I didn't want any misunderstandings between us. I remember, he gave me this strange smile, but didn't say anything. That night, he called Afshan over and resumed fucking her. The next day, the inspector general summoned me and told me my services were no longer required in the Sindh police, and that I had been posted to Gilgit, about as far away from Karachi as was possible. When I asked him why this had happened, he told me the Don had complained that I was acting unscrupulously, trying to take advantage of my personal friendship in order to secure a lucrative posting. I was considered unscrupulous, while

Tariq Colombowala, who was appointed deputy mayor, started openly asking for kickbacks on municipal contracts from the first day he took over. No one said anything to him, because he started bankrolling the Don's lifestyle. But I was shut out.'

'Because he wanted you out of the way so he could carry on with the girl.'

'No. He had no interest in the girl. He fucked her a couple more times and threw her right out again. It was just to show me his power. To put me in my place. It took me almost fifteen years to get posted back to the city. Till the Party was in power, they wouldn't hear of it, and then when the operation began against the Party, I was doubly damned as I was considered suspect because of my earlier loyalty to the Party.'

'What happened to the girl?'

'I don't really know. I didn't want to go near her again, for fear that it would worsen my predicament. I heard she had a nervous breakdown. Never quite got over this episode.'

'And how did you get over this "episode"?'

'By keeping my mouth shut about all my previous associations in public. And grovelling and kissing the Don's ass in private. And also, thanks in no small part to you.'

'Me? Saala, what the fuck did I do?'

'I kept assuring him that he needed me to run Special Branch, so that he could be made aware of any threats to him in a timely fashion. I was the one who first broke the news to him about the existence of a secret organization called the Others that had sworn to destroy him, even when no such organization existed. He was so paranoid that he easily believed it. Subsequently, fact followed fiction and the Others came into being.'

'Saala bhenchod, but you created us! How could you tell him that there was a threat when there wasn't one?!'

'I didn't create anything. This was an idea whose time had come. The Party has destroyed so many lives, hurt so many people in this city, a group like this would have formed sooner or later. History tells us that tyranny is ultimately always opposed. People tolerate getting screwed only for so long. I was merely like a gardener, nurturing a plant that was always going to bloom in this environment.'

'So this is a fucking sham! Just to keep you in this shit job?'

'Of course not. The Party needs to fall. The Don needs to fall. I am convinced of that goal now more than ever. But sitting on this perch gives me a vantage point, to view the entire field of play.' Guddu picks up a stack of files from his desk and throws them over to Byram. 'Look, this is the truth about the Party. Every day, my officers compile a daily situation report, which is given to the CM and passed on to the Party. These are the things I leave out of the official report.'

Byram picks up the top file, which is the thickest. A Post-it note on the cover, easily removable in case of detection, has the word corruption stenciled on it. Inside, the file is divided according to the ministries that the Party currently holds, with a picture and the name of the relevant minister attached. He spends several minutes perusing the file, chuckling from time to time.

'You people are responsible for last year's malaria epidemic as well?'

'The health minister sold off the government's reserves of anti-malaria medication on the black market, so when the cases started occurring, there were no stocks in the government hospitals. That meant the government ordered more, under emergency procurement rules, and the minister got more kickbacks from buying from the most expensive vendor.'

'And how much goes to New York?'

'There is a formula. The Don gets half of any kickback fee, the CM or minister concerned gets 30 per cent, and the Party gets 10 per cent, with the rest being shared by the relevant government officials. That's why the CM insists on holding on to so many important ministries himself. It maximizes his earnings.'

'Saala, after being in the police your whole life, suddenly you've become a moralist?'

'Not at all. I believe in corruption. It is what keeps the wheels turning in a country like ours. I indulge in it from time to time. But the problem is one of proportion. If you eat the whole pie and don't distribute at least some of the crumbs to the wider populace, you start to have problems. This city's infrastructure is falling apart. Crime increases, disenchantment with the system increases. The Party has only made things worse since it came to power on its own. Ever since the Don got a big pat on his back from the Americans and from Islamabad when that DSP Akbar Khan rescued the American journalist a couple of years ago, there have been no limits. All the ministers eat as if there is no tomorrow.'

'Saala bhenchod, you're not in this for the fucking good governance! You're in it for your personal ambition. You figure that either the Others will succeed in killing the Don, or you can always turn them over to the Party if it doesn't work out. Either way, it's your ticket to become the Don's golden boy once again. If you find out who the Others are, he'll definitely make you the IG.'

'Yes, I am not in it for good governance. But I do believe the Party is out of control. Like a rabid animal, it has to be put down. Forget the corruption. Look at the other files. Our Party members perpetrate every single imaginable crime on the denizens of this city every day. Rape, murder, robbery, blackmail. There has to be a reckoning some day. This is no longer the Party I founded. It does not stand for my ideals any more. If I thought that there was something salvageable about it, believe me, I would try to salvage it. But the Party has to be destroyed in order to save it from itself. There are others who feel the same way I do. My friends in the Agencies, the Kaala gatewallahs and Bleak House. They would also appreciate the Party cut down to size.

'And you're wrong about me selling out the Others for my personal advantage. There is no advantage, only risk for me if I were to try and do that. I'm walking a tightrope. Do you think I would live, forget survive in this job, if the Don had an inkling that the Others were my brainchild? You think he would have any hesitation to order my murder, or indeed the liquidation of my entire family? Look at what he just did to Asad Haider. So I'm in this as deep as you are.'

Byram stares at Guddu for a long instant, as if trying to judge his sincerity. Apparently satisfied, he finally speaks. 'So why did you call me here?'

'Asad Haider. He is the key to everything. So far, we have been doing nothing better than throwing stones at the Party. We didn't have the muscle to take them on directly. But Asad changes everything. He was head of the Party's militant wing for over twenty years, for God's sake. He is a walking, talking, killing machine. He was the Don's one irreplaceable acolyte. It's a testament to the Don's foolishness that he killed Asad's family before ensuring that Asad was dead. Asad Haider is a man who will never forget, or forgive. And many of the ward bosses owe more to Asad than to the Don. This can be the beginning of a civil war within the Party, if we can only get to Asad before anyone else does. I need you to find a way to make contact with him.'

Byram's face grows cold and impassive, then suddenly, with a growl, he shouts, 'No! I will not work with that murderous bastard Asad Haider.'

'Byram, I know how you feel about him after what he did to your son, but politics makes the strangest bedfellows. You have spent so many years, fuelled by your hatred of the Party, doing everything you could to make a dent on them. Now, we can punch a hole in them, using him. You can't let your personal feelings get in the way of this opportunity. Please.'

'Saala, get someone else to do it. Ali Raza or that Deobandi terrorist who works for you.'

'If I use anyone else, the Party will see it coming from a mile away. You are the only one who has the requisite experience and contacts, and can fly under the radar.'

Byram rises from his chair violently, his eyes bulging out of their sockets and his hands shaking with anger. 'You are a bastard.'

7

ISMAIL

I realized that after what I had witnessed, it would be difficult for me to return to my old life. What I hadn't realized was exactly how difficult it would be.

I didn't return to the office immediately. Instead, I went home and took the next day off. I had half a notebook full of notes, but I didn't start the article. I wasn't sure if I should inform somebody about the murder of the three workers. It was hardly an anonymous event. The bodies had been found almost immediately and the TV channels went crazy discussing the contents of Baba's 'open letter' to the Don. The Party called for a 'partial strike', which meant that they only burned a couple dozen vehicles instead of several dozen. But noticeably, the wards did not try and make an entry into Lyari. To me, the Party's response seemed unnaturally mild. It was as if they were holding back for something.

Exactly what the 'something' was became apparent when I reached the paper's office a day and a half later. As soon as I sat down, my editor came over to talk. I thought he would give me an earful for having bunked work the previous day, and having come in late today, but instead, he was extremely solicitous, asking if I was all right. Then, he took me to his room and shut the door. Inside sat a thin man, sipping a cup of coffee, wearing a smart black waistcoat and starched shalwar kameez, along with the sort of supremely self-important air that only comes from being a public representative in the Indian subcontinent.

'Ismail, let me introduce you to Mian Mithu sahib, he is …'

'I know who he is. He is the United Front's media spokesperson.'

'Exactly. It's a pleasure to meet you, Ismail. Your editor has told me a lot about you.' His eyes were cold and calculating as he shook my hand, scanning me for any sign of weakness.

'Did you hear about the boys from the ward?'

'Yes sir. That's why I got in so late. I couldn't get a bus from Jauhar due to the Party's transport strike.'

'Terrible business. The boys were barely out of their teens. Engineering college students. One of the bodies was found without a head. Imagine telling a mother that her son's body was found without its head. Savages.' The way Mian Mithu sipped his coffee and licked the malai off his lips, it didn't seem as if he would have had much difficulty talking about the headless teenager to his mother.

'You were in Lyari yesterday, right, Ismail? You had gotten that exclusive interview with Baba.' I should have realized that my editor was in on the plan. After all, he was a fervent Party supporter, often suppressing negative news about the Party while highlighting the flaws of their political opponents. There were some rumours circulating in the office that he was angling for a senate seat in the next elections. But the greater reaction came from the spokesperson, who raised his head and viewed me with predatory interest.

'Uh, yes sir, I was.'

'Did you get your interview?'

'Well, uh, yes and no. I mean we had started, but then something came up and Baba got up and left. I assume it must have been to do with the issue with the ward boys. He never came back after that.'

'So, you mean to say that you actually met Baba Dacait yesterday?' The questioning was now being done directly by Mian Mithu.

'Yes, I did. But, as I said, only very briefly.'

'Where did you meet him? In Lyari?'

'Yes, as I told Editor sahib, his people had arranged for me to be taken into Lyari for the interview.'

'This story was a very big coup for you, Ismail. I had our media cell do some checking on you. You haven't gotten such a big scoop ever before, have you? How did you manage it? How did you get in touch with Baba?'

Now, at this point, I had a choice. I could be truthful and tell them about Rafiq Rangoonwala, or I could make a case for journalistic ethics and refuse to name my source. I wasn't a big fan of either Rafiq or ethics, but I didn't want to reveal all my cards just yet, until I knew where this was heading. So I chose to stall by telling a half-truth.

'I got in touch through an old acquaintance, who knew somebody who knew somebody close to Baba. You know he's a big fan of football, so he's always hanging out with these old footballer types, and I got the interview through one of them, who asked him for a favour. He had actually been looking to talk to the media, and my approach came at a good time. Why, is there a problem? I mean I know he is your political opponent, but for me it was a good story, and I had informed Editor sahib before …'

Mian Mithu started stroking his moustache. 'No, no, don't worry about *that*. We are not concerned with your meeting him, although he is *not* our political opponent. He is a terrorist. But it's interesting, I didn't know that he was a football fan. And he met you well? He opened up to you, was comfortable with you?'

'Well, I mean, he's a professional criminal, so I don't think he'll ever warm up to a total stranger, but he was nice enough to me. Offered me chai and cold drinks, and was forthcoming enough when I asked him questions. Although, as I said, we couldn't get very far because he left.'

'And what was his security like?'

'I don't know, I'm not a police officer, I don't know how good they were, but there were plenty of men with guns standing around, if that's what you mean.'

'Ismail, do you think you will be invited back? You said you didn't finish up.'

'Well, uh, yes, he did say that he would continue the conversation and arrange another time to meet.'

'Excellent. Excellent. Editor sahib, I must say, I am really impressed with Ismail's intelligence and journalistic commitment. I think he has a tremendous future in this business, *if* he makes the correct *decisions*. I foresee him becoming a huge name in journalism. Maybe anchoring his own show on one of the channels, in the not-too-distant future.'

'What decisions?'

Mian Mithu smiled, the trap now set, the prey cornered. 'Well, Ismail, we need your help. Baba Dacait, as you would have gleaned from today's headlines, has become a major irritant for the Party and for the city. He believes he is above the law. It is our civic duty to make him realize that he is not. Now, you know that part of the issue is the failure of the police and our Party cadres to gain entry into Lyari. Baba has made it a no-go area, so he cannot be arrested. But, if he were to somehow be lured out of Lyari, say on the pretext of giving an interview to a foreign news channel, by a journalist with whom he has established a rapport, then the problem could perhaps be *eliminated*.'

'What do you mean by eliminated?'

'We both know that you aren't that naive, Ismail.'

'But why me? You have plenty of journalists on your payroll. Get one of them to do it.'

'We have, but none of them were able to get an interview with Baba Dacait. You were.'

'But what can I do? Why would he come out of Lyari on my saying? And if he were to even suspect that I was involved, he could have me killed then and there. Sir, I am a simple man, please leave me out of this.'

For a second, his eyes blazed and his jaw became taut. 'Editor sahib, I thought you said this one was smart. But he doesn't seem to be understanding my gist. Do you really think Baba is the one you should be worried about, Ismail? Your wife teaches at the government secondary school in Gulshan Iqbal, right? Her principal informs me that she is a very bright teacher. It would be a shame for the schoolchildren to be deprived of her. And your own children? One has to be very careful with children these days, what with all these express kidnappings going on and sexual perverts on the loose. You wouldn't want anything to happen to yours, would you?'

'What are you saying? I ...'

'Look, I'm not saying anything, Ismail. I'm just pointing out that this is a *very* dangerous city. Things *happen* here every day. *Sick* things, *painful* things. It helps to have powerful friends in this city, and I am telling you that the Party wants to be your friend. We will not only ensure the security and safety of your family, we will open doors for you. Like I said, you seem to be a talented man. Editor sahib won't be in his seat forever. We could easily arrange for you to take over here, or go to another paper or a TV channel. We could make you the most respected columnist in the city, by giving you special access to the Party. Hell, if you can pull off this Baba plan, we will make you a hero. Ever thought of joining politics? We're always looking for bright people. A safe seat, with a guaranteed majority of 50,000, could be given to you. The Don likes to reward loyalty and bravery. Think about it.'

I swallowed hard and looked at my editor, who gave me no sympathy at all. I wasn't sure whether that was part of the plan to scare me, or his anger at the package I was being offered by the Party – a package that he, presumably, would have wanted for himself. So I turned to the source of my predicament, Mian Mithu, and started pleading with him, hoping to at least buy time. 'But sir, to do this, I need time to build a connection with Baba. It's not like he'll come running out of Lyari tomorrow at my say-so. He will only come if he trusts me. Give me some time, please. And sir, if I succeed, you know his people will know it was me, so I will need some kind of financial compensation, you know, to relocate to another neighbourhood, perhaps go to Dubai for a while. I would be obliged if you could work something out for me.'

Mian Mithu looked at my editor, a triumphant glint in his eyes. Then he downed the remaining coffee in his cup and stood up. 'Of course, we also realize that an operation of this delicacy will not happen overnight. Go and see Baba again. Take your time to build up his confidence in you. Then, when he is ready, deliver him to us. And don't worry, we will look after your financial requirements. I knew Ismail was a sharp man, Editor sahib. Give him any support that he may require in this matter. I look forward to hearing from you soon, Ismail.'

And with that, he walked out of the editor's cabin, his bodyguards, who had been stationed in the newsroom, in tow behind him. I had gotten a stay of execution, but I would need to figure a way out of this situation. My editor agreed to clear my schedule so I could concentrate on this story, and also gave me ten thousand rupees for expenses. This, from a man who had never given me ten rupees for a cup of tea. Obviously, a visit from Mian Mithu opened doors and wallets. I told him I would need to go in deep with the gangsters, be with them day and night, to make the plan work. I didn't want to have to keep coming back to the office to give progress reports to either Mian Mithu or my chutiya editor on a daily basis.

Having done that, I spent an hour or so at the office, pretending to go through the motions of a normal day. I secretly packed up anything of value in my desk. There wasn't much to begin with, but I did have a few files that would be good for future blackmailing prospects. I put them in my bag, and, on the pretext of getting a bite to eat, left the office.

I had a genuine choice in front of me. It was obvious I had to choose a side in this war for Karachi. There were risks on both sides, but alongside that risk came opportunity. A chance to play the big game. Other, lesser, men might have worried about their lives or their families, but not me. I had waited all my life for such a chance. All I needed to do was leverage this properly. The Party's offer was pretty good. The only downside would be having to put up with idiots like Mian Mithu.

I had decided that my first move was to get rid of my liabilities. I got home and told my wife to prepare to leave for the village with the children, on the pretext that my mother was ill. Once I got them packing, I walked over to the opposite tower block to mine, to get some insurance. I had known Qudratullah Mehsud for many years. He had been a street tough all his life, known for extorting hundreds and hundreds of rupees from the fruit and vegetable sellers in the area. He was handy with a knife, which had earned him his nickname of Chaaku. But, as times changed, so did Chaaku, taking shelter in whichever political party afforded him protection from the police. Initially, he had even joined the United Front, but when they didn't make him the local ward boss, he suddenly remembered his ethnicity and switched to the Pashtun nationalists. As the years went by, he kept expanding his portfolio, going from petty extortion of shopkeepers to major extortion of builders, and then, in a natural progression, to land-grabbing. A few years ago, as the Taliban established themselves as another force in the city, and more importantly, when his cousin became a senior Taliban commander in North Waziristan, Chaaku had a revelation and discovered religion. Or at least those aspects of religion that were profitable to him. So he grew a beard and let his hair grow long in the Taliban fashion, and now he planted black Taliban flags instead of red or saffron flags on the plots of land he snatched, but the fundamentals of his business remained the same. The Taliban wanted money, the same thing as everybody else. And Karachi is like an ATM machine that constantly churns out cash. But the advantage that Chaaku got from joining the Taliban was that now he had bigger guns and explosives at his disposal. You could say that his company's infrastructure had improved.

We were old friends because I had always used my sources to highlight potential extortion targets for him. So the minute a builder got approval from the municipal government for a new project, I would find out through my contacts and pass this information on to him, for a small consultancy fee. Chaaku would then present his demands to the unfortunate builder.

Right now, I needed him, as I said, for insurance. He had set up a baithak in a ground-floor flat that he had illegally seized. A couple of his Taliban men were usually there while he held court. Everyone knew Chaaku was there, but no one bothered to raid the place. It was rumoured that Chaaku had once sent a message to the local police station warning them to stay away or else he would send a suicide bomber to the gates of the station. Since then, even the normal police patrolling in front of Rabia City had stopped. Chaaku met me immediately and, over a cup of tea, I explained to him that I was in trouble and would rely on him to protect my family, in case either the Party or the Lyari gangsters came after me over here. Chaaku was thoroughly decent about it and told me not to worry. To be honest, I wasn't that worried because I knew that word of Chaaku and the Taliban's presence in Rabia City was spreading and it would be foolhardy of anyone to attempt to muscle their way here.

Reassured, I slept on my problem, still not sure which side I wanted to choose. In the morning, I dropped my wife and children to the coach station, ensuring that they got on to the right bus. I then took another taxi to the PC Hotel, in the centre of town. I knew my editor always took people he wanted to suck up to for lunch there. And I still had a large chunk of his money burning a hole in my wallet. So I figured, as I thought about the most momentous decision of my life, I might as well do it while tucking into a five-star buffet meal.

The Party's offer was a good one, no doubt. I could certainly see myself as an MP or a senator. As I tucked into my second helping of chicken boti and mutton chaap, I had a vision of myself, wearing a starched white, pure cotton kurta with gold cufflinks, sitting in a government number plate sedan with a flag on it, a police escort following me everywhere with a wailing siren. It would be a good life, a massive upgrade from my current circumstances.

But there was a downside. They say once you enter the Party, the only way out is in a coffin. The Party takes over your life. Everything you do, everything you say, is run through Darul Sakoon, the headquarters. Someone once told me that the Party made all newly elected parliamentary candidates perform menial chores at the Don's house like domestic servants, just to ingrain into them that they belonged to the Don now. Refusal to do any of these tasks resulted in a visit from the local ward boss. The threat made by Mian Mithu against my family hadn't been a casual one. Nor was it limited to my not cooperating in the plan to kill Baba. The same threat would hang over my head even if I became one of the Party's chosen ones. In effect, everyone in the Party was held hostage by the Don. Was all the money and power in the world worth that? Perhaps.

I finished my meal and got in touch with Jheenga again. He arranged for me to be picked up from Botal Galli, near Rafiq Rangoonwala's shop. As I stood outside waiting to be picked up, Rafiq seth wandered out and was shocked to see me. 'Relax, Rafiq seth,' I said. 'This time I've called Baba myself. No need for you to spend two rupees making the call.' He got an even bigger shock when he saw Jheenga's sheedis pull up and open the door for me to get into their car.

I was told that this time we were going to Baba's house in Afshani Galli. It was already evening by now and the route was dark thanks to a power cut. At first glance, Afshani Galli seemed to be a typical Lyari street, narrow, with barely enough space for a single car to pass through, and ramshackle two- or three-storey houses closely packed together, on either side. However, that was the only normal thing about the street. The entrance to Afshani Galli had been sealed by a massive steel gate, manned by Baba's M-4 rifles-toting sheedis wearing combat fatigues, bulletproof jackets and the compulsory fashion sunglasses, even at night. There were more sheedis on the rooftops, manning morchas with light machine guns and rocket-propelled grenades. Everybody walking through the steel gates was body-searched, including myself. But once inside, the galli was colourfully lit up with fairy lights strung from the electric poles. A massive generator hummed silently and ensured that the whole street had uninterrupted electricity, courtesy of Baba. Boys played night cricket on the road, not needing to be mindful of passing cars. Painters had painted huge murals on the house walls, paying tribute to Baba. One of the paintings, the largest one, depicted him wearing the traditional robes and turban of a Baloch sardar, holding up an AK-47 in one hand. Slogans in praise of Baba, painted in letters five feet tall, calling him a hero of the people, Lyari's last, best hope, and one that compared him to an F-16 fighter jet, adorned the walls. Further up the road, at the entrance to Baba's house, a ten-foot-tall TV screen had been set up, and a football World Cup match was being screened, with an audience of about a hundred people watching, screaming encouragement and reprimands to the players on the screen. In the middle of them sat Baba, wearing a fake Barcelona shirt on top of a shalwar.

I raised my hand in salaam and he acknowledged me with a grunt, but made no other attempt to communicate. He remained focused on the match, oblivious to all else. Somebody got me a chair to sit on, and soon a trolley with tea and snacks was rolled out, from which I helped myself. But Baba remained interested only in the football for the entire ninety minutes. I don't pretend to be a fan of football, but from the oohs and aahs of the crowd assembled in Afshani Galli, it seemed to be a pretty good match, though only one goal was scored in it. One of the crowd members informed me that it was Brazil's opening match in the World Cup.

After the match, Baba got up and gestured to me. We walked into his house alone. Although the house seemed cramped from outside, I discovered that inside, several of the surrounding walls had been knocked down to create more space. At the back of his house was a big indoor swimming pool. Baba sat down at the edge of the pool, lighting up his standard bhara hua cigarette and dipping his feet in the pool. I sat down on an uncomfortable cane chair that was precariously close to the edge of the pool.

'Salaam Baba. Good match. Although the one you should definitely see is the Argentina one. I have heard they have this player, Messi, who is supposed to be the new Maradona.'

Baba grunted and nodded in approval, as if in agreement with my assessment of Messi's footballing skills. 'He's good, very good. But he's no Maradona.'

I shrugged. That was probably a view of Messi shared by thousands of fans across the world, not just a gangster in Lyari. 'You know, Baba, I've been thinking. I didn't know you had put up a screen for the whole street. It's a fantastic idea. I think you should do it on a bigger scale. Maybe set up a giant screen in Gabol Park throughout the World Cup, and we can highlight your love for both football and the local community. Show everyone that while violence continues in other parts of the city, Lyari is so safe that you can watch football at one in the morning and nothing will happen. It will be a great PR victory over the Party.'

Baba stroked his beard in the way that I was now beginning to realize he did when he was attracted to an idea.

'Uh, you can invite select members of the media and talk to them about football things. You know, like you just did with me, comparing Messi to Maradona, Brazil's chances in the World Cup. Show everybody that you are not the demon that the United Front tries to portray you as.'

Baba remained silent for a long time. Finally, he responded with a single sentence. 'Good. You set up the interviews and the screenings, and take any expenses you need from Jheenga.'

I realized at that moment that I had suddenly become a de facto member of the Baba Dacait gang. It was a strangely liberating feeling, and it was perhaps that feeling that influenced what I did next.

'Baba, there is something I wanted to talk to you about. When I went back to my newspaper yesterday, Mian Mithu, the Party's spokesperson, was waiting for me in the office. My editor had told them about my meeting with you. They threatened me and told me that I should come up with a way to lure you out of Lyari, on the pretext of an interview with a foreign news channel. Their plan was that once you were out of Lyari, I should inform them and a hit team would come and kill you. I am sorry I didn't tell you earlier, but this only happened yesterday. I didn't know what to do. They threatened my family. But I do know that I want no part in any plan to kill you.'

Baba's only reaction was to take another drag of his teriak cigarette. It was as if I had told him who had scored for Brazil in the match we had just watched. If anything, perhaps telling him that would have elicited more of a reaction.

'You put your family at risk by telling me this.'

'Well, I sent my family away to our village this morning, so they should be okay, but I don't know if I will be able to go back to my flat.'

'What did Mian Mithu say about me?'

'He called you a terrorist, and he said you had become a thorn in the Party's side.'

Baba nodded, finished his cigarette and stubbed it out on the floor. Then he called out for his men. Jheenga and several others came running into the pool room.

'Jheenga, Mian Mithu was making a plan to kill me.'

'But how would they have done that, Baba?'

'They were going to get Naich to lure me out of Lyari. I want to send a message to that madarchod. I will pay ten petis to the man who gets me Mithu's tongue. He enjoys speaking so much, let's see what he can do without his fucking tongue. I don't care how many others you kill to get to him.'

Jheenga shrugged. 'Ten lakhs. Good money. Don't worry, Baba, it will be done. But what do you want us to do with him?' He pointed his pistol, which was perpetually in his hand, at me.

'Naich is a good man. He was loyal, even though he didn't have to be, and these Party bhenchods threatened his family.

I admire and respect such a man. He's one of us now. We will take care of him. And if one hair on his family's head is harmed, I will personally go and buttfuck that bastard Javed Gringo in front of Darul Sakoon.'

Why did I choose Baba over the Party? There were risks on both sides, and opportunities too. But the Party was the more established force in this city, while Baba was considered by most to be just a common criminal. The Party sat in the corridors of power, Baba just watched football in Lyari. That is the way most conventional people would have viewed this problem. Then why did I do it? In that moment, while watching the Brazil match in Afshani Galli, I had a vision. A vision of limitless possibility, of being able to shape the image of Baba Dacait, making him a player, not just in this city, but in this country. The Party's vision had already been shaped. I would just be another peon, albeit a well-compensated one, at Darul Sakoon. With Baba, I would be the scriptwriter and director of this movie. Besides, Mian Mithu's arrogance just pissed me off. What a chutiya.

8

BYRAM

'The shutdown in the city went into its third day today, as the United Front workers continued to observe a mourning period following the murder of the Party spokesperson Mian Mithu on Wednesday. All shops and businesses in the city remained closed and no public transport was available. Common people have started to complain that rations are running low, with stores remaining shut for such a long period and no delivery of essential everyday items like petrol, milk, ghee and eggs due to transport remaining off the roads. But the Transporters' Association has demanded protection from the police and guarantees from the government that its trucks will not be damaged before resuming service. The transporters claim that more than sixty buses and trucks were burnt by members of the United Front during the strike period. The Chamber of Commerce and Industry has claimed that the strike has caused the economy a loss of ten billion rupees. Chief Minister Tariq Colombowala has assured business leaders who called on him at the Chief Minister House today that the Party would call off the strike tomorrow and all businesses would reopen. The chief minister has said that the United Front has always worked for the interest of Pakistan, and has overlooked all the grave injustices that have been committed against it by other governments and parties. It has never taken revenge for the extrajudicial murders of its workers that had been committed in the previous government because the Party has always believed in the Don's message of reconciliation and forgiveness. However, the chief minister also warned that it would be difficult for the government or the Party to restrain its workers in the face of blatant provocation from criminal and terrorist groups like the Baba Dacait gang, and any business or political interests that continued to support such miscreants. He said that even more than the murder itself, the manner of the Party spokesperson's killing was horrendous, and he has ordered the inspector general of police to arrest the culprits within forty-eight hours.

Mian Mithu was a member of the national assembly and had been the national spokesperson for the United Front for the past two years. He was kidnapped by armed assailants who took his police escort hostage as he came out of an unidentified apartment complex in Defence, on Tuesday night. The policemen were deprived of their weapons and let go after several hours, but Mian Mithu's severely mutilated body was recovered the following morning from Mauripur Road, near Lyari.

On the other side, notorious gangster Baba Dacait has released a statement to the press stating that the killing was in retaliation for the hundreds of innocents that the Party has killed over the years in the city. Baba Dacait also stated that he was a peaceful man, and his supporters only resorted to violence to protect citizens from the gangsterism of the United Front Party. In a personal message directed at Mr Mohammed Ali, the founder of the United Front, Baba Dacait has said that the Don was no longer the only Don in this city. He declared that he was in Lyari, and would remain in Lyari, and if the Don wanted to fight him, he should stop hiding in New York and come back to Karachi.

In the light of what can only be termed as escalatory statements by both sides, the city is bracing for an extended bout of violence, despite the chief minister's assurances. Families are planning to stock up extra household supplies as soon as shops reopen, because they are unsure of how long shops and businesses may be closed again in the event of another incident between the two groups. From Karachi, with cameraman Latif Warsi, this is Nazish Brohi for Super News.'

Byram grunts and flicks to another channel, where the content of the news report is more or less the same. He has watched this bulletin, on different channels, five times already in the last couple of hours. That's the amount of time he has been waiting in this small two-by-four cabin that serves as the booking office for the cable TV business run by the local ward boss, Saquib Shatroo. Byram doesn't mind though. It's good to be out of the house. Especially after having been cooped up there the last few days because of the tension in the city. At least in the office of a cable TV operator he has the luxury of being able to actually watch the news. At home, all he has been able to get is the Party's own in-house channel showing non-stop coverage of the tributes being given to the slain spokesperson by Party members at Darul Sakoon, the Party headquarters.

Finally, the door of the cabin opens and a middle-aged overweight man, with long oily hair and lips bright red from constantly chewing paan, walks in. He has an air of authority around him, as if he is used to being obeyed by all. But his greeting to Byram is an unexpectedly warm one.

'Arre Uncle, sorry I got delayed. It's been crazy these past few days. Meeting after meeting, instructions from headquarters – the wards should do this, the wards should do that. The wards should ensure no vehicle moves on the roads, the wards should ensure that people only watch the Party channel. Oof, what am I to do? I am the ward boss of Soldier Bazaar but I am also a businessman. And I have a queue of customers complaining that they can't watch their favourite TV dramas because we have switched off the feed.'

'Yes, saala, all I've gotten on TV the past three days is that drivel from your headquarters. When are you going to restore normal service?'

'Tonight, Inshallah, Uncle, tonight. I'm sorry for the inconvenience. I would have switched back the regular channels for my customers the first day, but the problem is one of my competitors would have gone and complained at Darul Sakoon that the ward had made them shut off their normal programming but Saquib Shatroo's cable business was continuing to show Bollywood movies in this time of mourning. Karna parta hai, you know how it is. One complaint to the wrong person and you end up in a gunnysack.'

'Tell me something, how did they get him so easily? Didn't he live near here? Don't you have your ward boys patrolling everywhere?'

Saquib takes a paan out of his pocket, unwraps it from its shiny packaging of glittery paper and old newsprint, and delicately places it in his mouth. 'Arre Uncle, he lives near Martin Quarters, but these bhenchods can't control their dicks. He had a girlfriend in Defence. Some hot burger bachchi. He couldn't resist going to fuck her. And as for the police escort, God save everyone from those bastards. Must have been high on booze or charas. Once they become part of a minister's escort, they think discipline doesn't apply to them any more. I'm sure one of them only must have tipped off those Lyari madarchods. Told them, come now, there's no security cover. And when Baba's men showed up, the thullahs didn't even offer token resistance. Arre bhai, at least you fire a few rounds from your weapons to make it look like you put up a fight. Nothing. Just handed over their Kalashnikovs like Eid presents. I tell you, Uncle, times are bad. In our days, the police used to be something. People like Akbar Khan, Inspector Dilawar, okay fine they were mostly hunting us down, but we respected them. They were real men. Now you have all these bloody Party-appointed sifarshis in every thana, and these chutiyas couldn't wipe their own assholes.'

'Did they really mutilate the body?'

'Cut his dick and balls off, and shoved them in his mouth. Fucking animals, these Lyariwallahs.'

'So what's the Party going to do now? Send the police to Lyari?'

'Arre Uncle, the police will do fuckall in Lyari. Baba is so fucking entrenched there, it would be like fighting a war. Remember last year, the great Akbar Khan, scourge of the United Front and the Taliban, went in and even he failed. Baba blew up two of the police's armoured personnel carriers with his armour-piercing rockets. The bhenchod seems to have cornered the market for all the American weapons that they scavenge from Afghanistan. Baba buys them wholesale from Quetta. Mines, night vision goggles, M-4, M-5 sniper rifles, God knows what else.'

'So are you going in?'

'Very difficult. They want us to go in, but these sheedis with Baba are fucking self-trained commandos. Always tanked up on teriak and ready to fight like junoonis. We can burn buses and beat up shopkeepers for extortion, and get up close and blow someone's brains out, but we can't fight a war. I explained to Javed Gringo, if we went in we would have to fight for every alley, hand to hand, with Baba's men. On their home turf. It would be a massacre. Not only would we lose men, we would lose face. So far we have maintained our control on this city because everyone thinks we cannot be challenged. If we were to fail in Lyari, it might open the floodgates. Others might decide to assert themselves. Baba might decide to expand out of Lyari. The Taliban in Sohrab Goth and Kuwari Colony might also decide to take advantage of our weakened position. So no, we're not going in, but some response has to be given. Mian Mithu was a chutiya, but he was our chutiya. We can't let his death go unanswered. I really wish Asad bhai was around. He would be able to figure out exactly what to do. Gringo doesn't think like that. He's a killer, not a general.'

'And what news of Asad Haider? Has anyone been in contact with him? It's confirmed that he survived in New York, right?'

The expression on Saquib Shatroo's face turns to one of sheer terror. He gets up and opens the cabin door, to ensure that no one is within earshot. Then he sits back down again, huddling over his small desk inches from Byram's face.

'Arre Uncle, you will get me killed. Don't take that name in public, for God's sake. They are looking for anyone with any further information about Asad bhai. It's a complete black-out as far as he is concerned. Half the cadres aren't even sure whether the incident in New York actually happened or not.'

'But you do have information about him. I know you messaged him when you boys killed his family. Didn't he reply?'

'I didn't kill anybody, Uncle. None of my boys even went along. That was all Gringo's doing. He brought in a team from another ward. We couldn't do it. Asad bhai's family was our family. How many times have we all eaten haleem at Nani Amma's house? The old woman fed me with her own hands. I've done many wrong things in my life, Uncle, but this bharwat even I couldn't do. And then after that, there was the whole deal with Aleem bhai as well. Tobah, God forgive us.'

'Was it Javed Gringo who went after Aleem as well?'

'No, he tasked it out to some externals because it had to look like it was the Lyari gangs that did it. Couldn't take the chance of one of his boys being recognized by local ward people. It would have blown the whole cover story.'

'So tell me, honestly, why did you bother to contact Asad if you are so scared of me even mentioning his name?'

Saquib Shatroo stares down at the table, sincerely pondering the question, as if it is a conundrum he has never thought of before.

'How long have you known me, Uncle?'

'Saala, since you were a boy who used to try and steal cream rolls from the old bakery.'

'Yes, you've seen me all my life. You've seen me grow up in this neighbourhood. You know then, that everything I am is thanks to Asad bhai. You said it yourself. I was a street urchin, playing gully cricket and stealing from people like you. My father worked in a tannery all his life. The only thing he ever brought home was the goddamn smell which never seemed to leave his body. Asad was the one who stopped me in the street one day and asked me if this was what I wanted to do with my life. He inducted me into the Party, as a tea boy in this same ward office that I now head. Look at me now. I am one of the most powerful men in this city, boss of the Party's important Soldier Bazaar ward, a successful businessman in my own right. My kids go to an English-medium school, my wife wears imported perfumes and once a week we go to Dolmen Mall and sit in 500-rupee seats to watch an English film. I have finally managed to get rid of the stink of the tannery from my life. Asad bhai changed my life. He changed all of our lives. I remember the old days, when all the Party cadres would be hiding around, scared shitless that the maulvis would catch hold of them and whip their asses. Asad bhai was the one who was strong when we needed him to be. Where would this fucking Party be without him? Do you think the Don could run this city by remote control for twenty years if Asad hadn't been around? Even that bastard Gringo, who now goes around calmly executing people he's known all his life without even breaking a sweat. Ask him, where would he be if Asad bhai hadn't saved him! He'd probably still be getting buggered in that orphanage that Nani Amma got him out of. And that madarchod didn't wince when the Don ordered him to kill her.'

Saquib Shatroo wipes the tears from his eyes with a dirty sleeve, and runs a hand across his balding head. Byram is silent, but puts a consoling hand on Saquib's forearm.

'Listen to me, Saquib. If you feel this way, why don't you reach out to Asad? You know he's still alive. He can challenge the Don.'

'Uncle, he is one man alone against the killing machine that he built. What can he do?'

'But he is the right man, Saquib. Look, there are others, other ward bosses like you, who owe him everything. You yourself admit this, right? The Don could perhaps dispense with everyone else in the Party, but Asad is different. He understands every inch of this organization. He can take it over, get rid of these corrupt fellows at the top. And now he is in America, probably under police protection. The Don can't strike him again. With your help, and a few other people that I might know, he can take over this Party. Contact him.'

'Arre Uncle, fairy tales. Many people have used the same line over the years, but the Don is still here. Who are these others who will supposedly support Asad bhai?'

'Trust me. There are others. I can't name names, but there are. Within the Party. Who feel exactly as you do.'

'If they feel exactly as I do, then they will *do* exactly as I do. Which is absolutely nothing. Arre Uncle, do you know what the biggest drawback is of becoming such a powerful man as I have become? You lose your balls. You think about every move you make, because the stakes are higher for you. When I was a junior member of the ward I could do as I pleased because I didn't give a shit. I didn't *have* a shit to give. But now, you see all this prosperity around you, this office, the flat I just bought in Boat Basin, investments in land near Memongoth. All rely on my current position. So I will cry in front of you and I will have a Quran khwani at my house for Asad bhai's family, but quietly, lest any Party informer find out. And then I will go back to business as usual. That is the cowardice that comes with success. If, as you say, there are others in the Party who feel as aggrieved about what has happened to Asad as I do, they will also quietly drink their anger. This politics na, Uncle, is a very bhenchod thing.'

'Eh look, I'm not advocating you do anything. I'm just saying, if you do get in touch with him, or if he contacts you, let me know.'

'You seem very impressed with Asad bhai, Uncle. Have you ever met him?'

'I didn't need to meet him to know he was a real son of a bitch.'

Byram's tone suddenly turns sharp, the bile in his heart seeping out before he has a chance to regain control of his emotions.

'Arre Uncle, after all this talk about Asad Haider being the only one who can save the Party, you don't even like him? What's this all about?'

'I never said I liked him, Saquib. But it's as you said. This politics, it's a real bhenchod business. The bigger the bhenchod, the more useful he is.'

*

It's quite late by the time Byram finally leaves Shatroo's office. As he gets into his brown 1982 Toyota Corolla, perhaps the last of its kind left on the road, it strikes him that his conversation with Shatroo was risky. Shatroo could expose him if he were to report their conversation. But there was no other way to accomplish the task given to him by Guddu. And if there is anybody in the Party whom he could come close to trusting, it would be Shatroo. He has after all known him since he was in short pants. Besides, he has plenty of dirt on him as insurance. If it ever came to that, he could always tell his interlocutors about Shatroo's skimming of ward funds, always a capital offence in the Party. He has all the proof, since he was the one who taught Shatroo the creative accounting that enabled him to hide the pilfered money in the ledger books. Then there's the little matter of the text message to Asad Haider, another little peccadillo that the Don would not ignore.

The streets are empty as he drives instinctively towards old Soldier Bazaar and the site of the original bakery. London Bakers, one of the oldest and proudest retailers in the area. His grandfather had come up with the name at a time when any business with the word London in it instantly became more attractive to customers. In his time, Byram fulfilled all his dreams of expanding the original bakery into a full catering business, but at his father's insistence they had left the old bakery as it was, continuously serving meetha buns, macaroons, fruit cakes, lemon tarts and chicken patties to the residents of Soldier Bazaar for close to eight decades.

After the violence of the day, shops cautiously lift only half their shutters, like veiled women wanting to take a peek at the world around them. Business is conducted furtively so as not to attract the attention of the local ward, on whose orders the shops had forcibly been shut. But even downed shutters cannot stop the smell of freshly baked bread from wafting outside. Since he was a boy, Byram has always loved this smell.

He parks on the curb and walks round to the back of the bakery, where the night shift has started production for the morning. In an old neigbourhood like this one, people still prefer their fresh loaves of bread or zeera biscuits hot from the oven, over the sterile, packaged products that are available in every corner store and supermarket. Once upon a time, when Byram had made a success of the bakery and the catering business, Cyrus had told him to look into packaging his cookies as a way of expanding the business. Byram had laughed in his face. Wrapping the biscuits in cellophane and putting them in a cardboard box for every chutiya to buy from every store would take away the soul of the biscuits and the business. That's what he had told Cyrus at the time. Cyrus had looked at him as if he was crazy. In truth, it did sound a bit mad, biscuits having a soul and all that, but Byram believed it. Every item in the bakery had character, an individuality and history that was sacred to him.

But now, as he sees the run-down condition of the bakery, with a handful of workers stripped down to their banyans, sweating over the ancient ovens, he thinks that perhaps he had made a mistake that day. Perhaps he should not have been so dismissive of Cyrus's idea. He could have become rich. Byram Dinshaw, the biscuit king of Karachi. Maybe that would have solved their problems. Freny would still be alive, and perhaps Cyrus wouldn't have had his … incident. Perhaps wealth could have protected them from the madness of this city.

At the back door, he is greeted by Karim Bux, his bakery manager for the past thirty years, standing with a small pineapple cream cake in his hand. 'Sahib, I knew you would come tonight. You always come on this day without fail. That's why I had this made for you special. It was Freny madam's favourite, wasn't it?'

Byram stares at the cake as if it is a newborn child, marvelling at the evenness of the frosting and the symmetry of the pineapple chunks that decorate it. He half smiles and nods to Karim Bux, taking the cake from his hand. 'How is business?'

'We're managing to stay afloat, but nothing more. The bakery does all right, but the catering business is struggling with so many competitors. Apparently, there's some minister who wants to buy up all the commercial land in the neighbourhood. He sends his people to negotiate terms, but it's hardly a negotiation. The ones who don't accept his offer start having problems. Party boys from the ward bringing exorbitant extortion demands, food inspectors showing up, excise officials asking for audits. It happened to the Modern Bakerswallah. He put up with it for about a month, and then sold, for one-tenth the value of the business. Just his land was worth more than what he got from Minister sahib.'

'Modern Bakers is gone? Saala, all my life I wanted to find out his recipe for jam tarts. Poor bugger. What are they going to do with it now?'

'They're tearing it down to build another shaadi hall. Big business, shaadi halls. The advantage of living in a city of eighteen million, someone's getting married every day. You ought to think about selling the catering business. People these days don't want these old-fashioned weddings, with three-tiered cakes and brass bands. They just want their oily kormas and biryanis, and a DJ to play the latest Bollywood hits on the sound system. You ought to take more interest in the business, Byram sahib. It will help us and it will help you. You can always find someone to take care of Cyrus baba. This will keep your mind occupied. After all, it's been what, ten years since Freny madam …'

Byram glares at Karim Bux but does not respond. Instead, he shuffles around the bakery for a few more minutes, watching the workers put the final touches on the various confections. 'What's the problem? Everything is working fine here, why do you need me? Keep running things as they are. And don't worry, I have plenty of things to occupy myself with,' Byram grunts and shuffles off towards his car, not giving Karim Bux an opportunity to respond.

The house on Britto Road is only a short drive from Soldier Bazaar, but this late at night, with no street lights and the city carrying a deserted look, Byram feels nervous while driving.

The Party has had its men on the streets throughout the day, stopping cars on the road and burning them, just to further reinforce the perception of an absolute shutdown. The few who are brave enough to be out despite the presence of the Party are usually worse than the ward boys. Car jackers and mobile phone snatchers looking for easy prey. Byram wouldn't want to run into either type at this hour.

His eyesight isn't what it used to be, so he bends over the wheel and peers into the darkness. He has driven on these streets all his life, but at night, a wrong turn here or there can lead you into a very different part of the city. After all, Lyari isn't too far away. It is pitch-dark now, a massive power cut having doused the street lights as well and added to the aura of absolute desolation.

Up ahead on the road, a man with a flashlight flags him down. Byram's hands shake and he feels a dull pain in his chest. He prays that it's not a heart attack. Since Freny's death, he has made an effort to take care of himself, not out of any desire to live a long life, but just to survive long enough to take care of Cyrus. And to complete his mission. Nothing else matters.

He can see the man now, blocking the road, forcing him to stop. He has a pistol in his hand, which he taps on the windowpane to get Byram to lower his glass.

'Bhenchod, the Don gave a strike call, did you not get the message? Now you'll wish you had stayed at home chutiyay … arre Uncle? Is it you? What are you doing here?'

Byram recognizes the man as a member of the local ward. 'Saala Panjwani, you scared me. I just came from meeting your ward boss. He had called me for some work.'

'Who the fuck is it? I thought I told you to keep the road clear of any traffic for the next ten minutes!' a second voice rings out from the darkness.

'It's okay. Its only Bhenchod Chacha, an old Parsi from the area. He's just going home.' Panjwani turns back to Byram and smiles apologetically. 'Sorry Uncle, we're working with a team from another ward. The matter is a bit sensitive, so they're jumpy.'

'Is it some new lafra?'

'Arre no, Uncle, it's these fucking Lyari gangsters. First, they drilled holes in the knees of our college boys, and then, this latest thing with Mian Mithu. Saquib bhai said we had to give some response since our ward is the LoC.'

'LoC?'

'The Kashmir border. Between the Party's strongholds and Lyari. So we are at the front line of all the action. We found out Jameel Jheenga comes to the Makki Masjid in Garden on Thursday nights. So Gringo bhai sent in a special team, I think they're from Landhi or something, and we snatched him an hour ago. We're just finishing up the formalities now. These Landhi boys were worried that the police will show up, but I told them, this is Soldier Bazaar. The police doesn't leave their thana without checking with us first.'

'You got Jheenga? Baba's second-in-command?'

Panjwani swells with pride. 'Yup, just did him in that alley. Five shots in the head. Saala madarchod. Good fucking riddance. Say, Uncle, this killing-shilling makes me very hungry. You wouldn't have anything to eat, would you?'

Byram stares at the cake box on the passenger seat and wordlessly offers it to Panjwani, who opens it greedily, and in the absence of a knife, breaks off a piece with his fingers.

'Thanks Uncle, that hit the spot. You should get moving now, before those Landhi boys come by and demand the rest of your cake.' Panjwani smiles at his little joke as he returns the box, his fingers still smudged with cream and bits of pineapple sticking out of the side of his mouth.

Byram rolls up his window and restarts the car, turning the corner from Britto Road, into Katrak Colony. As he parks, he hears the low hum of the generator in the next house. Like all the houses here in Katrak Colony, it was once owned by Parsis, but is now rented out by a small business that makes and packs potato chips on the premises. Most of the original families have moved out of Katrak Colony, going to more tony locations like Clifton or the Parsi colony in Mehmoodabad. They started moving about twenty years ago, claiming that Soldier Bazaar was getting too crowded and too violent. Freny never wanted to move, even though he had suggested it several times. She used to argue that Soldier Bazaar had always been crowded, even when most of Karachi was a desert, because it was the heart of the city. After her death, it became more important to Byram to stay on and preserve her memory in the old house.

As for the violence, well, they were mostly correct on that point. As Panjwani put it, Soldier Bazaar was a fault line in the city, a boundary zone where the competing interests of the city's powers overlapped. Religious parties, both Shia and Sunni, staked a claim to it, as many of their most significant madrasas were here. The Party, of course, had strong ties because Asad Haider had been a local chokra and a lot of the Party's initial muscle had been recruited from here. Besides, the Don's house, Darul Sakoon, now the Party headquarters, was just across the road in Lines Area. And now, of course, there was Baba Dacait, the latest generation of Lyari thugs, but the first one who dreamed of citywide domination. Like a fast expanding medieval empire, his outposts had stretched out from Lyari and now touched the peripheral localities of Patel Para and Garden East.

The Party considered Soldier Bazaar as very much their heartland, but the truth was a little more complicated than that. True, they had won every election from here in the past twenty-five years, but vote counting was not a true measure of power in the city. More importantly, Soldier Bazaar was one of those areas where the other groups were unwilling to accept the Party's hegemony. And the Party could not afford to be challenged so brazenly. And so the violence had escalated over the years, the area becoming like cold-war Berlin, a prestige point that no side was willing to give up on.

He enters the pitch-dark house and lights a few candles. With Cyrus's medical bills, he can't afford to buy a generator. The hospital equipment runs on batteries, so the monitors are the only source of illumination in the house. But Byram prefers the darkness. He embraces it. Especially today.

The nurse is fast asleep in Cyrus's room. A gentle breeze blows in from the balcony, cooling the entire house. In the glow of the monitors, he can see Cyrus's face. Even with the various tubes running out of his nose and mouth, it is an innocent-looking face. Freny used to call him her little angel. She died of cancer, but Byram knows it was really of a broken heart. For five years, she struggled to come to terms with what had happened to her only son. She had tried everything – Eastern medicine, Western medicine, faith healers of all denominations. By the time she had exhausted all the options, she had also exhausted herself.

He pulls up a chair, and by the glow of the monitors, opens the cake box. Panjwani's dip in the box has left the cake in a mess. Byram uses a knife to tidy the debris of cream, pineapple chunks and cake, trying to restore some kind of structural integrity to it. At length, he takes a piece of cake and holds it against Cyrus's lips. Byram knows his son hasn't had solid food in fifteen years, but it is still important for him to try.

'Eh Cyrus. Wake up, you lazy bugger. Always sleeping. Always late for school. Have some cake. At least today eat something. Saala, it's your mother's birthday. It's her favourite cake. Have a bite for her sake.'

For a moment, just for a moment, the façade that Byram Dinshaw has worn for almost ten years drops. He holds back a sob, and tears roll down his cheeks on to Cyrus's chest. Just as suddenly, he regains his composure when he hears the nurse stirring. He takes a bite of the cake and puts the rest back in the box. Then he finally kisses Cyrus's forehead, tousles his hair and walks out of the room.

He reaches his own room and lights another candle on top of the file cabinet. His hands are still jittery after his encounter with Panjwani, and it takes some effort for him to take his daily pills. Only after downing two glasses of cold water does a semblance of calm return. He lies down on his thin mattress and picks up an old scrapbook lying by the bedside. Freny's scrapbook. Her idea to document their life together, for their children to keep for their children, so they would know where their family had come from. There are dog-eared pictures of the bakery, vacations, weddings, births. Tiny souvenirs from a life left behind. At the time, keeping a scrapbook seemed like such a good idea. A record of the good times. But what about the bad? One never thinks to document the things that go wrong, even though they often provide greater insight. Thus, there are no pictures displaying the horrific and permanent nature of Cyrus's injuries, no medical reports outlining the progress of the cancer cells as they ate their way through Freny, and no balance sheets showing the advancing decline of London Bakers and Caterers.

Byram tosses aside the scrapbook and picks up a folder lying beside it. Another of Freny's projects. A collection of all of Cyrus's articles. Byram had always known Cyrus would never join him in the business. He was marked for bigger things. He loved reading, and he always wrote beautifully. They had both been so proud when he got his first job, as a gossip columnist for one of the leading English dailies. When Cyrus got his first pay cheque, a measly 10,000 rupees, he had insisted on taking them out for a grand dinner, one that probably cost him an entire month's salary. They had gone to the Chinese place in the Avari. Of course, where else would Parsis go? He had been so bubbly and full of life, discussing plans for what he wanted to accomplish and how he would go about it. The polar opposite of the lifeless piece of meat that lies in the hospital bed next door. Not a day goes by that Byram does not think about pulling the plug, but he is cursed by a promise made to a dying woman. Freny had forced him to swear an oath to do everything he could for Cyrus's recovery, even if it seemed hopeless. She had made him promise that he would have to keep trying till either Cyrus got up from that hospital bed, or the Don went to hell, whichever came first. The first option is never going to happen, so he has focused these past ten years on making the second one come true.

He takes a well-thumbed newspaper cutting from the folder and starts to read it. It is from the November 1996 issue of *Glamour Mag*, a Karachi socialite magazine that Cyrus had helped to set up and establish, serving as its first editor.

Greetings Pussycats,

A little bird tells me that all is not well in Madam Deputy Prime Minister's house. Madam has, of course, been busy in Isloo, selflessly serving the people, while her gallant husband, a certain moustachioed provincial minister, has had to bear the burden of excruciating loneliness in his constituency in the badlands of Ghotki. Finally, Mr Minister grew tired of having his dinner alone in front of the TV and only seeing his wife on the nine o'clock Khabarnama. He decided to be a bit more social and invited a female cabinet colleague, an Adviser on Women's Affairs no less, to advise him on his personal women's affairs over dinner. The two were spotted canoodling at the Lotus Room in the Sheraton, and thereafter, apparently a room was booked for the night at the hotel. Talk about takeaway tushy.

The plan would have been perfect, if not for the fact that Madam Deputy Prime Minister decided to take the red-eye from Isloo. Arriving home in the very early hours of the morning and discovering hubby wasn't there, she made furious inquiries from her husband's loyal personal secretary, who was forced to spill the beans about the minister's sleeping arrangements at the Sheraton. Whereupon, Madam descended upon the hotel, with her police escort and retinue in tow, and demanded to know from the night manager which room her husband was shacked up in. Caught between a rock and a woman scorned, the poor manager was able to buy enough time to call Mr Minister to warn him that Madam was on the way up. Apparently, our Casanova was just able to sneak away a blushing adviser down the service elevator before Madam showed up and gave him hell! Wags say that the minister's magnificent moustache wasn't the only thing to wilt in the face of an earful from the missus, and he was hauled off to his own single bed by his guards. As for the blushing adviser, we can safely say that the Deputy Prime Minister is one man she will certainly not be advising any time soon.

And speaking of Casanovas, I hear that our very own desi Don Corleone has also developed a roving eye. We all know that running the city by the sea with an iron fist can be a tiresome task. All those extortion calls to make, all those strikes to order, ministers to bully and what not. Recently, the Great One has started taking a break by watching a little TV. One show seemed to catch his eye in particular, a new drama serial starring the newest sensation on the city's showbiz scene, the multi-talented Songbird from London. The Songbird and her brother grew up in good old Blighty, and while he became a record producer, she attended the prestigious Royal Academy of Dramatic Arts in London before deciding to return to the Land of the Pure.

Well, Pussycats, it seems her talents didn't go unnoticed. For the debonair Don was enamoured of her from the minute he saw her on the idiot box. My pets tell me that he expressed a desire to meet her and, ahem, more. When told that, well, she wasn't exactly that sort of girl and wouldn't necessarily come running to him, especially as she was engaged to a young banker, he threw a tantrum, berating his long-suffering deputy leader, the bespectacled Imam. He reportedly told his followers that he would not be able to bear it if the Songbird got married to somebody else. Finally, the Party's enforcer-in-chief was called in to solve the problem. Said enforcer paid a visit to the Songbird's house, and, I am told, gently but firmly explained to the young woman's family the error of their ways in having refused the Great Man's advances. Do you remember the line from the movie The Untouchables where the character says, 'A kind word can get you far, but a kind word and a gun can get you further.' Well, sports fans, without going into the details, let me just say that it was that kind of conversation.

The result, of course, was that, as expected, the Songbird agreed to see the Great Man. In his excitement, all the flower sellers in Nursery were ordered to cover every inch of the Markaz with red roses. Hai, how romantic, no? Unfortunately, the Great Man's gentleness did not extend to the other activities of the evening, which I'm told were of the bed- breaking variety. A week later, his lusty ardour having been sated, the Great Man had his men deliver the Songbird back to her family, not quite chaste and untouched, but at least in one piece. Well, once she had been marked as the Great Man's conquest, her banker fiancé broke off the engagement. My pets tell me that the experience has shaken her up so much that she has suddenly lost her knack for singing or acting, and in fact, the family may well move back to London. Ah well, such is life in the fast lane of old Mai Kolachi …

Your beloved Cyrus will see you next month, Pussycats.

Reading it never fails to bring a smile to Byram's face. It was Cyrus's last article. He picks up another clipping, the last one in the folder. This one is not a gossip column, it's a news report, and it's not written by Cyrus.

140   Omar Shahid Hamid

JOURNALIST ASSAULTED, FIGHTING FOR LIFE

Karachi: 27 December 1996. Journalist Cyrus
Dinshaw was rushed to Civil Hospital last night
after receiving severe injuries as a result
of an assault by unnamed assailants. Dinshaw,
twenty-nine, who is the features editor at
Glamour Mag, our sister publication, was on
his way home from the magazine's offices
on Abdullah Haroon Road when his car was stopped
by armed men near Pakistan Chowk. According to
eyewitness accounts, the men forced Dinshaw
out of his car at gunpoint, confirmed his
identity, assaulted him briefly and then took
him in another vehicle to an unknown location.
Several hours later, Dinshaw was recovered
from near the Radio Pakistan building on
M. A. Jinnah Road, having suffered severe
injuries. He was rushed first to Civil Hospital,
and then shifted to Aga Khan, where doctors
continued to operate on him through the night.
Although the full extent of his injuries
has still not been determined, the Medical
Superintendent at Civil Hospital confirmed
that Dinshaw had suffered partial paralysis
as a result of a broken spine, a ruptured
spleen, kidney failure and a degree of brain
damage, in addition to severe loss of blood.

The police have registered a case at Arambagh
police station against unknown persons, as
no group has claimed responsibility for the
attack. However, sources claimed that the
FIR was not lodged at the police station for
several hours after the incident, allegedly
because of pressure from certain political

quarters to not allow registration of the case. Mr Dinshaw also writes a celebrity gossip column every month for the magazine, and came to prominence as a result of his latest column in the November issue. In it, Mr Dinshaw had poked fun at a figure who is alleged to have been the Don, suggesting that he had a recent liaison with an actress. The United Front Party had taken offence at the article and threatened to take legal action against the magazine unless a retraction of the article was issued. Sources within the magazine confirmed that over the past few days there had been several heated meetings between members of the Party politburo and the editorial team. The Party's head of discipline, Asad Haider, was seen visiting *Glamour Mag's* offices on Tuesday and is reported to have threatened Mr Dinshaw. But no one at *Glamour Mag* was willing to verify this report. Some eyewitness accounts also indicate that Mr Dinshaw was transported to a Party ward office in Ranchore Lines after being abducted. The Party has vehemently denied any involvement in the assault on Cyrus Dinshaw and has condemned the incident as an attack on a member of a minority community. The Party's general secretary, Imam Qutbuddin, said in a statement that the Party had always fought to give all communities, Muslim or non-Muslim, equal rights.

Editor's Note: The writer of this article recently resigned from the newspaper and moved to pursue other career opportunities in Turkey due to threats to his life.

9

ASAD

Anthony Russo has never managed to master the art of eating a burrito. As usual, his first bite causes the saucy filling of salsa, black beans and guacamole to spray onto his shirt. He sighs as he grabs a tissue, and reflects that perhaps his second ex-wife Maria was right when she used to make him eat burritos standing naked in front of the kitchen sink. Sauce-filled sandwiches and Anthony Russo just do not mix well together.

Out of the corner of his eye he spots Cardenas walk into the precinct's lunch room. Cardenas sees him and cannot resist breaking into a smug self-superior grin, as he grabs a chair opposite Russo and takes the plastic top off his plate of salad.

'Ooh, another one crashed and burned, eh Tony? Man, I know your second wife was Colombian, but you didn't pick up any Latino skills. Eating a burrito is an art.'

'Really, Charlie? That's rich, coming from a guy who never eats a burrito. You eat more leaves than a fucking goat.'

'Hey man, just because I don't like to eat it doesn't mean I don't know *how* to eat it. That shit ain't good for you, Tony. You've been off the wagon since the divorce.'

'Which one? My last two wives insist I fell off after the first one.'

'Seriously, Tony. You're gonna harm yourself, man. You eat like a teenager. Burritos, donuts, and don't even get me started on the stash of candy in your locker. If the perps ever found out, they wouldn't try to bribe you with money, they'd throw a box of Three Musketeers at you. Come over to the house, Juanita'll cook you a proper, healthy meal.'

'Jeez, get off my case, Charlie, you're beginning to sound like my mother. It's my thing to take the edge off. Some cops drink, some smoke, some fuck around, I eat candy.'

Charlie Cardenas smiles indulgently at his partner. 'When did you get like this? High school?'

'No, actually it was in the Counter Terrorism Bureau. Long hours, the constant stress of thinking about the fact that the one little thing you might miss would end up becoming the next major attack on the city. Especially in the months straight after 9/11, it was so tense. Everyone else started popping pills, I started popping Tootsie Rolls.'

'You were there a long time. Why'd you get out?'

'I got sick of it. It wasn't police work any more, it was always the shadowy world of our friend, Simon Sole. I don't like that cloak-and-dagger shit. I wanted to get back out into the real world and not worry about how some asshole in Pakistan may have been thinking of blowing up Times Square.'

Cardenas smiles. 'Yeah, so you come here to the 20th, and end up with the case where some asshole in Pakistan is committing murder in front of the Natural History Museum. Funny how the world goes around.'

'Well, in this case, I don't know if it's some asshole *in* Pakistan. Looks to me more likely that it's an asshole in Brooklyn.'

'Straight up, Tony, it's been a week since we went to see the Don, and you haven't told me what your impression is.'

'I haven't had a chance to discuss this with you because our friend Simon has shown himself to be endlessly cooperative. He's so helpful, he's snowing me in with stacks of confidential reports, citing threats to the United Front and its beloved leader, the Don. I can't move from my desk to take a leak before another pile of dogshit comes my way.'

'You think he's covering something up?'

'Hey, I'm not accusing anyone of anything, Charlie. But here's what I think. I think all the documents he's feeding me as "evidence" are a little one-sided. Now you and I know this United Front party isn't exactly 100 per cent kosher, but the CIA seems to be running their PR campaign, trying to single-handedly negate all the negative propaganda against the Party. I have a serious problem with Simon Sole being the Don's biggest cheerleader. Why is that, I ask myself? What do these guys do for the CIA that gets them this kind of service? And why, in the first place, is the CIA taking such an inordinate amount of interest in a murder investigation? This isn't a terrorist incident, this isn't the World Trade Center or the Times Square bomber. What's it to them?'

'Sole admitted he was from the Company?'

'No, but I can smell Langley on him from a mile away. I worked with these guys in the CTB. I had a friend do some digging on Mr Sole. Turns out he was posted in Karachi, from 2003 to 2006. So he goes back a ways with the Don and his party. The problem with being that close to a subject is that you allow your biases to cloud your professional judgement. That's why I don't buy his theory of this being a hit by the Pakistani intelligence services. That's the Party line. I'm not saying the Pakistani spooks don't do this kind of thing, but they've had this situation with the Don for ages. Why would they bother with him now?'

'And what's your take on our visit last week?'

'I think that guy in Brooklyn deserves an Oscar for acting, for one thing. I don't know, maybe I'm biased. What have you come up with?'

'Okay, so I've been talking to some people in the State Department. They did some checking for me. Asad Haider's visa was approved in two days by the Consulate in Karachi. Even though he was residing in Dubai at the time. And on top of that he was exempted from the screening and vetting process that would normally take up to two months.'

'And why would the Consulate do that?'

'There's no paper trail, but my source tells me that from time to time the Consulate will waive the screening for individuals considered "politically important". This is usually for politicians or senior civil servants whom the Consulate wants to do a favour. Asad Haider was in that category. Apparently, the request for granting his visa came from the chief minister's office.'

'And, of course, the chief minister is the Don's appointee.'

'Exactly. But remember, the Don said the Party had voted to expel Haider months ago, and that the chief minister had complained that Haider was interfering with his good governance plans. So how come the same chief minister is getting his office to call up the Consulate to issue Haider a visa a month ago? At a time when, according to the Don, Haider had been thrown out of the Party? It doesn't add up. And here's another thing. In the past ten years, the Party has been able to get asylum for four hundred individuals. That's more than anybody else in the entire system. Apparently, they've got some channel in which their asylum candidates get approved immediately. They've got a better success rate than people who were persecuted by Saddam Hussein.'

'And that wouldn't happen unless they had somebody giving them a supportive recommendation from within the US government.'

'Exactly. So all of this confirms your suspicions about this cosy relationship with the CIA.'

'Anything else on Haider?'

'Yeah. A journalist friend in the *New York Times* asked their Pakistan bureau chief to do some digging. Haider is bad news. All the stuff about him on those websites is all true. The *Times* guy claims that he's supposedly directly involved in more than sixty murders in Karachi. He was known as the Party's enforcer. The way it worked was that the Don gave an order and Haider went and whacked the people.'

'Okay, so here's what we've got so far. This Party, the United Front, is bad news in Karachi. The Don lives up to the name and runs the party like a mafia boss, and Haider was his chief hitman, who was supposedly thrown out of the Party months ago. And yet, he walks into the US Consulate, gets a visa in two days, for which he is recommended by the chief minister, who it seems is also a political rival. He shows up here, has a meeting with the Don, which by all accounts is an unpleasant one, and two days later someone tries to kill him in Central Park. What's wrong with this picture?'

Cardenas is about to start digging into his salad when a uniformed desk sergeant comes into the lunch room.

'Hey, Detectives Cardenas and Russo. There's a call for you guys from New York Presbyterian. You got a witness who was wounded in the Central Park shootout there? Well, he wants to talk about a confession.'

Russo and Cardenas stare at each other dumbfounded, until Russo shrugs his shoulders. 'Dump the goat food, Charlie. This case just took a new turn.'

*

The doctors remain in awe of Asad Haider's powers of recovery. Barely two weeks since his surgery and he is back on his feet.

Still extremely weak, but all his other body functions seem to be returning to normalcy. The only thing with him is he doesn't talk much, preferring to answer the nurses and doctors in monosyllables. Still, most of the staff in the ward has heard of the tragic story of the message on his mobile phone of his entire family being killed. And they assume his reluctance to talk is based on his grief.

Which is why his request to speak to the detectives comes as a surprise. That's the most he's spoken in two weeks. What's even more surprising is when he says he wishes to make a full confession. That brings the NYPD boys running. Cardenas and Russo are in the hospital within thirty minutes of receiving the request. Nurse Ratchet greets them at the nurses' station in her usual reserved manner.

'How's our boy doing, Nurse?'

'Detective Russo. Mr Haider has recovered remarkably well from his injuries.'

'Uh, Nurse, we are going to need to speak to him in a private place. Is there a single room that you could wheel him into, so we can interview him?'

'As it happens, Mr Haider's ward is empty at this moment, as the last patient checked out this morning. So there's no need to move him. But he is still very weak, and his vitals haven't stabilized. You can talk to him but you can't upset him in any way. His body is still in a state of shock.'

She leads them into the ward. Asad Haider has the bed closest to the window, and he stares out, seemingly engrossed in the magnificent view of the East River and Roosevelt Island. He turns and looks at them with a blank expression as Russo and Cardenas take seats opposite his bed.

'Mr Haider, my name is Detective Anthony Russo and this is my partner Detective Carlos Cardenas. I understand you made a request to speak with us. Is that correct?'

'Yes. I wish to make a confession.'

'A confession of what, sir?'

'A complete confession of my crimes.'

'Okay, sir. At this point, I have to make you aware of your rights. Any statement that you give to us, in which you incriminate yourself or others, can be used against you as evidence in a court of law. You have the right to take legal counsel. If you cannot afford one, the city will provide one for you. If you still wish to proceed to speak with us, you will be waiving those rights. Do you want to continue or would you like to call a lawyer?'

'If my statement implicates others, will they be arrested?'

'Yes sir. Anybody else implicated in your statement is also liable to be arrested.'

'And there will be no political interference from your government in your investigation, no matter who I name?'

'Mr Haider, this is New York. The US government cannot interfere in a homicide investigation in this city. It just doesn't happen that way. I guarantee you that.'

'Then I would like to proceed. I waive my right to a lawyer and want to make a full confession.'

'Okay, Mr Haider, what would you like to tell us?'

'For the past twenty-eight years I have been affiliated with the United Front political party. In that time, I have committed scores of crimes at the behest of the Party, and in particular, the leader, Mohammed Ali Pichkari, who was known to all within the Party as the Don. For the past sixteen years, Mr Pichkari has resided in New York, having claimed political asylum. He alleged that he and our Party were being persecuted by the state agencies in Pakistan, but the truth was that the Don has continued to control the militant activities of the Party from New York.'

'So you're saying that Mr Pichkari has orchestrated crimes in Pakistan while sitting here?'

'Yes.'

'What kinds of crimes?'

'Murder. Extortion. Terrorism. Rape. Kidnapping. Government corruption. If it was wrong, we did it.'

'What proof would there be of such crimes being ordered from here?'

'I am your proof. I was the Party's head of security and internal discipline. Over the years, I received thousands of direct instructions from the Don in New York ordering me to execute these criminal acts. I organized the Party cadres into teams, which we call wards, and all of the Don's instructions were executed through the wards. I have personally killed sixty-four people on the instructions of the Don. And I have ordered the deaths of hundreds more.'

'What was the motive behind so many killings?'

Asad Haider coughs and takes a sip of water. Speaking so much at one go has taken a toll on him, but his voice is still strong, burning with an inner conviction. 'Do you know anything about Karachi, Detective?'

'I know a bit, from our investigations into this case, yes sir.'

'Then you will know that the Don is the uncrowned king of Karachi. His will cannot be challenged, and any who do, do so on pain of death.'

'I'm sorry, Mr Haider, but at present our pressing concern is the events here in New York. What can you tell us about this incident? How is it connected to what you are saying?'

'It is all connected. The Don ordered my execution when I refused his command for the first time in my life.'

The nurse taking Asad Haider's readings, who has totally ignored their conversation till now, looks up, startled. Cardenas looks at Russo, whose face is, as always, expressionless, a true poker player's face.

'Mr Haider, I'm going to back up for a minute, so we get all the facts straight. You arrived in this country fairly recently.

The JFK immigration entry stamp on your passport reads 5th March. You were given a ten-year visa by the US Consulate in Karachi even though you have never visited this country before. What was the purpose of your visit?'

'The Don had summoned me. He said he needed to speak to me personally as he had a very delicate task for me. Usually, in the past we would communicate in code, over the phone, on Viber or Skype. Although I spoke to him virtually on a daily basis, I had not met him physically for sixteen years. But this time he said the task was so sensitive that he needed to talk to me in person.'

'Okay, walk us through what happened from the point that you flew in to New York.'

'When I landed at JFK Airport, the Party had sent a car to pick me up. The driver was a former ward boss who has taken asylum here. He said the Don wanted to see me immediately, so I didn't even stop at a hotel. I went straight to the Party offices in Brooklyn. When I got there, Raja, the Don's personal secretary, ushered me into a conference room, where the Don was waiting for me. He hugged me and congratulated me and took a sweetmeat from a plate and put it in my mouth.'

'Why did he congratulate you?'

'He told me that I was going to become the Party's second in command, officially. He was going to announce it at the next meeting of the politburo. I just needed to do one thing before that meeting. I had to kill Aleem.'

'Who is Aleem?'

'Aleem was one of the founder members of the Party, and he was responsible for introducing me to the Don. He was a member of the Party's politburo for many years, and made many personal sacrifices for the Party. He was one of the Don's closest confidants.'

'If he was so close to the Don, why did he want him dead?'

'He told me he suspected that Aleem was conspiring against him. He claimed Aleem wanted to take over the Party for himself.'

'Do you think this was true?'

'No, it was absurd. Aleem is a businessman. He had been out of Party activities for several years now. He has never betrayed the Don's trust, and had no interest in taking over the Party. I had met him recently in Dubai, just before I came here. When he heard that the Don had summoned me, he predicted that the Don would order me to kill him. At the time, I didn't understand why Aleem would make such a ludicrous assumption. But he was right.'

'So Aleem had obviously suspected something. Why would the Don want to kill one of his oldest friends?'

'Because the Don has become a pheron.'

'Excuse me? A what?'

'Pheron. In English you call it pharaoh, I think. A man who thinks he is a god on earth. Power has driven him mad.'

'So what did you do when the Don ordered you to kill Aleem?'

'For the first time in twenty-eight years, I refused. I said I could never believe that Aleem would ever have plotted against the Party.'

'And, uh, what was Mr Pichkari's response?'

Asad Haider feels his breathing become heavier and the dull pain in his chest return. He hesitates, before answering. 'He became silent. He didn't say a word for several minutes. And then he told me to leave and never come back to the Party ever again. He told me I was a traitor, that I had betrayed him like everybody else. And then, he took … he took the aqeeq, the ring that my grandmother had given to him for protection, and he threw it at me.'

'Is that the ring that was found in your possession, sir?'

'Yes.'

'What happened after that?'

'I knew I was a marked man. That is the way it has always been in our Party. He who is considered a traitor to the Don, is considered a traitor to mankind. In the past, it had been my job to hunt down and kill such people. I knew that the Don would order someone else to do the same to me. So I left the Party headquarters and checked into a hotel near Times Square, where no one would be able to find me. I called Javed Gringo, who was my most trusted operative in Karachi, and told him to warn and protect Aleem. He assured me that everything was under control, and that he would send one of his people to meet me and ensure that I got back to Karachi safely. We arranged a meeting at the Museum of Natural History. But when I got there, the man whom Gringo had sent to meet me took out a gun and started firing as soon as he saw me.'

'So, your people turned on you. And do you know whether Aleem is still alive or not?'

Asad feels his breath constricting once again, as he recalls the most painful memory of his life. 'I don't know. But when I awoke in the hospital, I found a text message on my mobile phone. The Don had ordered the killing of my eighty-five-year-old grandmother and my mistress and her family. They didn't spare a six-year-old child. They didn't even spare an old woma …'

The display starts beeping manically as Asad's vitals drop, he feels his chest is about to explode out of his body. Nurse Ratchet comes running and pumps some sort of injection into him as he starts going into convulsions. 'Detectives, I told you not to upset him! He's going into cardiac shock! I need you to get out of here, now! Nurse, escort these men out and beep Dr Bose stat!'

*

Asad feels the darkness creeping in along the edges of his consciousness. He is no longer aware of his surroundings. The only thing his mind focuses on is the image of his grandmother's aqeeq, the ring that the Don threw back in his face. The same one that Nani Amma had put on his finger the first time he had visited Asad's home. That was before he became the great Don, when he was just Mohammed Ali Pichkari, a second-rate student being bullied by Jamaatiya thugs.

His mind feels like it is wrapped in damp cotton wool, and takes him back to his childhood. To his grandmother, Nani Amma, the unshakeable matriarch of the family. To her stories about the family's tradition of having been the caretakers of the Bara Imambara in Lucknow, virtually Shia royalty in pre-Partition India. Of how she had arrived in Karachi as an almost penniless refugee in 1947, abandoning a 110-room palace. And how, slowly but determinedly, she re-established the grandeur of Lucknow in the Bara Ghar, the Big House, a mansion abandoned by some Hindu businessman heading in the opposite direction. It was the largest evacuee property in Purani Numaish, and Nani Amma was allotted it as compensation for the losses she suffered as a result of migrating from India.

The centrepiece of Nani Amma's calendar was the observance of Muharram. The family's strong Shia tradition dictated that Muharram always had to be observed on a grand scale. Nani Amma would host a majlis on each of the first seven days, culminating with a bigger majlis and matam on the eighth day. The Shia elite of the city came to the Big House to listen to the majlis because Nani Amma always called the best zakirs of the city, who delivered the most eloquent sermons. The sermons would be accompanied by the constant cooking of deghs and serving of tea, and would continue late into the night, reversing the regular routine of the household, which would sleep during the day and wake at night. It was one such eighth of

Muharram, two and a half decades ago, when Asad Haider had committed his body and soul to the service of a charismatic young man named Mohammed Ali Pichkari.

He will never forget that day. He remembers being woken late in the afternoon by a servant girl, informing him that a friend of his was waiting at the gate. This in itself was unusual, as Asad would normally cut himself off from the world for the ten days of Muharram. No college, no cricket, no friends. After all, as the only grandson of the great Begum Naqvi his presence was expected at all times in the house. His only expedition to the outside world would be to participate in the Maqami Jaloos, the major Shia procession on Ashura, the tenth day, that wound its way from Numaish through the heart of the city, Saddar, to the Hussainiya Iraniyan Imambargah at the edge of the old town, Lyari. His friends all knew this, and would thus never disturb him during the ten days.

Intrigued about his visitor, he raised himself out of bed and walked out of his room into the old black-and-white tiled ballroom at the centre of the house. All of Asad's childhood memories were linked with the house. His father had died when he was very young, prompting his mother to move back into the Bara Ghar. The Bara Ghar was always full of visitors, aunts and uncles and family friends taking advantage of Nani Amma's hospitality, moving in for weeks on end. There was very little privacy in the house, and Asad only got a room to himself when he started college. He had been awarded a small, cupboard-sized chamber that had served the previous inhabitant of the house as a temple room. He didn't mind, the privacy was worth it, but it did mean that he had to trek across the great hall, the centrepiece of all activity, to get to the gate. Already the arrangements for the evening's majlis were being readied. Servants covered the black-and-white tiles with white cotton sheets and draped black curtains on the windows.

His mother sat on a chair, supervising everything. From her stern expression, Asad knew that she did not approve of his receiving a visitor. His mother and grandmother had become suspicious of all his friends since the police had showed up at the house a month ago. His support and protection of Aleem's friend, Mohammed Ali Pichkari, had prompted some of the Jamiat activists to file a complaint against him in the local thana. The police's visit had come as a surprise, as he had not informed anyone at home about his political activities. He had only managed to avoid the lockup because the police superintendent was a fellow Shia and an ardent admirer of Nani Amma's. But since then, the family had forced him to stop taking part in Party activities. After all, it wouldn't do for Begum Naqvi's only grandson to become a street hoodlum.

He had told Aleem of his decision to withdraw from the Party and subsequently had not had any contact with any Party member. Which was why he was shocked to find Mohammed Ali, standing at the gate with a duffel bag slung over his shoulder.

'Where the hell have you been, Asad?'

'Bhai, I told Aleem I can't do it any more. There's a lot of pressure from my family, especially after the Jamiatwallahs sent the police to my house.'

'So what? I thought you were a dedicated political worker. Things like this are a regular part of our lives. How can you just walk away from everything we are trying to establish? This isn't a game, a cricket match where you can throw away your wicket when you don't feel like batting any more.'

The Don never raised his voice, even for an instant. His only gesture had been to take off his sunglasses and look straight into Asad's eyes. But that was enough to overwhelm Asad with guilt and shame. He didn't understand how this man, whom he had only known for a few months, could have such an effect on him. He lowered his eyes to stare intently at the pebbles on the ground.

'Mohammed Ali bhai, I really can't talk about this right now. It's Muharram, and I have family duties and responsibilities. We have a majlis tonight, and I really have to get back to helping out with the preparations.'

'I know you have a majlis. I know it's the eighth of Muharram. I'm not an idiot. I thought your mother and grandmother would need help around the house, so I came by. Here, help me store this bag in your room.'

Before Asad could articulate a response, Mohammed Ali was inside the gate, dragging him along in his wake. Nani Amma had by this time arrived in the great hall, and flanked by his mother and uncle, stood with arms folded, staring disapprovingly at the dark, long-haired young man in a kurta and pyjama, both appropriately black for the occasion.

But that afternoon, Asad had received his first true lesson in politics. Mohammed Ali Pichkari had walked into the Bara Ghar facing a hostile audience, and by evening he had won over every single one of them. He pitched in wherever he was needed. No task was too menial, whether checking the sound system or heating the coals for the matam, or wrapping portions of lal roti and kebabs in paper parcels to distribute as niaz. Even the servants commented that Asad baba's friend had done more work around the house than Asad baba had ever done.

The first sign of a thaw on the family's part came when Asad's mother asked Mohammed Ali to stay for the majlis. This was an unheard of honour, as the majlis was for women only and the only men allowed were family members.

The pace of activity became more frenetic after the late afternoon Asr prayer. Dusk saw the arrival of Khajjan Begum, a betel-chewing 200-pound apparition wrapped in a black chador, and her two sisters, each one a sumo wrestler in her own right. Khajjan Begum was one of the most emotive zakirs in the city, someone to whom even Nani Amma accorded respect by receiving her at the gate. It was said that the sisters' recitation of the tragedy of Karbala could reduce grown men to tears. They were in great demand during Muharram, with many people willing to pay handsomely to hear them. But for the eighth, Khajjan Begum always came to the Bara Ghar. It was tradition and her way of acknowledging the family's pre-eminence as the former caretakers of the Lucknow Imambara.

The majlis began in earnest after the evening prayer. The house lights were dimmed and Asad and Mohammed Ali took up positions near the main gate of the house, to act as ushers and guards. Even in those relatively peaceful days, Muharram was always a tense time for sectarian relations in the city. Khajjan Begum and her sisters took centre stage on the elevated dais in the hall and started relating the tale of the tragedy of Karbala, how on these same dates 1300 years ago, Hussain, the favourite grandson of the Prophet of God, began his journey from Medina to Kufa with his band of seventy-two followers. And how they were intercepted by the army of the usurper, Yazid, on the barren field of Karbala. With growing spectacle Khajjan related the story of the courage of Hussain and his followers on Ashura despite overwhelming odds and terrible privations, and of their eventual martyrdom.

'Ya Hussain! You could have bowed your head against Yazid, just as everyone else did! But in the face of overwhelming opposition, you showed inimitable courage to stand up for justice! This is the fundamental essence of Hussainiyat!

'Ya Hussain! Did the cruel forces of Yazid have no consideration for the family of the Prophet of God? The man who ushered light into the darkness of this world! Oh, you cruel butchers! Could you not have at least spared the women and children? Were your hearts made of stone that you could not even spare the life of Hussain's six-month-old son? Had you no remorse that you dragged away Bibi Zainab, the granddaughter of the Prophet, and forced her to march to Damascus?

'Ya Hussain! Till when will the Yazids of this world perpetuate injustice? There is no torture that they can give us that would be more painful than the sacrifice of Hussain! For a Momin, every day is Ashura, and every place is Karbala!'

For Khajjan Begum, it was more than just a sermon. It was a performance. Her dramatic portrayal of the day of Karbala was so riveting that even outside, at the gate, Asad could hear the low moan of women weeping. He had listened to the recitation of the tragedy of Karbala since he was a child, and it never failed to move him. It was, after all, at the heart of his family's tradition and creed. But he had been surprised that day to find Mohammed Ali standing next to him, sobbing unashamedly.

Khajjan Begum's rhetorical gifts achieved their objective. The women, worked up into a frenzy of emotion, stepped into the garden for the matam. Nani Amma led the way, being the first one to walk across a pit of glowing red coals. She did it without flinching and following her lead, dozens of others stampeded across the pit, ultimately reducing the coals to cold grey ash.

As the matam concluded, the guests started to drift away. Asad and Mohammed Ali had to ensure that all the departing guests took home their hissa, a portion of the food. Nani Amma was always very particular about the dispersal of the hissas. Thus, it was quite late by the time Asad and Mohammed Ali slipped away to the roof to eat their own packets of lal roti and kachchey keema kebabs. It was a cold January night but one of the servants had set up a brazier on the roof, using some of the still-warm coals from the matam. Wrapped in shawls, both men sat in silence for a long time, exhausted by the day's exertions and enjoying the warmth of the coals near their feet and the food in their hands.

'Thank God, Muharram won't fall in the summer for another few years at least.' Asad scooped pieces of kebab from his plate with scraps of lal roti.

'Why?'

'Because it's intolerable to walk in the Ashura procession for miles in the summer heat. Much more bearable in the pleasant winter weather.'

'That was amazing.'

'What?'

'The matam. The passion of it, the junoon. Your grandmother is truly a remarkable woman. To still be leading the matam, at her age, without any fear or hesitation.'

'She says she prays to Imam Hussain and she doesn't feel a thing. It's very important to her. All of this. It reminds her of the old days in Lucknow.'

'Lucknow is a very important part of your tradition.'

'It's been drilled into me all my life. Sometimes I think I know more about pre-Partition Lucknow than I do about modern-day Karachi. The shadow of tradition has always stalked this family. Nani Amma once told me that the first time she walked on the coals she was just a girl of twelve. But it was expected of her then and it is expected of her today. They say that in our family it is the women who are strong. Perhaps that's why they worry so much about me. Because there's another tradition in our family, of the men falling off the wagon.'

Asad took out a small ball of black resin from his shirt pocket and rolled the charas into a joint. It was the one habit that he could not forsake, even for Imam Hussain. He lit it and took a long drag. 'She's seen a lot in her life. Partition. Losing everything they owned when they came over. Then spending years trying to recover from that loss. Her husband, my grandfather, never fully did. He was but a shell of a man for the last twenty years of his life.'

Asad passed the joint to the Don, who hesitated for an instant before taking a drag. 'What happened to your father?'

'Another example of the unreliability of the males of the household. He was a charlatan, a con man, who tricked my mother into marrying him. He convinced my grandmother by telling her of his Syed background. They only found out afterwards that he had lied. Nani Amma wanted my mother to divorce him. But they had only got as far as a separation before he was killed in the riots in '72.'

'Was he active in the Urdu language movement?'

'He was a born rabble-rouser. The cause wasn't important to him. It was the tamasha, the spectacle that he enjoyed. Or so I'm told. I was very young when he died. That's why they worry so much about my working with the Party. They're scared I might have inherited my father's genes in this regard.'

Mohammed Ali took another drag of the joint. 'Tell me, what do you want to do with your life?'

'I want to play cricket. I want to play for Karachi, and then I want to play for Pakistan. The only time I'm truly at peace is when I'm out there batting. But I don't know how far I'll be able to go with that.'

'Why? Aleem tells me you're a very good player.'

'Nani Amma and my mother feel that being a professional cricketer is not an appropriate career for our family. Besides, I'm not exactly a favourite with the local selectors. Since I've never kissed their asses, they go around telling everyone that I'm a drugged-out goonda, not fit for selection for any serious type of cricket. Saale bhenchod. They've decided that no matter what I do, they're never going to pick me for the Karachi team.'

'It seems to me that a lot of other people decide for you what you should do. What do you want? You want to idle away your life dabbling in one thing or another? Is that what the Party was for you? A passing fancy? So when you tell your children about your wasted life, one of your anecdotes will be that for about five minutes you were a member of the United Front? Or do you want to actually accomplish something?'

The words had stung Asad like a slap in the face, but Mohammed Ali Pichkari had held his gaze with dead, unflinching eyes, refusing to back down. Till that moment, Asad had never met anyone he had not been able to intimidate. Apart from the women in his life. Mohammed Ali snatched the joint from his fingers and took another long drag.

'Look Asad, I'll be honest with you. I need you. You are a natural at politics. You know what to say to people to get them to do what you want. The others don't have this ability. Aleem has a generous heart, but we all know that ultimately he remains under his father's thumb. Guddu is gone already to the Police Academy. At some remote point in the future, his contacts in the government will prove useful, but he can't help in organizing the Party on the streets. And Imam, well, he is a good debater, but you and I know that politics isn't a debating society. Its brutal and you have to be able to give as good as you get. They all have big hearts, but they lack courage. It takes courage to do terrible things for a greater purpose. That's how we will succeed. Aleem and Imam can't do the things that have to be done. Only you can.'

'Do you really think that this Party of ours can go somewhere? You think you can change anything? Look at this country! We don't even know if that bastard Zia will hold these elections in March! He'll probably find an excuse to delay them again, just as he has every time these past eight years! What are we going to do? The five of us and Zaibunissa and maybe a handful of other chutiyas who have nothing better to do.'

Muhammed Ali had looked into the far distance and smiled. 'That woman, Khajjan Begum, really moved me. I started crying back there. I know you saw me, I didn't try and hide it. I also know that seeing my tears shocked you. It's not considered manly, is it? But I cried because I heard the message behind Khajjan Begum's words. You listen to her sermon, and many others, every Muharram, but you do not hear them. I am not a Shia, but the story of Imam Hussain inspires me. All great things come from small beginnings. What is it Khajjan said? We should treat every day as Ashura and every place as Karbala! That is how you change the world. Look at this city with its millions of citizens, who fight for a meagre existence every day. They are begging to be led. I will provide that leadership, but I need you with me.'

He had paused, running his fingers through his moustache contemplatively. 'Yes, I don't deny that we haven't done anything more than talk till now. But you are the catalyst. You will be my sword as well as my shield for the battles that we must fight in the days ahead. I cannot do this without you.'

Asad Haider cannot now remember what exactly he had said in reply. But that night they talked on that cold roof, wrapped in their shawls, until dawn. They had talked about anything and everything. Mohammed Ali had told him about his dead father, a clerk in the military accounts department, whose scrupulous honesty and diligent dedication to duty had dug him an early grave, leaving behind a small house in Lines Area, and a widow and three sons on the verge of penury. His elder brother had managed to secure a job as a stenographer in the deputy commissioner's office in Hyderabad, and his mother had sold most of her jewellery to ensure that her youngest son was able to finish university. They talked about family, politics, girls and cricket. Asad could not remember opening up to someone like this ever before. In the space of a few hours, Mohammed Ali became the elder brother he had never had.

Finally, with the muezzin's call booming from the loudspeakers for the morning prayers, they picked themselves up from the freezing concrete floor and descended back into the house. Asad had led Mohammed Ali to his room, to get the kit bag he had brought with him. Mohammed Ali beckoned him to lock the door, and then, with great ceremony, unzipped the bag and removed several layers of old clothes to reveal, wrapped in a cotton cloth, a freshly oiled AK-47. Lying in the hospital bed decades later, Asad still remembers the almost sexual exhilaration he felt when he held the cold gun metal in his hands. An instant feeling of absolute confidence and calm swept over him, as if he had ingested some fast-acting narcotic. The Don recognized the look on Asad's face and smiled. 'This is how we will gain power in this city. The only kind of power that matters.'

'Bhai, where did you get this from?'

'Remember Lala? From the Pukhtoon Student Union? A few months ago I had asked him for help in fighting against the maulvis. He's now working in his father's transport company, and they run a lucrative side business smuggling weapons from their village in Waziristan into the city. I bought this from him.'

'But how did you afford it? It must have cost a lot.'

'Well, let's just say I didn't pay my tuition fees for this semester. I know it's only one weapon, but it's a start. I want you to have it. Take care of it and become our defender. There is no one else I would trust with my life.'

Asad remembers having tears in his eyes for some reason. He picked up an old wristwatch, with a battered leather strap, that lay on his bedside table. 'This is the only thing I have of my father's. I want you to have it and I want you to know that I will always stand with you, come what may.'

On the way out they had run into Nani Amma, who had just finished her Fajr prayers. She beckoned them and tied an Imam Zamin on Mohammed Ali's forearm, and took off an aqeeq ring from her finger to give to him. She didn't say anything. This simple act had signified her approval and support. At the gate, the two men embraced like long-lost brothers, and from that moment, Mohammed Ali Pichkari ceased to exist for Asad Haider. There was only the Don now, his guiding light for the next twenty-eight years.

In his hospital bed, lying awake at night with nothing but the beeping of monitors to keep him company, Asad thinks about what may have happened if he had not accepted that AK-47 that day. If he had not allowed the Don into his house. If Nani Amma had slapped him, instead of hugging him to her breast. Would the world be a better place? Would he have nightmares about all the people he has killed? Would Mumtaz and Nani Amma be alive today? They say destiny is made in a matter of seconds. Seconds to have slammed the gate in Mohammed Ali Pichkari's face, on that eighth of Muharram. He knows regret is useless, but retribution is not. There can be no going back, but he can at least try to make amends. Ensure that future young men and their grandmothers do not become victims of the Don and his Party.

*

It is a couple more days before the hospital staff consider him fit enough to call back the detectives. Luckily, he has not suffered a full heart attack, but they are still sceptical about his overall mental and physical condition. Asad knows though that his mind and body are healing. He can never overcome his grief, but he is managing it. A lifetime of killing people makes one's mental shock absorbers particularly adept.

When Russo and Cardenas enter his room, he is sitting up in bed, heartily tucking into a bowl of jello.

'Detectives. Thank you for coming back.'

'How are you feeling, Mr Haider?'

'Stronger. Much stronger.'

'Detectives, I warned you last time that Mr Haider wasn't prepared for a complete interview. You have five minutes and no more today.' Nurse Ratchet's expression is stern and uncompromising.

'Nurse, it's all right. I'm much better now and would like to have the opportunity to speak with the officers. Please. Would it be possible to get another bowl of jello?'

'Of course.' Nurse Ratchet walks away, thwarted in her attempt to curtail the meeting, continuing to glare disapprovingly at Russo and Cardenas.

'Mr Haider, I'm sorry, what I have to say may upset you again. We did some checking and you were right. An Aleem Siddiqui, who was an ex-Party official, was shot dead, along with his wife, in his home a few days back. According to news reports, the local police reported the crime as an attempted house robbery. The United Front has publicly condemned the incident and held a one-day strike in protest. Your friend, the Don, has apparently refused to accept the police version and claimed that Mr Siddiqui was murdered by gangsters from Lee-ya-ree. Is that how you pronounce it? Apparently, your friend in Brooklyn has alleged that the murder was committed at the behest of some kind of underworld figure called Baba Dacait. Does any of this make sense to you?'

'Perfect sense, Detective. In the Party, we have always been very good at killing our own and then crying at their funerals.'

'So you believe that these Lyari gangsters had nothing to do with Mr Siddiqui's death?'

'I told you who killed Aleem bhai, Detective Cardenas. Aleem lived in North Nazimabad. If you understand Karachi's geography, you will understand that the Lyari gangsters couldn't even dream of entering that enclave. Our ward boys have pickets all over the area. No one can move without the Party knowing of it. There hasn't been a robbery in that area in thirty years. So both the police and the Party are lying.'

'Why did the police put up this story of a house robbery?'

'Because the local police station in charge is our man and it was probably his feeble attempt to cover up the real crime. The police will never investigate this case. They don't want to end up in a gunnysack by the side of the road. The Party will dictate what goes into the investigation report. It seems as if the Don wants to make some political capital out of Aleem's death by blaming the Lyari gangsters.'

'Yeah, seems that way. The Party sent a delegation to meet the prime minister in Islamabad, to complain that some of his coalition partners and some intelligence agencies were patronizing these Lyari gangsters. The delegation also apparently talked about you and asked the prime minister to take stricter action against the Taliban in light of the attempt on your life here.'

'Of course. Why wouldn't they take the opportunity to tilt against both their enemies. Blame the Taliban for trying to kill me, blame the Lyari gangs for Aleem. Blackmail the government into doing whatever we want them to do. Play up the Taliban card for Americans like you. It convinces people that there is only one party standing up to the extremists. It's brilliant.'

'Well, now that you mention it, your Party does seem to share a close relationship with some organs of the US government. Care to shed some light on that?'

'It's very simple, Detective ... sorry, I forgot your name.'

'Russo. Anthony Russo.'

'Detective Russo. The Party has had a long-standing relationship with your CIA. We provide all sorts of services for you. I'm surprised they haven't contacted you with regard to this case.'

'What kind of services?'

'I'm sure, Detective, that the CIA is better placed to tell you about these things.'

'Humour me. What kind of services?'

Asad Haider takes a big blob of jello and puts it in his mouth, taking his time to swallow it. 'We find things for you. Things, documents, people. You tell us what to look for and we find it. Sometimes, we also clean up for you.'

'What does that mean?'

'Come on, Detective, you know what I mean.'

'I want you to say it.'

'We occasionally kill people that are of interest to your government.'

'Why?'

'Just before 9/11, we were in a bad state. There had been an operation against the Party. The police had killed most of our ward bosses in encounters. They had informers everywhere within the Party. There was a police officer, his name was Akbar Khan, we used to call him Terminator because he just kept hunting down our boys and killing them, like a machine. The Don had been gone for some time, and the Party structure was tottering. I had to operate from Dubai because the risk of me getting captured or killed in Karachi was too great. So I had to run the network by remote. Every time the police hit one of our ward bosses, we would try and hit right back by targeting and killing a police officer. But we were losing people so fast that we barely had anyone left on the streets. At one point, even I had given up hope of the Party surviving.

'Then 9/11 happened. Whatever its repercussions internationally, it was a blessing for us. We were welcomed into the governing coalition because we were no longer the focus of the government. They had to deal with the jihadis, and since we opposed the jihadis, we became their natural allies. And that's not all we did. Since the Don was here, he was in a position to make contact with the CIA and other agencies and offer our support to them. He told them that we could give you Americans information from the ground, information that the Pakistan government may or may not have shared. And because our wards were all armed and experienced death squads, we could even hunt down anyone that the Americans wanted. Since we controlled Karachi, we were very useful to you. So you see, many of us used to thank God for Osama bin Laden.'

'Mr Haider, I'm sure you can appreciate that such sentiments naturally don't go down very well in this city. A lot of us lost good friends when the towers fell.'

'I am sorry, Detective. I didn't mean to offend you, I was just trying to point out how the Party was able to take advantage of the situation after 9/11.'

'So what exactly did you hand over to the Americans? And how did you know about all of this? I presume the Don's arrangement with the CIA would not have been publicized a lot.'

'It wasn't. Of course, in Karachi everyone is a conspiracy theorist, so everyone thought the Don had some deal with the Americans, but only Raja and I knew the extent of our dealings. Even people like Tariq Colombowala, who is our chief minister, was kept out. Raja or the Don would tell me in Dubai to meet an American official from the Consulate in Karachi. He would pass on a list of instructions to me. Sometimes they were looking for verification of addresses, sometimes they wanted information about certain government departments, or the port or airport. These were all things that we could provide quite easily because we had our people on the streets and in every government department. I would send ward boys to madrasas that were located in places where the Americans couldn't possibly go, to do ground checks. At the height of our cooperation, I was meeting Simon every couple of weeks.'

'Simon?'

'Yes. That was the name the official gave me. I assumed it was a cover name. He would fly in from Karachi and arrange to meet me either in a mall or in a hotel coffee shop. Always a public place.'

'What did Simon look like?'

'He was a heavy-set man. Crew cut, definitely ex-military. He wore a thick ring on his finger. I asked him about it once because it was not a normal ring. It had some kind of insignia on it. He said it was a class ring from the Air Force Academy.'

Russo and Cardenas exchange a meaningful look, but do not make any comment.

'What else did Simon ask you to do?'

'We traced down a few individuals for them. They were jihadis, mostly Arabs, who had fled from Afghanistan and were hiding in Karachi. Our boys were able to pinpoint their hiding places, and then the Americans would use the Pakistani police or Agencies to capture them.'

'What happened to these individuals?'

'None of this was ever made public. I assume they must have been taken to Guantanamo.'

'You said that you killed people at the behest of the CIA. Who did you kill?'

'Mufti Namakzai. He was a very senior cleric at Bajauri Town. Bajauri Town is one of the oldest and largest madrasas in Karachi, and a lot of these jihadi types have studied there. Namakzai was a very well-respected man. They say Mullah Omar and Osama had both been his students.'

'Was he Al Qaeda? I've never heard of his name.'

'No, I don't think so. But he was in touch with everybody. Simon seemed to think he was very important. He got very excited when I told him we could easily get him. You see, I had known him for years. Not personally, of course, but by reputation. Bajauri Town is not too far from our family house in Purani Numaish. In my youth, when I was with the Shia students' organization, we often fought with the students from Bajauri Town around Nishtar Park. Namakzai was known to be a rabid Shia hater. He had given fatwas against us. So when the order came, I was very happy. It would be like killing two birds with one stone.'

'So how did it go down?'

'When Simon gave me Namakzai's name, I passed it on to the Don. I knew killing Namakzai would be a huge step, even for the Party. He had a massive following around the city, and his death would bring half a million madrasa students out on the streets. They would also link it to the Party, because Namakzai had been publicly critical of the Don for a long time. It didn't matter to me, but it would create a … what do you call it when things get really messy … a shitstorm, yes, that's the word. The Don was obviously weighing the situation, because it took him twenty-four hours to call me back. But he must have calculated that getting him out of the way was worth it, because when he did call me back the next day he told me to go and meet Mufti Namakzai. That was our code for assassination.'

'I gave the job to Gringo. He was my most trusted subordinate. He got a team from the Malir ward, because we didn't want the local ward involved. After all, they roamed around that area on a daily basis, there was a risk that they could subsequently be identified. We couldn't afford to let this to be directly linked to the Party. Gringo's team watched the madrasa for a week. The thing about Namakzai was that he was a man of very fixed routines. Very punctual. Very bad idea in our line of work. It makes you an easy target. Every morning after Fajr prayers, he would go for a walk around the neighbourhood. Numaish is a very busy part of town, but at that time in the morning the streets are empty. He always walked alone, didn't take any bodyguards. And always did the same circuit. On to Business Recorder Road, circling around Hanifia Hunter beefwallah, past the gate of Jamshed Quarter police station, then back inside the gate of Bajauri Town. He did this circuit about three times, regular as clockwork.'

'Having watched him for a week, the boys decided to take him. There were four of them, two on a motorbike and two in an ambulance. We got the ambulance from the Party's charity wing. It's a great cover to transport weapons. The boys on the bike wore helmets to cover their faces and dressed in shirts and ties, so that it looked as if they were commuters going to office. When Namakzai turned the corner at Hanifia the second time, both the ambulance and the pillion riders emptied their pistol clips into him. There were two witnesses on the road at the time, street cleaners or something. We shot them too. Gringo was one of the riders, he had me on his phone live throughout. I kept directing them, telling them which escape route to take, where to throw the guns, everything. I managed the whole thing from Dubai.'

'You seem quite proud of yourself.'

'I never said I was a good man, Detective.'

'What happened after Namakzai's murder?'

'The city went crazy for a few days. His students protested very violently. I think they burned two hundred cars in two days, or something like that.'

'Was there any suspicion about the Party's involvement? Or the Americans?'

'Initially, there was some talk that the Party had done it. But the Don was smart, he was one of the first people to come on the media and condemn the murder. I think he did it even before the news had properly broken. Besides, Namakzai was a controversial figure. Everybody hated him, the Shias, the Barelvis, everybody. The list of suspects was long enough for us to cover our tracks.'

'What did Simon say?'

'Simon was happy, but he was a little shocked at the violent reaction in the city. Which was naive of him, because we had always expected that Namakzai's disciples would wreak havoc when they heard the news. When I met him next he said he hadn't expected us to be so direct in killing him. I told him, what did he think, that we would put cyanide in his tea? I told him those sort of elaborate plots only happened in the movies. But I do think they were a bit taken aback, because they didn't ask us to kill anybody else for a while after that.'

'How many people did you kill for the CIA after Mufti Namakzai?'

'A handful of others, but they were nonentities. Nobody knew who they were. The boys told me a couple of them were foreign, Arab or something. But no one else of the level of Mufti Namakzai. In every case referred to us by the Americans, I used Javed Gringo's team.'

'And what did the Party get in return for doing the CIA these "favours"?'

'A free hand. We were allowed to expand our operations in America, and our people were given visas and asylum here.'

'Money too?'

'Yes. These offices and condos that the Don lives in, the chauffeured limousines he drives, don't come cheap. The CIA paid us for all the work we did. The lion's share stayed with the Don, but he sent me some money in Dubai too. Enough to establish myself.'

'Your friend Javed Gringo is the same person who you say killed your family? And set up the trap for you here?'

'Yes. Same man.'

'Are you willing to testify in court?'

'Not only am I willing to testify in court, I am surrendering myself to the New York police. I want to be prosecuted for my role in hundreds of acts of terrorism that were ordered by the Don, while he sat in America. I will accept any punishment that is handed to me by a court of law, but this reign of terror that people like myself and your government have perpetuated must end. And I want the Don to face trial in America, where he cannot intimidate witnesses or prosecutors.'

'Why did you carry out the Don's orders all these years?

'Because I believed in him. I believed in him more than I did in God.'

'So what's changed? Is this regret? Because, frankly, it's a bit late for that, don't you think?'

'I know I cannot take back all that I have done. Which is why I am willing to accept whatever punishment comes my way. But this is for revenge. For myself, and all the others whose lives the Don has destroyed.'

10

ISMAIL

Jameel Jheenga's death, while tragic and quite gruesome even by Karachi standards – he didn't have a face left by the time they found his body – turned out to be quite good for me personally. I entered Baba's circle at the very moment when he lost his closest confidant. Jheenga and Baba had come up together from the streets. Jheenga had been a shrimp wholesaler in the Fishermen's Cooperative Society when Baba was first trying to make a name for himself in Lyari, and he was the first one to throw his lot in with the fledgling gangster. No one else amongst Baba's men shared the same kind of connection that Jheenga and he had. Faced with this vacuum, Baba started turning to me in order to fill it.

My first job was to familiarize myself with all the gang's operations. Who controlled which part of Lyari, what money came from where, how much came from drugs, how much from kidnapping, how much from extorting the municipality. Everything was done on zaban, on word of mouth. As a result, the death of one man, Jheenga, who kept all the strings together, was enough to paralyse the entire organization. In truth, it was run a bit like our newspaper. At one point, our owner Mr Khujli, had gotten sick of the confusion and had foisted a fresh-faced MBA graduate upon us to sort out the paper's complex financial affairs. The poor boy had gone crazy and run away in a week. There were times when I felt the same way.

I also had to implement my strategy of changing Baba's public image. This became even more important in the light of Jheenga's death because the United Front were painting Baba as a terrorist and criminal, and we had to show everybody that we were more than that. Thus, we immediately started setting up the football World Cup screenings. Overnight, the boys kidnapped a group of engineers who arranged huge screens for fashion shows. Once they got over fearing for their lives, the engineers were very good at setting up a twenty-foot screen at Gabol Park. The next move was to clean Lyari up a little. The reason for the mountains of trash on the sides of the roads in Lyari was that the gang sold off the local municipality's petrol quota, so the trash collection trucks had no fuel to run on. I spoke to Baba, and immediately he instructed Ghaffar Langra, who was in charge of extorting from the municipality, to start giving back the fuel. In three days, Lyari got cleaned up. In fact, so intimidated were the shopkeepers by our boys riding on the trash collection trucks with their weapons that instead of adding to the mess by throwing their garbage on the street, as they had done for decades, they actually started throwing it in the assigned dumpsters.

My strategy became an instant success. The local people were awestruck by Baba's efforts to clean up the neighbourhood and to let them enjoy football for free. But it wasn't just the locals who were impressed. Soon, helped by my reaching out to media contacts, word started spreading of the 'revolution' in Lyari. They heard about the fact that they could enjoy football, in total security, guarded by Baba's men, in the middle of the night without having to worry about power cuts or anything else. In fact, to capitalize on the football theme, I had all of the gang members dress in football jerseys to make them clearly identifiable.

I knew we had succeeded beyond our wildest dreams when one of the English papers picked our screenings as being the best venue in the city to watch football, better than the screenings at the five-star hotels. That really got the Defence–Clifton burger crowd flocking to Lyari. The long-term benefits of this image transformation became evident to Baba, especially when the Party copied our idea and announced that they too would set up a giant screen for the semi-finals and final of the World Cup outside Darul Sakoon.

Despite my success, I knew that Baba's men were still not convinced of the value of my image-rebuilding project. They had grudgingly gone along with my schemes because no one had any alternative ideas, but they didn't trust me. One evening, I was smoking on one of the rooftops of Afshani Galli when Ghaffar Langra approached me. It was just before sunset, the best time in Karachi, as the air begins to cool down and the breeze from the port starts blowing across the rooftops. After the death of Jheenga, Ghaffar was now technically Baba's senior aide. But Ghaffar had never been considered a bright fellow by Baba, just an extremely loyal one. He had been made in charge of extorting the local government authority because it was the simplest scheme, unlike drug or gun smuggling, where one often had to think on one's feet. There was literally nothing to it. Baba's gang used the municipality like a bank, going in to withdraw funds whenever they needed them. It was thought that even Ghaffar Langra couldn't fuck this up.

Now, I had already had a couple of run-ins with Ghaffar, and I knew I was probably not his favourite person, so I was surprised when he limped up to me that evening and asked me for a cigarette.

'Eh Ghaffar bhai, why do they call you Langra?'

'Because I limp.' Langra stared at me as if I had asked the stupidest question in the world.

'No, I can see that, but why do you limp? Some kind of bullet injury?'

Langra laughed, displaying a set of discoloured teeth that would have made a dentist salivate at the prospect of six months of steady employment. 'No, I fell off the roof of my house. I was chasing a kite, you see. The bone never set properly, because the doctors we had at Lyari General Hospital at the time were chutiyas. So I ended up with this permanent limp.'

'Didn't anyone tell you it was a bad idea chasing a kite on a rooftop?'

'I thought I could catch it. That's the way it is with us Baloch. If we think we can do something, we do it.'

He took the lit cigarette and looked at me with a suddenly serious expression. 'What exactly are you trying to do here? Baba seems to trust you, but I don't. What's your angle? Around here, people don't think I'm very smart, but even I can figure out that anybody in your position would have backed the Party. So why did you decide to come here?'

I had been expecting this question for some time, so I took my time to answer it, taking another drag of the cigarette before I threw it onto the floor. 'Look Ghaffar bhai, I chose to come here because I think Baba can become a real force in this city. People even outside of Lyari are sick and tired of the Party's chutiyapas after twenty-five years. No one wants to listen to that bhenchod Don making speeches from New York and giving orders by remote control. Karachi is looking for alternative leadership. Your fault has been that you have thought small so far. Limiting yourself to crime and to Lyari when the entire city is ripe for the taking. We can have a finger in everything, just like the Party does right now. We can replace the Party as the pre-eminent force in this city. And Baba can replace the Don. But to do that, we need our image to change. Most people in this city have only one opinion of Baba, and that is the one shaped by the Party, that he is nothing more than a terrorist and a criminal. But if we show people that he is actually a leader, a man who has taken the initiative against a corrupt system to clean up his own neighbourhood, who has brightened up the lives of the people of Lyari, then we can turn the Party's narrative against them. And once we have political power to go along with our street power, then no one will be able to touch us. That is why I did all these dramas with the road clearance and garbage pickups and football matches. To show to the world what we can do in Lyari. If you are worried about the police coming back here and chasing you, you needn't be. Even the Party admits that after Akbar Khan's failure in Lyari last year, the police no longer have the balls to try and make an entry here. Neither does the Party. Why do you think they were so keen to hatch this elaborate plan to use me to lure Baba outside of Lyari so that they could kill him there? They know entering Lyari would be suicidal. But we need to do these other things so that people think we are more than just a bunch of gangsters.'

I didn't know whether I had gotten through to Langra or not, because he just shrugged his shoulders, grunted and walked away. But the next day, I did notice that Ghaffar himself was standing on the road from Mauripur to Gabol Park with a garbage truck, exhorting the municipality workers to do their jobs with greater enthusiasm.

'This is good. It is working.' That's all Baba said to me, the night of the Germany–Brazil semi-final. That was the first indication that he was pleased with my efforts. Baba had never been a great talker and after Jheenga's death he had become more withdrawn. He was greatly affected by the murder of Jheenga. He had never expected the Party to commit such a brazen act, and never expected it to hit so close to home. But to be honest, it was stupid of him to think this way. After all of Baba's provocative actions, why *wouldn't* they go after Jheenga, especially if he was stupid enough to not take appropriate security precautions. But I knew it wasn't my place to say any of this out loud.

'This is just the beginning. I am going to make you the most popular man in Karachi. You said you had some landholdings in Balochistan, right?'

'Yes, near Wadh. Why?'

'Because I am going to make you a Baloch sardar in the eyes of the people. A noble man who cares only about the welfare of the people.'

'How the hell will people forget my origins? Everyone knows where I am from.'

'People are chutiyas, Baba. They will always believe what they want to believe. It's all marketing. Trust me. And that's not all we're going to do. We will change the face of Lyari. These fucking Partywallahs keep going on about what they do for their constituents. We will show them what we do for our constituents. We're going to open a new college here. And we'll totally revamp Lyari General Hospital. We are going to build a platform that allows us to expand your empire beyond the borders of Lyari. And the United Front will never know what hit them.'

Baba eyed me for a long moment with that emotionless expression of his that always made me wonder whether I had gone too far. Then he got up from his seat and beckoned me to come with him. He looked in the mirror and donned a Sindhi cap before stepping out. I had noticed that he was dressed better than usual, wearing a crisp white cotton shalwar kameez, with his beard and hair trimmed and perfumed with attar. Obviously, it was an occasion of some sort but I had no idea as to what it was.

Outside, a convoy of jeeps was waiting for us, the men had already climbed in and were on high alert. Baba slowly ascended the SUV closest to the door, and I sat down in the back seat with him. We swiftly travelled till the edge of Lyari, near the timber market, where even at this hour the narrow roads were clogged with traffic. Just as the convoy ground to a halt in the traffic, Baba signalled me to jump out with him. I had barely recovered from the shock of tumbling out of the jeep when suddenly Baba, now sitting on a Honda 125 bike, tapped me on the shoulder with a grin on his face.

'What are you doing, Baba? What about your security?'

'Sitting ducks in this traffic. And so obvious the Party madarchods would see them coming from miles away. The motorcycle is much better. No one would even think that Baba Dacait would be riding around alone on a motorbike. I've survived this long not because I'm braver than everybody else, but because I'm smarter.' He had a toothy grin on his face as he gestured me to jump on.

But he was absolutely right. The motorbike allowed us to navigate the choked traffic in a matter of minutes, and with total anonymity. We were one of thousands of motorcyclists on the roads. As soon as we passed beyond the electronics market, Baba accelerated, making me hold on to him like a girlfriend, heading in the direction of Clifton Bridge. Just before the bridge we turned off on one of the side roads, finding ourselves in a quiet, leafy street with huge old houses. I knew the neighbourhood well. Not from personal experience, but because I had seen it hundreds of times on TV. This was where Chandio House was located.

Now, Chandio House is one of the most important addresses in the city, right up there with Darul Sakoon – the Don's house – the US Consul General's residence and the Corps Commander House. It is acknowledged as a place where history has often been made. This is because for close to a hundred years it had been the home of Sindh's pre-eminent political dynasty, the Chandios.

The Chandios had already produced a prime minister, a governor, two provincial chief ministers and a handful of individuals who were once upon a time knighted by the Queen of England. They had also produced three generations of Oxford University graduates, and one from Oxford Polytechnic School – Nawaz Chandio was apparently more inclined to parties than exam papers during his time abroad. As a Sindhi who grew up in the dark martial law days, I had been taught this family's history as a child. I had also grown up on tales of the family's courage and on the belief that they were the only solution to all of Sindh's problems. In every election in my lifetime, my entire extended family, in fact our whole village, had always voted for the Chandios or their representatives every single time.

But Chandio House now wore a sorrowful look, as if its glory days were perhaps in its past. The fronds of the palm trees were withered and dry, the bougainvillea hedge overgrown and falling over the walls, and the old iron gate, with the remnants of decades of political posters still stuck on it in bits and pieces, looked rusty. Indeed, the house had seen much sorrow. It had received the body of a patriarch who had been hanged by the army while he was prime minister, and more recently, a scion shot to death in a badly planned and poorly executed encounter with the police.

In fact, the fortunes of the Chandio family seemed to have set in permanent decline since the tragic killing of Nawaz Chandio more than ten years ago. His brother Yousaf, who had lost his chief ministership as a direct result of the incident, had never been able to win back his premiership. Two elections had passed with only worsening results for the Chandios. And while Yousaf remained the leader of the opposition in the Sindh assembly, he led an opposition with a constantly diminishing number of seats, as the United Front consolidated its position and expanded its governing coalition.

It was here at Chandio House that Baba stopped his bike and disembarked. A wave of humility, that I had never seen Baba display ever before, swept over him. He calmly waited at the gate as the guard went in to announce him, and then stepped gingerly into the Chandio compound, as if overawed by its grandeur. For grand it was, there was no denying that. We were led to an annexe that served as a camp office for Yousaf Chandio, and I have never seen such a magnificent room. Now admittedly, my experience of grand offices was limited to my editor's shitty little cubicle, but I would challenge if even Sardar Obama has such a nicely decorated office. There were animal heads on the walls, old black-and-white photos showing the elder Chandio during his time as prime minister, carpets so plush and soft that I just wanted to keep on standing on them, and a huge, highly polished desk that dominated the room. To one side of the desk was a small seating area adorned with huge leather sofas, and it was here, rather than behind the desk, that we found the great Yousaf Chandio.

The man in front of me looked much older than the face I had seen so many times on TV. I was shocked to see his hair so dishevelled and white, in contrast to the perfectly groomed, dark-haired personality we always saw in the media. His entire appearance was quite untidy. He wore a crumpled kurta, and his hand shook slightly as he raised a glass of whisky to his lips. He looked like a slightly doddering grandfather, rather than the charismatic politician he had once been. In recent years, especially after his brother Nawaz's death, his public appearances had become fewer. It was rumoured that Nawaz's demise had shattered him not only politically, but personally as well. It was said that while it was the police officer Akbar Khan who went to jail for the killing of Nawaz, it was actually Yousaf who was awarded a life sentence. His mother refused to speak to him, his sister-in-law called him a murderer in the press, and half of the old family retainers turned on him because they believed him complicit in Nawaz's death. He was even briefly shut out of Chandio House, as Nawaz's family had been living here, while Yousaf had inhabited the Chief Minister House when the fateful shooting had occurred. And Nawaz's angered fedayeen had refused Yousaf entry for many months. It was only after the intervention of one of Nawaz's lieutenants, the underworld boss-turned-politician Shashlik Khan, that Yousaf had managed to broker a deal with Nawaz's widow, who was paid a princely sum, Nawaz's share of the Chandio empire, to move to Dubai. My father had told me at the time that the sum was so large that Yousaf had to mortgage large chunks of the Chandio lands to Shashlik, who had advanced him the money to give to his sister-in-law.

It could be argued that this was ironic, since it was Shashlik's arrest by Akbar Khan that had arguably triggered the entire sad sequence of events that led to the death of Nawaz Chandio. By that logic it could be said that Shashlik's culpability was as great as Yousaf's. But Shashlik was nothing if not a born survivor, and he had somehow managed to avoid suffering from the fallout of Nawaz's death. In fact, he had prospered from it. At the time, he had been in Akbar Khan's custody, but he was released soon after the incident and acquitted of all charges by Akbar's arch-rival, Maqsood Mahr. And soon after that, he agreed to join a coalition led by the United Front, became labour minister, and made even more money selling visas to poor fools who wanted to work in Dubai and Oman than he had from all his gambling dens. That's Karachi politics for you.

And here he was again, sitting next to Yousaf Chandio on the plush leather sofa. His jet-black hair was slicked back, and his pale skin provided a dramatic contrast with his baggy black

silk kurta. I had heard that once upon a time Shashlik Khan
prided himself on his fitness, but now even the baggy kurta
couldn't hide a paunch that made him look eight months
pregnant. I was amazed to see him here, because Shashlik
remained officially a member of the government, even though
his lucrative ministry had been taken away recently. Chief
Minister Tariq Colombowala, who has always had an eye for
making money, decided that he had underestimated the value
of the labour ministry, especially in light of the fortune Shashlik
was able to make from it. So he had taken it over himself
and given Shashlik a sukha ministry, Women's Development,
where the opportunities for both moneymaking and the actual
development of women were extremely limited.

It had long been rumoured that Baba had powerful political
patrons, but no one knew who they were. Of course, Lyari
had been a traditional stronghold of the Chandios, but there
was never an obvious link between Baba and Yousaf Chandio.
Besides, Baba's rise had coincided with Yousaf's loss of interest
in politics, so no one had ever bothered to make the connection.
As we approached the sofas, Baba bent low and touched Yousaf
Chandio's feet. My greeting was a little less humble, just a simple
bow and salaam as Yousaf bade us sit on the sofa opposite him
and Shashlik. An attendant served us tea and snacks, and I could
sense Baba's nervousness as he sat next to me, trying to hold
his cup properly. During this period, Yousaf Chandio made no
attempt at small talk, as would be customary at such occasions.
Nor did he bother to inquire about who I was. After another five
minutes, in which Baba succeeded in adding to his nervousness
by dropping a sandwich on the floor, it was Shashlik who finally
broke the silence.

'Baba, Adda Yousaf wants you to stop these attacks on the
Party. It's spoiling the political atmosphere, making the Don
nervous, and it serves no purpose.'

Suddenly, I noticed Baba's body stiffen. Till now, he had been the picture of meekness, but in one second Shashlik's tone changed his attitude completely.

'If Adda Yousaf wants me to do something, he can ask me himself. Who are you to tell me what to do or not to do?' Baba stared at Shashlik with a killer's dead eyes.

'Look Baba, I'm saying this for your own good. I see the Party's ministers in cabinet meetings. They are very nervous. I spoke to the CM. He told me they don't want to start a fight over Lyari, but you know that they aren't in control. The Don runs them from New York by remote control. If he is provoked, then they will have to come after you. Your making all these public pronouncements, abusing him and calling him a coward, doesn't help at all. Look, I'm speaking from experience. It isn't pleasant to have the entire weight of the Party and the government after you all at the same time.'

Baba suddenly laughed humourlessly and fixed a crooked smile on his face. 'I haven't lost my balls like you, Shashlik Khan. What is your experience? That the first time that policewallah Akbar Khan came knocking on your door, you shat your pants? Bhenchod, you couldn't last two days in his interrogation, you went whimpering to your pimp police officer, Maqsood Mahr, to beg him to get you out! And the minute the Khakis offered you a deal, you allowed them to put their dicks in your ass to get out. I've heard the stories, Shashlik Khan. The whole city knows what you did. The whole city also knows what I did. When Akbar Khan came to my neighbourhood, you know how we greeted him? With bullets. I personally fired a rocket at his armoured car. Ask him, where the fuck is he now? I humiliated him so badly that he put his tail between his legs and ran off to Lahore. I'm Baba Dacait, Shashlik, don't try and tell me what to do, saala bharwa.'

Shashlik bristled at Baba's comments, his pale face turning bright red. He clenched his fist, and again Baba's body tensed, as if ready to stand up and fight. But before Shashlik could say anything further, Yousaf Chandio spoke up.

'Baba, calm down. Shashlik is right. I told him to speak to you first. This vendetta that you have with the Party is not good for anyone. What do you hope to achieve? You think they will back down after you killed their minister? They are a political party and you are a gangster. They can destroy you if they want.'

'Adda, I respect you, but they are no more a political party than I am. We all know that. They have put out this image that no one dares to challenge them in this city. And everyone kowtows to them, because they are in with the faujis, and the Americans. Everyone knows that the Americans back that bhenchod Don because he got Asad Haider to kill the old cleric Namakzai. I could have done that. That's no big deal. Why should I back down? I'm not afraid of that prick. If he has a problem with me, maybe he should stop pissing himself in New York and come back here. Besides, Adda, why are you worried? This is between me and the Don. You are not involved in any way.'

'But it does involve me. Everyone knows that Lyari is our old family stronghold, and when things start going wrong in Lyari, people, big people in this country, not just the Party, look at me questioningly. And when they start to think about political retribution, they will take it out on me.'

'Arre Adda, why are you scared of the Party? You are allowing yourself to be misled by idiots like Shashlik, who go running with their tails between their legs at the first sign of trouble. You are a Chandio, you don't need to bow before the Don or anyone else. Nothing will happen to you, it's my guarantee. My men are willing to give their lives for your family.'

'I am a Chandio, and I am still the political master of Lyari. And I am ordering you to stop this feud with the Party. Don't forget that if I choose to do so, I can make it impossible even for you to stay in Lyari.'

The rebuke was given in the tone of a man used to having his instructions obeyed. But as Baba's shock and anger at such an open threat welled up within him, I chose to speak up. 'Sir, I think you haven't visited Lyari recently. If you had, you would find that the ground reality is very different now. Everyone has tremendous respect for you and your family, but the people love Baba. So I don't think you can make it impossible for him to stay in Lyari, although he can certainly make it impossible for you to win five votes there without his support.'

'How dare you be impudent with me! Do you know who I am? I am Yousaf Chandio, I have been chief minister of this province twice! Who brought you into this meeting!'

Now, all along I had thought that Yousaf hadn't asked about me because perhaps Baba had told him beforehand that he was bringing me, but it became apparent that he hadn't asked about me because he considered me irrelevant, more or less like a cushion on the sofa. I had taken a big risk by speaking out because there was no guarantee that Baba would support me, but now, from the corner of my eye, I saw the sly smile on Baba's face.

'Adda, this is Ismail Naich, my … political adviser. I have brought him in recently to help change the image of the gang, and to help us implement some social welfare projects in Lyari.'

'Sir, no one is trying to be disrespectful of you. But at the same time, we would appreciate it if you were respectful of the new political realities. Yes, you were chief minister, twice. And you did have a constituency in Lyari. But you haven't been chief minister for ten years, and you haven't visited Lyari for probably fifteen. Baba is the new reality for the youth of Lyari. They see him organizing boxing tournaments. They see him setting up huge TV screens in public parks so common people can enjoy watching the football World Cup. They see him eliminating petty crime from the streets, even though he is accused of being a gangster. And they will vote ultimately for whoever he tells them to vote for. Up till now, it has always been the candidate of your party. But that could change.' I let the sentence hang in the air, to allow its implications to sink in.

'And who would he throw his support to? The United Front? Don't be ridiculous. He knows I am his only choice.'

'You *were* Baba's only choice, sir. Don't forget, he could always stand himself. And that would become humiliating for *you*.'

Yousaf Chandio stared at me with new-found interest, and I could almost hear his astute political brain working, weighing the options, making complex political calculations. When he spoke again, it was once again in a calm and measured tone.

'Look Baba, Ismail, I understand what you are trying to do. And I agree with it. The Party does need to be challenged and the Don does need to be taught a lesson. But no matter how many ward bosses or ministers you kill, it won't make any difference to the Don. His downfall will come only when he is defeated politically. That is why this violence is senseless. And it will give the Party an advantage in this Soldier Bazaar by-election that they have just announced to fill Mian Mithu's seat. They will play the sympathy card with their supporters, claiming that the Baloch hordes will slit everybody's throats if the Party isn't around. And they will justify extra police deployments at polling stations on grounds of the threat from Baba, but all the time they will use the extra security to ensure their ward boys are able to stuff the ballot boxes without anyone stopping them. Look, I am trying to unite the opposition parties by getting everyone to agree on supporting a common candidate against the Party. We won't win, but if we can cut into the Party's share of the vote, this will give me a potent political weapon to claim that the Party's popularity is waning, and to push them to call for early elections.'

'And what if you were to win?'

'Don't be preposterous. Soldier Bazaar is a safe seat for the Party. That idiot Mian Mithu won it by 20,000 votes last time round.'

'Sir, what if we ran the election campaign? What if we used all the tactics the Party uses in elections, but what if we did it better? Do you agree that it would be a huge upset for the Party to lose the seat?'

'Yes, it would be a political tsunami. But I tell you, it's just not possible.'

'Sir, the election is due to be held in three months, right? Give us three months. You have nothing to lose. The worst-case scenario is that your candidate will lose, but he will still have reduced the Party's winning margin. So, in essence, the worst-case scenario is your best-case scenario right now. And if the Party loses the seat, well, then anything is possible.'

'So what do you want in return for performing this miracle?'

'We want you to support whatever we do in Soldier Bazaar during the election campaign. We want you to keep the other opposition parties in check by ensuring they all support a common candidate. And we want to be the ones to select that candidate. And if our man wins, we want you to give us the discretion to award your party's ticket to whoever we choose, for all of Lyari's provincial and national assembly seats in the next election.'

'Who will you run? I know that both the Shia and Sunni parties are advocating that I should pick one of their candidates, a learned scholar, Maulana Noorani or somebody like that.'

'Sir, forget these Noorani–Sheerani, Pathani Islamic scholar types. They will never win because the public in Soldier Bazaar never connects with these sorts. We will take a cue from the Party's playbook. We are going to pick a fresh face, a candidate who everybody can get excited about.'

'And the killings will stop?'

'The killings will stop during the election campaign.'

Yousaf Chandio turned to look at Shashlik, who seemed to be in a state of bewilderment. This meeting had taken a turn he had never expected. Then, suddenly, Chandio got up and hugged Baba warmly. 'Then good luck to both of you.'

When we got back on to the street, Baba tapped my shoulder. 'Ay chutiya, you've made big promises inside. How will we do all this?'

'Trust me, Baba, we can succeed. This way, when our man wins, everyone will know he won because of you. You will become the political godfather of not only Lyari, but Soldier Bazaar as well.'

'And how will we do this without killing anyone during the campaign?'

'We promised Adda Yousaf we wouldn't kill anyone. We didn't say anything about not kidnapping people.'

At this, Baba laughed loudly and heartily. 'Saala, your mind works like a computer, Naich. Well done. Now, what's the next step?'

'Well, now all we have to do is find a candidate.'

11

ANTHONY

'Forty-three pages. Forty-three goddamn pages of testimony, and you don't want us to touch it?'

'What's the evidence?'

Anthony Russo raises his eyebrows in astonishment, picks up the thick folder lying in front of him, and somewhat dramatically pushes it towards his questioner, the woman from the District Attorney's office. 'It's a history of the crimes committed by Asad Haider on the orders of Mohammed Ali Pichkari, aka the Don. Pichkari ordered these crimes while remaining based here in Brooklyn. The crimes include literally hundreds of murders, not to mention numerous acts of terrorism, arson, rape and assault.'

He stares at the people sitting around the mahogany conference table, trying to see if the implications of what he is saying have sunk in. Unfortunately their expressions confirm his own analysis that this meeting is a rat fuck.

New York's finest have sent their finest representatives to this meeting, being held in a magnificent wood-panelled conference room on one of the higher floors of One Police

Plaza, the headquarters of the New York Police Department. Russo tries to work out how much support he and Cardenas could rely on if things get difficult. He quickly concludes, from the high quality of bureaucratic pencil pushers sitting across the table, that it wouldn't be a lot. There's his precinct captain, Brian Ash, a silver-haired Irishman and recovering alcoholic, a throwback to an earlier NYPD, who's just looking to quietly finish his career in the pre-retirement rest home that is the 20th Precinct. Russo can tell from his expression that he hates even being in this meeting, as it's something that could cause ripples on the last stretch of his journey to earning a comfortable pension. On the other hand, next to Ash is the borough commander, Nick Santapio. He's the kind of guy who barely keeps from tripping over his own ambition. He's spent most of the meeting looking past Russo and Cardenas, staring at the pictures and plaques on the wall, as if sizing up where he would put his things whenever he inherits this office. He's on the fast track, the youngest borough commander in the city, looking to soon earn a corner office here in Police Plaza. But such rapid promotion doesn't come without an absolutely mercenary attitude, and a healthy propensity to be able to eat your own young, if the need arises. Russo has no doubt Santapio would gladly throw him and Cardenas under a bus if that helped him in any way. The third person across the table is Hunt, the thin, bespectacled chief of detectives. Russo doesn't even bother glancing at him. Everyone knows Hunt is a prick. The joke in the locker rooms is that if you ever meet Hunt and a gangbanger with an AK-47 in a dark alley, be sure to shoot Hunt first.

There are three other people in the room, on whom the course of the meeting will ultimately depend. There's the DA office's representative, whom he has just passed the file to, Anna Sara something or the other. Russo hasn't caught her last name but he knows she is the DA's chief adviser and hatchet woman. She's a pure politician, trying to sniff out the big media case that she can ride all the way to the governor's mansion in Albany. Then there's the man whose conference room they are all sitting in. The chief of department of the NYPD is the highest-ranking uniformed officer on the force, just below the commissioner in terms of rank and protocol. His presence at this meeting is a clear indicator of the stakes that seem to have been raised by Russo's and Cardenas's investigation. Put it another way, they must have really stirred the shit for the chief to have summoned them.

More likely, the excrement stirrer is the final participant of the meeting, who sits on the far corner of the table. Simon Sole has still not officially admitted that he's CIA, but he isn't exactly denying it either. Russo and Cardenas stopped taking his calls after the meeting with Asad Haider. They just can't trust him. As the investigation has progressed, the calls have grown more frequent, the messages more frantic. The final straw, thinks Russo, must have been their decision to bring in the Don for a second round of more intensive questioning. The minute they made their intentions public, this meeting got suddenly called. It has to be Sole pulling the strings.

'And these forty-three pages represent the statement of this guy Asad Haider, who was the intended assassination target in the shooting incident at the Museum of Natural History?' The question once again comes from the DA office lady.

'Uh, we're not comfortable referring to it as an assassination yet. We're still treating it as a murder investigation.' Even Cardenas, who has kept a tight leash on his emotions throughout this meeting, rolls his eyes at the borough commander's effort to remain politically correct at all times. As if not using the word assassination somehow changes the facts of the case.

'Yes, Counsellor. His statement provides us the motive.'

'And he gave this statement in the presence of legal counsel?'

'No, he waived his right to legal counsel. He was also aware that his statement is self-incriminatory, and he is willing to face the consequences of that.'

'And where is he now?'

'He's still in hospital. We've got a police guard on him there, but the doctors say he should be okay to check out in another couple of days. When he does, we'll take him into custody.'

Russo understands that all of these questions are frivolous. All of these details are already in the report that he and Cardenas submitted. The lawyer is flummoxed, not sure where to take this, not sure whether pursuing this is good or bad for her career. She takes off her glasses and looks questioningly at Simon Sole, as if trying to get some direction from him. 'There are some very serious allegations here against the CIA.'

'First of all, those are all allegations, there's no proof in there. We get conspiracy theorists saying stuff that's much worse than this every week. This is nothing. Hey, we're the CIA, if somebody isn't trashing us, it means we're not doing our job. Secondly, even if I were to hypothetically concede the point that some of these things happened, they all happened in a foreign country, and pertain to national security. There is a jurisdictional issue here.' Simon Sole remains the only person in the room who isn't flustered.

'Oh, so you're finally admitting that you are, in fact, working for the CIA, and not the State Department. Hypothetically speaking, of course.' Cardenas can't resist getting that jab in, drawing a tight-lipped smile from Sole.

'We have to maintain a low profile, Detective, keeping in mind the sensitivities and media hype generated by this case.'

'What about this character in Brooklyn? Pitch-ka-ree? The Don? If we proceed, this has to be handled very carefully. He has a very impressive legal team. The DA himself has been getting calls from several of his Harvard law school classmates on this one. All the big firms are lining up to defend this guy. And we haven't even decided to do anything yet.'

'Yes, Counsellor, that's precisely where this case gets a little *delicate*. Now we have a relationship with Mr Pichkari, obviously that relationship involved some very sensitive issues that I cannot reveal here on grounds of national security. Suffice it to say that if any legal action were taken against Mr Pichkari, there is a strong likelihood that overseas US assets would be put in danger. Now, far be it for us to interfere in a criminal investigation in the United States, but we do want to point out that Mr Pichkari has never been accused of any sort of illegal activity in this country in the fifteen or so years that he has lived here. He hasn't even gotten a parking ticket. And in terms of character reference, we can certify that he has been extremely patriotic in his support of US interests overseas. I don't see why we need to drag a man with such an exemplary record into this case on such flimsy evidence.'

'Wow, you guys must really have had a hard-on for Namakzai, if you're going to this length to cover for the Don.'

'I can assure you, Detective Russo, that any stories that Asad Haider may have told you about a fanciful CIA plot to kill Mufti Namakzai are just lies. The truth is that in fact, as Mr Pichkari mentioned to you in his interview, Asad Haider has for some time been involved in criminal activities for personal enrichment. This is something that has been documented by our Karachi station as well. The list of people who want Asad Haider dead is long and distinguished, and now he's making things up for you guys so that he can stay on in the United States instead of being deported back to Karachi.'

'He's got another five months to run on his stay. He's in no rush to go anywhere. And he is volunteering to go to jail. I don't see any advantage for him in wanting to stay here.'

'Compared to the alternatives in Karachi, trust me, jail here would be far more preferable. The minute he lands there, somebody is going to try and finish the job, whether it's the Pakistani intelligence agencies, or the Taliban or whoever. Asad Haider isn't exactly Mr Popular back there. And also, he doesn't have five months here, and he knows it. We did some checking on his visa and found that it was obtained illegally, without having gone through the security vetting process. Also, he got a visa issued from Karachi while he was living in Dubai. Our Karachi office figures he must have bribed one of the local employees to get the visa. The Consul General is initiating an inquiry there, but in the meantime, the Karachi Consulate has sent us verification of the cancellation of the visa, which would mean that, as of this moment, Asad Haider is in this country illegally and liable for instant deportation.'

'That's bullshit and you know it. He got the visa because your friends got him the exemption. The chief minister's office called up the Consulate and requested an expedited service for him, because he was a Party big shot.'

'Detective Cardenas, I can only tell you the information I've received from the State Department. This is from them, not us.'

'Can he claim asylum here?'

'Well, technically he could, Counsellor, but the State Department isn't very hot on that idea. You see, the Pakistan government has informally made a request for Asad Haider to be handed to them. As he himself admits in this statement, he is culpable in several dozen murders, including those of military personnel, and those folks take that pretty seriously back there. I can confirm that the ISI has also approached our station chief for help in this matter. State feels that, considering the critical level of cooperation between the United States and Pakistan on counterterrorism issues, it would be really bad form for us to grant asylum to a man who the Paks have tagged as a terrorist.

I mean, we can hardly blame them for covering up bin Laden if we were to do this. That's why, State, and we, are keen that Asad Haider should be removed from the United States before he has an opportunity to force his way into the legal system here. He hasn't made an overt appeal for asylum in any of the forty-three pages of his statement, so I think that provides us with some cover.'

Reassured that somehow Sole has saved her from landing her exquisite Christian Louboutin heels in a deep pile of dogshit, the lawyer puts her glasses back on and resumes in a more imperious tone. 'I'm looking at this statement, Detective Russo, and I can't see any admission of an offence committed in the United States. These are all crimes pertaining to Pakistan. Heinous, no doubt, and sensational, but there is a jurisdiction issue. We can't charge him with anything based on this statement.'

Russo lounges back in his chair and laughs. 'You tied this one up nicely, Simon. Good way to get rid of a loose end. First, you get him to do your dirty work in Karachi, whacking whoever you want whacked over there, and then you fix it so he gets deported back to Pakistan where, knowing their track record, his own Party will bump him off for you. No one else to rat out your little secrets. Except the Don, and you don't need to worry about him. He's here, and he's your boy anyway.'

'Hey, I resent the implication, Detective. We want the Natural History Museum shooting solved as much as you do. You think we like the fact that an American has been killed on American soil, and that it is loosely linked to one of our operational assets? I have been trying to be as helpful as possible with your investigation but you guys are the ones who aren't even taking my calls.'

'You could give a rat's ass about our investigation, all you want is to save your fairy fucking princess Don so that you can continue to use him for whatever horror shows you're running in Karachi. Let's just cut out the bullshit here, the fact of the matter is that the CIA has been actively trying to subvert a murder investigation in New York.'

'Detective Cardenas, that's enough.' It's the first time the chief has spoken in the meeting, and Russo is surprised by the raspy quality of his voice, coming out like it's from a badly tuned radio. It serves its purpose and shuts everyone up. Daniel Esposito is a tall, broad-shouldered man with a pockmarked face and a sober moustache, who still looks sharp in his uniform despite his sixty-one years. He's a living legend on the force, a hero cop from an earlier era, the man who brought to light and investigated one of the worst corruption scandals in the department's history. The Mr Clean who's never really played the political game with the mayor's office. This has resulted in him having seen off four commissioners in his fourteen years as chief of department, without ever himself having been considered for the top job. He purses his lips and looks at Russo and Cardenas for a long moment. Then he turns to the file in front of him.

'Detective Russo, how long have you been on the force?'

'Twenty-five years, Chief.'

'Good. Then you can appreciate what a big deal this case is. A woman is killed, and five other persons wounded, in a shooting incident on the steps of the Natural History Museum, in one of the safest parts of New York. This isn't the Bronx, this is the Upper West Side. It's been over a month, and we have made no discernible progress on this case.'

'That's not true, sir. I believe we have made very significant progress, thanks to the cooperation of Asad Haider.'

'What exactly do you think he has given us? Explain to me what exactly you think happened here.'

'Yes, Chief. It's real simple. Asad Haider was the chief enforcer for the Don, who has run Karachi while sitting here in Brooklyn for the past fifteen years. Haider committed numerous murders at the behest of the Don. The Don summoned him to New York, and the Sindh government which the United Front heads, officially facilitated the visa for Haider. The purpose of summoning Haider was to give him instructions for another hit, on one of the old Party stalwarts, whom the Don feared might become a rival for himself. Haider refused to carry out the hit, so the Don ordered him to be whacked here in New York. At the same time, Haider's family were all murdered in Karachi by the Party. These forty-three pages provide us with a solid gold motive. Haider was the inside man, the guy who knew where all the bodies were buried. He was also the only one who knew about the Party's relationship with the CIA. Once he reneged, the Don had to kill him to hush things up.'

'Counsellor, can we legally prosecute for any of the crimes mentioned in this statement?'

'No sir. Haider may be screaming our door down, confessing to things that he did in Pakistan, but even if those crimes involve the Don, who is now a US citizen, there's nothing there for us to prosecute him here. And if, as Mr Sole claims, his visa has been revoked, we are obliged to deport him. His only role in this case would be as an intended victim. We can't keep him in the United States till the case comes to prosecution. Who knows how long that may take. We can always arrange for him to come back as a witness, but that would only be when the case comes to trial. As I see it, we have to send him back home now.'

'Hunt?'

'There isn't enough in this file to go forward on, Chief.'

'Nick?'

'Chief, this is a very sensitive case, and there …'

'I'm aware it's a sensitive case. What's your opinion?'

'If there are external considerations, as the CIA says, then we should probably keep them in mind. This whole thing is very messy. Maybe we should also transfer the investigation to a specialized unit that has more experience of liaising with the intelligence community. Russo and Cardenas have done a good job, but this is out of their league.'

'The commissioner wants this case solved and so do I. It seems as if we don't have enough to continue working in the direction we've been working in. Mr Sole, if you forward the State Department's visa cancellation letter to us, we will process the deportation proceedings and put Mr Haider on a flight to Karachi as soon as he is physically able to make it. Detectives Russo and Cardenas will personally escort him to the airport and put him on that flight. But the investigation stays with them. And they will continue to look into all sorts of leads, irrespective of where they may take them. Thank you, gentlemen. And lady. That'll be all.'

'Excuse me, sir, but can I get a guarantee that Mohammed Ali Pichkari won't be harassed any further? Of course, if the police want any legitimate information, we are happy to facilitate that process.'

'Mr Sole, the only guarantee I'm gonna give you is that the NYPD will do a professional job of investigating this case, just as they have done so far. I'm sure that if the officers need your help, they will reach out to you. And when I say that'll be all, that means you can go now.'

If Simon Sole is stung by the rebuke, he doesn't show it. He smiles politely, picks up his papers and shuffles out. Russo and Cardenas also get up to leave, but the chief motions to them to stay. 'Hang on. I want to talk to you two. Alone.'

Russo and Cardenas sit back down while their superior officers exit the room, unsure of their fate. Chief Esposito takes another look at the papers in front of him, and then raises his head to stare out through the window at the Lower Manhattan skyline.

'Too bad you can't smoke in here any more. I miss smoking in my office. Either of you smoke?'

'I have the occasional cigar, sir.'

'Cuban?'

'Yes sir.'

'Where do you get them from?'

'Uh, it's a connection at the airport, sir. But I'd rather not say more than that.'

Esposito smiles, once again stroking his moustache. 'Don't worry, I won't rat out your source. I've read your file. You're a good cop. You did that thing in the Bronx, as a rookie, when you saved that kid. And then 9/11. You went into the towers and saved those three firemen. Worked four days straight. You're a damn good detective too. In counterterrorism, you had a natural feel for that stuff. The one thing I look for in a cop is sound instincts. And you've got that. So tell me, what do your instincts tell you about this Don character?'

'He's dirty, Chief. He's essentially been running a criminal empire from here for years, right under our noses. And the CIA, to the best of our knowledge, has been complicit in it. He ordered the hit on Asad Haider. We know he did, we just can't prove it. Yet.'

'What would you need to prove it?'

'Surveillance. Phone taps, a sting operation. Most importantly, a little bit of time, Chief. This guy isn't going to fold easily.'

'I don't know about time. There's a lot of heat on this case. I haven't seen the CIA so far up its own ass since the 1993 World Trade Center bombing. And the commissioner's worried that this case might spoil our good working relationship with the Agency. Plus, the media's going crazy.'

'Sir, I understand that there's a lot of media pressure ...'

'I don't give a shit about media pressure or CIA pressure. I give a shit about why this happened on our watch. I don't care who the fuck these people are or where they come from, but I'm not going to tolerate their politics spilling onto our streets. You might hear different from the commissioner, and that's his prerogative. I'm not looking to become the next Secretary of Homeland Security. I'm a cop and I believe our job is to solve crimes. So you let me know what resources you need, and I'll make sure you get them. And I'll also square it with your bosses, so that the two of you do nothing but work on this case.'

'And what about the Don, sir? Can we bring him in?'

'If you do it immediately, Cardenas, his lawyers are going to raise hell. And the commissioner and mayor may not be able to take the heat. But you build the case, with wire taps or informants, or whatever, and you pitch it just right, no one will be able to block you. Not even the fucking CIA.'

*

Three days later, the doctors at New York Presbyterian give Asad the all-clear. But instead of being taken into custody, Russo and Cardenas are there to inform him that they will have to escort him immediately to the airport. Simon Sole has been remarkably efficient in getting confirmation of the cancelled visa from Karachi. In fact, everything has been handled with clinical efficiency. Even Asad's hospital bills have been paid up fully by the time he starts changing out of his hospital gown, courtesy of the Party. Simon Sole tells Russo and Cardenas that despite everything, the Don has not forgotten his commitment to bear all of Asad's medical expenses. Just for old times' sake. Brilliant, Russo thinks. Make the grand selfless gesture, and ensure that there is no excuse for Asad to stay in New York. Besides, if his calculations are correct, thirty grand is probably a day's take for the Party in Karachi. No big deal.

Asad Haider accepts the news about his deportation without any form of protest. He doesn't cry, he doesn't shout and scream at them, he doesn't curse the fact that life is unfair. He just listens with an expressionless face and starts packing his few belongings as soon as Cardenas finishes speaking. Once he's done, he raises his hands to be cuffed, and silently walks out of the hospital to the unmarked police car parked right outside the hospital's main entrance.

They are past the Triboro Bridge before he finally speaks. 'So, Detective, what was it you said to me about things being different here than they were in Pakistan? It appears that your faith in the US government not interfering with your investigation was somewhat misplaced. Apparently, Uncle Sam also makes exceptions for the Don.'

That single sentence brings to the fore what Russo and Cardenas have been privately feeling. Their frustration is evident. Cardenas grips the steering wheel so tight his knuckles turn white, while Russo continues to stare straight ahead, without answering.

'Can you at least tell me what flight I'm going back on?'

'It's a Pakistan Airlines flight, straight to Karachi. Your ticket is being covered, courtesy the State Department. Leaves at nine.'

'Detectives, you know what will happen to me when I land in Karachi. I am a dead man.'

Russo sighs and nods. 'How will they do it? Get the local cops to pick you up and bump you off?'

'I'm too big a liability to leave in the hands of the police. Your CIA friends must have already told them the flight number. I wouldn't be surprised if they put someone on the plane to watch me and point me out as I come out of immigration. Gringo will have his team ready outside. They'll grab me as quietly as possible, then take me to a ward office to finish me off. That's what I would do.'

'Is there any way you can survive this?'

'You could let me go.'

'Sorry. That's the one thing we can't do.'

'I understand. It was worth a shot.'

Cardenas unexpectedly takes the exit off the expressway and pulls up in a quiet Queens neighbourhood. Both Russo and Asad look at him with some surprise as he turns to face them.

'If you were to evade capture in Karachi, what would you do?'

'If I survive somehow. I swear I will bring the Don and his Party down.'

'Look, we can't let you go here. Sole would have us by the balls, and the investigation would go to somebody else. But what can we do to help you get out of Karachi Airport alive?'

'Let me make a phone call. Just one phone call.'

Cardenas takes out a roll of quarters from his pocket and points to a payphone across the street. 'Here, take these, and go make your call. But you try and run, and I'll shoot you myself.'

'I understand. Thank you, Detective Cardenas.'

Russo looks at Cardenas again, then unlocks Asad's handcuffs and opens the rear door for him. 'What the fuck do you think you're doing, Charlie?'

'This is bullshit, Tony. I'm not the Don's fucking errand boy. They wanna kill him, they can find him on their own. If he gets away in Karachi, then good luck to him.'

'He's not exactly Mother-fucking-Teresa, Charlie. He's a cold-blooded killer, he *was* the Don's cold-blooded killer till a month ago.'

'I know that. And if they get him, maybe he had it coming to him. But I'm not going to gift-wrap him and hand him over on a plate just because Simon Sole wants it done that way. They'll probably find him and kill him whether we let him make a phone call or not. But maybe, just maybe, he gets away. And then we have a valuable ally to help us nail the Don over here.'

Asad returns to the car, and they resume their journey without further comment. Approaching the turn for JFK Airport, Russo finally turns towards Asad. 'Can I ask you a question?'

'Of course. You want to know who I called?'

'No, actually I'd rather not know that. All the years you worked for the Don, all the people you killed, all the other bad things you did, you ever feel any remorse?'

Asad Haider looks out of the car window and thinks about the question for a moment. Then he turns and looks Russo straight in the eye. 'No. Never.'

'At least you're honest, I'll give you that. Here's my card. If you survive, and if you still want to nail the Don, give me a call.'

12

ASAD

Seventeen hours on a plane gives you plenty of time to be introspective. Especially if you are pretty certain that you will be killed the moment you reach your destination. Asad Haider watches his fellow passengers eat the nauseating, reheated food, trying to sleep on uncomfortable seats, flooding the toilets and attempting to watch the inflight movie with headphones that don't work, and wishes he could join in with them.

Instead, he thinks about Anthony Russo's question. He didn't lie when he said he had never had remorse for his victims. Well, not until he found himself lying on a hospital bed fighting for his life. He may remember all of their faces, but he would be lying to himself if he said he had ever hesitated for a moment when killing them, or ordering their deaths. For him, each crime was a bureaucratic task, to be carried out efficiently, and for an appropriate compliance report to be generated to the Don. It wasn't as if all the victims were unknown to him. Many of the Party workers that were sentenced by him for the smallest infringements were very well known to him.

And of course, there was the murder of Imam. Imam, with his wild, electro-shock hairstyle, pointed goatee and pince-nez glasses perched on his sharp angular nose, always dressed in a crumpled sherwani and tight churidar pyjamas that made his legs appear as if they were white sticks, looking like a veritable Lucknowi Trotsky. Imam the thinker, who constructed the Party's ideology, but bitterly opposed the cult of violence that Asad and the Don embraced as the Party grew. Imam had dared to soar as high as the Don. He was extremely popular with the Party rank and file, in many cases, even more than the Don. That was why he had to be brought down. And that was why it had to be a deep dark secret, known only to Asad and the Don.

Asad had always detested Imam for his intellectual airs and graces and his smug self-righteousness. And he knew Imam hated him. But he also understood that no matter how much they held each other in contempt, they were two sides of the same coin: Imam the humane face of the Party, and Asad the nasty underbelly you prayed you would never get to see. It is even more ironic that both are now victims of the Party they spawned.

He recalls the day the Don finally voiced what he had secretly felt for a long time. It was a hot afternoon, and the two of them were alone on the rooftop of Darul Sakoon. As the Party grew into a behemoth, Mohammed Ali Pichkari's simple two-storey lower-middle-class house was converted into the Party secretariat, with all the trappings of power. To get away from the legions of ward bosses asking for instruction, ministers wanting to pay their respects and civil servants petitioning for lucrative postings, the Don would resort to spending evenings on the roof. It was an old-fashioned mohalla rooftop, with the cool evening air blowing amidst the drying clothes hung on a washing line. In those early days, the Party had not yet taken over the buildings surrounding Darul Sakoon as they would do later on, so the Don still had regular neighbours. The buildings were so close together, he would often look into their houses as he strolled on the rooftop.

'Do you know anything about training pigeons?' Back then, the Don had developed an interest in raising pigeons and a number of pigeon coops had been placed on the roof.

'What? No, Don, the only thing I know about pigeons is that they shit on you a lot. Why would I know how to train them?'

'Someone in your family must have raised pigeons back in Lucknow. Kabooterbazi was a pastime for nobles back then. I really enjoy these birds. But I still haven't figured out how to train them to be carrier pigeons. Find out from Nani Amma if there's someone who can teach me how to do that. It has something to do with clipping their wings.'

'I will ask her. Is this why you summoned me?'

'Interesting. That pigeons need to have their wings clipped. I think all of us should have our wings clipped once in a while. Some *more* than others. Some people feel that just because they set up the organizational structure of this Party, they have a right to constantly question and second-guess me. That's not good.' He had paused and looked at Asad. 'It almost makes me think that someone who does that so regularly is like an actor, taking direction from *somewhere else*.'

'Imam? He's a chutiya, but he would never get in bed with the Agencies. Would he?'

'They promise you the world. It is easy to get swayed. Especially if you are ambitious and vain, like Imam.'

'You really think so?'

'They would like nothing better than to get rid of me, because I don't always go along with what they want. And Imam would like nothing more than to have to manage this Party without me in his way. Common interest makes the strangest of bedfellows.'

'What do you want me to do?'

'What you always do to protect the Party.' Having announced his momentous verdict, the Don had immediately changed the topic. 'But forget this for now, this isn't the only reason I called you here. Look here, the Flower Seller's Association made me this gigantic bouquet of the rarest flowers in the city.'

On a small table there had been the most exquisite bouquet Asad had ever seen, with lilies, tube roses, orchids and marigolds. 'Don bhai, thank you, but what will I do with these flowers?'

'Well, for one thing, you can give them to that travel agent you're fucking. What's her name, Mumtaz?'

'How do you know about her?'

'I run this fucking city, you think I don't know who my security chief has fallen for? Especially when the romance began at one of our jalsas? Now when are you going to make an honest woman out of her? I mean, you've been going out longer than we've been in government. So, what's your problem?'

'If it were up to me, I'd marry her tomorrow. It's Nani Amma. She won't accept me marrying someone who's not Shia.'

'Have you spoken with her?'

'Well, no. I, uh, I'm a bit scared to raise the issue. You know how devout she is. In her eyes, me saying I want to marry a Sunni is as bad as saying I want to marry a gori.'

The Don had broken into uproarious laughter. 'You know, if anyone outside this room were to find out that Asad Haider, the Party's much feared Head of Discipline, was terrified of his grandmother, we'd be dead in this city. The mullahs would come and hunt us down in our homes. For God's sake, talk to Nani Amma. Do you want me to do it? Although, on second thoughts, I'm pretty scared of her too. If she were to drag me outside the Big House by the ear, that wouldn't reflect too well on me either.'

Both men had laughed. The Don had put his arm around Asad. 'But seriously, let me know if you need me to do

something. Now go and take that girl for dinner or something.
And go to a nice place, don't take her to a fucking dhaba. Tell
them it's on me.'

That conversation summed up Asad's dysfunctional
relationship with the Don. Asad complied with both of the
man's instructions. That same night he had taken Mumtaz for a
romantic dinner at a five-star hotel. And the next morning he went
and murdered Imam. He arranged everything himself, not even
trusting Javed Gringo for this particular job. It couldn't look,
even to Party insiders, as if the Don had ordered Imam's death.
So Asad had worked a clever ruse, luring Imam for a private
meeting near Malir Cantt. He had made it sound sufficiently
conspiratorial that Imam had come alone, dispensing with his
ministerial car and police guards. Perhaps he had thought that
Asad was going to confess his own differences with the Don.

Whatever his reasons, when Imam did show up, Asad had
shot him six times, with a 9mm pistol that could conveniently be
traced as being a military issue weapon. The obvious implication,
of course, became that having been shot by such a weapon,
virtually outside the front gate of the largest army base in the
city, Imam's death had been arranged by the Agencies.

In Party circles a whispering campaign began with people
questioning what Imam had been doing alone so close to Malir
Cantt. The rumour quickly became that Imam had been in
league with the Agencies, who had killed him because of a
disagreement. It was enough to tarnish his legacy, especially
when the Don accused the Agencies of complicity in the
murder, confirming everybody's suspicions. Thus, even in his
death, Imam had proved useful, providing plenty of kindle for the
Don to set fire to, precipitating the confrontation between
the Party and the State.

What was often left unsaid about Imam's death was the
collateral damage caused by it, the peripheral lives destroyed as

surely as if by a missile fired from a drone. His wife was thrown out on to the street penniless, because unlike all of the Party's other ministers, Imam had actually never partaken in any corruption. He had never siphoned off millions for a rainy day. So that when the storm broke, the only shelter his family had was the minister's bungalow that had been allotted to him. And even that was taken away from them as quickly as possible. The Don never intervened, when all it would have taken was a raised eyebrow to stop all the injustices being perpetrated by the Party against its own creator. In fact, he had encouraged all the actions taken against Imam's family, as if killing him weren't enough. Imam and his entire family had to be wiped out from the history books.

Asad didn't follow up on what happened to them subsequently. He had heard that the wife had found a job giving private tuitions to rich kids for a while, barely making ends meet, living in a hovel somewhere in the Rafaa-e-Aam society. The children, a girl and a boy, bereft of a loving father, drifted through a life of hopelessness and despair. Asad remembered the boy well – he would on occasion play cricket with him in the gully in front of Darul Sakoon when Imam brought him along for some meeting or the other. Gringo once told him that a few years back the boy had tried to apply for a government job on the Party's quota. The job was a minor clerical one, and the boy was qualified, in fact overqualified for it. He had gone to the local ward office and requested that he be considered on the basis that his father had been a martyr of the Party. The ward boss had torn up the boy's neatly typed résumé, and given the job to the first person who was willing to pay the bid of a hundred thousand rupees. It was hard to imagine that the son of Imam, the man who had given thousands of jobs to the deserving all over the city without asking for a penny in return, could not even get an interview for a peon's job. This is what the Party did for its martyrs.

It wasn't just the Don's vindictiveness or the ward boss's avarice that were to blame. Asad had known everything and never lifted a finger to help. Because he had accepted the Don's assessment that Imam had become an enemy of the Party, and in his code all enemies had to be crushed beyond recognition and without mercy.

*

He is brought back to the present by the thump of the plane's wheels hitting the tarmac. They are in Karachi, and the next thirty minutes will decide whether he lives or dies. His fellow passengers are in a hurry to get off the plane as quickly as possible, falling over each other to get their hand luggage from the overhead compartments. He keeps sitting, weighing his options, waiting to see if his phone call has worked. At length, the stewardess, who has been incredibly obnoxious to everyone else throughout the flight, comes to him and gently asks if he is Asad Haider. When he replies in the affirmative, she asks for him to stay seated, as a wheelchair is being arranged for him. He is not sure if this is his escape plan kicking into motion or the Party's kidnap plan. Sweat beads form on his brow because he knows that if it is the Party trying to get to him, there is no way out from here. But the stewardess senses his unease, and in a low voice tells him not to worry as she is a fellow Momin. It is only then that he is reassured that this is his ploy, and not Gringo's.

The call he had made earlier from Queens was to an old Shia acquaintance of Nani Amma's who works for the Civil Aviation Authority. Asad Haider has, over the years, maintained a parallel network of sympathizers based on Nani Amma's Shia admirers. He has maintained and nurtured this network, deliberately keeping them apart from his Party accolytes, not because he ever thought that his Party would turn on him like it has, but more as an insurance policy in case the Agencies and police ever tore down the Party's network. This was his backup plan, to be able to function in the shadows, with his people placed everywhere, in all sorts of departments and businesses. Not even Gringo knows about these people. That was supposed to be the fail-safe, so that if the ward bosses, or Gringo or anybody else ever got caught, Asad's private network would remain protected. He thanks God for his foresight, as it is this secrecy that may be the only thing that keeps him alive today.

He is wheeled off the plane on the courtesy wheelchair. He is glad that the ravages of his long invalidity in the hospital are still evident in his appearance. It helps to build the fiction that he is just another ill passenger. His contact is a middle-aged, mid-ranking airport official called Shahji, who meets him in the Arrivals hall. He bends close to Asad, as if inquiring after his health, and asks if he has a hundred dollars. Asad, glad that Detectives Russo and Cardenas had returned his wallet to him before he boarded, hands Shahji three hundred. Shahji manoeuvres the wheelchair away from the main lines of passengers waiting to clear immigration and goes to the far corner of the room where there is a separate counter for VIP arrivals. He slips the hundred-dollar note inside the passport and slides it across to the immigration official. Without a second glance, the official deftly slips the note out and stamps the passport, waving Asad's wheelchair through. The entire operation takes less than a minute, and most importantly, no one recognizes Asad and nor is his arrival officially documented.

Instead of wheeling him towards the baggage claim area, Shahji wheels Asad to a door marked Restricted Access meant only for airport personnel. The wheelchair avoids all suspicion as anybody watching would assume that an airport employee was helping an invalid passenger. Once out of the main hall, the man hands Asad a woman's shuttlecock burqa that will conceal him from head to toe. Being wheeled around in the chair with the burqa on, Asad looks like any other incapacitated old woman. In short, nothing to arouse the suspicions of anybody watching.

Shahji wheels Asad past the baggage carousels, not bothering to stop to pick up any bags. Using the wheelchair as an excuse, they head towards a nondescript side door. The security guard on duty doesn't give them a second look and opens the door for them. And just like that, after a decade of exile, Asad Haider is back in the city.

13

BYRAM

Byram mops his brow with a handkerchief that has been soaked through with his sweat. The heat is unrelenting. With temperatures touching 50 degrees, this has been the hottest May in fifty years. That would be formidable enough on its own, but in Karachi one has to deal with the humidity as well. It washes over Byram, drenching him in waves of sweat. There is hardly a dry spot left on his safari shirt.

He looks up again, scanning the arrivals terminal systematically, studying every person in the crowd, and especially observing all the passengers coming out of the Arrivals gate. He spots at least thirty ward boys that have specifically been deployed to pick up Asad Haider. They're not even trying to be particularly discreet. All the ward members are wearing sunglasses, most are wearing some kind of Party identification, whether a T-shirt, a lapel pin or saffron-and-black sweatbands, and they all walk with a swagger derived from having kicked people around for years. They might as well have all come wearing 'I Heart the Don' T-shirts, thinks Byram.

The Party is out here in force today. Apart from the men posted at the Arrivals gate, Byram has seen several vehicles with official municipal government number plates and Party stickers plastered on them, stationed in the parking lot. Another couple of ward boys stand at the front of the taxi queue, checking everybody who gets into a cab. It's all informal, of course. These men have no official authority to do anything, but their T-shirts, with the Don's face on them, are enough to dissuade anybody from objecting to their actions. And the collective aura of menace they exude ensures that regular passengers try and keep their distance. It's clear that Javed Gringo isn't taking any chances today.

Neither is Guddu, who is as invested in keeping Asad Haider alive as Gringo is in killing him. Which is why he has insisted that Byram go to the airport personally to make contact with Asad. Byram had tried to avoid this, suggesting that Guddu should get someone else to go. Perhaps Ali Raza, the Shia leader who is Asad's childhood friend. But Guddu was adamant about Byram's going, arguing that anybody else would stand out like a sore thumb. Besides, who would suspect an eighty-year-old man at the airport would have anything to do with one of the city's most notorious killers.

Apart from the professional risks, Byram has very personal reasons for not wanting to be here right now. He feels his heart thumping in his chest. The heat and the tension aren't good for his condition, but Byram knows that somehow he must get through this. And not just the immediate situation. He is going along with Guddu's plan, but he still doesn't know what he will do when he comes face to face with the man who destroyed his son. He takes a pill from a small packet in his pocket and chases it down with a big sip from a mineral water bottle. He tells himself that he only has to hold out a little longer, do this for the greater good. And then once all this is over, he can join Freny again.

Guddu's plan is a simple one. His trusted Special Branch staff inside the airport will be alerted when Asad's flight lands. They will identify him and discreetly bring him out to Byram. Nothing simpler.

Too simple for Byram. Which is why he rejects the plan. Guddu may trust his Special Branch men, but Byram doesn't. Everybody in this city is scared of the Party, scared enough to even violate the instructions of their boss. It risks exposure, and besides, if Byram knows Asad Haider as well as he thinks he does, Asad would never go along with such a ploy. He would know, after the circumstances of his ejection from New York, that the Party would have put out a strong fielding for him as soon as he landed. He would never trust one of Guddu's Special Branch men. Or anyone else for that matter. Asad Haider knows he is landing behind enemy lines, and no one is to be trusted. Which is why he would have devised an alternative escape plan for himself. Some way in which he could get past the horde of Party workers without being detected. He is not sure how Asad Haider will manage to do this, but he assumes that Asad must have sources, other than the Party's network, working for him. It would be the smart thing, and the one thing Asad Haider has always been over all these years is smart. Until now, he has proven himself to be a masterful player in the deadly game that is Karachi politics.

And so Byram waits. And watches. Standing on one side of the Arrivals gate, pretending to be just another family member waiting to receive a passenger, he looks at the people standing around him, trying to detect something, anything, out of the ordinary. The heat seems to have sapped the energy out of the entire landscape, and people standing around the entrance seem to be going about their business almost in slow motion.

The girl is here as well, sent by Guddu to be another inconspicuous aid for him. It's the first time she has been on an operation like this one. Although she stands silently next to him, Byram can feel her body is taut with nervous tension. She daubs the perspiration from her upper lip with the corner of her dupatta, and her eyes flit around nervously, taking everything in, especially the Party thugs. But the good thing is, she doesn't complain. About the heat, or the risk. Besides, her presence further solidifies his cover as just another old man come to pick up a son or daughter coming back from overseas.

He closes his eyes for thirty seconds to steady himself. Then he opens them again and focuses on the crowd once more. He still doesn't know exactly what he's looking for, but he keeps scanning, looking for something out of the normal. And then he sees it. Just for an instant, but that is long enough. Something inside him tells Byram he has found his man.

What he sees is an old woman in a burqa being escorted out of a side door at Arrivals, universally ignored by both the airport security staff and the Party's ward boys. And indeed, there is no need to pay her any attention. She's just an old woman in a wheelchair, after all. But there is something about her that doesn't quite fit. Her frame is bulky, straining against the material of the burqa. Byram can see it even with her sitting. It doesn't gel with her otherwise frail appearance. What intrigues him even more is why she has been brought out of a side door rather than the main gate. There is nothing in the main exit that impedes wheelchairs. Indeed, as he watches this curious pair, two other women in wheelchairs come out of the main exit. To get a side door opened like that, especially in the present security environment, would require connections. The sort of connections a man like Asad Haider might have perhaps?

Byram nudges the girl and silently bids her to follow him. The woman and the man pushing the chair take a circuitous route into the parking lot, momentarily turning towards the taxi queue, and then turning away at the sight of the ward boys checking the line. They meander their way into the middle of the parking lot, away from any Party personnel. Byram is still unsure if his instinct is correct, and for a moment the thought crosses his mind that by abandoning his observation post in the Arrivals area, he has taken a big risk, especially if this woman turns out to be a red herring and Asad Haider slips out while he is here in the parking lot. But then he catches a glimpse of her shoes. As the man parks the wheelchair and walks away, the hem of the woman's burqa rises from her ankle as she turns to watch the man go. And Byram can see that the footwear she has isn't ladylike at all. It isn't a heel, it isn't a sandal, or a plimsole, it's a man's patent leather Oxford. That's when he knows his hunch was right.

Byram quickens his pace, dragging the girl with him and pointing out the old woman to her. The woman has been abandoned in her wheelchair, and Byram isn't sure if that is permanent or temporary. He doesn't want to wait to find out. As they approach the wheelchair, Byram nervously pats his trouser pocket, and feels the sharp edge of the kitchen knife. He feels the cold steel and it sends a shiver down his spine. The knife is his insurance policy, to ensure Asad's compliance. At least that's what he's told himself. For a millisecond he thinks about using it, once and for all putting an end to Asad Haider's life. It would be so easy, gutting him in the neck and walking away. After all, this is the man who is the embodiment of everything that is wrong with the Party and with this city. The man whose downfall he has plotted for years, whose death he has fantasized about. What a relief that would be. For about five minutes. And then what? Byram knows Asad is not the problem. It is the system that has spawned him, the Party that nurtured him, and the man who for all these years has controlled his life and that of countless others from thousands of miles away, callously making choices about who should live and who should die.

The girl reaches the wheelchair first and asks the old woman if she requires a lift. The woman in the chair is startled, not expecting someone to come up and speak to her. It takes her a moment to respond and she does so in a voice that is barely audible.

'Asad Haider, saala, I know it's you. Don't try and hide it. I am here to tell you that your Party is searching every inch of this airport to find you. You know the Don has ordered your death. The fellow who helped you, how much more will he risk for your sake? He has gotten you till here. Only we can get you out of this airport. Now don't make a fuss and let the girl push you towards our car. Come quietly, or I swear I'll alert the Party goondas myself and leave you to die in this bhenchod parking lot.'

'Who are you?'

'You don't need to know our names. All you need to know is that we are the people you have been hunting for years, and right now we are the only thing keeping you alive in this city. Now get in the car.'

14

ISMAIL

Baba and I had three months to win the Soldier Bazaar by-election and break the myth of the Party. Three months, and not even a candidate to start with, and against the most ruthless electoral machine in South Asia. Forget all these BJP Modi–Shodi types in India, or the Begums of Bangladesh. People think they are ruthless, but the United Front would run circles around all these people with their sheer bloodthirstiness.

If there is one thing that the United Front can claim credit for it is perfecting the art of stealing elections. Twenty-five years of unbroken success in elections in this city meant that the Party had fine-tuned its tactics into an art form. Other political parties activated their election cells a few months before an election and then packed them up immediately after the results were announced. The Party's cell operated through the year, 24/7. It was constantly updating voter lists, analysing voting trends, monitoring, through the wards, which ethnic group had moved into which locality and whether or not this was an opportunity or a risk. If new migrants were thought to be beneficial, they were courted, with the ward assisting them in settling in and immediately registering their votes. However, if a community was thought to be against the Party, then they were targeted. Their members were threatened and assaulted, and occasionally targeted and killed. The Party's lawyers challenged the establishment of their abadis in the courts, while the wards made life hell for them by denying them municipal amenities. Until, of course, that community finally swore allegiance to the Don.

Two nights before election day, the local ward always collected the ID cards of all new voters in the area. Their votes were then cast by the Party's proxies, and if anyone had a problem giving up their ID card, or was overly enthusiastic about exercising their right to vote themselves, they ended up in hospital. According to the electoral rolls, even I had voted for the Party several times. Or at least the man with my ID card had.

This was how the Party had kept its grip on the city for so long. On top of all this, the United Front was in government, which meant they could use the entire machinery of police, civil administration, returning officers, everyone, to ensure that they won. But I had a plan.

There are a few rules for success in electoral politics. They are as follows:

a. Find an exceedingly charismatic candidate – or, failing that, an exceedingly dull candidate that you can control completely.
b. Have lots of cash to spend.
c. Always be on attack, rather than defence. If an allegation is to be made, better for you to make it first, no matter how outrageous it may seem. Most are true anyway.
d. Make sure the voters know that your use of 'power politics' is more effective than your opponents'.

For point (a), if you don't have someone really famous, then it's better to go for a total unknown, someone picked randomly from obscurity. Voters sympathize with someone who has come from their background. It makes them think that perhaps one day they too can become an MNA or MPA. They are chutiyas, I know. But that's politics.

So I settled upon a fellow called Faisal Nagori, a local businessman with nothing to recommend him except for his ownership of several popular milk shops in the locality and a desire to enter the big game. The only exceptional thing about him was his recipe for milk with almonds, for which his shops were famous. I am told that people get in line in front of his shops from six in the morning to have it every Sunday.

Even better than the popularity of his milk, was his intellectual ability, which was more or less at the same level as the buffalos from whom he got his milk. He couldn't string together a sentence when we summoned him to Afshani Galli. He thought he was going to be punished for some omission on his part, and so he kept begging Baba for forgiveness even after we had given him the good news that he was going to be our candidate. But that was just the sort of candidate I wanted. One who just did as he was told.

Having told him not to worry about anything, we sent him on his way and got down to point (b). Money was, of course, not an issue for us. Baba decreed that he would spend whatever it took to win the seat. True, the Party could call upon the resources of the government, since they were in power and this would have represented a significant hurdle for anybody else opposing the Party. But we were Lyari gangsters. If we ran short of money we just went out and stole some more.

And the advantage of a by-election like this one was that we could concentrate our resources on one constituency. We didn't have dozens of competing MPs demanding resources and assistance from the chief minister. If Nagori needed posters to be printed, we just kidnapped a printer and made him print as many as we needed. If he needed buses to transport voters, we hijacked them. The Party's problem was that though it had grown up using the same tactics as us, now that it was part of the political establishment, it couldn't afford to be as crude as us in their methods.

We accomplished point (c) on the third day of the campaign, when we sent Nagori to Soldier Bazaar police station to file an FIR against the Party's workers for having kidnapped his nephew. Now, in truth Nagori's nephew had never been kidnapped. We packed him off to Dubai for a month. But his disappearance allowed us to create an issue, alleging that the Party was trying to intimidate our candidate. At the same time, we actually kidnapped three of the Party's key constituency workers from their homes.

Because we had accused the Party of kidnapping Nagori's nephew first, their attempts to blame us for the disappearance of their workers sounded like a counter-allegation made just to respond to our charges, and the media soon lost interest. Meanwhile, the men we had kidnapped were some of the Party's most experienced activists. It unnerved the other Party workers as this kind of thing had never happened to the Party before. They had gotten so used to being the bullies in situations like this, they had no idea how to react when we started giving them a taste of their own medicine.

The Party ranted and raved, but to no avail. Their home minister instructed the police station in charge at Soldier Bazaar not to entertain our complaint. But Rauf Kaala Coat, Baba's lawyer, got a court order forcing the police to register our case. The Party's candidate, a fresh-faced IT engineer, went and registered a case naming Baba as the mastermind behind the kidnapping of the Party workers. It didn't make the slightest difference to Baba, who already had about sixty cases pending against him. Case no. 61 would be no different. As the late Jameel Jheenga had memorably remarked, to apprehend Baba the police and the Party needed to grow the balls to enter Lyari first.

The ward boss of Soldier Bazaar tried to go to one of Nagori's shops to threaten him. But when he got there some of Ghaffar Langra's boys opened fire on him, forcing him to flee with his tail between his legs. Then Nagori went and registered another case, claiming that the ward boss had tried to cause damage to his shop. Finally, even the Don got involved, recording a speech from New York, blaming his own government for failing to stop the rampant terrorism being perpetrated by Baba Dacait in the by-election campaign. That was the biggest endorsement for us, because it showed voters that we had become so powerful that the Don had to complain about us personally.

Which brings me to point (d), the use of power politics. The thing to understand about elections in Pakistan is that the voters tend to flock to the candidate who creates the perception that his power is limitless and hence his victory is inevitable. This is how the Party has held on to power for so long. It had nothing to do with its popularity or its manifesto. Election after election, it had shown everybody who was boss in this city. That was the aura of the Party's power, the mentality we had to break.

It started with rallies. If an unknown candidate starts gathering large crowds, he creates a buzz about himself. The chattering classes start chattering about the candidate's powerful institutional backers. The Agencies themselves, who it seems to me measure political support solely by counting how many people show up at a corner meeting, start revising their estimates and the candidate gets some momentum behind him. Pretty soon, the illusion becomes a reality.

No one was better at gathering crowds in this town than the Party. But we started using its own tactics – buying or bullying large numbers of people to show up at Nagori's rallies. It didn't matter what the idiot did or said at the rally, the only thing that mattered was that the powers that be saw large crowds coming to listen to our candidate. People started thinking this election was actually going to be a contest.

The next thing was wall chalking. Wall chalking is a fine and underestimated art in South Asian politics. In a city like Karachi people spend a lot of time on the road. Walking long distances from home to work and back again. Waiting long hours on the footpath for a diminishing number of buses and taxis. Or, if you are lucky enough to get into one of those horrible buses, taxis or rickshaws, you are then stuck for hours in one of the city's interminable traffic jams. So while the poor man is stuck on the road in the heat, with the sun bearing down upon him, he likes to have something to read. Not too long, after all, nobody has the time to read a newspaper article or a novel. But something short, punchy and humorous. Karachi's graffiti fills this void. It is a public service, providing the citizens with informed political opinions in single phrases. Like that thing that all the Defence–Cliftonwallahs are using on their mobile phones these days. Twitter. Wall chalking is like Twitter for the masses.

This was another area that the Party dominated. Normally, you cannot drive or walk for more than three minutes anywhere in this city without being confronted with the image of either the Don or an airplane – the Party's electoral symbol – on a poster, or sticker, or as a painted mural. At times, it feels as if the Don's sunglasses-covered eyes are watching your every step in this city.

In Soldier Bazaar, we went on the offensive. We planned it like a military operation. Late one night we sent out a platoon of plasterers and painters, guarded by a horde of gun-toting gangsters. Tearing up the Don's posters and replacing them with images of Nagori and Baba becomes a lot easier when you flood the streets with armed men. By morning, there wasn't a wall or gate left in the constituency that didn't have our poster stuck on it. So much so that even the gate of the apartment complex where the ward boss lived ended up with three of our posters plastered on it. I think the Party called him in for an explanation after that.

This was all gimmickry though. Everyone understood that the real test of power politics would come on election day. The real battle would be about which side could put in the most number of thappas in the ballot boxes. We knew, for all our efforts, that we could not stop the Party's machine from stamping thousands of fake votes. The trick was to ensure that somehow our tally of fake votes exceeded theirs. We knew that there were certain areas in the constituency, like Martin Quarters for example, which were genuine and complete Party strongholds. The polling stations were controlled by the ward, as were the polling staff, which meant that the ward boys could sit inside the polling station all day and stuff as many ballot boxes as they wished. We had to similarly take total control of the polling stations in our areas. And then we had to somehow disrupt the Party's ballot-stuffing operations.

The first task was easily achieved. The polling staff arrived on election day to find that our boys, toting their Kalashnikovs and pistols, had already taken over several polling stations. The staff was informed that they would have a very comfortable day as long as they cooperated. They happily traded in the ballot papers and special ink for a hearty breakfast, the promise of an even heartier lunch and the relative comfort of a back room where we had even temporarily installed an air conditioner for their comfort. All they had to do was sit at the polling station and verify all of the votes that we stuffed as genuine at the end of the day. So, we got to work stamping ballots. To ensure that there was no interference with our process, our men took up guard outside the station as well.

In theory, police officers are deployed outside every single polling station on election day. But on that day the poor policewallahs have only one problem in life – who will feed them. Their own bosses eat up the food charges meant for them, and the poor constables starve in the heat all day. So essentially, they can be bought for the price of a bag of biryani and a bottle of Pepsi. We gave them that and they were more than happy to sit in the shade and sleep all day. Every two hours or so, one of them would send a message on the police wireless, reporting that all was calm and voting was going on in an orderly manner.

Having secured our own polling stations, we now had to disrupt the Party's vote stuffing. The best way to do this is to ensure that some incident occurs which stops the voting process. We knew that the Party's polling stations were as well protected as ours, so it was no use sending out teams to do aerial firing in front of them, or to instigate fights in the polling camps outside the stations. The Party would be wise to these sorts of tricks already, having used them themselves for so many years. Besides, whatever else happened outside the polling station, their ballot stuffers would continue to work inside. No, we had to do something that would genuinely get them to stop.

And then I seized upon an idea. I went back to my flat in Rabia City and met with my Taliban friend, Chaaku Mehsud. For twenty petis, Chaaku agreed to lend us one of his bomb makers. He would make small, improvised bombs that would be placed near several polling stations that were Party strongholds. We would detonate the bombs remotely, thus triggering a panic that the Taliban were attacking polling stations and bringing a temporary halt to voting at those stations, while our stations ran up the score undisturbed. Chaaku didn't care, he was in it for the money. And the fact that the bombs were made by a Taliban expert was the greatest guarantee of their safety. You see, the fellow who made them was a genuine artist who understood precision and collateral damage. He wasn't some doped up Lyari Baloch who would accidentally blow up an entire building just because he didn't notice how much explosive he was putting into the bomb. In this city, if you want something done right, always go to the Taliban.

Sure enough, on election day my plan went off like clockwork. Towards the afternoon, when most people come to cast their vote, bombs went off near several United Front polling stations. A handful of people were injured in the blasts, but nothing serious. The casualties were actually lower than the average daily casualty toll in Karachi. The bombs were left in plastic shopping bags in garbage heaps outside the polling stations. They served their purpose, setting off a panic and temporarily stopping the polling, as even the Party's battle-hardened election veterans abandoned their posts and evacuated the stations. In the time it took for the bomb disposal squad to search and clear the buildings, and for the polling to restart at those polling stations, our ballot stamping operation had run up a sizeable lead. Chaaku was nice enough to even get some chutiya maulvi to claim the attack, so the blame wouldn't come on Baba.

But despite all this, come election evening, as the votes were being counted, I was nervous. I was the one who had sold this idea to Baba, and despite all our efforts I didn't know if the plan would succeed or not. And if it did not, I didn't know how much credit I had with Baba. Would a failure mean the end of my time in the gang? Or on this earth? It was thoughts like this that made me sweat even more. Our polling agents seemed confident on the phone, but then this was Karachi. Anything could happen right up till the last moment.

In my nervous state, I was chain smoking on the roof of Baba's house in Afshani Galli. When Ghaffar Langra found me, I must have been on my twentieth cigarette. He simply told me that Baba had summoned me, not revealing whether we had won or lost the election. I feared the worst when, downstairs, in his swimming pool room, Baba greeted me with a grim expression.

'Naich ...' Perhaps it was my paranoid state, but I felt Baba took my name in an accusatory manner. 'We've won. We've fucking won, you brilliant bhenchod!'

I collapsed into a chair with relief. Baba turned up the volume of the TV, which was reporting the stunning upset victory of Faisal Nagori over the Party's candidate. The anchorperson on the channel said that the reason for the defeat was most likely the bomb blasts which had deterred voters from coming to vote. The fact that they had happened so unexpectedly took the Party by surprise and they hadn't had enough time to organize a response.

'Naich, have you ever drunk beer? Here, try this, it's imported, it's called Hine-Kin. You deserve it. But what do we do now?'

I had barely collected my thoughts as I caught the green can that Baba had flung at me. It opened with a refreshing pop, and as I took my first sip, even though I knew nothing about beer, I knew that this Hine-Kin, or whatever it was, was good. The alcohol and the sound of exploding fireworks as the celebrations began brought back my confidence. 'Now, Baba, you watch. This is just the beginning. I will make you the biggest leader in this city since the Don himself. First, we get old Yousaf Chandio to honour his pledge. Have you ever thought of becoming a senator?'

Baba laughed heartily and took a swig from his can. 'Actually, I have.'

15

ANTHONY

After six weeks of surveillance, they get their man. Six weeks of mind-numbing, round-the-clock stakeouts, using six different officers positioned close to the Party's Coney Island Avenue headquarters. The one thing that Russo and Cardenas have learnt in these six weeks is that this is no ordinary political party. These people understand this business, and take counter-measures that could have come from the CIA's playbook. The Party deploys watchers all over the neighbourhood, forcing the team to constantly change location and appearance in order to avoid detection. It's a real pain changing vehicles and covers every day – using a cable repair van one day and a produce delivery truck the next.

It's a miracle this operation has lasted this long. Chief Esposito's intervention gets them the manpower and technical support without the bosses asking too many questions, but you never know how long that's going to last. It's a credit to the skill with which Tony Russo has run the entire operation that they have managed to fly under the radar, avoiding detection from the Party as well as the bureaucratic wrath of their own bosses who seemed quite content to accept Simon Sole's logic about this case without question. Tony has worked like a man possessed, never taking a single day off during the last six weeks, working fifteen–eighteen-hour shifts. Even when he is away from Coney Island Avenue, Cardenas knows that he's been at the precinct, trying to put together other pieces of the puzzle. Cardenas has never seen Anthony Russo so consumed by a case.

It is Tony's idea to follow the Don's bodyguards. He is convinced that the key to get to him is through them. The Don doesn't spend a moment without them. But the problem is, they all seem to be boy scouts. They conduct themselves with the discipline of the former Spetsnaz troopers that they are. No drinking on the job, no illegal display of firearms, not even jumping a red light. Nothing that would allow them to be entrapped by the cops.

All, except one. Tony calls him Alexei the pimp. This is because he's the one responsible for bringing girls to and from the Don's apartment. Three days a week he brings the Don's 'nurse' around. Cardenas is sceptical about her even being a nurse, because she comes dressed in a nurse's outfit that looks like it was purchased in a sex shop. And Cardenas doesn't know of any New York hospitals that get their nurses to dress like 1950s' sluts. But that's just Alexei's day job. Every night he brings a girl to the apartment for the Don. On Saturdays, he brings two. They are almost always Latinas, except for Thursdays, when the girl is a demure Oriental.

Procuring the women isn't what gets Alexei into trouble. Russo and Cardenas run a check on the escort agency supplying the girls. Very high class. Thousand dollars a night. Alexei isn't exactly soliciting on the corner of Broadway and 42nd Street. But what makes Alexei stand out, and what ultimately also leads to his downfall, is his demeanour. For Alexei, unlike his other colleagues, is a cheerful guy. Too cheerful. He has the sort of bubbly personality that can only be procured through a few grams a day of Bolivia's finest exports. That's what gets him busted. After playing it straight for six weeks, he makes one mistake. Running low on his supply, he places a call to a dealer who does deliveries, not realizing that his cell phone is being monitored. The dealer shows up for the drop in a very respectable-looking Toyota Prius on the corner of Prospect Park to find a phalanx of uniformed officers, and Alexei with his face in the gravel and his hands cuffed behind his back. He doesn't look too happy any more.

Russo and Cardenas give the drug bust to the local narcotics squad as a favour, but keep Alexei for themselves. They let him cool his heels in a holding room for five hours, where officers question him only about the drugs and nothing else. Then, just when the pressure has built up to breaking point and Alexei looks like he is about to start crying like a baby, Russo and Cardenas step in.

'Alexei Melikishvili. Is it Alexander or Alexei?'

He recognizes them immediately, from their earlier interview with the Don, and suddenly the perspiration on his forehead goes into overdrive. 'I … I know you …'

'Yeah, yeah, I get that a lot. People say I look like Jose Calderon of the Knicks. But that isn't important. What's more important is that we know you, Alexei. We know you've been a naughty boy. But, let's put it this way. Maybe we can help you out, if you help us out.'

'Help you with what?'

'Tell us about the Don.'

An expression of absolute physical terror sweeps across Alexei's face. 'No, no, I cannot. It iz my job, ve have to be discreet, ve cannot talk about client … I signed non-disclosure agreement. They can sue me.'

'Non-disclosure agreements don't cover criminal activity. But if that's the way you feel, we understand. Good luck getting a job in private security with a rap sheet that has you for possession of 200 grams of coke. I think there might be a mall in Peramis that'll hire you.'

'You would tell … but I have unblemished record at work.'

'I'm sure you do. But we did some digging on your firm. I don't think they want to attract any attention. Considering that their only client is the United Front Party. And we know the Don doesn't want any kind of negative publicity. Certainly not the kind that he'll get from one of his bodyguards getting busted for drugs. All sorts of questions. Like, were the drugs just for the bodyguard or for others as well? You can see how this doesn't end happily for you. Tell you what, you have a think about this. We'll be outside the door if you need us.'

Russo and Cardenas walk out of the precinct to a diner across the street, where Detective Gary Li, another member of their team, has already commandeered a booth. Within five minutes of sitting down, they receive a message that the suspect wants to talk. Russo ignores the beeper, preferring to concentrate on his cheeseburger.

'What do you figure, Tony?'

'Let him sweat for an hour more. Get him real nervous, the sort of shitting-your-pants nervous. Then we go in and have a chat and use him to nail the fucking Don.'

'You've really got a hard-on for this guy. What gives, Tony? Is this a race thing? You don't like Pakistanis after 9/11 or something? Hey, you can be honest with a spic and a gook sitting in front of you.' Detective Li chuckles at his joke, while Cardenas looks more contemplatively at his partner.

Russo puts down his burger and wipes his ketchup-covered fingers on a napkin before answering. 'No, it's not a racial thing, Gary. It's an attitude thing. I don't like people like the Don and his Party.'

Li chuckles again. 'So what you're saying is, you don't like politicians.'

Russo smiles indulgently. 'When I was a kid, my old man was a dock worker. He used to work his ass off and they'd pay him peanuts. Every payday, they'd line up and the foreman would hand them over their salary in cash. Right next to the foreman would be this other guy, wearing a broad-rimmed hat and an expensive suit. All the dock workers would receive their pay packets and immediately turn around and give that guy a share of their hard-earned salary. He was a mob guy, and they had a finger in every piece of action that went on at the docks. Nobody could do nothin' about it. That's just the way it was. I used to go down there sometimes, to pick up my Dad, and I saw this going on every time. This prick in the suit never worked a day in his life. But he thought he could intimidate his way into making a living off other people's hard work. People like that piss me off. They think they're untouchable because they've got so many levers to pull. The United Front and the Don, they're exactly like that mob guy. They believe they're above the law, and they prey on the weak and helpless. On top of it, this asshole comes to America and thinks he can continue to pull the same shit over here as he was doing in Pakistan. Like I said, I don't like the attitude.'

When Russo and Cardenas get back to the precinct an hour later, Alexei is indeed a nervous wreck. Sitting in an antiseptic interview room in the police station, where the only smell is that of his body odour – vodka mixed with sweat – and the only sound is the tapping caused by his leg shaking uncontrollably against the metal table, he can barely control himself. Rivulets of perspiration fall off his wide, balding head onto his now crumpled shirt and tie. He looks up with trepidation as Russo and Cardenas enter the room.

'How are you, Alexei? Had enough time to think things over?'

'Yes, Detective. I cooperate. But pleez, you must keep my cooperation secret. Discretion iz very important in our business. If thiz gets out, I never get another job az bodyguard.'

'Don't worry, Alexei. We'll keep our little chat very hush-hush. We just want to verify some facts from you. We don't want you to get in trouble with your Russian countrymen.'

'They are not my countrymen. I am Georgian. Polizman in Georgia, like you. Not Russian mafia FSB thug like others.' Alexei spits vehemently on the floor.

'So why do you work with them if you don't like 'em?'

'Money waz very good. Two thousand dollars a day for each man on Don's detail. Plus, I was on deliveries, I got tips from him for that too. He iz very good employer, Mr Don.'

'What all were you delivering?'

'The Don doesn't like to go out. He doesn't even meet too many people. So he likez everything home delivered. So it waz my job to get the fun stuff. Girls and drugs. He has strange working hours, because he iz speaking to Pakistan. So, he wants girls at four in the morning. It'z my job to ensure he gets what he wants. Iz not easy. He has very specific taste and requirements.'

'What do you mean?'

'Well, he wants Hispanic girls only. Brown with big breasts. It reminds him of Pakistani women. I had to find escort agency that has large stock of Hispanic women. And that iz open for business at all hours. Luckily, with the amount of money he pays, people are willing to accommodate.'

'What about the Oriental girl on Thursdays?'

Alexei laughs proudly. 'Ah yez, Chinese Thursdays. My suggestion, to change menu once a week.'

'What about the nurse, she a hooker too?'

'No, to best of my knowledge, she iz genuine nurse. Therapist. He just likez her to wear revealing uniform when she iz around.'

'And I take it the drugs that you got busted with weren't just for your personal consumption. Some of those were for the Don too?'

'Yez. He sleeps very little, he needs pick-me-up. He likes to do coke when he wakes up in the afternoon. He does it with his drink, vodka and Pakola.'

'What the fuck is Pakola?'

'Iz Pakistani soft drink. Green in colour. Party gets special supply shipped in, just for Don. He only has vodka with Pakola. Never anything else.'

'Is there a stash of coke lying in his apartment? If we have a probable cause to search, will we find some?'

'Oh no. He iz very careful. Only takes what he uses immediately. Stash iz kept with Raja, his secretary. Raja also snorts, secretly, never in front of Don. Raja keeps everything, makes all payments. All in cash. Even ve get paid in cash.'

'He must need a lot of cash to make all these payments. So where does he get it?'

'Oh, cash no problem for Party. They get shipment. Every three days. From Pakistan. Bagman, he bring plenty of greenbacks in gym bag.'

'Wait a minute. How much money comes in and how often?'

'I don't know how much. All I know iz, every Tuesday and Saturday, ve go to JFK to pick him up and bring him to Raja. Bag iz filled with money, big wads of dollars.'

'And Mr Raja runs the entire operation?'

'Yez, he keep all accounts.'

'Let me ask you something, Alexei. How come you boys have never been tempted to hijack the cash on one of your airport excursions?'

'Oh no, no. Why ve would do that? Nothing better than working for Party. They pay well, I am becoming wealthy man wery fast.'

'Tell us more about the bagman. Same guy?'

'Different guy on Tuesdays, different on Saturdays. Sometimes, there is third guy when other two are on vacation.

But not more than that. Iz sensitive job. He take direct flight from Karachi.'

'Well, it's your lucky day, Alexei. It's Tuesday today, so you get to ride with us to JFK and identify the bagman.'

'But you say you only want information. What if someone spots me? This is more than information.'

'What this is beginning to look like, Alexei, is a criminal conspiracy. And if you don't come with us, then you're obstructing an investigation into a criminal conspiracy. Your possession charge is gonna look like small potatoes compared to this. Don't worry about being spotted. We'll take you inside, real quiet. Ever seen the restricted parts of JFK Airport? You'll love it.'

The direct Pakistan Airlines flight from Karachi lands two hours later. With Alexei in tow, the bagman is identified within minutes. He is a nondescript fellow, as all good bagmen should be, with a receding hairline and spectacles. He is dressed in a plain shirt and jeans, with a baggy jacket in his hand, devoid of any kind of flashiness that would make him stand out in a crowd. His only hand luggage is a gym bag, as Alexei said.

Russo and Cardenas have him pulled in for secondary questioning, but he seems unfazed by that. After all, half the men on this flight go in for secondary questioning. It's only when he is asked to unzip his bag that panic sweeps over his face.

Sure enough, the search reveals, under a pile of old clothes, neatly stacked piles of hundred-dollar bills. The customs agent conducting the search informs them that the amount is exactly $10 less than the $10,000 maximum that is allowed by law.

'What do you reckon, Charlie?'

'I think somebody knows US customs laws very well to ensure that he comes in just under the maximum mandated limit. But the problem is, we've got nothing on him now. He can walk out of here and laugh in our faces. What do we do now?'

Russo stares at the open gym bag, with the stacked currency notes clearly visible inside it. Suddenly, he takes out his wallet, withdraws a $20 bill, and drops it into the bag. 'Well, let's just help our friend over the limit, and see how cooperative he is when he's told he is in violation of US currency laws.'

'Tony, what are you doing, man?'

'Relax, Charlie, I got this. These assholes aren't getting off on a technicality.'

It takes the bagman about forty-six seconds to start spilling everything once he is taken in for questioning. He's still talking four hours later when Cardenas leaves the interview room to join Russo outside. It's past midnight, but it is a balmy New York night, and the air feels oppressive, pregnant with humidity. It's the sort of night that makes New Yorkers wish for the bone-chilling cold of mid-January.

'He still talking?' Russo smokes his cigar, filling the air with the rich smell of Cuba's finest tobacco.

'Yup. He's shitting himself. Thinks he's going to Guantanamo. Especially after the customs guys discovered another ten grand hidden in secret compartments in that jacket of his. We should have looked harder, you could have saved your twenty bucks.' Cardenas stretches and loosens his tie ever so slightly, his only acknowledgement of the heat.

'So, who's he giving up?'

'He says he works at the Party headquarters in Karachi. His only job is to bring the money. They picked him because he has family in the States, so it looks natural for him to make such frequent visits. Got a brother in Jersey city, and a sister in Chicago.'

'Where's the money coming from?'

'Raja's brother keeps the accounts in Karachi. It's all dirty money. The Party's ministers drop off the Don's share from the kickbacks they receive. The ward bosses deposit their shares of extortion payments from the city. The accountant converts the money into dollars, and sends our friend in there on his field trips.'

'But why the fuck wouldn't they use hawala or something like that to get the money here?'

'Well, that's the other interesting part. They use that as well, and they use regular bank transfers too. But they use those methods for official Party funds. This arrangement is for the Don's money. He wants his cash in his hands, not in some bank. And get this. The courier arrangement allows Raja and the accountant to skim off the top. They cook the books. The Don usually accepts whatever Raja tells him, and even if he or anyone else were to check, they wouldn't be able to trace anything, 'coz there's so much money coming in from everywhere, no one knows what the fuck is going on. No paper trail. They're robbing the Don blind and he doesn't even know it. They give the couriers a piece of the action to keep them quiet, but no one else knows.'

'And this guy was supposed to hand the money over to Raja?'

'Yeah, like Alexei said. Apparently, they keep it stashed at the Party offices. But if we go in and search the premises, that prick Simon Sole and the rest of the brass will be up our asses again. So, what do you wanna do now?'

Russo takes another drag of his cigar and smiles. 'This is where it gets interesting.'

*

'Fuck me.'

If there's one thing Tony Russo has learned over a long career, it is that if you want to stir up a shitstorm, you should do it in style. The evidence of his success in doing so is laid out in front of him, on the front pages of all three major New York newspapers. There are full-page photos in the *Post* and the *Daily News* showing a phalanx of cops raiding the Party building on Coney Island Avenue. The *Times*, ever the paper of record, has a front-page article with the headline 'Who is the Don?' The Don's two separate worlds, in Karachi and New York, have collided sharply, jolting everybody with the impact.

They're all back in Chief Esposito's office, sitting around the same polished table as they did seven weeks ago, when no one wanted to touch Asad Haider's testimony. Russo and Cardenas are there, as is the chief and the lady from the DA's office, and their borough commander and precinct captain. The only one not present is Simon Sole.

'Couldn't you have been a little less dramatic, Detective?' Santapio, the borough commander, is clearly pissed. He had been hoping, like everyone else in the room, that the problem of the Don could be simply wished away. And now it's hit them in the face with the force of a pickup truck.

Russo shrugs, enjoying watching his bosses squirm. Fuck them. 'Sir, the last time Detective Cardenas and I went there we were confronted by armed men who refused to back down despite our showing them our badges. Under the circumstances, my only option as a responsible officer was to go in heavy and take every precaution available at my disposal.'

'Was the presence of five TV channel trucks also part of your precautions?' Russo isn't sure whether Santapio is angry about the presence of the media or their presence in his absence. Everybody knows he's a showboater.

'Sir, I have no control over the the media. You know they always get tipped off whenever we do any kind of major deployment or movement in force.' Russo knows this to be a lie. In truth, tipping off the media is part of his insurance policy. He figured Simon Sole wouldn't be able to hush everything up if the press saw them recovering tons of cash from the Party offices. And that's exactly the way it played out. The city's press can't get enough of the story of how the NYPD busted an organization in Pakistan that seemed to be laundering millions of dollars and has possible links to terrorism. Money and bombs. The mother's milk of modern media.

The raid itself is wildly successful. It catches the Party by surprise. The bagman has told them where the cash is, and the look on Raja's face is priceless when they cuff him and haul out over a million dollars from the office pantry. Stored in hundreds of brown paper bags, when the money is brought out it looks as if the cops have just bought groceries for the entire precinct. The *Post*'s front page has a picture of the cops bringing the bags out, with a headline that says, in typically humorous fashion, 'Paper or Plastic?'

The woman from the DA's office nervously clears her throat. 'What about probable cause. This raid is going to cause problems.' It's clear she's crapping herself because of the calls her boss is getting from the city's top law firms, which having seen the stash of cash coming out of Coney Island Avenue, are just lining up to get a piece of this case.

'We got a tip-off related to our murder investigation that led us to detain an individual at JFK, who was bringing in illegal amounts of money into the country. His information led us straight here, and he was proved to be correct. Mr Raja, the Don's secretary, who was arrested from the premises yesterday, could not give a reasonable explanation as to the origins of the $1,062,436 that was discovered at the location. These recoveries substantiate the testimony recorded earlier by Asad Haider. I think that counts as very reasonable probable cause to support our investigation, which is increasingly pointing to an international criminal conspiracy, involving the commission of crimes by the United Front, at the behest of their leader, the Don, both in Pakistan and right here in New York. I don't think the Don's fat-cat lawyers can have any objection to any of this. What would you have us do? Give the money back?'

The lawyer is taken aback by Cardenas's vitriol and is momentarily stunned into silence.

Russo nods benevolently. 'Besides, what are you worried about, Counsellor? This is a great case as far as the DA is concerned. You get to show that your boss is a crusader against terror financing. I would think that would put his next election in the bag, as well as a future run for the governor's mansion in Albany. Christmas came early for you guys, right?'

For the first time, Russo's comment makes Chief Esposito smile. 'All right. It's decided then. Keep working the case, Detectives, and do what you gotta do to solve the murder. That is all, good job, men.'

'Sir, the CIA has some objections to the, uh, tactics used by the officers. And they still have some questions about whether or not this Don character is going to be arrested.'

Chief Esposito looks at Santapio with cold, dead eyes. 'Nick, I don't recall the CIA having jurisdictional responsibility for investigating crimes in the city of New York. When they get those powers, then we can have a talk. Till then, the detectives will use whatever tactics are appropriate to work this case out.'

The chief's cold response shuts Santapio up in a hurry, and everyone shuffles out of the meeting room. Russo breathes a sigh of relief as he steps out of the office suite. His gambit of raising the media profile of the case and turning it into a political football to keep the CIA out has worked.

'Good job, Tony.' Cardenas fist bumps Russo in the hallway, out of sight of their bosses. Then, out of the corner of their eyes, they spot Simon Sole walking towards them, looking pissed. For the first time, he seems to have lost his cool. Russo decides he is definitely going to enjoy this encounter, despite the fact that Sole standing at his full six feet four inch height, poking a finger at his chest is an intimidating sight.

'You fucking flatfoot pricks. You think you pulled a fast one? You think you can piss all over us like this and embarrass us?'

'Why Simon, whatever are you talking about? Surely, you know how much Charlie and I share your spirit of inter-agency cooperation?' The smirk on Russo's face just makes Sole more pissed.

'Inter-agency cooperation, my ass. You gave the *New York Times* the story about the Don's links with the CIA. It's all in there, the Namakzai hit, everything. You fucking gave it to them to humiliate the Don.'

'Simon, in case you didn't notice, we've been a bit busy counting all the Don's illegally laundered cash. Besides, any half-decent reporter could have made those connections. It's not like you guys have been very subtle in hiding your links to the United Front. I also hear Asad Haider gave your death squads the slip in Karachi. For all we know he could have called this one in over the phone, just like the Don does.'

'You can't arrest him. It'll be a disaster for the Party in Karachi. And on what fucking grounds? You don't have a fucking case.'

'Listen Simon, in case you haven't figured this out yet, I don't give a flying fuck about whether or not the Don feels humiliated or whether you think I have a case or not. And as far as our investigation is concerned, we will do whatever it takes, whether that means arresting him, or arresting you. So do me a favour, take your finger out of my chest and shove it right up your ass. All the way up. And tell your buddy to start packing. I'm having a real nice cell prepared for him on Ryker's Island.'

And that, thinks Russo as he walks away, has been the most gratifying part of the last two days.

16

ASAD

Sadia Ali wishes she could die. She hasn't slept all night, praying, hoping that the arrival of the cool morning will wash away her ills. The morning does arrive and brings its coolness, but it does not bring the relief Sadia seeks. The last two weeks, leading up to last night, have been torture for her. Throughout that period, she has known this moment was approaching. Indeed, at some level she has perhaps understood its inevitability for the past two months, but that doesn't make it any easier.

It has been two months since Asad Haider's arrival here in the Dinshaw house in Katrak Colony. Two months in which circumstance has thrown together these three strangest of allies, forcing them to live under one roof. Guddu had felt that the most nondescript hiding place for Asad would be at Byram's. And to help Byram, and to monitor Asad, Guddu also has Sadia placed here. So a cover story is constructed in which Asad is supposedly an extra hand, hired by Byram as a nightwatchman and general handyman to watch the parts of the house that lie empty. Byram also temporarily lets go of his son's nurse, so Sadia has a reason to stay in the house 24/7.

But while Guddu's plans seem sound in theory, their practise is very different. Sadia has seen the pain etched on Byram's face every single day for these last two months. Sitting with Asad, explaining to him who they are and what their mission is, giving him food and shelter, all the time knowing that the man sitting across him is responsible for destroying his son's life. Even worse, knowing that one phone call would solve his problem, would guarantee him the satisfaction of seeing this evil man suffer as cruel a fate as he has forced upon Cyrus Dinshaw.

Asad, for his part, is quiet, taking everything in, trying to piece together the puzzle. Part of that is because he is still recovering from his injuries. Thinking as he used to do, using what the Don called his 'shaitani dimaag', his devil's mind, is much harder now. One of the first observations that Byram feeds back to Guddu is that the physical and mental trauma inflicted by the Don on Asad Haider may have had a permanent effect. He may never again be the man he once was.

But another reason for Asad's slowness in piecing things together is deliberate. He has not been told everything, on grounds of operational security. He only knows that Sadia and Byram belong to the Others, the group that has sworn to avenge itself on the Party. And on the principle of an enemy's enemy being one's friend, they are his allies. But Guddu has forbidden them to reveal their personal histories, and he has forbidden them to reveal his identity. So Asad does not know who the cranky old man's son is, nor does he know that the pretty young girl who conducts herself with a maturity and confidence well beyond her years is the sister of the famous Inspector Dilawar Khan. All he sees is the pain in their eyes.

Sadia also now knows that Asad is not the ogre she has imagined him to be. She realizes this the first week he is here. Walking alone in Byram's garden one night, she hears wailing. It comes from the abandoned downstairs portion of the house where Asad has been given a room. Following Guddu's instructions to be observant of everything, she approaches the room and spies him crying like a baby, calling out the name of his grandmother. Perhaps she is naive, but she cannot understand how a man who weeps so earnestly for his grandmother can be the cold-blooded killer everyone says he is.

She watches him cry like that every night. Guddu has told her to befriend him. Contemplating that task becomes easier when she sees him lying so helplessly each night. So she starts sitting with him, eating with him, listening to him, answering those of his questions that she can answer without giving too much away. It's not easy, getting him to open up. Asad Haider has trusted maybe four people in his entire life, and three of those are dead, killed by the fourth. But no man can remain an island when surrounded by such pain, and talking to the girl is soothing. She doesn't want to know anything about the Party and she doesn't seem to be interested in his past. She talks about everything and nothing in particular. She tells him about the city, this city that he has returned to after so many years, a city he has helped to rule like a feudal fief, but a city that now he cannot see beyond the iron gate of this old Parsi mansion. He realizes that he is living in his old neighbourhood, just a few streets away from the house he was born in. But he knows he will probably never see that house again.

The richest irony is that when Sadia talks to him about Karachi, it is a Karachi that is unrecognizable to him. He has prided himself on his intelligence network that was able to give him minute-to-minute information about who was plotting against the Party and which minister had privately criticized the Don over a drink at his home in the evening. But for so many years, he has been so fixated on these things that he has forgotten that there is a Karachi that exists beyond Party intrigues. Her Karachi is a city of young people, of roadside cafes competing to serve the best doodhpatti chai in town; of boys and girls dressing up in green-and-white and getting together to watch the soap opera that is the average match involving the Pakistan cricket team, sharing the exhilaration of a victory and the despair of a defeat; of the anticipation of a first date, of wrapping your arms tightly around his waist and feeling the wet monsoon wind blow in your face as you ride a motorcycle down to Seaview. Her chatter is a balm, because it reassures him that there can be a world outside the nightmare that is his life.

And things would have remained this way, with Sadia slowly inching her way into Asad's consciousness, had the New York Police Department not intervened. Karachi holds its breath at the news of the raid on the Party's headquarters on Coney Island Avenue. Its citizens expect and fear an explosion of wrath from the Don that never comes. Confusion prevails in Darul Sakoon as well as at the Chief Minister House, as the Party's spin doctors seem unsure of how to spin this. After all, hasn't the Don always supported the Americans? Why have they now turned on him? The chief minister himself remains remarkably silent, preferring to go on a tour of Upper Sindh to inspect preparations for the coming flood season. A city that has been held hostage for so long becomes fascinated with events unfolding in New York. Ratings for the evening news talk shows go through the roof, and within a week, residents of middle-class localities like Gulshan and Nazimabad have become fully conversant with the finer points of US criminal and police procedure, as practised in the city of New York.

But the raid also has a direct impact on the house in Katrak Colony. Suddenly unsure of the future, Guddu needs information that can be of use to him. And quickly. So for the past two weeks, he has pumped Sadia up to get more from Asad. To use whatever means necessary. Guddu makes it sound casual, as if he is instructing one of his police officers to beat up a suspect to gather information. But for a woman, it is not so simple. The only weapon at her disposal is sex. And that creates a moral quandary for Sadia Ali.

It's not like Sadia is a prude. For her generation, sex is no longer a taboo subject. Almost twenty years of the Internet and online chatting have ensured that casual sex, or 'affairs' as they are popularly called, is no longer the preserve of the rich and famous in Defence and Clifton. Sadia too is no virgin. She has had two lovers, ex-boyfriends, and she slept with them not because she was madly in love with either, but because the experience excited her. Planning everything like a military operation, from arranging the pickup and drop-off points with her boyfriend to creating an impenetrable cover story about her whereabouts that would fool even a brother who was a cop. And, of course, the sex. Afternoons spent exploring each other's bodies in a stranger's bed, in the house of some friend's friend. Cleaning up afterwards like a professional killer at a crime scene to ensure no telltale evidence is left behind, no condom wrappers in the wastebin, no panties left under the bed.

So the sex isn't a big deal. In fact, she had slept with her first boyfriend while her puritanical brother was still alive. And from a purely physical attraction point of view, Asad is pleasant. He has retained the lean toughness of his youth and, in fact, looks more appealing with age. He has grown a beard since arriving in Karachi, but even that gives him more of a roguish air. She cannot deny that even before Guddu's suggestion, she has had the occasional lustful thought about him. It's only natural when you're living in such close quarters for an extended period of time. But it sickens her. Because at the back of her head she cannot stop thinking that he is the man who ordered her brother's death.

Which is why what she did last night is even more revolting to her. Finally, she succumbs to the pressure of Guddu's demands and, late in the night, enters Asad's room. This is not unusual, for she often chats with him at this time, but this night she enters and takes off her kurta, wordlessly offering herself to him. His reaction stuns her even more. There is panic in his eyes, total shock at what she is doing. He clumsily hands her kurta back to her and turns his back to her, shaking like a frightened animal. And so she has spent the past night feeling that she has debased herself, and unsure of which is worse, that she offered her body to her brother's killer, or that he rejected her.

Sadia has never been particularly religious, even less so since her brother's murder. She stopped praying that day because she could not accept that a merciful God could have intended such a fate for a good man like her brother. But this morning, for the first time in over a year, she kneels to pray with the muezzin's call at first light. There is no prayer mat, so she prays on the moist, dew-covered grass in the lawn. As she rises from the wet grass, she sees him, limping unsurely towards her. It is the first time she has seen him in natural light, as he seldom ventures outside his room. He somehow looks even older.

'I am sorry. I am truly sorry for my reaction last night. I … well, something like this has not happened to me in a very long time.'

'Why? I thought you lived in Dubai and I heard you were rich. I would have thought lots of women would have thrown themselves at you.'

'I … there was someone in my life for a very long time. I was in love with her and I never thought of anyone else.'

'Oh. I'm sorry, I didn't realize you had a wife.' If it is possible, Sadia feels even worse than she has so far.

'Not my wife. I never married. She was my … well, honestly, I don't know what to call her. If you have been in a relationship for almost twenty years, calling her a girlfriend sounds very childish. And calling her a mistress sounds very sordid. She was the only woman I ever loved.'

'Why didn't you marry her?'

'Something always came up. Finally, she got tired of waiting and married someone else. But we continued to be together.'

'That's a strange relationship.'

'To the world it sounds very strange, but it worked for us. Anyway, I … I've never been with anyone in my life except her. So when you came to my room last night I didn't know how to respond. I am sorry if I made you uncomfortable. I didn't mean to be ungrateful, you have really helped me these past few weeks, and you saved my life at the airport. But it's not you. You're a very pretty girl. But I'm not interested in … that. Not any more.'

'Where is she now?'

'She … was one of the people whom the Don had murdered when I disobeyed him. Her whole family was killed.'

'I'm very sorry. I don't know what to say.'

'Do you mind if we sit? I find that I get tired very quickly these days.' Asad plonks himself into a garden chair. 'Look Sadia, I think it's time we were honest with each other. I may be an old fool, but even I know that what you did last night was not out of choice. Someone told you to do that. I also know that you and the old man have not been completely truthful with me. I know you work for an organization that is plotting against the Party. But you have never told me why you do this.'

'What do you mean why? We do it for the good of the country …'

'You say that, but I can see in your eyes that there is a much more personal reason. For both of you. I sense you have a far more personal grievance against me.'

Suddenly, the tears start to flow. The pent-up emotion comes bubbling out, and Sadia weeps loudly. 'Because you killed my brother, Dilawar Ali.'

Asad stares at the grass pensively for a long moment, allowing her to get it out of her system, and waiting till she is composed again. 'Inspector Dilawar Ali, SHO of Korangi. Last posting was SHO Clifton. Killed on 4 December 2013. Ambushed near his house, in Gulshan Iqbal.'

'But how do you remember ...'

'I remember all of them. Each and every one. The ones I killed myself and the ones I gave the order for. Every date, every location. That is the burden I shall carry till my dying day. Sadia, I have done horrible things in my life. And perhaps, it is right that I should suffer as I now do. And I also know that there is nothing I can say to you to make you hate me less, or not wish for my death. In fact, I wish for my own death. But I only want to live so that I can in some way atone for my sins, and that atonement will only come when I rip this Party apart. So I ask you to help me till that day. I know you are committed to this cause, you know of the evil of this Party and the Don. If you weren't committed, you wouldn't have gone to the length you went yesterday. That's why I need you. Please help me to end this.'

Sadia wipes her tears and contemplates the seemingly broken man sitting in front of her. How many men would have the guts to admit to their sins without offering any justification? There is a terrible strength within him. A strength that may be enough to even shatter the Don. Perhaps Guddu is right about him.

'What do you need?'

'I need to speak to the Shia leader, Ali Raza. He still lives here in Soldier. And I need you to take me to a ladies' Quran class.'

*

The Birjees Colombowala Ladies' Community Centre is clearly visible as you enter Hijrat Colony from the PIDC bridge side. It's the only double-storey building, and as you come down the bridge you can see two massive posters, one of the Don and the other of Chief Minister Tariq Colombowala, hanging down from its roof and covering one whole side of the building. It has expanded considerably in the past five years, from the original one room it was started in, to cover the fairly large local government amenity plot upon which it now sits. Large painted pots are placed alongside the freshly whitewashed walls on the street to counter betel-chewing pedestrians who feel that it is their right to spit the red betel juice onto public buildings.

The centre and its inhabitants are proud of how far they have come in the past five years. From teaching little girls how to read the Quran in the original one room, it now offers a range of sevices, including much larger Quran interpretation classes for women, as well as vocational courses to teach young women sewing and computer skills. But in truth, luck has played a huge part in their success. There are hundreds of similar projects in the city that never take off for lack of funds or lack of interest from patrons. Three things worked in favour of the Birjees Colombowala Ladies' Centre, or BCLC as it is termed on the police wireless system. Firstly, it lay in the constituency of the chief minister. Secondly, the chief minister's mother died six months after he took office, so he felt an overwhelming desire to dedicate something to her memory. After all, Begum Birjees had prayed fervently for every crooked deal that her son Tariq had ever made in his life as he climbed the slippery slope of power within the United Front. And lastly, the chief minister's wife, known locally as Zaib Apa, has taken a personal interest in the development of the centre. That's a knockout combination by any standard.

Zaib Apa's commitment to the centre is laudable. She visits every week, usually on Saturdays to attend one of the Quran lectures. And she inspects every part of the centre, making sure that there are adequate resources. Of course, being the wife of the CM, her definition of 'adequate' is considerably larger than other people's. The CM's secretariat has an unlimited budget for the BCLC, and standing instructions that the centre must get whatever it asks for. Hence, the city government allots the land for free, the Public Works Department constructs the building from official funds, the IT ministry provides computers that were part of an American aid package for the uplift of rural Thar, and one of the chief minister's wealthy industrialist buddies donates two hundred sewing machines, in exchange for a thirty-million-rupee tax write-off. The Horticultural Authority even plants a magnificent garden, wth exotic plants and sprinklers tending to the lush grass in the middle of a locality where the surrounding houses do not have running water. Of course, all of this has to be protected. After all, the residents of Hijrat Colony are known to be covetous by nature, so an eight-foot-tall wall is thrown up, illegally encroaching upon and halving the width of the street. And the local police station establishes a police post right next to the wall. Truly, the ladies of Hijrat Colony have never felt so safe before.

The wonder of all of this is not that all of these resources have been given to the BCLC. Every chief minister has a vanity project or two to waste government funds on. The real wonder is that it all works as it should and that all the resources are actually utilized appropriately. And that is due to Zaib Apa. It is, of course, widely known that Zaib Apa had been a founding member of the Party, the first head of it's women's wing. But then love intervened and she married a dashing young Party volunteer called Tariq, who through his sheer dedication and hard work rose through the ranks to the apex of power. Being the selfless and supportive wife, she chose God and family over the cut and thrust of politics. At least, that's the official version. No explanation is ever given over why Zaib, the ultimate feminist in the university, chose to recant her beliefs so completely. Nor why she additionally abandoned her jeans and kurtas for a hijab and chador.

If an inquisitive journalist were to ever ask this question – which is highly unlikely since Cyrus Dinshaw's fate is a cautionary tale whispered about in the Press Club to this day – the standard reasons given by a spokesperson would be health. It is true that Zaib often looks ill and withdrawn on the rare occasions that she does make a public appearance. To those few who meet her at functions at the CM House, she seems spaced out and distant, and is often observed compulsively popping pills. But a small circle of Party insiders know that this is not the full story behind Zaib's withdrawal from public life.

Which is what makes her commitment to the BCLC even more admirable. It is the one public project she allows herself to participate in. Many privately concede that her management is far more effective than her husband's. There is no waste, and no skimming off the top in any of the works related to the BCLC. One only needs to look at the neighbourhood around the centre for proof of this. The road in front of the centre remains half paved, and the sewage flows in uncovered drains despite the fact that the chief minister has allocated 200 million rupees for uplift projects in his constituency in this fiscal year alone. When she once had the temerity to ask him about this state of affairs, her husband had coolly informed her that while the BCLC symbolized his commitment to charity and she was welcome to play with it as she chose, the roads and drains of Hijrat colony were his business, where no interference would be tolerated.

There is no indication that this Saturday will be any different from every other. Zaib Apa arrives promptly at 4 p.m. to participate in the Quran class. Her security detail doesn't usually follow her inside the BCLC on her own direction, since she doesn't want a bunch of policemen to be staring lewdly at the young women there. Besides, it's not like a threat is going to materialize from within a ladies' community centre. The only difference this Saturday is the attractive young girl, who obviously doesn't look like she's from the locality, who approaches Zaib Apa at the end of the Quran class. She introduces herself as a social worker who works in the nearby Reti Lines neighbourhood, and requests that Zaib Apa meet a poor impoverished maulvi who is excellent in his recitation and interpretation of the Quran, but is unable to secure a job anywhere. It is an unusual request but not alarming in any way. Many maulvis, knowing of Zaib Apa's passion for Quranic education, often petition her for all sorts of things. So she allows the young social worker to lead her to an empty classroom where the preacher is seated. It is only when she sees him that Zaib Apa lets out an involuntary gasp. She immediately recovers her composure, realizing that the head of the centre is also standing with her, and orders everyone out of the room on the pretext of wanting to listen to the maulvi's recitation and interpretation.

'The beard really doesn't suit you, Asad. What on earth are you doing here?'

'I could say the same of your hijab and chador, Zaib. I've been lying for the last four hours. You've been lying to yourself for considerably longer.'

'What do you want, Asad?' Zaib sits down on one of the chairs and starts absent-mindedly twirling the lapis lazuli rosary that she always carries.

'I want him dead. He took my life away.'

'He took all our lives away, in one way or another. Look at me. You think I wanted to end up like this? Tariq's decoration piece for him to wheel out when necessary? Of course not. But the mistake I made was to fall in love. With the Don. And when he tired of both my body and my mind, he parcelled me off. He sold me like a slave to Tariq because it was inconvenient for him to have me around, either as a lover or a politburo member. I had no say in the matter. I kept my mouth shut because Mohammed Ali said if I didn't go along he would release pictures and tapes of me, and ensure that my entire family was dragged through thanas and courts for the rest of their lives. For all my feminist sentiments, at heart I am still a Pakistani woman. I couldn't bear for my family to be humiliated. So I swallowed my pride and accepted his decision. And then when I started seeing what you and he had turned this Party into, I really started to feel scared. Did you think it was normal for a political party to have death squads? To drill holes into your opponents' knees? You were happy to go along with him on everything. For God's sake, you murdered poor Imam just because he raised his voice against what was going wrong in the Party. Now, just because it's happened to you, you feel aggrieved.'

'How did you know about Imam?'

'I shared Mohammed Ali's bed for three years, Asad. I know exactly how he thinks. I knew he would not be able to stomach Imam's dissent for long. And I also knew that you were his mindless tool, through which he could get anything done. It was after Imam's death that I really turned to religion. I decided somebody had to atone for all our sins.'

Tears start to stream down Asad's face. His shoulders shake as he sobs. 'Nani Amma, Zaib. There wasn't even anyone to bury her. No one to even read siparas on the soyem. I was her last male relative. I should have been there ...'

'I know, Asad. I told Tariq it would look strange if no one even acknowledged her passing. He agreed, so I went to the Bara Ghar, made the arrangements, ensured that she should be buried in a plot next to your mother in the Shia section of Mewa Shah. I even went to condole with that poor girl Mumtaz's family.'

'Do they know what happened?'

'They have no clue. They believe the police version, that it was a particularly gruesome house robbery. Obviously, I didn't tell them why I was there, I just pretended that I had read about it in the papers and was so horrified that I had to come see them.'

'Did you see … her face? Or had that bastard Gringo destroyed it?'

'There's no use thinking about these things, Asad. You made that poor girl so miserable in life, I am sure the afterlife will be better than this world ever was for her.'

'I loved her, Zaib. Do you really think that I made her miserable?'

'I know you loved her, Asad. But look at the cost she paid for your love. The things we women do for you men. She knew you were a monster and still loved you. She waited for you for years, denying all of her family's entreaties to marry. And even when she did, she didn't do it for love, she did it for your convenience, marrying a simpleton so you could keep carrying on with her. My God, she loved you so much, she even agreed to sleep with the Don during the operation, because she feared that he would give you up as part of a deal with the government. How could her life have been any good?'

'She did what?' Asad's blood runs cold at Zaib's comment.

'You know the Don always needed new playthings. If he could play with me and that poetess of Guddu's, why do you think he wouldn't play with the one person you loved? With him it was always about manipulating all of us.'

Asad's voice is barely a whisper as the import of Zaib's revelation washes over him. 'Who else knew?'

'Tariq knew. The Don boasted about it to him. That's how I found out. Not that Tariq shares his discussions with me, but he blurted it out at a point when he thought I was drugged out. That bastard Raja almost definitely knew. And your boy

Gringo must have known. She apparently approached the Don through him. She had heard a very strong rumour that he was going to hand you over to the Agencies in Dubai as part of a deal to ingratiate himself with them. Tariq said the Don told her he would guarantee your safety if she slept with him. So she did. To protect you.'

Although the tears continue to flow down his cheeks, there is a new inflection in Asad's voice, a hardening that sends a chill down Zaib's spine. 'So Gringo knew everything?'

'You always treated him like your younger brother. You brought him into your home, into your family. But you were wrong about that one, Asad. I never liked the look of him. You raised a snake whose ambition and bloodlust is matched only by that of the Don's.'

'Evidently, I was wrong about a lot of things.'

'Why did you come to see me, Asad? Why do you put my life at risk, along with your own? Did you think I would agree to join you in a revolt against the Don? I am not the person you knew when we founded the Party, Asad. He broke me a long time ago. And now he has broken you. You cannot win. I am an old woman who just wants to look forward to her jaanemaaz and her drugs every day. There is nothing else I can do for you, except put a new chador of flowers on your grandmother's grave every week. Please go from here.'

'Thank you, Zaib. For all that you have done for me. I will not bother you again.'

*

You cannot win. Zaib's words are still in his head as he takes his position in the third row of the Friday prayer congregation. It has been ages since he has attended Friday prayers. And perhaps the first time ever that he has stood in a Sunni mosque.

In all these years he has never had the feeling of impotence as he has had these past two weeks since his visit to the BCLC. He imagines this is what the Party's opponents must have felt like for years in the face of the onslaught that people like him and Gringo unleashed upon them.

You cannot win against him. Her words eat into his soul like a cancerous growth. That's not true, Zaib. I won't allow it to be true, he tells himself. Unlike the thousands of victims who have silently borne everything that the Party dished out to them, he will not go silently. He will hurt that bastard in New York in ways that he didn't even know he could be hurt.

As he listens to the khutba in the mosque, he fingers the cold metal of the pistol that is hidden in the folds of his shalwar. It's been a while since he has held a gun, but its touch is reassuring, as it has always been.

The presence of the weapon is a result of his other meeting. Ali Raza is a prominent leader of the Shia community. Well, to call him a community leader would be a stretch. He's more of a rabble-rouser, the stick that the city's Shia leadership pulls out when it wants to pressure the government on some issue or the other. What is a less well-known fact is that Ali Raza is one of the biggest players in the city's underworld. He's connected to everyone because he does business with everyone. Whether it's partnering with Baba Dacait to smuggle Iranian diesel across the border to be sold in the city's petrol pumps, helping the United Front to canvas for votes in Shia strongholds like Ancholi, Rizvia and Shah Faisal Colony, or loaning out hitmen for freelance contract killings. Ali Raza has a rate card for everything.

Asad knows all of these things because Ali Raza is his oldest friend. He remembers the two of them playing marbles in the street even before Asad started playing cricket. Ali Raza was his mischievous friend from the wrong side of the tracks, the one whom Nani Amma and his mother always disapproved of.

Which always gave Asad even more incentive to hang out with him. They came up together in the Shia youth organizations that proliferated in Solider Bazaar in those days. That is until Asad went on a radically different path and joined the Party. At the time, Ali Raza had discouraged him, arguing that the Party was a non-starter, and besides, it was always much safer to stick to your own kind. Asad, bewitched by the genius of Mohammed Ali Pichkari, had gotten angry and refused to speak to him for the next two decades. It would have been hard to argue with Ali Raza's logic twenty-five years ago, but who knew that Asad Haider would be the catalyst who would change the Party's fortunes? Such is the way of politics.

Because of that old childhood link, and because of the fact that he had stopped one of the Party's ministers from expropriating the Bara Ghar after Nani Amma's death, Ali Raza is one of the few people in the city that Asad can go to without fear of being handed over to the Party. He doesn't stay for long. He knows he is toxic and doesn't want to put any greater burden on Ali Raza. All he asks for is a single pistol, a reliable one that won't jam after three shots. Without asking another question, Ali Raza gives him one of his own, a Turkish Stoeger with a full clip.

It's lightweight and fits easily into his baggy shalwar, allowing him to mingle without suspicion with the Friday congregation in the mosque. The mosque itself is a small nondescript one in Ranchore Lines with no ostensible security. There is nothing special about it, except for one fact that is known only to Asad. Every Friday, Javed Gringo comes here to offer his prayers. It is near the orphanage where Gringo spent the first fifteen years of his life, before Asad took him out and made him the perfect killing machine. That's where he got his name, Gringo, because he was so fair-skinned that he looked like a foreigner. On account of this, it was assumed that he had been an unwanted issue of one of the prostitutes from nearby Napier Road, who had abandoned him at the orphanage. The older boys in the orphanage had made fun of Gringo for this little titbit. But the thing about Gringo, even back then, was that he was a vicious fighter. Nobody made fun of him for very long. Asad had found him on a visit to the local ward, when Gringo had beaten up one of the ward boys for making fun of him, not caring about the consequences of his actions. Asad had realized then that such a fearless boy could be turned into an excellent weapon.

The Friday prayer visits are Gringo's only acknowledgement of his former life. He prays at the mosque and then gets a degh of biryani for all the children in the orphanage. The only one he has ever told about these visits is Asad. It's rare for him to miss a visit. It only happens if there is some extremely pressing Party business. Last Friday was one of those occasions. Asad had come then too, but Gringo did not make an appearance. It allows Asad to familiarize himself with the surrounding environs, not only of the mosque but of the area as well. It allows him to prepare better. And these things always come down to your preparation.

Gringo is there today. Asad sees him in the first row. He prays just behind the khateeb. Since he's a bit of a local celebrity, they always reserve a place for him in the front row. Asad struggles to keep up with the prostrations of the rest of the congregation. He hasn't prayed in a very long time, and on top of that the gestures of the congregation here are different to the Shia fashion that he is used to. One false step on his part will raise suspicions about him. Regular mosque-goers have become ever more suspicious about individuals who seem out of place in the congregation these days. Everyone, regardless of their denomination, has become wary of potential suicide bombers blowing themselves up in the middle of a jamaat.

The prayer ends and the crowd starts to disperse, with a few staying on to read the optional nafils after the obligatory raka'ats. Asad starts moving forward, towards Gringo, who has his back to him. Although only two rows separate them, it still takes a few minutes as Asad is swimming against the current of the majority of people who are trying to exit the mosque in the opposite direction. This is the crucial moment. If Gringo were to turn and recognize him, that would be the end of it. The tension of the moment raises his heartbeat, and he slowly eases the gun out of his shalwar and cocks it. He tells himself to relax. It's something he's done on innumerable occasions in the past. Despite the afternoon heat, he wraps a dirty shawl tightly around his face to conceal himself. His physical appearance has changed so dramatically with his now flowing beard that he doubts if Gringo would recognize him even without the shawl, but it's an extra precaution. If Gringo were to suddenly turn, it would take him a moment or two to figure out his identity. That's all Asad will need.

But Gringo doesn't turn. He is having a word with the imam of the mosque, handing him some money. Asad draws up right behind Gringo and plants the muzzle of the gun gently on the base of his neck. Then, almost imperceptibly, he whispers one word.

'Mumtaz.'

Gringo flinches slightly as the cold gun metal touches his skin. And that's all he ever feels. Asad pulls the trigger and the bullet tears through Gringo's throat to lodge itself in the foot of the poor imam. The sound of the fire and the screaming of the imam stun everyone momentarily. Ignoring the commotion around him, Asad looks down at Gringo's twitching body now lying at his feet. He fires again at Gringo's cheek, causing his brains to spatter all over. This time, the sound is amplified and the shock of seeing Javed Gringo's head explode triggers a wholesale panic, with all remaining members of the congregation running towards the entrance. Asad fires two more shots in the air to create more panic and fear, and then turns and heads in the opposite direction further into the mosque. He has scouted a back way out, and in no time he is able to scale a short wall and exit onto a side street. He tucks the pistol back into his shalwar and takes off the now blood-spattered shawl he had worn to cover his face and protect his shirt. A passer-by asks him what has happened, and he tells him that a group of armed men just opened fire in the mosque. As the man rushes off to see if he can help, Asad Haider calmly walks away, hailing a rickshaw from near the main road.

17

GUDDU

In November, as the days become shorter and the evenings in Karachi become noticeably cooler, Aunty Park fills with walking and jogging enthusiasts, keen to work on their physical fitness. The core group of regulars will, of course, come in all seasons, but the casual fitness buffs, having avoided the stifling heat and humidity of October, flock to the park to enjoy the first tidings of winter. Aunty Park, as the name suggests, is mostly a preserve for middle-aged members of the fairer sex. Of course, the Cantonment Board that administers the park did not have the temerity to come up with such a sexist and ageist name by themselves. They had originally named it, with far greater political correctness, Ladies' Park, but some wag decided Aunty Park was a more appropriate name, and it has stuck ever since. So much so that even the Cantonment Board has been forced to change the name to Aunty Park on its website for ease of explanation.

That does not mean Aunty Park does not admit men. In fact, between 6 p.m. and 7.30 p.m. on most weekdays, the empty plots of land that surround the park swarm with official Government of Sindh limousines, as their owners, all senior civil servants, like to take their evening constitutionals in this park. It is said that many an important policy decision has been made between profusely sweating, Nike-wearing bureaucrats on their tenth or eleventh round of the walking track.

So it is no surprise to see Guddu sitting on one of the park benches wearing an orange tracksuit that makes him look like an inmate of an American penitentiary. He has just finished his ten rounds of the track, and sips from a bottle of mineral water, enjoying the light breeze as it cools the sweat from his brow and neck. He smiles slightly as a bearded man approaches him. It isn't the beard that makes him stand out. There have been an increasing number of beards in the park for some years now. Guddu finds that bureaucrats especially tend to grow beards as they grow older, as a lifetime of bad decisions and the prospect of their professional mortality, more commonly known as retirement, flashes before their eyes. But this particular bearded fellow is unique because he is the only one in the park who comes without the appropriate kit. No ugly tracksuit, no shiny Nikes or Reeboks. Just a plain white shalwar kameez.

'It's good to see you again, Asad. Thank you for coming at my request.'

Asad Haider curls his lip in a contemptuous snort. 'Guddu. Can't say the same for you. I must be getting old. Or maybe it's because of the bullets that the Don pumped into me. Five years ago, I would have figured this whole thing out in half an hour. I should have guessed that the old man and the girl were just patsies. They would need a central source of direction and that could only come from you. The Party would have found them and killed them years ago had they been on their own.'

'You mean *you* would have killed them. Still, give them some credit. They've been operating for years under your nose, even before your current health problems and your falling out with the Don. You didn't figure them out even then.'

'Perhaps you've gotten a lot better at the game than you used to be.'

'Perhaps. Or perhaps the Party has been rotting from the inside for a very long time, and hasn't been as good as you assumed it was. By the way, my condolences for Nani Amma. She was a wonderful lady, a true matriarch. The city will be a sadder place for her absence. You will, of course, understand that I couldn't attend the janaza. Wouldn't have been good form for the intelligence chief of the province to attend the funeral of the grandmother of the Don's chief adversary.'

'Of course. I wouldn't have expected anything different from you, Guddu. But I'm curious. What's your game in all of this? Why haven't I been handed to the Party? Why would you risk your own neck to meet me face to face?'

Guddu gestures to the spot on the bench next to him. 'Do sit down, Asad. It attracts needless attention to us if we keep conversing while you stand to attention in front of me. I'm here to tell you that you made a terrible mistake in killing Javed Gringo. It's scared the shit out of the Don and the entire party apparatus. Gringo was a big wicket, and frankly, they're not quite sure what to do without him.'

'Why would you think I give a damn? I want that bhenchod to be scared. I want him to know that I'm coming for him.'

'Well, if that was your objective, you really fucked it up. You see, the old man now has a real problem in New York. The officers pursuing the investigation into your shooting are not relenting and it seems as if either the Don's connections in America aren't what they used to be, or they're just not working. They've already arrested Raja and a bunch of other people from the offices there. The rumours are they found money, drugs and all sorts of interesting trinkets. And they apparently have some statement given by you against the Don which ties everything together very neatly. The old man is so shaken that he called the chief minister last week and told him to start making preparations for him to return to Karachi. But now, after you bumped off Gringo, he's petrified. So you see, if you want to kill him, how do you plan to do it if he keeps sitting in New York? Were you hoping that your curses would have some kind of viral effect on him?'

Asad reflects on Guddu's words for a moment. 'I hadn't realized the police there would keep pursuing this. When they deported me, I thought that was the end of it. I figured the CIA had bailed the Don out.'

'Evidently not. The police have the old man by the balls and they're squeezing hard. Are you still in contact with them? Perhaps we can discreetly feed them some documents that might aid in their inquiries.'

Asad takes out his wallet and searches for the card that Russo had given him before he boarded the plane. He finds it and hands it to Guddu. 'They told me to get in touch, but I never did. Was he actually going to come back? After all these years?'

Guddu wipes a bead of sweat off his trim moustache. 'If he were to come back, could you kill him? It wouldn't be easy. He'd be protected by the government and the Party.'

'I'd find a way. Some way. You forget, this is what I do. It's what I'm good at. It is my only objective in life, till I draw my last breath.'

'Well, then what I am about to tell you will absolutely delight you. You are the fourth person to know this secret, after the prime minister, the chief minister, and myself. Not even the home minister has been told yet. The Don has decided to return. Gringo's death made him jittery, but the CM and I convinced him that he could be adequately protected in Karachi. Plus, to be honest, he doesn't have too many choices. If he stays in New York and they haul him down to a police station to get a mug shot, that's the end of his mystique right there.'

'How soon will he be back?'

'Within the next ten days, most likely. The CM is informing the Party politburo tomorrow, and they'll make it public soon after. But they want as little time as possible between their public anouncement and his actual flight. They don't want the Americans to start expediting charges against him if they find out he's planning to bug out. Also, the quicker they do it, the less time there is for any group to plan an assassination attempt.'

'Unless that group already has advance knowledge of his plans.' For the first time, Asad turns and smiles at Guddu.

'Precisely. But there are certain conditions. I have a plan, and you must adhere to the plan. It's the best way to ensure that the old man does not survive when we hit him. Once he dies, what you do is totally up to you. If you want to challenge for the leadership, I'm fine with that. If you decide to strike a deal with the CM, I'll arrange for you to meet Colombowala. Or if you decide to spend the rest of your life sitting by Nani Amma's grave and reciting prayers, I will ensure that no one bothers you ever again.'

'Why, Guddu?'

'Why do I want to bring the Don down? Well, I suppose I could give you a bunch of rubbish about protecting the larger interests of the city and the country, but you and I both know that would be a lie. Let's just say this, I still miss that poetess. I pretend that I don't know what happened to her, but I do. She threw herself out of a window on the sixth floor of the State Life Building. That wasn't right. He shouldn't have played with her life. Or mine. Fifteen years in Gilgit is a very long time to punish a man just for having expressed his ambition. In my own way, I'm as bitter as you. And if you're worried about me double-crossing you, don't be. If I wanted to do that I would never have exposed myself by meeting you.'

'All right. I agree to your terms. How do we do it?'

'I have some contacts in jihadi circles. Let's just say they are happy to loan me a suicide bomber. I will get the bomber false accreditation from Special Branch. It will look like he was one of our officers. We can't get him into the airport, the security is too tight. And we won't be able to get him near Darul Sakoon, because police personnel aren't allowed to come near there. But there's another option. I am sure the Party will roll out a legendary extravaganza to welcome the Don home. Millions of people lining the streets, that sort of thing. A show of strength, a sign of his continuing popularity. They will naturally arrange for a bus with a reviewing stand, so the Don can wave at his beloved supporters all the way from the airport to Numaish. The place to do it is his bus. It will be parked outside the airport's security cordon. I will send the bomber, under the guise of doing a secondary sweep of the bus to check for explosives. That will allow him to infiltrate the security cover that the Party puts up around the bus. Our man will wait there till the Don boards the bus, then he will blow himself up. We will make sure his jacket is packed with enough explosives to wipe out everyone there. I can't take the risk of the Don just losing an arm or a leg.'

'So what do you want from me?'

'We cannot afford to leave anything to chance, because it'll be my neck if the Don survives. I need you to ensure that the bomber does his job. He will be an illiterate Pathan, so you will need to be there to guide him, get him close to the bus, past the inner cordon of Party security. And then, you disappear and get a safe distance away. I will get you a Special Branch ID as well.'

'What if someone recognizes me?'

'Ah, now that's where we can benefit from Gringo's death. There is confusion among the ward bosses right now. No one knows who is in charge. Many of them feel that what was done to you was unjust, and many of them owe you everything. If Gringo were alive we wouldn't have a chance. That bastard would put a bullet through your head the minute he saw you. But the others are in awe of you. If they see you, they will waver, hesitate. I will ensure, through the CM, that one of your loyalists is put in charge of the inner security cordon. I'll try and get that fellow from Soldier Bazaar, Shatroo. He's in disgrace after the Party's defeat in the by-election. It will give you time to escape, leaving the bomber in position as you become the decoy for him. Look Asad, I know there's a risk to you, but we have to take this chance. If the Don reaches Darul Sakoon, he'll be safe for the rest of his life. The Americans won't be able to do anything to him, and no one else will be able to get to him because they'll turn the place into a fortress.'

'I don't care about the risk. I want him dead. Whether I die alongside him or not is inconsequential. There's nothing left for me to live for.'

'Don't try to become a martyr, Asad. It doesn't suit you. All you need to do is guide the bomber to where the bus is parked, and then get out of there. You may not want to think about this right now, but remember that someone will have to pick up the pieces after the old man. It's not just a matter of personal ambition. You and he created a monster. You will need to control the wards before they lay waste this city. The police can't do it. The CM can try, but he doesn't have the sort of clout with the ward bosses that you have. So for all our sakes, don't be a hero. Stay alive.'

'Just tell me where to meet your bomber, and how to recognize him.'

'My people will set up a command post outside Madam Apartments, just as you turn on to Shahrah-e-Faisal from the airport compound. It will be pretty close to where they park the Don's bus. Get to the command post, and the bomber will be there. He will recognize you from the ID that I will give you. I will arrange the time as soon as we have the details about the Don's flight. But do not be late, because I don't want the bomber hanging around on his own. It'll raise suspicions. Do this right, Asad, and you will have done an incalculable favour to all of us. To this entire city.'

'I'm not doing this for anyone else, Guddu. This is just for me.'

18

ISMAIL

I witnessed Mallick sahib's entire conversation with the bearded man. I took his photo as discreetly as possible, as I had been told to do, with the camera in my new smartphone. Arre bhai, there are some perks to becoming the right-hand man of Baba Dacait. The day after the Soldier Bazaar election result, the president of the Electronics Dealers' Association came to Baba with a 'donation' of five lakhs and six brand new dabba pack iPhones, as a mark of respect. I got three of them as my reward. I sold two, but I kept this one.

Anyway, you will ask what I was doing in the hi-fi Aunty Park that evening. Well, Mallick sahib had asked me to come. It wasn't easy, I can tell you. The guard at the gate stopped me because he thought I looked like an eve teaser. It took the intervention of one of Mallick sahib's bodyguards to get me in. But Mallick sahib didn't really want to talk to me. He just wanted me to get the picture. I kept walking on the track, pretending to talk on my phone. I passed them three times, but then I got exhausted and sat down on the grass, like a lot of the other tired joggers. I don't know who the bearded fellow was, but once he left, Mallick sahib just confirmed that I had gotten the picture, and then he also left.

You see, he and I had already set things in motion. The 'jihadi' contact that he had spoken of was me. I went to Chaaku Mehsud and rented a suicide bomber from him for Mallick sahib. Well, I suppose rent is the wrong word, since that implies you are going to return the item, and this item was definitely not coming back. Chaaku, being the entrepreneurial sort, had started a roaring side business, offering suicide bombers to customers at the right price, to solve their tricky problems. It was a very effective solution. I mean sure, if you wanted to be old fashioned, you could still pay a ward boss or one of Baba's gangsters to rough up a business rival, or convince someone to give you a theka that they weren't willing to give otherwise. But that was never a permanent solution, and you, as the customer, would be left having to carry out the fatigues of the party you had hired. With one of Chaaku's bombers, the problem disappeared for good. All for a convenient one-time payment.

It was also fantastic because the police never came after the person who had hired the bomber. All such cases were classified as terrorism cases with no personal motive. If a Shia, Christian or Barelvi businessman was killed, the police would say it was a sectarian killing. And if your rival was a Sunni Deobandi, they could always say it was a general act of terror. Perfectly believable for Karachi. As far as Chaaku was concerned, he had a virtually limitless supply of human bombs. He fed them some line about how the target was an enemy of Islam. These chutiyas believe anything.

So anyway, it was easy enough to arrange a bomber from Chaaku. Baba was happy enough to front the fee of ten lakhs when he heard the target would be the Party. He was so enthusiastic he told me I should negotiate the rates for bombers in bulk, as he wanted them to keep blowing themselves up in front of ward offices. I had to calm him down and convince him to start with one. After all, it would be bad for business if dozens of bombers blew themselves up in the city on the same day.

Still, I could see a new self-confidence in Baba since the election win, a belief that he was now equal to the Don. He wanted to challenge him head on, something he could never do while the Don sat in New York. Back here was a different story. As Baba said, the Party may still have the numbers, but he was the one who had the guts.

And indeed, the Party seemed to have actually wilted in the face of Baba's ferocity. Their boys had started steering well clear of Lyari. In Soldier Bazaar, we had established a new 'Public Contact Office', next to Nagori's milk shop, as a counter to the local ward office. Ghaffar Langra put in a bunch of tough-looking thugs to man the office, but on my insistence we put in one mild-mannered, polite fellow to deal with the public. We soon found that a number of people started showing up at our office looking for solutions to their problems, instead of going to the ward. Buoyed and somewhat stunned by our success, Yousaf Chandio announced that Baba would be responsible for candidate selection for his party's Lyari seats in the next election. We had finally arrived.

The only ones who didn't seem to get it, much to Baba's irritation, was the media. Once the announcement was made about the Don's return, the TV channels ran nothing but analysis about this political earthquake. I could see Baba glowering at the TV screen every evening. Despite all his success, he had been relegated back to being a two-bit hoodlum, while the channels gushed and speculated about every aspect of the Don – what was going on in his case, how would he come back, what security arrangements the government would make for his return, how was the Party preparing to welcome him.

One idiot producer ran a whole segment on the renovations that were being done to the Don's bedroom in Darul Sakoon.

It got to the point where even the plans for the suicide bomber stopped bringing a smile to Baba's face. A couple of nights before the Don's scheduled arrival, while I finalized my plans on the phone, Baba's anger boiled over. 'Bhenchod Naich, what good is the suicider for us? If he succeeds, everyone will think the jihadis killed the Don. There will be no credit for Baba Dacait.'

'Arre Baba, try and look at this strategically. With the Don out of the way, you will inherit this entire city. Why do you care about who kills him?'

'I do care. I want everyone to know it was me. That way these Party madarchods will never have the balls to challenge me again.'

'Baba, the Party has become a joke. Even more so since that madarchod Gringo was killed. You know what someone told me? That Gringo was killed by some pissed-off husband who wanted revenge because Gringo fucked his wife. That one man walked up to him inside a mosque, alone, in front of hundreds of witnesses, and blew his brains out. How will they challenge you if they can't even find a cuckolded husband? The wards can't think of entering Lyari, they can't even operate in Garden, or half of Soldier any more, and you think these fuckers can even dream of challenging you after the Don dies? Arre, Mallick sahib told me their shit is packed because the Don insists on holding a rally at Nishtar Park. He says it's historically significant since the Party's first jalsa was there, but the wards can't guarantee security because it's so close to Soldier Bazaar. They're worried you will come and throw grenades at them or something. So for the first time ever, the Party is begging Special Branch to set up metal detectors at Nishtar Park. It's literally their backyard and they can't secure it.'

Suddenly, there was a gleam in Baba's eye. 'Naich, that's it. That's perfect! I will go and attack their venue. I will go and throw grenades in Nishtar Park on the morning of the jalsa.

They will have to call it off, which will be embarrassing enough, and on top of it if the Don is killed the same day it will be an absolute disaster for the Party.'

'What? No Baba, that's not what I meant! I agree it will be hugely embarrassing for the Party if their jalsa gets cancelled, but how will you get through the security? The police will set up checkpoints and roadblocks in the entire area leading up to Nishtar Park, from early morning. The minute they see your convoy of Vigos coming, they will open fire.'

'I won't be travelling in my Vigo. Remember when we went to meet Adda Yousaf, I switched to a motorbike and no one noticed us? That's what I'm going to do again. Just a couple of riders on a motorbike, like the hundreds who regularly pass by Nishtar Park. And we'll do it early in the morning, when the police shift will just be coming on duty, and the Party workers will still be groggy from the night before and not really alert.'

I rubbed my temples with worry. I must have looked horrified because Baba burst out laughing.

'Naich, why are you so worried? Are you scared of coming with me?'

'Well, Baba, I mean … I don't know … but if you insist …'

'Arre chutiya, what will you do there? You don't know how to ride a bike and you don't know how to throw a grenade or fire a pistol. Don't shit your pants just yet, Naich. I know you are very useful to me, but I also know that you're not capable of doing this type of work. Tere bus ka kaam nahin hai. I will go alone, with one of the boys. You will stay here.'

I breathed a sigh of relief, which made Baba giggle some more. 'Okay Baba, but I insist you don't go alone. Take one other motorbike with you. Take Ghaffar on a second bike to watch your back. Isn't that right, Ghaffar?'

Ghaffar Langra grunted, and everyone assumed that was him agreeing to my suggestion, though I thought the grunt was somewhat non-committal. But it didn't matter because Baba nodded vigorously. 'Okay, we will take two bikes. But stay at a little distance from me, Ghaffar. If they see two bikes coming together, they might suspect something.'

'And there is one more thing I can do, Baba. I'll go and speak to Mallick sahib and find a route for you to follow into Nishtar Park, where there will be the least police presence. Maybe he can even delay the deployment slightly, allowing you to get in and out without risk.'

'Will he agree? I thought all those policewallahs were terrified of the Party.'

'Mallick sahib is different. He is with an Agency, so he's no normal policewallah. After all, he is the one setting up the suicide bomber scheme. I think he will agree to our plan. If we attack the jalsa and the Don is killed the same day, the Party will never recover.'

The following night, having already met with Mallick sahib again and given Baba a route on which there would be minimum police presence in the early morning, I left Lyari. I needed some time to myself. The tension of what was happening and what was about to happen was getting to me. After all, even the greatest men do get nervous sometimes. The next morning was the big day. The day of decision. I couldn't sleep, so I wandered the streets like a vagrant. As the darkness of the night turned to the greyness of dawn, I found myself drawn to Nishtar Park. Like a man watching a train crash, I couldn't stay away.

Nishtar Park had remained a hive of activity all night long. The new ward boss had personally supervised the assembling of a stage and the testing of the sound system, and a deluge of cabinet ministers had kept showing up at the venue through the night to offer their own advice to the ward boss, whose patience, I am sure, would have been worn thin by the end of it. But as morning broke, the exhausted Party workers crept away to snatch a few hours of sleep. After all, it was going to be a big day for them.

Security was tight, but I still had my press pass. I told one of the ward boys that I was doing a story on the arrangements to greet the Don, so they allowed me to wander around unhindered. Despite my role as Baba's right-hand man, very few people had seen me anywhere, so I was absolutely anonymous. In fact, a couple of the ministers even came to me to have their quotes recorded, so they could later point to my article as proof that they had gotten their hands dirty in setting up the stage and supervising the arrangements. The Don liked these sort of personal touches, apparently. Some were even disappointed that I hadn't brought a photographer along. Visual evidence was so much better.

Seventeenth of November was a cold morning. The dew had made everything damp as I made my way to a small chai shop a short distance away from Nishtar Park, on the side of the route that Mallick sahib had picked out. I ordered breakfast, but I couldn't eat a bite. Only the hot tea in the chipped porcelain cup warmed my hands and my spirits.

I spotted a big grey Toyota Land Cruiser with police number plates arrive at Nishtar Park. It was obviously a senior officer because the monstrous vehicle was accompanied by two escort pickups. I was surprised though, to see Mallick sahib himself descend from the back door of the jeep. His escort vehicles took up positions on the street on which I was sitting. In fact, one of them parked literally right in front of my little tea stall.

From this distance, I could see Mallick sahib make a big fuss about checking the security arrangements, having the bomb disposal squad sweep the premises and berating the local SHO for not having properly deployed policemen on the surrounding rooftops. As this went on for about ten minutes, I felt waves of tension sweep over my body. If anybody had been paying attention to me, which they weren't, they would have noticed my hands trembling quite visibly. After all, I hadn't participated in anything like this in the past.

After another five minutes or so I heard the low rumble of motorcycles, with their silencers taken off. I turned my back to Nishtar Park and saw two bikes approaching. Even from this distance, I could make out Baba's distinctive features, his dark skin and his curly hair. In a moment of panic I looked around to assess whether he would be able to recognize me. But I needn't have worried. The police mobile parked in front of me would obscure his view, and anyway, why would he be staring randomly at chai shops just as he came in to lob grenades at Nishtar Park. He was on the lead bike, and just as he turned the corner and the park came into view, I could see that the second bike seemed to hold back.

The policemen in the mobile, as if by prearranged signal, suddenly became alert and took up positions on the road. The escort commander, who was one of Mallick sahib's most trusted subordinates, executed the plan perfectly. He raised his hand as if signalling for the motorcycle to stop, but then without really giving them the time to slow down he gave the order to fire. As the first round of the policemen's AK-47s went off, everybody at the tea stall ducked under their tables for cover. Except for me. I couldn't look away.

Baba had no chance. As the spray of bullets hit them, the rider – a young boy called Latif Pappu – was propelled off the seat of the now skidding bike. The bike dragged on the street for a couple more feet before crashing into a pole. Baba's body was still half on the bike and as it came to a halt, his right leg was pinned under the frame of the motorcycle. The entire incident took less than thirty seconds. I turned to see if there was going to be any return fire from the second bike, which Ghaffar Langra should have been riding. But after having slowed down at the corner of the road to allow Baba to take the lead, the second bike was now nowhere to be seen. I don't think the policemen even noticed it, or if they did, they didn't care. The escort commander calmly walked up to the overturned motorcycle, kneeled and raised Baba's head. I think Baba was still alive, but I couldn't be sure. Anyway, without looking up, the officer shouted out, asking if this was Baba. In response, I shouted back in the affirmative. The escort commander turned to me and nodded, then very carefully stood up, took two steps away from the body – to avoid the splatter, you see – and fired two shots in Baba's chest. I was later told they wanted to preserve the face for identification, and more importantly, for the media slides. One of the other policemen walked up to where the boy Pappu's body had fallen and fired another burst from the Kalashnikov into him.

I slumped back in my chair and breathed a sigh of relief. A posse of policemen and Party workers were rushing to the scene and the chaiwallah was pulling his shutters down. I inconspicuously joined the crowd gathering on the sidewalk, and saw Mallick sahib, wearing his suit and tie even this early in the morning, approach the crime scene in a deliberate and unrushed manner. The escort commander whispered something in his ear and Mallick sahib scanned the crowd. For a brief instant, our eyes met, and he half nodded.

That was it. My role was done. I turned and started walking away, wanting to be far away before the police or Party workers decided to start asking questions from bystanders. As I reached M. A. Jinnah Road from one of the side streets, I found myself at Numaish, just opposite Lines Area and to the entrance of Darul Sakoon. It was still early, not yet even 7 a.m., and I passed a battered old police pickup that was one of hundreds that had been deployed in the area for the protection of a jalsa that would never occur. I had never seen such a concentration of policemen and vehicles in such a small area. But then, it's not every day that the Don comes back home.

The policemen in the pickup were standing around the hood of the car, drinking tea and listening intently to their wireless. From the frequency of the incoming messages and the tone of the dispatcher, I could sense that something else had happened.

Feigning ignorance, I approached them and flashed my press pass. 'Bhai sahib, has something else also happened in the city, or are they talking about this firing incident?'

The portly sub-inspector in charge of the group looked up from his tea in an irritated fashion, as if I had interrupted his philosophical musings on life. 'I don't know about any firing incident here, but there's been a bomb blast near the airport.'

19

GUDDU

For days, the city has been painted saffron and black. The Party's colours dominate every kind of object, moving and stationary. Telephone poles and street lights are draped with Party flags. Every inch of available wall space in the city is covered with posters of the Don. With the notable exception of Lyari, every shop and office block from West Wharf to Port Qasim, and from Boat Basin to Katti Pahari, sports either a photo of the Don or a banner welcoming him home. And well they should. The wards are keeping tabs on who did how much in their respective areas on this unique occasion.

Obviously, displays of sycophancy come hand in hand with such devotion. Cabinet ministers fight with each other over the right to illegally expropriate the most prominent billboards in the city, where they can put up massive personal panaflex paeans to the Don. The ones in most demand, and the ones which create the greatest amount of inter-ministerial bloodletting, are those on Shahrah-e-Faisal, the road that leads from the airport to the city. Everyone knows that the Don is definitely coming down this route. The owner of a mithai shop in Gulshan who has had the innovative idea of offering boxes of saffron-coloured laddoos and black gulab jamuns has to call for police protection when his stock runs out and he starts receiving phone calls from the irate wives of Party members, threatening to burn his store to the ground unless he makes a new batch of the sweetmeats.

Of course, the official reason given out for the Don's decision to return home makes no mention of a New York police investigation, or the arrest of the Don's personal secretary, Raja. It highlights the Don's undying love for his city and his determination to walk the streets of Karachi again, regardless of the security threats to him. Privately, the chief minister briefs the top columnists and news anchors and tells them that the Don's decision is in response to the rising threat from the gangster Baba Dacait and from the Taliban. He is determined that all such antisocial elements will be banished from the city.

This is the day that the Party faithful had thought would never come. Fate has made it so that the Don, who himself has stated so many times that he didn't think he would ever see his home town again, must now return. And so the Party cannot afford for the spectacle to be a damp squib. But just applying tonnes of saffron and black paint to the city is not enough for a political victory. As in each of its electoral triumphs, the Party has always believed that the margin of success must always be overwhelming. Thus, each of the Party's sixty-four wards receives instructions from Darul Sakoon to muster at least 20,000 people each to line the route of the Don's cavalcade from the airport to Nishtar Park. Anything less than a million-man march is unacceptable.

From before dawn the crowds are brought in by bus. Each ward boss has been given a quadrant to fill along the route, all the better to know instantly who has failed and who has succeeded in meeting their targets. A ward boss who does not have a ten-row deep crowd on either side of the road in his quadrant might as well shoot himself in the head, instead of going back to the ward and having someone else do it to him.

On top of all the concerns for creating the appropriate awe-inspiring spectacle is, of course, the overwhelming problem of security. The security threat surrounding the Don is a real one, even more so after the rise of Baba Dacait and the bomb blasts during the Soldier Bazaar by-election. Chief Minister Tariq Colombowala hands over the entire 30,000-strong police force of the city to the Party, and further reinforces them by calling in the police forces of the neighbouring districts of Thatta, Jamshoro and Dadu. An enterprising criminal could have a field day robbing the city blind, if he could actually make it from one part of the city to another. All public transport is commandeered by the Party. All roads leading to the main artery of Shahrah-e-Faisal are sealed by shipping containers, thus cutting the city into two halves. It is decided that the best way is for the Don to fly in by charter jet, so that flexibility and secrecy can be maintained about his arrival time till the last minute. In light of the Don's temporary liquidity problems, the Sindh government generously picks up the bill for such extravagance. The CM promptly declares a public holiday and announces that he and his cabinet will wait at the airport for as long as it takes till the Don arrives.

It is this milieu into which Guddu finds himself driving, at eight in the morning, on 17 November. He sits in the back seat of his official SUV, taking great care to appear completely professional and disinterested. But the pounding inside his head testifies to his growing anxiety. The first part of the plan has gone off beautifully. Naich's successful luring of Baba to Nishtar Park has resulted in the first victory of the day. On the pretext of diligently checking security at the jalsa venue, Guddu's presence and the action of his escort commander will ensure that he will personally get the credit for the death of Baba Dacait.

The second part of the plan also seems to have kicked off, although it is not immediately clear whether it has been successful or not. Guddu receives the same message on the police wireless as the policemen whom Naich interrogates – there has been a bomb blast near the airport. But the subsequent details of the incident are sketchy, with the inspector general having ordered radio silence to avoid creating a panic. The problem is, with mobile phone signals being jammed for security reasons all along the route, the only way to learn about exactly what has happened is to reach the scene first. Guddu knows that the first officer on the spot will be the one to spin the subsequent story to everyone who matters. And so he leaves immediately for the airport, stopping only to send a text message to the chief minister and a wireless message to the inspector general, a man two years his junior and a choice imbecile even in a long line of fawning buffoons, informing him that he is on his way to the crime scene to report personally on the incident. He knows that it will tickle the IG to have the additional inspector general of Special Branch running to the scene like a junior superintendent of police.

But Guddu doesn't care about that. Right now, the only thing that matters is getting to the spot to verify what has happened. If he makes it and if things have gone according to his plan, he will never have to worry about his moronic boss ever again. His advantage is that unlike everyone else he knows exactly where to go. He orders his driver to reach the Special Branch command post where he had instructed Asad to rendezvous with the bomber. The driver is taken aback by Guddu's precise knowledge, but he figures that the boss is, logically, heading to his own unit's command post to get more information.

Guddu's biggest problem is time and the crowds along the route that he has to take to reach the airport. Logically, the Don's intended route is the shortest way to the airport. But that is without taking into account the sea of humanity that has been assembled to greet the Don, and the fact that in their overenthusiasm to pack the route with as many supporters as possible, the ward bosses have dismantled the barriers that were meant to keep the crowds off the actual road. People have overflowed onto Shahrah-e-Faisal, and despite the constant and loud entreaties by the sirens and flashers in Guddu's motorcade to make way, the best they achieve is moving at a snail's pace through the mass of people. The only comfort Guddu draws from this is that any other officer trying to reach the scene will have to contend with the same logistical problem.

He notices a speck of blood, probably Baba's, on his polished shoe, and vigorously wipes it with a piece of cloth. Guddu has taken extra care in his dressing this morning. If this is going to be the biggest day of his life, then he is determined to look perfect. Hence, despite the early hour, his charcoal suit and bright blue tie look pristine. He takes out a comb and runs it through his hair, ensuring that not a single strand is out of place. Then he picks up the file lying on the seat next to him and idly flips through the papers, at the same time trying to assess the current situation. The wireless has no update on the Don, but Guddu knows that his plane has already landed at six in the morning. It was felt that the Don could rest and freshen up after a long flight while remaining on board, while the chief minister and the politburo, who have set up their own temporary headquarters in the airport's VIP lounge, could deliberate on what was the best time for the Don to disembark and begin his historic journey home. Therefore, Guddu had not expected news of the blast so early. He had hoped that he would have had time to reach the airport beforehand. So this means that either something has gone wrong, or the Don decided to move out of his plane far earlier than expected. The first possibility is the more likely one.

It takes the convoy about thirty-five minutes to get to the Madam Apartments command post, where chaos still reigns, despite almost an hour having passed since the blast. The air is thick with smoke and the smell of cordite, while shell–shocked ward members, covered in the blood and guts of their friends, are carrying AK–47s and trying to direct ambulances through the mass of humanity, to take away the wounded. Despite his having arrived in an official vehicle with a police escort, Guddu is stopped at the entrance by a heavy–set man, whose long hair and saffron T–shirt are caked with blood. Guddu recognizes Saquib Shatroo, the former ward boss of Soldier Bazaar.

'Shatroo, let me through. I am the head of Special Branch. The CM has sent me to find out what has happened. Are you hurt? Is this your blood?'

Shatroo is dazed and confused, so Guddu takes him by the hand and sits him down on the side of the road. 'I … I think I saw Asad bhai.'

'Where did you see, Asad, Shatroo? Is he dead? Was the Don here when the blast happened?'

'No … no Don. But I saw Asad bhai. I'm sure of it. He wasn't a ghost, he was flesh and blood. I'm not imagining it, am I?'

'Where is Asad now, Shatroo?'

'I think he blew up.'

'Shatroo, for your own sake, don't mention Asad's name to anyone else. Now go and get some treatment.' Guddu whispers the last words in Shatroo's ear and then enters the tent – now torn to shreds – that had been set up as the command post. Blood and limbs are strewn everywhere, and Guddu's eyes start scanning each body part, as if looking for something in particular.

One of his Special Branch officers comes up to him holding a plastic bag which seems to have the remains of a head in it. 'Sir, four of ours were killed, and one uniformed officer. And there are two others, but we're not sure if they are ours or civilians. We've found the remains of what look like Special Branch IDs, but we're checking our duty lists. Oh, and we recovered the head of the bomber from inside Madam Apartments, sir. It must have flown off when he blew himself up and the velocity carried it into the parking lot of the building. Looks Pathan to me. One of the bodies must be his, and I found part of a Special Branch ID card that doesn't seem to match our lists. He may have forged some kind of official identification …'

Guddu gives the officer a look that makes him shut up immediately. 'Where's the other unidentified body? Show me.'

'Sir, this way.' In one corner of the tent a depression has been created in the ground. Guddu assumes this to be the blast epicentre. A body, or what used to be a body and is now just a pile of human remains, lies next to it. 'Sir, it's impossible to identify this body. We think there are parts of the bomber's body mixed with this one as well.'

Guddu carefully and deliberately gets his officer to lift each and every piece, to look for any form of identification. A detached finger has an aqeeq ring still in place on it. Taking his handkerchief, Guddu carefully strips off the ring and examines it. A thin smile breaks out across his face. Nani Amma's ring.

Guddu places the ring in a small Ziploc bag and tells his officer to put the finger in a separate bag. Then he speedily walks out of the tent towards his jeep. 'Where is the Don's bus?'

'Sir, it was parked on the other side of the road. It had bombproof glass and B-6 armour, so nothing happened to it. Just the tyres burst. They're trying to get replacements. The ward members are guarding it themselves, they're not even allowing the police to come near it. I've tried to explain to them that we need to collect evidence …'

'Don't bother. We've got all the evidence we need. Keep that finger secure and secret. Don't mention it to either the ward boys or the investigation police. We will need it for fingerprint ID. I believe it belongs to the bomber's handler, the real mastermind of this attack.'

'Uh, yes sir. What about the bomber's head, sir?'

'That? That's worthless. Hand it over to the investigation team. Special Branch has already solved this case.' Guddu turns and looks at his officer, as if sizing him up. 'Your name is Ahsan, isn't it?'

'Yes sir. Inspector Ahsan, from the district Malir office.'

'Ahsan, you play your cards right and I will ensure that you get promoted for solving this case single-handedly. And one more thing. Hand me those IDs you said you recovered from the bomber, and don't mention a word of them to anyone, not even your supervisory DSP. Do I make myself clear?'

'Yes sir.' Ahsan takes the charred piece of paper from his pocket and hands it over. Guddu takes a lighter from his suit pocket and sets the paper on fire, holding it till it burns into ash.

'Very good, Ahsan. Carry on.'

In contrast to Shahrah-e-Faisal, the road leading up to the airport terminal building is empty. Airport security has ensured that the crowds brought by the wards do not spill over towards the terminal, and following the blast they have sealed the road altogether. His official vehicle makes it past the barricade and speeds towards the Arrivals terminal. He has radioed the Special Branch staff at the airport to alert the chief minister about his coming, and as soon as his jeep pulls up, the CM's staff officer and the head of airport security are there to take him in. The airport itself, strangely enough, carries a deserted look. The car park is empty of vehicles, and a solitary traveller, having no way of getting home, sits and eats a burger at McDonald's. Though flights are still operating, experienced Karachiites, anticipating the logistical madness that would no doubt be caused by the Don's return, have opted not to travel on this day. Only a handful of foreigners, those poor souls with no experience of the city, sit on top of their luggage trolleys, hoping against hope that a taxi will brave the hordes and venture out to the airport.

Guddu is led through the baggage area into a sealed-off VIP lounge, which is too small to accommodate the massed leadership of the Party and the government bureaucracy all at once. No one who is anyone in the government wants to be left behind in kowtowing to the Don. Thus, provincial secretaries perch themselves on sofa arms and uniformed senior police officers find themselves virtually boxed into a janitorial closet. With all communications cut off, Guddu is the first person in hours to have come from the outside world, and the room rises almost in unison, looking at him expectantly for news. His boss, the inspector general, and the Party's home minister, Pakora, a thoroughly corrupt fellow with a pudding bowl haircut, approach him, but the CM's staff officer turns them away and says that the Don and the CM have ordered Guddu to come straight to the aircraft without talking to anybody. A side door leads out onto the tarmac, and the CM's Mercedes is waiting to take him out to the private jet parked on one side of the apron. It's a luxurious aircraft, a Gulstream G-5, the sort you see Hollywood celebrities travelling in, thinks Guddu. Airport security staff surround the aircraft and no other vehicle is allowed to come close.

As Guddu begins to mount the stairs alone, trepidation starts building. He has not met the Don face to face for fifteen years. How will the old man react to seeing him? Guddu recalls their last meeting, shortly before the Don left for America. Guddu had by that time spent half a dozen years in Gilgit and was desperate to return to Karachi. He had literally begged Raja to get him five minutes with the Don, but the second he had entered the meeting he had regretted having asked for it. The Don had been imperious and fierce, giving him none of the respect that a founding member of the Party deserved. He had castigated Guddu for having had the impudence to have asked for a meeting, and told him that if he even opened his mouth about coming back to Karachi for another five years, his family would be wiped out. It was a time when the Don was at the height of his powers, and having recently seen Imam murdered, Guddu came out of the meeting petrified. He had promptly taken the next flight back to Gilgit and had not broached the idea of coming back to Karachi with anybody for another eight years.

The interior of the plane is even more luxurious than the outside. A massive couch runs the length of one side of the plane, while comfortable leather seats are fitted on the other side. A centre table is overladen with snacks and a pot of coffee. Apart from a very pretty stewardess who stays close at hand in case she is needed, there are only two people on the plane. The Don sprawls on the couch looking like a beached whale. Guddu notices that although the plane has a private cabin and a fully equipped bathroom, the Don has obviously not even started grooming himself for his public appearance. He is still in his night clothes, in this case a white flowing Arab-style jooba, and his hair is ungelled and dishevelled, while a light, white stubble covers his chin. A glass of his favourite green Pakola and vodka is sitting on the table in front of him, despite the earliness of the hour. In contrast, the chief minister, who sits on one of the oversized leather chairs, is immaculately attired in a well-cut suit with matching red tie and handkerchief. He sits smoking a fat Cuban cigar and sipping coffee.

Before Guddu has had a chance to collect his thoughts, the Don speaks out. 'Guddu. Has it been so long that you have forgotten your old friend? Does Tariq keep you so busy that you cannot even show up to receive me at the airport?' The Don gets up and envelops Guddu in a bear hug that feels more like having his life squeezed out by a python. 'Tariq tells me you have been doing some good, keeping close tabs on the people who want to harm me.'

Tariq Colombowala takes one last puff of his cigar and stubs it out in the ashtray. 'Yes, Guddu, I have been apprising the

Don of the very extensive surveillance programme you had put in place to ferret out the Party's enemies. What do you have to report? All we know is that there was a blast near here.'

In spite of the aircraft's air conditioning, Guddu wipes beads of perspiration from his brow. 'Yes sir. My Don, my humble apologies for not having been present to receive you, but at approximately six this morning, on my way here, I decided to personally supervise a security check that my bomb disposal squad were doing at the event venue at Nishtar Park. I was particularly anxious to do this myself, as I had received information that the gangster Baba Dacait would try and attack the venue, to try and disrupt your speech there. As luck would have it, while I was there one of my informants inside Dacait's organization called me and told me that Baba was on his way to Nishtar Park to personally lead the attack there. I had no time to inform anybody else, so I told my personal escort to take up positions to engage Dacait and his men. I am happy to inform you, sir, that my escort managed to shoot Dacait and one of his accomplices dead before they were able to cause any damage to Nishtar Park. Just as I was about to organize a pursuit of the remaining assailants, I received word that a bomb blast had occurred near the airport. I immediately rushed to the scene and found that a suicide bomber, mistaking the Special Branch camp to be the spot where your reviewing bus was supposed to have been parked, had blown himself up, killing six police officers and at least two civilians. I personally went and reviewed the crime scene and found that the bomber is most likely to have been a Pathan from the tribal areas. But that is not the most alarming thing, sir. Among the remains of the bomber, I found the remains of a second individual, who I believe was the bomber's handler and navigated him close to the point where you were supposed to have been. I have found evidence that this handler was Asad Haider.'

Guddu hasn't even bothered to stop for breath while recounting the morning's events, but he can see that what he has said has jolted the occupants of the aircraft. There is stunned silence from the chief minister, while the Don wordlessly collapses back on to the couch, staring incredulously at Guddu.

'Asad? Can this be possible? What evidence did you find, Guddu?'

Guddu removes the Ziploc bag from his pocket and takes out the ring. 'Don bhai, I found this ring on a severed finger at the blast site. I think you will recognize it as Nani Amma's ring, which she had given to you. Only Asad would have had this ring. In any case, we have the finger, we can always match a fingerprint or dig up his mother's body for a DNA sample.'

The Don holds the ring in his palm, as if looking at some other-worldly invention. 'Yes. This is Nani Amma's ring. I gave it back to Asad when he came to see me in New York. You are absolutely right, Guddu. Asad must have been with the bomber. But what does this mean?'

Guddu looks at the chief minister who nods at him to continue. 'Don bhai, since the honourable chief minister tasked me to investigate his, and my own, suspicions about traitors working against the Party from within, I have been working only on this task. I believe I have uncovered a massive conspiracy to get rid of you and destroy your vision of the Party. I believe that a cabal of Party members, possibly in very senior positions, have been orchestrating a campaign against you, and they have allied themselves with both the Taliban and the gangsters from Lyari. I now believe that Asad was a part of this cabal, but I am not sure that he was leading it. I do not know yet which other senior Party figures are involved, but this corruption has spread like a virus to the lowest rungs of the Party. I know that my story may sound crazy to you, my Don, but today's events are starting to bear out my hypothesis.

Besides, the chief minister has had his own doubts about the Party as well.'

'Yes, Don bhai. As you know, according to your instructions, we bifurcated Party affairs from government affairs, so that since I have been chief minister my job has been to push forward your vision of governance and to collect revenue. I am completely isolated from Party politics. But in recent months, I started to notice an ... inconsistency in the decisions that we were told were made by the Party. When I questioned people about it, I never got a straight reply. People like Raja would always invoke your name and say such and such directive had come from you, and that it was not to be questioned. But I have had my suspicions that it was others trying to manipulate things by using your name. Unfortunately, since Raja controls all access to you, and these matters were of such a sensitive nature that we could never bring it up over the phone, I had no way of contacting you. But Guddu's investigations bear all of this out. Someone is trying to take your Party from you.'

'Betrayal. I am betrayed. You think that snake Raja is involved?'

'Don bhai, before we accuse anyone, we need to have proof. We cannot say definitively who is involved in this conspiracy, but I can say this: after all that has happened today, I don't trust anyone in the Party structure, not the politburo, not the ward bosses, not Raja. I cannot even be sure of my own cabinet ministers. Of course, I do find it curious that Raja, who is supposed to manage your secretariat in New York, was so careless – even when he knew a police investigation was under way – as to leave hundreds of thousands of dollars in the office in a place where the police could easily conduct a raid and seize the money. And who is being made the fall guy for whatever is happening in New York? Certainly not Raja. Everyone is pointing fingers only at you. Like I said, I don't have proof, but if you want my opinion, you are being setup by your enemies.'

'Sir, what Chief Minister sahib is saying is absolutely correct. Look at the evidence just from today's incidents. Baba Dacait was able to approach within throwing distance of Nishtar Park before we were able to stop him. It was pure luck and the courage of my sources, that I was able to be there to stop the attack. But I should not have been needed. Where was the security? At our Party's jalsas, we never invite the police to provide security. We have always done our own security. So where were our much-vaunted ward bosses? They should have had pickets set up halfway to Lyari to detect any kind of movement from the gangsters. But instead of going into Lyari to spread your mission, these so-called loyal Party workers have been withdrawing, pulling back in the face of Baba Dacait's assault. I now believe that they deliberately connived to make us lose that by-election in Soldier. After all, the Taliban took responsibility for the election day bombings, right? Well, we know from today's evidence that the Taliban are working hand in glove with these Party traitors. There is no way that the bomber or Asad should have been able to get so close to your bus. The wards don't allow the police to come near such areas, so how could a Pathan wearing a heavy shawl, a man who so obviously looked suspicious, and Asad Haider, whom everyone recognizes, or should recognize, get in? I did some checking and found that the ward boss who was made responsible for security around your bus was a fellow who was very close to Asad. Saquib Shatroo I think his name is. How was a known loyalist of Asad Haider given such a sensitive role today of all days? It was pure luck that one of my Special Branch officers stopped the bomber and caused him to explode prematurely, otherwise we would have been mourning you at this time.'

The Don takes a heavy swig from his Pakola vodka and empties the glass. He gestures to the stewardess who immediately brings another one. 'They would have been scraping bits of me off the pavement. Me. The Don, the man who liberated this city, being washed into the gutter by a hosepipe.'

'My Don, today we got lucky, but how many times can we rely on Guddu to shoot and kill someone like Baba Dacait, or some conscientious police officer to stop a suicide bomber? These people have tasted blood, and they will not stop until they kill you.'

'Guddu. Guddu will be responsible for my security. Just like the old days. Tariq, I want you to immediately issue a notification, making Guddu the Karachi police chief, in addition to his job at Special Branch. I was misled all these years, Guddu. People kept telling me to keep you away, but now I realize what a mistake that was. Never again. I want you to sniff out all the bastards, Guddu. I don't care how high it goes. There are no sacred cows in the United Front. And I want you to crush them. Issue the order now, Tariq.'

'Don bhai, I am humbled by your confidence in me, but it will not be so easy. I cannot touch Raja, even to clarify whatever role he may or may not have in this conspiracy, because he is in the custody of the Americans. I doubt even you would be able to talk to him. And until we weed out all the traitors, we cannot trust anyone in the Party. It makes my job impossible because for all these years we have relied on the wards to be our sword and shield. As a party, we never trusted the police or Rangers. But now, how can we protect you if the threat comes from those same ward bosses who were our strength? They killed off Gringo, who could have flushed some of them out. Now we have nobody. Can you imagine what would happen if you go to Darul Sakoon, your own house, under their protection? Your enemies would virtually hold you hostage. They could slit your throat in the night and the chief minister and I wouldn't even know until the morning. The police can't set up pickets within two blocks of Darul Sakoon.

It has always been the Party that provided protection to you. Can you imagine what our political opponents will think if they get wind of the fact that the Don is replacing his own wards with the police because he cannot trust his own people?'

'But ... but what are you suggesting, Guddu? That I not stay in Karachi? How can that be? Where will I go? The situation in New York is bad. Those haramkhors in the NYPD aren't listening to Simon Sole. They want to put me in a cell. I will not go to some American jail to be gangraped by a bunch of Mexicans!'

'Don bhai, please calm down. I know this is a very stressful time. Here,' Tariq says, taking out a pill from his jacket pocket, 'have this with your drink. It's a concoction that my personal hakeem does for me and Zaib. It's fantastic for relaxing. But please, listen to us. For our sake, for the sake of millions of your supporters, you cannot remain in Karachi. It will be suicidal in the present climate. Guddu and I will need some time to identify and eliminate all the traitors. I know you have legitimate apprehensions about being humiliated in America. But I believe I can help you here. I have recently been having a number of discussions with the American Consul General, and the ambassador in Islamabad. I have discussed your case and have highlighted all the support that we as a Party have given them during this war on terror. I told them, how would anyone ever support them in the future, if they allowed their police to treat you like some kind of common criminal. The diplomats here are sympathetic. The ambassador, in particular, had his legal attaché do some research, and they are convinced that the police don't have any case against you. The matter will never go to court. He has also said he will talk to the CIA, to underline once again the Party's value as an asset in the region. We can even point to today's bombing as an example of how the extremists will do anything to kill you. I am confident that your troubles in New York will end very shortly. You can go back, take control of Party headquarters over there, get rid of Raja, while Guddu and I sort things out over here.'

'Yes, the CIA *have* to see that the attempt on my life means I am the biggest target for the jihadis, don't they? They have to see the logic of that.'

'Absolutely, sir. Give us some time to identify your enemies. Once we have taken back control of the Party, you can return whenever you want.'

'But what will the media say if I fly back from the airport? What will the Party faithful think? That I am a coward?'

'Don bhai, you have a perfectly good excuse. In light of the two attempts on your life, we can say that after consultations with the politburo we forced you to return as the security situation in the city is so obviously precarious. I will conduct a shake-up in the bureaucracy and the police. We are already replacing the Karachi police chief with Guddu, and that will further reinforce the point that you had to leave because of circumstances beyond your control. We will receive some criticism in the short term, but the minute we have seized back control of the Party, we will reassert ourselves and everything will go back to normal.'

The Don sighs and sinks deeper into the couch. He takes off the sunglasses he has been wearing throughout and puts his hand on his forehead. The stewardess appears again with another Pakola vodka. The Don hands the drink to Guddu, who raises his hand to decline, but has the drink forcibly thrust into his hand. 'Drink with me, Guddu … the way we used to do in university. Remember? The only way we could get alcohol was through that friend of your father's, that old Parsi. He had a permit since he was a non-Muslim. Drink with me again. We will need to build this Party again, the way we once did. Only this time, there is no Aleem, no Imam and no Asad.'

Guddu pats the pen in his jacket pocket and discreetly puts down the green-liquid-filled glass after taking one nauseating sip. He looks again at Tariq who smiles understandingly. He is far more used to the Don's soliloquies.

'Asad. It all comes down to him. I made a mistake, you know, Tariq. I will never admit it outside this aircraft, but I will admit it to the two of you. I made a mistake by ordering his killing in New York. I shouldn't have told him to kill Aleem. I should have let Gringo handle that, and I should never have gotten that rank amateur to try and kill Asad. Maybe Asad didn't need to die. Maybe if I hadn't tried to kill him, he would not have joined this conspiracy against me. On the other hand, maybe he was always part of the conspiracy. But even then, I should have managed things better. Gringo could have killed him in Dubai, or I could have gotten professional contract killers, Russians or Colombians, to do it in New York. I thought I would save money by getting it done in-house. I've started thinking like an accountant after spending so much time with Raja.'

'Nothing is irreparable, Don. We'll fix everything.'

'Yes, nothing is irreparable or irreversible. As long as you keep sending me money from your ministries, I will have the resources to rebuild this Party.'

'Don bhai, I had already anticipated your financial difficulties because of the police raid, so I have asked my staff to bring $200,000 in cash for your personal expenses. Arre, Don bhai, you have come home after so many years, how could I send you off without a present? Consider this a "shakal dikhai". It's in my car, I will have it loaded onto the plane and you can take it back with you.'

'Ah Tariq, Tariq. Your greatest quality has always been your thoughtfulness. Once again, you have saved your Don. I must thank you, Tariq.' This time it is Tariq's turn to be enveloped by the Don. 'And I must also thank you for this magical pill you gave me. It is miraculous. It immediately relieves my stress. What's in it?'

'Morphine, I think, and some muscle relaxants, I'm not sure what else. It's something I had made especially for Zaib. You know how hyper she can get. It keeps her mellow. I take it once in a while when I'm stressed. I have a case of it in my car. I'll have that put aboard as well, so you have a comfortable flight back.'

'Thank you, Tariq, my loyal friend. And Guddu, remember, find my enemies.'

Two hours later, the plane is fully refuelled and loaded with its new cargo of pharmaceuticals and greenbacks, and takes off for its return journey, leaving Tariq and Guddu on the tarmac. As Tariq turns to go back to the VIP lounge to address the cabinet and politburo as well as the media contingent, Guddu taps his pocket again.

'Bingo.'

20

ANTHONY

Anthony Russo is searching for coffee in his apartment when the bombing occurs. It's a small one bedroom, off Amsterdam and 110th Street. It's an unusual area for a middle-aged Italian–American cop to live in, surrounded by the chi-chi new money of the Upper West Side, the intellectualism of Columbia University and Barnard College, and the grittiness of black Harlem. Russo doesn't fit into any of these demographics. Which is exactly why he is here. After his last divorce, which saw him lose his house in Howard Beach, he wanted to get away from all the vestiges of his old life. He enjoys the vibrancy and cosmopolitanness of this area, compared to the closed, white middle-class, ethnic-Italian bubble that he has lived in all his life in Queens.

He hasn't been home a lot recently, and the state of his apartment is testimony to this fact. Empty pizza and takeout boxes litter the dining table and a mountain of unwashed dishes lies piled up in the sink. The fridge is empty except for a bottle of vodka and a carton of expired milk. Every morning Anthony tells himself that today he will definitely go to the grocery store, but every night he returns home too exhausted to bother. This has been his routine since the raid at Coney Island Avenue. He has pored over the tonnes of evidence collected, trying to make sense of the actual scope of the Party's operations. It is a far bigger beast than even he originally imagined. The Party is truly global in its reach, creating a trail of business, crime and politics around the world. There are bits and pieces of evidence that point to involvement in human trafficking in Australia, dubious real estate deals in Dubai and gang-related violence in Mozambique. There is even some suggestion that the Party is involved in extortion from Pakistani businesses in Chicago and right here in New York. The Don's moniker of being the mayor of 'Little Pakistan' isn't just an empty title.

What makes it harder for Anthony is that half the documents are in Urdu. It takes ages for a translator to render them into English. Anthony even resorts to acquiring an Urdu-to-English dictionary to see if he can speed up the translation himself. And he starts monitoring Pakistani news channels on the Internet, looking for any snippet of information that can help him understand this case better. He can't make sense of most of what is being said, but after three weeks he is now able to pick up on when the Party is being discussed.

Which is how he finds out about the bombing. His laptop is streaming a news telecast from a Pakistani channel, as he digs deep in the bowels of his bare kitchen cupboards to find a sachet of instant coffee. He is alerted to the fact that something has happened by the excited tone of the broadcaster, and the use of the words Don, United Front and bombing, are enough for him to understand the gist of what's going on. He forgets about his coffee and starts watching the telecast, trying to decipher what he can from the images and the few English words used by the reporters.

He is so engrossed in this that he doesn't hear Charlie Cardenas knocking for a full three minutes, until Cardenas resorts to banging on his door.

'¿Qué diablos, Tony? Where the fuck were you? I thought I'd swing by after the DA's office to brief you, and also to make sure you eat something half decent. I got Chinese.'

'Something's happened in Karachi, Charlie. There's been an attack on the Don's procession. Suicide bombing, I think.'

'Jeez. Is the fucker dead? 'Coz that would solve half our problems.'

'No. I think he's fine. From what I can make out, they're saying he never got off his plane. But they keep mentioning Asad Haider's name. I think there's some connection between him and the bombing. I think he may even have been killed in it.'

'You think Haider was the bomber?'

'No idea, but I need to talk to the translation guy to figure out exactly what's happened.'

'You're never going to get him, Tony. The translators are long gone from the precinct. It's almost 9 p.m., man.'

'Okay, then the next best thing is to go to Midtown, Lexington Avenue, where they have those Pakistani eating joints. We can get the cabbies who hang out there to translate for us. They have the Pakistani news on there all the time.'

'Tony, let it go, man. We'll find out in the morning. You're becoming obsessed with this case. Look at yourself, man. Look around you. This place is a mess. You've been home for three hours, and you can't get away from this shit. Look, I wanna bust this asshole too, but it's just the job, buddy. You can't let the job take over, compadre.'

Anthony stares at Cardenas, trying to decipher him. 'What's the matter with you? This is our case. I thought you were on board. We said we were going to nail this son of a bitch.

Hang on a minute. What happened at the DA's office? Is that high-heeled bitch backing off from prosecuting?'

'Calm down, Tony! Now I know why you keep getting divorced! Why you live in this empty fucking apartment! The job possesses you like a fucking demon or something!'

Almost as soon as the words are out of his mouth, Charlie Cardenas regrets them. He knows he has crossed a line. 'Look Tony, I'm sorry, man, I didn't mean that. I'm just tired. You know I love you, hombre.'

Anthony Russo exhales slowly and then gives a weak smile. 'Don't worry about it, Charlie. You know, maybe you're right. Maybe I do need a break. Hey, you want to get a drink? We'll go down to the bar on the corner of the street. Do me some good, getting out of this place.'

The bar is quiet, even for a Wednesday night. Neither man says anything to the other for a while, quietly sipping their drinks. Cardenas is still feeling guilty about his outburst, but Anthony is just pensive, observing his partner's discomfort.

'So, what did she say? Ms Anna Sara whatever, queen bee of the DA's office.'

'She says there isn't enough there yet. Raja's in trouble, he's looking at some serious time on the laundering beef. He was in charge of the office. All the little receipts we found for the money were signed by him. But he ain't giving up the big man. He's singing about everyone else in Pakistan because he knows that shit is worthless to us. It's just like the Mob. He's scared and he wants a future here, even after he gets out. He probably figures if he keeps his mouth shut, the Don'll get him a hotshot lawyer, get a minimum sentence at some country club type of facility for a couple of years. If he breaks the omertà, he's fucked. They won't do shit for him then. And on the murder, we got nothing still. No weapon, no statement from anybody about knowledge of it and no connection to the Don. Nada.'

'Just like the Mob, huh? Then why don't they try them all for racketeering, like they do with the Paisans? If the DA uses the racketeering laws to go after the Party, that would make it a crime just to be a member of such an organization. We can nail the Don on that.'

'She's reluctant to do that. Gave me some bullshit about putting out a perception that they were criminalizing South Asians, like they had Italian Americans. She says state's trying to put a lot of pressure saying the NYPD should limit its investigation to crimes committed in the city, rather than trying to act like some kind of global investigative agency. I think it's that cocksucker Simon. Doing his bit to save the Don. She's also pushing us to wrap this up quickly. What did you dig up at your end, in the Urdu language project?'

'There's some scraps here and there about extortion threats made to local merchants in the Coney Island area, and in other cities. But it's going to take fucking years to translate and decipher all the shit that we pulled out of their headquarters. And then it'll probably take a task force to chase down all these half leads. That's probably why the bitch wants us to hurry. Simon doesn't want to give us any goddamn time to be able to dig up anything else.'

'And now, if your interpretation of Pakistani TV is correct, Asad Haider just blew himself up, so we got no hope of him sending us anything useful. Fuck.'

Anthony leans back in his seat and rubs his eyes. 'All of that fucking work for nothing. This motherfucker is going to come laughing back and set himself up once again, exactly where he left off.'

'We did a lot of good, Tony. It ain't gonna be *exactly* as he left. For one thing, he's lost a shitload of cash. And it's going to get harder to get the money back in now that Homeland Security and customs have been alerted and are going to be watching for this stuff. So are we. Their biggest advantage was that we didn't even know they existed, so they could do as they fucking pleased. It's not going to be like that any more. Everyone knows who they are now.'

Anthony looks out of the grimy bar window and frowns. 'Yeah, I suppose you're right, Charlie. What I don't get is, why did the Don run? He didn't need to, Simon would have put things right eventually, as he has done.'

'Maybe he just lost his cojones. Didn't want to have to deal with even the remote possibility of a couple of flatfoots like you and me hauling him down to the precinct. What's the word Haider used to describe him? Pheron. Hey man, these pharaoh types don't like slumming it with the rest of us.'

'You were right about me, Charlie. I let this job consume me. I need to get a nice hobby. Gardening or playing chess or something.'

'You got to get yourself a new chica, hombre. Hey, let me talk to Juanita, I'll tell her to fix you up with one of her girlfriends.'

'You sure Juanita will even vouch for me, Charlie? I'm not exactly Mr Reliable.'

'Hey, you're family, Tony. Of course she will. She loves you.'

'You're a good man, Carlito. Let's have one final drink. A toast to that motherfucking cocksucker, the Don, may he die of liver failure from that crap he drinks. Hey, who knows, maybe we can get the food and drug guys to check the ingredients of that drink of his, Pakola. There's got to be something wrong with something so green.'

'That would be hilarious, man. We couldn't get him on murder, but they finally got him for drinking some unhealthy shit. Hey, what's that buzzing? I think your cell phone's going off.'

'Shit, I really do need to get some sleep. I didn't even feel it. It's probably Santapio wanting to chew my ass over something.

Hang on, where is this number from? Looks like it's overseas. Hello? Who is this?'

'Take it outside.' While Anthony steps outside to take the call, Cardenas downs the last of his beer, idly thinking of what he will do this weekend. Maybe he'll take Juanita out for dinner and a show. They haven't done that in ages. And if they send the kids to her mother's, then there can be a separate after-hours show as well. Charlie is picturing the small of Juanita's naked back and the arch of her ass, when Anthony comes running back in.

'Charlie, get up, we gotta get back to my place stat. I got a call from Pakistan. A guy on the phone says he's from some kind of police intelligence agency. Says he got my card from Asad Haider, and he's sent me some kind of evidence, some recording or something, on my email. And you'll never believe what it is.'

Charlie has a gnawing feeling that he will not be seeing Juanita's naked back this weekend.

*

As the aircraft takes off and banks over Karachi's modest skyline before flying towards the Arabian Sea, Mohammed Ali Pichkari stares down at the city that he will never set foot in again. From 500 feet in the sky, it looks as if God himself has drowned the city in a sea of saffron and black. Mohammed Ali wonders if he will be able to spot his house from this height. And as he looks for it, a melancholy sweeps over him.

He thought he had come to terms with never returning to the city of his birth ages ago. He had left under a cloud, sixteen-odd years ago, as a result of the confrontation with the military establishment that was triggered by his ordering Imam's death and then blaming it on the Agencies. By that time, they too had had enough of the Don and his eccentricities. And so, like a married couple that has grown apart during their time together, the Don and the Agencies mutually decided upon a messy divorce.

For the first six years of his exile he had been willing and eager to come back, if only they would relent in their single-minded demolition of his Party. But then 9/11 happened, his relationship with the Americans deepened and it became evident that, on the one hand, America's tragedy drove the Party into the arms of a new military dictator, on the other, it ensured that the Don would never feel completely safe in his homeland. The Agencies would never stomach the extent of his closeness with the Americans, and, of course, the jihadis would view him as a tool of the West. By that time, there was too much at stake, too much money flowing, and too much of a good time to be had for him to risk it all for some foolhardy, sentimental desire to return home. Besides, it's not like there was anything he could do from Karachi that he couldn't do while sitting in his penthouse in Brighton Beach. Kill somebody, overturn a government, shut down the city, order some starlet to come to New York to give him a blow job. It was all just a phone call away.

But when his current problems overwhelmed him and the return became a probability rather than a possibility, the Don started to feel the old yearning again. Even the almighty Don could not keep that feeling bottled up inside of him any more. Not being able to go home for sixteen years is a terrible curse for anyone to bear, even the most powerful of men.

He doesn't realize that he has started to weep until the pretty stewardess brings him a tissue and a hot face towel, and rubs his shoulders reassuringly. Unlike lesser men, he is not ashamed of her seeing his tears. Only macho fools who have something to prove look to hide their emotions behind a veneer of false self-assuredness. Men who have experienced true power are not afraid of pretty girls seeing them cry. And when you know that anyone who dares to call you a sissy will be dead before they reach home that evening, you tend not to worry about these sort of things.

Still, he enjoys the pretty stewardess's hand on his shoulders. He accepts her offer of a massage, and as she kneads his back with her soft hands, he thinks about fucking her. She is *such* a pretty girl. Not his preferred Latina, but a dark-haired Eastern European. Good enough. He could do it, it would certainly make the flight go by much faster and make his worries go away. But unfortunately, this isn't that sort of charter. If Raja or that Georgian bodyguard of his had been around they would have ensured that the girls on board would have been inclusive of all 'services'. But this flight was arranged in a hurry by Tariq's people, and the stewardesses aren't whores. This is what happens when you make travel plans in haste.

He could still fuck her if he really wanted. She might still be up for it. After all, he has two gym bags full of hundred-dollar bills lying on the floor next to him. You don't have to be a whore to enjoy money. But there's the 10 per cent chance that she might not want his money, or his body, and might report the whole thing as sexual assault. And with his present troubles, the last thing he would need is another scandal. So, in the interest of self-preservation, the Don decides to keep his trousers on.

He looks at the opulent luxury around him and laughs out loud. If only his father could have seen all this. Saleemuddin Pichkari was a rarity among his Marwari caste, a man who actually failed at business. This failure led him to government service, in his case becoming a minor functionary in the military accounts department. Saleemuddin Pichkari had worked hard and died early, when his youngest son was only thirteen. He left his family nothing except the little 120 yard official quarter that had been bequeathed to him. To prevent the family from being thrown out on the street, Mohammed Ali's eldest brother had quit college and taken up an equally minor position as a clerk in the deputy commissioner's office in Hyderabad. At that point in time no one could have predicted that young Mohammed Ali would one day fly in a chartered jet with the spoils of the entire city at his feet.

Uncharacteristically for South Asian politicians, the Don never invited his family to share in his success. His brothers had discouraged and belittled his politics in the early days, and he never forgot it. Only his mother had glimpsed the future, as she saw her ne'er-do-well son hold a hundred thousand people spellbound at that first public meeting in Nishtar Park. By the time she died, a little over a year later, he was able to shut the city down for two days out of respect for her passing.

Many years ago, his eldest brother had visited him from Hyderabad and asked him if it was necessary for him to perpetrate all this violence. The Don hadn't answered. He was his brother, so he couldn't kill him, but he had gotten him suspended from his government job for three months. That was the answer right there.

Only the Don truly understood how to wield power. When they started this Party, all those years ago in a dusty dorm room of the university, they had all been equals. Mohammed Ali, Zaib, Guddu, Imam and Aleem. And, of course, later on, Asad. But only he would become the Don. As he had explained to Asad once, none of the others had the stomach to do the ugly things that had to be done. Only he had the strength to forge all of their destinies.

As time went on, they all outgrew their usefulness and slowly started becoming impediments for him. They all had to be removed from the picture, because the Don could have no equals. Guddu had been dispatched first, cut down to size so harshly that today he was nothing more than a snivelling civil servant, overjoyed at the crumbs he received from the Don's table. His gratitude on being appointed the city's police chief was testament to this. The Don had seen it in his eyes. A man who was so overjoyed at becoming a mere police chief was no more a threat than the pretty stewardess was.

Next was Zaib. Always a tricky one, because for all her militant feminism, Zaib forgot to draw the line between her cunt and her heart. She thought sitting on his cock empowered her to become his queen. Admittedly, she had been a good fuck at the time – although back then the Don had limited experience to compare her to – but it had been an amateur mistake to make, especially for a woman entering politics. She should never have presumed to hold his heart. Thus, she had been parcelled off to Tariq and crushed under the weight of domesticity. And Tariq himself? A man who had been chief minister for so long? Was he not to be feared? Not Tariq. The beauty of Tariq was his simplicity. He loved just two things in life. Money and cutting deals. He would never be the sort to stick his head out over the parapet.

Imam had been the difficult one. Imam was no fool. He had deliberately set himself up as a counterbalance to the Don. The puritan ascetic to his overindulgent cavalier. He knew there were people in the Party who spoke with awe of Imam's simplicity and honesty. No one ever actually contrasted it to the constant whispers of the Don's sexual peccadillos or even rumours of financial corruption, because no one wanted Asad Haider to come after them, but the implication was there. And Imam, that prick was sharp enough to play it up subtly. Imam was also a genuine Party hero, the only other person to be the public face of the Party. The organizational genius who had been the architect of victory. The man who put together the nuts and bolts while the Don made the pretty speeches. Yes, history *had* to be changed.

Aleem had been more a balancing of the books, an administrative exercise. He left the Party of his own volition but he had always represented the Don's conscience, even in the old days. As long as he lived, the Don could feel Aleem's disappointment boring into him. Aleem never said a word out loud, but the Don knew. And anyway, like a medieval king killing all rival claimants to the throne, no matter how unlikely their claim, it had to be done.

That left Asad. He had never seen Asad as a threat. Or at least, if he was one, as Guddu now seemed to think, he had hid it remarkably well. Asad had no ambition. The Don had often imagined himself to be a surgeon with Asad as his scalpel, removing the dangerous cysts from his body politic. But Guddu was right. At some point, a surgeon's scalpel can also be held to his throat. It's a weapon at the end of the day, just as Asad was. His anger had been legendary and something the Don himself would never have wanted to test. He thanks God that Asad never found out about him fucking that travel agent lover of his. Now *that* had been a risk he had been foolish enough to take. But ultimately he would have had Asad killed anyway, whether he had refused to murder Aleem or not. The Party needed fresh blood and fresh martyrs every few years, and a good surgeon also needs to change his tools with time, no matter how well they work. And now that too is done. He is left alone to rule, to rejuvenate his Party, to create a new history.

Over the Atlantic, he takes another one of Tariq's pills and that makes him dream pleasant dreams and pass out till landing. The plane lands at Teterboro Airport, far away from the commercial hustle and bustle of JFK or LaGuardia. Like the hundreds of VIP corporate and celebrity travellers who park their charter aircraft at Teterboro, the Don too does not expect to be hassled by such trifling formalities as immigration control or customs. He is still in the middle of his mellow buzz from Tariq's magic pills as he walks down the stairs on to the tarmac. A group of people are waiting for him at the base of the stairs, blocking the path to his limousine parked a few metres away.

In his slightly addled state, at first he thinks these must be minders sent by Simon Sole to debrief him about events in Pakistan. A couple of the men seem vaguely familiar. The fat one with no dress sense and the tall Latin fellow. He is sure he has seen them with Simon before. He must remind Simon to ensure his staff have some dress decorum. To work for the CIA and come dressed in such a rumpled state just cannot be good for your image. They flash some kind of badges at him, but his vision is blurred. His pills are helping him attain the seventh level of nirvana and the bright sunshine amidst the chill in the air just makes him feel even better. He smiles contentedly, nodding at whatever they are saying. One of the men is kind enough to take one of his gym bags from him. How polite, although he must ensure that none of them take out any of his cash. You can never be too sure about people these days.

They start escorting him away from the parked limousine towards the terminal building. It's awfully nice of them to greet him in this way, but he is a little tired. 'Gentlemen, perhaps we can do the ceremonies later. I've had a long flight and a stressful day, but do come by day after tomorrow and we'll chat.'

They persist in taking him inside, with one of them holding him by the elbow. It's a plain room, with just two long tables and more people in uniforms and wearing rubber gloves. In one corner he sees Simon, not looking very happy at all. Wait, something is wrong. This doesn't seem to be a reception committee. One of the men places his gym bags on the table, and a woman starts opening them. 'Hey, don't open that, that's private property!' He's seen enough daytime television in his time in America to know what his rights are. But for some reason they don't listen. Another man starts patting him down.

'Sir, sir, Mr Pichkari, are you on any kind of medication right now?'

The voice comes from a million miles away. He must focus now, this may be serious. The fat man has found Tariq's giant bottle of pills and is holding it up in front of the Don's face. Why doesn't Simon do something? He just stands there, dejectedly.

'Sir, are you aware that bringing in unauthorized foreign pharmaceuticals is a violation of FDA regulations? Do you know what's in these pills?'

By now, they have found his cash, and are stacking it on top of the tables. Not that it was particularly well concealed or anything. 'They, uh, they are painkillers. I don't know what's in them. Morphine, I think. Please, what are you doing with my money? Will you please just speak to Mr Simon Sole of the CIA, who is standing somewhere in this room. He will tell you, I have just returned from a sensitive diplomatic assignment on behalf of the United States government.'

'Okay sir, at this point I'm placing you under arrest for the murder of Nathalie Wlodachek in a shooting incident outside the Natural History Museum some months ago. You're going to have to come with us to answer some questions. And the officers from the customs service are charging you with narcotics trafficking and money laundering. If these pills do contain morphine, as you have claimed, that is an illegal substance that you cannot import in the United States without a licence. You also have on your person close to $200,000 in US currency, which is way more than the legal limit you are allowed to bring in. Please place your hands behind your back, Mr Pichkari.'

As the tall man handcuffs him, the only thought that comes into the Don's mind at this seminal moment in his political life is, what did the man mean when he said *close* to $200,000?

If Simon's face could sink any deeper into his shoulders, it would have. While Cardenas and the customs officials lead the Don away, Russo hangs back and walks over to Sole. 'I'm sorry you had to drive all the way out here for a wasted trip, Simon. But as you can see, your boy hung himself. I didn't exactly waterboard him.'

'Did you even have a taped confession of him owning up to the attempt on Haider's life, or were you just making that up?'

'Swear to God. Someone emailed me the voice file from Pakistan. When you've been shitting on people as long as the Don has, some people get tired of it and shit on you back.'

'That evidence isn't going to hold up in court. It's not credible.'

'Well, the same source told us about the drugs and the cash being on the plane, so I think his credibility's already established. Even if the murder charge doesn't hold up, it doesn't matter any more. The empire's crumbling. Second time in two months that the Don and his Party have been caught with large sums of cash and have no explanation where it came from. That's a pattern right there. Raja will start getting nervous. The Don'll try to pin this stuff on him, so he's got no reason to stay loyal any more. He might want to cut a deal. So you see, Simon, I might not even need my little magic voice file. Oh, and now there's the slightly uncomfortable fact that he took your name personally, and referred to his links with the CIA in a room full of about thirty people. Any bets on how quickly that bit comes out on the seven o'clock news? That'll mean you will have to steer clear of this case like the fucking plague. Hey, that's a nice suit, you should take it off and get it dry-cleaned, you might need it for the congressional hearings your boy triggers in Washington next week.'

Simon Sole has nothing left to say. The expression on his face is one of pure hatred. But as he turns to go, in one final gesture of defiance, he sticks his middle finger out to Anthony. Russo just laughs and walks out towards the tarmac. He instinctively goes for the cigar in his pocket, before a large fuel truck parked in front of him makes him put it right back. This job is tough. It brings you face to face with the nasty underbelly of humanity and it doesn't give you a lot of good days. Few and far between actually. But once in a while, when such a day comes along, it feels great and makes all the sacrifice worth it. And today has been a good day.

EPILOGUE

Ismail doesn't return to Lyari immediately. Needing time to gather his wits, he goes to a place where no one will think to look for him, the buffet at the PC Hotel. He finds the restaurant empty. After all, on the day that the Don is supposed to return to the city, no one wants to venture out to any kind of public place.

Ismail sits on a corner table, ravenously devouring fish tikkas and chicken jalfrezi, following the news on the restaurant's TV. He sees the report about the bombing, and how some commentators have started speculating that Party dissident Asad Haider might have had something to do with the attack, according to police sources. He has to admit that was a nice touch from Mallick sahib. Then, of course, is the even bigger news, a press conference by the chief minister in which he announces that, keeping in mind the security environment in the city, the entire politburo of the Party has begged the Don to return to New York immediately. No one raises the point that the entire episode has been a huge embarrassment for the Party, and Colombowala, skilled bullshitter that he is, actually manages to make it sound as if the day has not been a total disaster. Whatever the TV pundits might say, Ismail is sure the Party will never be the same again.

The news of Baba's death is only the third item in the list, having been crowded out by the other breaking events of the day. The report says he was shot in a police encounter and the body has been shifted to Civil Hospital. There is no news of any reaction in Lyari, partially because none of the channels are inclined to spare a van to go into Lyari on such a momentous day.

But Ismail knows that at some point he will have to go back to Lyari. Of course, he had planned all of this, so none of today's events are unexpected. But still, till now he had never thought beyond Baba's death. Now, he has a kingdom all ready for the taking. He just needs to grow the balls to take the final step. And he has to move fast before someone else stakes a claim.

Having finished eating, Ismail makes his way back to Lyari. It is a locality paralysed by the unexpected news of Baba's death. If the United Front hadn't been equally paralysed by the Don's comings and goings, they could have literally walked in and taken over. By the time Ismail gets to Baba's house in Afshani Galli, it is late afternoon. Several hours have passed since the events of the morning, but Baba's henchmen are all still in a state of shock. Ghaffar Langra and a bunch of the others sit quietly around Baba's pool smoking teriak, and occasionally sobbing.

'Arre, what the fuck is going on here? What are you people doing?'

'In case you haven't heard, Naich, Baba has been killed. Our father has left us. We are orphans today.' One of the younger boys, whom they call Shabbir Drama, weeps hysterically between puffs of the teriak-filled cigarette.

'Yes chutiya, I know. I have been at Civil Hospital for the past hour, trying to figure out how to get Baba and Pappu's bodies back.'

'What do you mean? We'll just go and get them.'

'Listen, idiot, you are all wanted men. The police has Civil sealed down. The minute you go, they will start picking you off like flies. Ghaffar, haven't you explained these things to these morons?'

Ghaffar doesn't answer for a moment, staring hard at Ismail. Then finally he turns to the others. 'He's right. What do you propose we do, Naich?'

'First things first. Even though the Party has been hurt by today's events, they are still dangerous. Organize all the regular checkpoints and patrols in our area. Nobody should even think of turning their eyes towards Lyari. Just because Baba has died doesn't mean we're weak. If any Party madarchod tries to enter Lyari or Soldier, shoot first and ask questions later. If we allow them to walk into Lyari today, tomorrow they will walk into our houses and kill us.'

'What about the police, Naich? And Baba's body?'

'It is very important that we make a symbolic show of Lyari honouring its leader. If we don't, then we will never be able to leverage either the police, or the Party, or that old fool Yousaf Chandio. Ghaffar, since none of us can go, I want you to gather all the old notables of Lyari. We'll send them in a massive procession to Civil Hospital, and they will demand the return of Lyari's son. The police can't arrest them, they haven't done anything wrong. And if the police refuses to hand over the body, we'll threaten large-scale unrest in Lyari. Once the delegation gets Baba and Pappu back, we will organize a grand funeral, with thousands of people coming here to Afshani Galli to pay their last respects. We will make Baba's funeral our showpiece, to tell everyone that the Lyari gangs are stronger than ever.'

Ismail's words act as a tonic for the men. They seem to be relieved that someone has taken the responsibility to take decisions. Finally, the gangsters of Lyari spring to action, leaving the room to carry out Ismail's instructions. Only Ghafffar stays behind, sitting on one edge of the pool smoking his cigarette. Ismail too nervously lights a cigarette and starts pacing round the pool.

'Ghaffar, today was a bloody disaster. I told Baba not to go. I told him this was a foolish plan. But did he ever listen? Fuck! And what about you? You were supposed to have a second motorcycle beside him. Why weren't you with him? You could have saved him.'

Ghaffar continues to smoke his cigarette, the smoke swirling around his face. 'I turned around when I saw what the real situation was.'

'What do you mean?'

'It was a trap. I suspected that beforehand. But when I saw you sitting at that chaiwallah, I knew it for a fact.'

'What? Are you mad? I was nowhere near Nishtar Park.'

'Yes, you were. You set the trap. You subtly pushed Baba to make this idiotic move, even as you covered your own tracks by publicly opposing his decision. I may not be the smartest guy, but I've been around long enough to recognize manipulation. I saw you. That's why I pulled back and let Baba go.'

'I … I don't know what you're talking about. I never manipulated Baba … I was never there …'

'Relax, Naich. We both betrayed him. You're right. I could have saved him, but I pulled back and let him go to his death. And you sat there and told the policewallah to shoot him. Baba died as he lived. Beholden to no one. But I'm curious about what your plan is now. What are you trying to do, giving out all these orders and getting everyone so fired up? You want to take over? Or do you plan to hand us all over to your friends in the police?'

Ismail stares at Ghaffar for a long moment, cursing himself for having underestimated his intelligence and trying to figure out what to say next. 'I would never bring the cops here, Ghaffar.

I chose to join Baba and all of you. I could have kept living my life as normal. I could have joined the Party but I didn't. I saw the greatest potential here. A chance to build something powerful. Look, Ghaffar, you and I know Baba was a hothead. He got carried away with his emotions. I don't think everything that we have built up in the past few months should be thrown away. Look at how successful we have been. The Don has run away with his tail between his legs. The Party is shaken to its core. We can take advantage of all this. I wouldn't presume to try and take over. Of course, I know you are the seniormost member of the gang. It is your right. All I'm trying to do is help, acting as a political adviser as I did with Baba.'

Ghaffar smiles in a way that makes Ismail think his ploy has failed. 'I don't care. If you take over that is. I hadn't thought of all the things you thought of right now. It's brilliant, I can see the logic of it. See, I can't think that way. Which is fine. I'm not an ambitious man. I don't want to be overlord of Lyari and I don't want to go for tea at Yousaf Chandio's house. So I'll back you. Baba always said that he wouldn't hand over all of this to anyone, whether they were his own blood or an outsider, unless they were worthy enough. I'll tell everyone that in my opinion you are the worthiest candidate to see us through these troubled times. If I back you, I guarantee no one else will oppose you. If they do, I'll take care of them. Besides, it's better for me to have you running the show. If I took over, I'd always be worried about you scheming against me.'

'What do you want in return?'

'All of Lyari's rackets. I want to be a rich man, I'm not interested in the politics. I want a finger in every piece of action that goes down here. Drugs, municipal corruption, extortion, Irani diesel smuggling. You give that to me, and I'll make sure no one puts a bullet in the back of your head.'

'Done.'

'Don't you want to think about it a bit?'

'No. What's there to think about, when both of us are getting what we want?'

'Excellent. Now, what are your orders, Sardar?'

'Sardar?'

'Well, I figure you need some kind of title. If you're going to be the boss, we can't keep calling you Naich or Ismail. That's not respectful. Didn't you tell Baba you were going to make him some kind of Baloch sardar? You can take that title now. Or do you want to come up with something else?'

'No, no, Sardar will do nicely.'

*

Cyrus Dinshaw dies one week after the traumatic events of 17th November. For those who have known the family, Cyrus's death comes as a relief. He has lived with the help of machines for over a decade. Not living at all really. Just breathing. The mourners who come to the house for the funeral prayers swear that they can almost see a half smile on the face of his father, Byram. It is a heavy burden to bury your child, but perhaps an even heavier one to see him disintegrate mentally and physically into mush.

Byram returns to an empty house, after Cyrus's body has been sent off to the Tower of Silence. Sadia has returned to her own home, her role in this little drama is finished. And, of course, Asad Haider is no more. But Byram enjoys the silence in the house. It brings him peace.

It's been a long day for him. Freny had made him promise on her deathbed to follow all traditional funeral rites when Cyrus passed away. 'I want him to die like a proper Parsi, not some godless duffer like you,' she used to say. Ah Freny. She really used her deathbed privileges to the hilt, binding him to all sorts of promises that he didn't want to keep. To stay alive for Cyrus. To not pull the plug on Cyrus, at least not until he had avenged him. She could never have imagined that day would actually come.

Byram wanders around the house, standing for a moment in each room, reliving his life. Here is his father's old study, where he first told his parents he wanted to marry Freny. The magnificent veranda with the black-and-white tiles, where Freny and he hosted so many parties. Formal parties, with tuxedos and gowns, and dancing. Oh, how Freny loved to dance. She always said it was his dancing skills that convinced her to marry him.

Then, there is his old boyhood room downstairs, the room he gave to Asad Haider to stay in. The few belongings Asad Haider had brought with him are still there. Some dollars in an old brown leather wallet lying by the bedside, and a few clothes that Byram had bought for him to maintain the cover, neatly laid out on the bed. It's not like Asad knew he wasn't going to come back.

It's surreal for Byram to accept that Asad Haider is no more. All these years he has hated Asad Haider more than he thought was possible for one man to hate another. What he hated even more was the fact that he was powerless to cause this man any harm. Even when Guddu assured him that Asad would not survive whatever they were trying to do, he had thought it was just a ploy. Guddu would say anything to get him to stash Haider at his house. So it was a shock for him to see the news broadcast announce Asad's death in the blast. It's almost enough for him to renew his faith in God after all these years.

The last three months have been the most difficult in his life, more difficult perhaps than watching his wife die, or cleaning his grown son's shit-filled bedpans. Keeping *that* man in his house, protecting him from the Party, *talking* to him. Every night, he has asked Freny if he was doing the right thing. If this wasn't some kind of betrayal of the promise he made to her. But now he is content in the knowledge that it was all worth it.

He climbs the old staircase, once again looking at the pictures that adorn the wall just as the girl Sadia had done when she first came to him. All of these memories will also have to go to somebody, just like all the furniture and the house itself. Then there is the bakery. He should give it to Karim Bux, the manager, as reward for all his years of service. Best to give him his chance, see what he can do with it. There is so much to do, but today Byram does not want to work or think about the future. Today, he just wants to savour the moment.

He reaches the top of the stairs and enters Cyrus's room. It looks completely bare. All the monitors and medical equipment have already been taken away. All that remains is the hospital cot that was Cyrus's home for the last fourteen years of his life. Cyrus's own room was on the other side of the house, but Freny had him placed here after his injuries, so that it would be easier to look after him. Byram remembers this room as originally having been the nursery. He had brought Cyrus here when he came home as a newborn from Uncle Saria Hospital. He had carried him up the stairs in his arms. It's funny that when they are so little that they fit in the crook of your arm you think you can protect them from anything in this world. How stupid a man is when he first becomes a father.

Byram Dinshaw shuffles to his room next door and lies down on his bed. He picks up the picture of Freny that has rested on the table next to his bed for fifty years. He traces the outline of her face with his fingers.

'I love you, pet. I kept my promise to you. I didn't pull the plug on Cyru all these years. I know you thought I would do it because I would be overwhelmed by taking care of him. But I never even thought of it. And I took care of him for nine years, you only did five. I kept Cyru alive right until those bastards got what they deserved. Asad Haider blown to so many pieces they couldn't even hold a funeral for him, and the Don rotting in some American jail. I did it, pet. I took revenge on all our enemies. But I had to do it now. I'm tired. All I want to do is join you. Besides, you hadn't seen him recently. There was nothing left of our Cyru. It was just a shell. And once I am gone, who would have taken care of him? Better that I should do it. Now we can all be together in your heaven.'

And with that, Byram Dinshaw places the picture on his breast, folds his arms on his chest, and is finally reunited with his beloved Freny. When the body is recovered days later, the notably unsentimental medico-legal officer at Civil Hospital remarks that in all his years of looking at cadavers, he has never seen such a look of contentment as he does on Byram's face.

*

The motorcycle outrider guides the armour-plated SUV through the gates and right into the porch of the Chief Minister House. As Guddu disembarks, the Chief Minister House security detail salutes him smartly, prompting a rather flimsy reply from him. He curses under his breath and promises himself that he will practise his saluting at home every night for ten minutes. He has spent so many years in the plain-clothes world of Special Branch, it's no wonder his saluting is rusty. Even the uniform that he once wore so naturally seems alien and restrictive. He keeps self-consciously looking at the new ranks on his shoulders, the crossed swords and crescent representing an inspector general. It all seems so new. He smiles to himself. If saluting properly and getting used to a slightly uncomfortable uniform are the extent of his worries from now on, then he has been a very fortunate man indeed.

The chief minister's personal secretary waits for him on the porch steps and leads him straight inside to the CM's private office. It is a modest office for the most powerful man in the province, reflecting the more modest personality of its occupant. The décor is simple, not like the old-world opulence of his predecessor Yousaf Chandio. There is a picture of the founder of the nation, but not the standard issue one with the Quaid in his Jinnah cap. This one shows the big man at home, wearing a seersucker suit and playing with his dogs, a cigarette dangling precariously from the corner of his mouth. A nod, perhaps, to the founder's more liberal proclivities.

There is a second picture in the room, this one coloured and blown up to a large size, showing the Don addressing a massive rally. It too is an old picture, and shows the Don as he was, young and restless and ready to take on the world. The picture makes him look quite dashing actually. Besides the pictures, the room is remarkably bare, dominated by a highly polished table which is empty, except for a gold-plated cigar cutter and an ornate wooden box of cigars. It is a well-known fact that Tariq Colombowala doesn't like paperwork. He prefers to do business verbally. In fact, he doesn't like putting his name down on anything, if he can avoid it. There's an old joke that even when he got married Tariq got someone else to sign on his nikah papers to avoid future incrimination.

But today, Tariq Colombowala is in his element. A gaggle of civil servants and some Party officials receive quickfire instructions, precise, direct and unambiguous. Observers have noticed a transformation in the chief minister these past few weeks. Previously, he was always a consensus builder, preferring dialogue and negotiations, and often vacillating over key decisions, deferring them till Party headquarters provided greater clarity. Whereas now he strides forward, making decisions without referring them to anybody else. His tone is more forceful and his entire demeanour exudes a new confidence.

Guddu again fails to get his salute right when he enters the room, but Colombowala is unconcerned and greets him with a warm smile.

'Out.' The simple command is barked out and it is immediately understood that the CM wants to talk with the new inspector general alone. Guddu takes the seat across from Tariq and places his cap and cane on the table.

'My dear Inspector General, you look sharp in the new uniform.'

'Thank you sir. It is all due to your kindness and support. You went out of your way to get me promoted and appointed as the IG, when the Don had only proposed me for the post of Karachi police chief.'

'I think we can drop the formalities when we're alone, Guddu. After all, we are co-conspirators. Cigar?'

'Thank you.' Guddu takes a fat Cohiba from the box and holds it against his nostrils, taking in the rich aroma of the tobacco. Tariq takes another and cuts off one end, taking his time to light it properly.

'So, where do we stand? Where is the investigation?'

'My man, Inspector Ahsan, who was first at the crime scene, is heading it. I have promoted him, so he will do as he's told. No one will find any link between us and the bomber. It will all point to Asad Haider attempting to kill the Don. Completely believable, after his assassination of Javed Gringo.'

'Good. And all the other loose ends? The girl and the old man? We don't have to worry about them?'

'No. The old man did us all a favour by dying a week after the bombing. Natural causes, nothing to do with us. But he wouldn't have said anything even if he were alive. And Sadia Ali didn't have any knowledge of our actual plans. She didn't know that I arranged for the suicide bomber through Naich and that I planned for Asad to die from the beginning. She just thought I was using Asad Haider to topple the Don. And now that Asad is dead and the Don gone, I have convinced her that she played a great role in avenging her brother's death and bringing down the Party. I told her it was God giving Asad Haider his just deserts. That gave her closure. Nevertheless, I will hire her as a civilian computer programmer in my office, just to keep an eye on her. You will have to approve the file, but I believe it is well worth it.'

'Of course. Consider it done. That's hardly any price for what we've accomplished. What else?'

'I have also located the former Soldier Bazaar ward boss, Saquib Shatroo, who saw Asad that day. He is in hiding, scared that the Party might be planning retribution. I wanted your permission before I arrested him. We'll book him in a number of terrorism cases. That'll ensure he'll be stuck in a hole for years. It's also good for the police to show a little bit of independence from the Party, sends the message that things are different now. With your permission, of course.'

'Absolutely. Throw that bastard in jail. And lock up a few more of these bhenchod ward bosses. Time to break their power and show them that no one is more powerful than the state.'

'Uh, you don't think the Party will react to such an extreme measure?'

'These madarchods have to realize that there is a new reality now. Me. If they want to continue to survive in the Party, they have to swear allegiance to me. Whoever doesn't, gets to face the law on their own. It's not like they're innocent. All of them have plenty of blood on their hands. But from now on, these dogs better bark for me. Not for Asad Haider or Javed Gringo or any other enforcer, and not for the Party. Besides, who is the Party now? The offices in New York have been shut down, Raja is incommunicado, probably preparing to go into the witness protection programme or something after he gives his testimony against the Don. And I'm cleaning out all of his appointees from Darul Sakoon and in the politburo, on the grounds that they have brought shame to the Party, and replacing them with my people.'

'And the Don?'

'The Don is only communicating with his lawyer. He's being held in some psychiatric facility and being evaluated on his mental condition. His lawyer thinks he can run a defence based on temporary insanity or something.'

'Will it work? The defence, I mean.'

'I don't know. Doesn't really matter either way. If it doesn't, the old man goes away for a long time and the city belongs to us. And if it does work, then I'm still paying for the lawyer and have taken over the Party apparatus here in Karachi, so the Don remains indebted to me, as his last loyal subordinate.'

'I have spoken to some American legal experts. They are of the opinion that even if the murder case stalls, the money laundering and drug offences will hold. It was brilliant of you to put the cash on the plane and to hand him the drugs.'

'Well, I was only being a loyal Party worker. It's not my fault if the Don can't get through US customs, despite having lived there for so long. Although, to be fair, after you sent off that audio file to those police officers, they were always going to be waiting for him. The Don always underestimated you, Guddu. You were always a sneaky little shit, but this time, you have surpassed yourself. He never saw it coming.'

Guddu chuckles. For once, the comment does not sound negative, but rather complimentary. 'So, what will we do now?'

'We will run this province. Without the Don pulling our strings from thousands of miles away. You will continue to head Special Branch and the Karachi police, in addition to being the head of the provincial police. I need you to hold all of these key positions until I have fully consolidated my hold over the Party.

You will use all the resources at your disposal to provide me with complete information about the Party, about my ministers, about my MPs and all my rivals. Information that I can use to blackmail and browbeat them into submission. In the absence of the Don's reign of terror, I shall use more "traditional" methods to keep everyone in line. Meanwhile, to the public and the Party faithful, I shall be the saviour. The man who kept the Party together after the disasters it had to suffer as a result of the Don's misjudgements. The straightshooter who broke the secret cabals within the Party and made everyone more accountable to the people. Yes, I quite like that one. Do you think your friends in the Agencies will go along with me?'

'Yes, I think so. No one wants another Don running a personality cult and a mafia organization rolled into one. It will be normal politics from now on. Whoever pays, wins. They might want you to purge some of the more "undesirable" elements within the Party. It's good from a marketing point of view, makes people believe that you've made a break with the Party's past.'

'Of course. I thoroughly enjoy a good purge, especially when I get to fuck my rivals in it. My only concern is Lyari. You're sure you have things under control there?'

Guddu breaks into a wide grin. 'Chief Minister, you have my word on it. The new head of the gangs is my informer, Ismail Naich. He's much smarter than Baba, and not a loose cannon like him either. He just wants a seat at the table and I think there's nothing wrong with that. He will keep the peace and will also cut us in on the lucrative Iranian diesel smuggling trade, as long as you keep the Party away from it. He will also serve as a check on Yousaf Chandio, because Chandio is now totally dependent on him to even enter Lyari. And all it will cost you is a single provincial assembly seat in Soldier Bazaar that the Party lost anyway due to its own incompetence.'

'Tell him not to worry, the Iranian diesel deal is just with us. I won't let the Party come near it. Believe me, I've had enough of the Party looking over my shoulder to check how much money I was making. And this Naich has political aspirations you say? That's perfect. The good thing about a politician is you can always negotiate with him. It's cowboys like Baba and ideologues like the Don whom you have to worry about. That's what I kept trying to explain to the Don. The "struggle" was long over. The Party had become part of the establishment. It was all about cutting deals now. He never understood that. He still believed that potential enemies couldn't be bought, they had to be crushed. It's a shame really.'

'Well, we are both free of him now.'

'Yes, we are. Thank you, Guddu, It's been a pleasure doing business with you. I look forward to a long and prosperous partnership.'

'As do I, Chief Minister. As do I.'

And with that, Guddu rises and finally gives a smart salute, before walking out of the office, into a new life.

ACKNOWLEDGEMENTS

None of my books would be complete without the love and support of my family, my wife Samar, and my son Suleyman, who have always generously given me the time to write; my mother, who has always been my greatest supporter; and my mother-in-law, who is my second greatest supporter. A special thanks to my agent Jessica and the team at Pan Macmillan India, who over the course of our collaboration on my books have become like family; and finally, a shout out to a small but intrepid band of policemen around the world, who work, usually against the odds, to provide justice to the powerless.

INTERNATIONAL BESTSELLER!

SOON TO BE A MAJOR MOTION PICTURE

'I strongly suggest that Western policy makers read *The Prisoner* before they next call for a military "crackdown" on Islamist militancy in Pakistan'

New York Review of Books

'An exhilarating crime novel ... Hamid's portrayal of the city, the police, and the byzantine political play is nuanced and sophisticated'

NPR

INTERNATIONAL BESTSELLER!

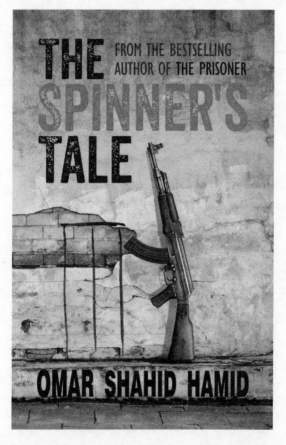

'Spinning his tale with intelligence and dexterity ... [this is a] gripping crime thriller with a heart-wrenching denouement'

The Hindu

'A book that one simply will not be able to put down'

Dawn